AUTONOMY

JUDE HOUGHTON

www.kristell-ink.com

Paperback ISBN 978-1-909845-96-1
Hardback ISBN 978-1-909845-480

Cover art by Ken Dawson
Cover design by Ken Dawson
Typesetting by Book Polishers

Kristell Ink

An Imprint of Grimbold Books

4 Woodhall Drive
Banbury Oxon OX1 69Y
United Kingdom

www.kristell-ink.com

For my family

WELCOME TO YOUR FUTURE . . .

PART I

2035–2042

1

SECTOR 2, CHURIN

L I Bao felt a pop between her legs followed by wetness. It was her fourth child, about to nose its way into the world. Silently cursing, she glanced across the Battery floor. A thousand pairs of hands worked in unison, but no Supervisor patrolled the lines.

Thank the *Faith*.

She had to get to the end of the shift. There was a bonus if they hit quota, and with the baby coming, she needed the credits. She gritted her teeth. The baby would have to wait.

The contractions came in short, agonizing bursts. Every time one peaked she had to stop, breathe and wait for the pain to pass. Twice a red warning light flashed in the corner of her viewer, telling her to speed up. The line could only move as fast as its slowest worker.

For almost ten years, Li had sat in the same seat assembling microchips. The components were something to do with iNet, but she had no idea what. Not that it mattered. Her function was to lay thirty-seven parts into the correct chip beds, each colour coded and thinner than a human hair.

The tricky part was manipulating each piece into exactly the right spot. Her iNet glasses magnified the components while her hands, enveloped in a rubbery gel, controlled robotic pincers. She didn't know what the gel contained and she hardly ever thought about it. She thought about it now as another contraction ripped through her body.

What if the chemicals penetrated her skin and travelled down the umbilical cord to infect her baby? Her other children were fine, but Li had not been on the line as long when they were born. The air was worse now too, not inside the Battery, where it was filtered, but outside where it was not safe to walk without a respirator, every breath filled with poison.

She shook away the thought.

Do not dwell on what you cannot change.

The teaching of the *Faith* gave her solace. To endure hardship was part of life; a small sacrifice when compared to the eternal bliss that followed. As she laid in another component, her mind wandered to a more practical problem.

Would she be able to hold her baby?

Li had held her other children, even if she couldn't nurse them, but recently her hands had become little better than claws, conditioned by daily shifts of at least twelve hours. She had the tell-tale folding-over of the wrist, the pincering of the fingers, the chapped red skin eroded by chemicals; what the workers called crab hands.

In the Stacks you could tell where someone worked by their particular deformity; the missing limbs of the machinists, the racking coughs and weeping eyes of the sterilization groups, the permanent hunch of the technicians and the crab hands of the assembly lines.

Her grip was poor and sometimes she dropped even the lightest loads. Perhaps it didn't matter. Their amah would look after the child while Li worked in the Battery.

She was not angry about her hands; neither did she blame her employers. The same repetition that curled her wrists made her efficient, and that meant she was allocated to a highly productive line, one that often qualified for quota bonuses. Li could lay a batch of components in less than fifteen minutes. Only enhanced workers earned more, those who had productive surgery such as a drill gun instead of a hand, a microscope instead of an eye.

Another contraction racked her frame and Li felt the baby's head push against her cervix. Sweat poured down her face as she struggled to keep her fingers steady. Singing under her breath, she rode the wave of pain, "A Grey, B Green, C Black bean . . ."

Li wanted to pull her hands from the gel and grip the desk, but that would set off an alarm. The robotic pincers shook and she almost dropped the half-completed circuit board onto the laminate workstation.

Two more red pulses flashed in the corner of her iNet glasses. She was a minute behind the line. If she lost any more time she wouldn't be ready when the device turned over, holding up the entire batch and jeopardizing the credit bonus for everyone.

Birth water began to seep from her leg, forming a puddle beneath the workstation. It wouldn't be long until the Battery's sensors detected the contamination. She prayed the shift would end before that happened.

Li didn't want to draw attention to herself. The Supervisors regularly identified stragglers to be replaced by new hands. After thirty, it was only a matter of time before the fingers became so crabbed they could no longer do the work. To that end, a thousand novices, trained and ready, came to the factory each day, filling in for temporary absences and waiting for the chance of a permanent seat. That was what kept the Battery so productive.

And the ex-line worker?

They were fortunate to be retained by the Battery at all. Some were relegated to lower grade sanitary work. Most had to be supported by their family or eke out a living as an amah; household servants, paid the price of their daily skaatch and no more. At least when Li was *Retired*, she could be the amah for her own home.

Li was thirty-two but she was fast, accurate, and safe for some time yet. Li had only held up the line twice in her entire career, and both times it was for just a few minutes. There was the day her brother died in a machining accident. She was distracted and couldn't keep up with the relentless assembly. Another time she had a fever and blacked out. The Supervisor slipped her synapse and she got through the shift.

Li rushed on with her work. Her pincers manipulated a purple micro flange into an orange chip bed.

By now, the rest of the line had finished. Li could sense her co-workers peering into their iNet display, wondering why the completed device had not been cleared and replaced by the last set of color-coded pieces.

Her status icon flashed another warning and she tried not to panic. Only three more pieces to go. Just three more! The robotic pincers pressed them together. Done!

A buzzer sounded signalling the line's completion. Compressed air shot across the device, removing any micro fibres that may have accumulated from the friction of the claws. She breathed a sigh of relief. Just thirty-seven more pieces to assemble and the shift was over.

But something was wrong. The new batch did not load.

The line opposite was already piecing together their next device; a hundred crooked backs, a hundred shoulders hunched. Her line, by contrast, was restless. Their routine broken, heads craned out of the workstations, jerking left and right like chickens.

Nobody spoke, any noise during the shift resulted in an automatic credit deduction, but Li could feel their anxiety. With every passing second, the prospect of hitting thirty thousand units for the week, and the associated bonus, became more remote.

As another contraction built, a pair of boots clicked down the aisle; the Supervisor. She tried to sit up straight for inspection, but instead creased over in agony, the contraction ripping through her. As the Supervisor reached her workstation, a groan escaped her lips.

The Supervisor spoke into his lapel. "Credit deduction for S17788."

Staring down, she could see his boot, tapping up and down in her birth water. A million microbes mixed and swam under her magnified gaze. The foot suddenly pulled away, conscious of where it had been.

"Disgusting," he said, and again spoke into his lapel. "Row 17, request clean up and gurney. S17788 is leaving the shift."

"I-I can finish."

"I don't think so," he said, impassive behind iNet shades.

There would be no bonus today, no pay for an incomplete shift and on top of that, a fine! Tears welled in her eyes. *Faith* give her strength! She would have to take another fourteen-hour shift tomorrow instead of staying at home with the baby.

The Supervisor did not move. He was not looking at her, but through her, reviewing data on his iNet lenses. "Your last component," he said. "The calibration reading shows the alignment off by nearly a degree. Sloppy. Very sloppy."

Her heart sank. A reject! The component was a reject!

The contractions had shaken her hands and she had not compensated enough. The baby was no excuse. Nearly all of the women on the line had laboured at their desk at one time or another. She had done it with Zhu and Min, checking into the triage centre at the end of the shift. With Zhu she came back to work the next day.

Her head swam. If it were a reject then . . . no, surely the Supervisor would forgive this transgression. Her record was clean, her stats outstanding.

This time when the Supervisor mumbled something into his lapel, she couldn't hear what he said.

A clean-up team scrubbed the ground. The odour of sanitizing sprays and chemical fluids filled the air, making her nauseous. A pair of orderlies eased her into a wheelchair while a young girl in an orange jumpsuit took her seat. The entire operation took under three minutes. The Supervisor clicked off and the line began again.

Li sat in the wheelchair, helpless.

"Look directly ahead," the orderly said.

Puzzled, she stared across at the far wall, past the rows of people, two thousand on this floor alone. Then she saw it. The golden circle of the retinal scan, her iNet glasses shining in on themselves; conferring her data to the Battery. The halo effect, they called it. It usually took a millisecond when iNet was registering you for something, so fast that you hardly noticed. But the halo was slower, a manual scan, for the official record. She had been *Retired*.

"Don't worry," the orderly said. "It's all over now."

"But I-I have to work!"

"I'm sorry."

"Please . . . call the Supervisor back," she begged.

The orderly wheeled her out.

"I just need a chance to explain. It won't happen again. I'm better than a novice, I swear I . . ." She raved on until another contraction broke the hysterics and with the pain, a new fear took hold of her.

Li had counted on using the Battery's triage unit for the birth of her baby. *Retirement* meant her employment ceased immediately, rendering her ineligible for medical care. She didn't even know where the nearest hospital was. She began to hyperventilate. "The-the baby!" she gasped.

The orderly smiled. "Don't worry. We'll take of that."

"Wh-what?"

"Just relax."

A latex hand pushed a soma capsule into her mouth. As it dissolved, a sense of well-being washed through her.

Yes, of course it would be all right. The baby was pre-contracted to the Battery as an employee, collateral for Zhu's *Aspiration*. The Battery had taken a sample of the amniotic sac at twenty-eight weeks to make sure the child was healthy, and then agreed to twenty-five thousand hours in return for the loan.

"That feels better doesn't it?" The orderly's voice was far away.

Li tried to nod, but her head was too heavy. The double doors of Triage opened in front of her. A dozen other mothers were in the process of giving birth, like her, caught short in the middle of their shift.

She was lifted out of the chair and onto one of the slow moving birthing stations that circumnavigated the room. There were five women in front of her, the conveyor belt powered by treadle bikes. The stations reminded her of an ancient fairground ride.

As she neared the delivery section, a nurse stepped onto the carriage and swabbed her arm. Li felt a prick and a massive dose of chemicals flooded through her. The nurse pushed a piece of rubber into her mouth. "Bite on this," she said, "you're up next."

Despite the dulling effects of the soma, Li screamed as the drug forced open her birth canal, propelling the baby through. She tried to visualize beyond the pain, to meditate on the greater good that the *Faith* encouraged. Instead, she let out a violent torrent of obscenities, spitting the rubber onto the ground. For once, the words of the *Faith* were no comfort.

Two minutes later the baby lay on her breast. Li's hands couldn't cradle her properly, but as long as Li didn't move, her daughter was unlikely to roll away.

Around her orderlies squirted liquid in the baby's eyes, pricked heels for blood and took a tissue sample.

Li thought it was unusual how the baby didn't cry. All of her other children had bawled, impatient and hungry while the orderlies worked on them, registering their vitals, checking for all the things they check for. Only when the tests were complete would Li be permitted to feed her, and then within half an hour she would have to leave Triage and walk home. Her husband, who was on a shift, could not be disturbed.

"We're almost done here," the orderly said, fitting a small respirator over the baby's mouth and nose. "The air is very bad tonight, so keep it on her at all times except when feeding, even indoors."

"Indoors?"

"That's the new guideline. First six months indoors, out of doors, always. We want to keep Balmoral fit and healthy."

"Balmoral?"

"Her name, Balmoral Murraine."

Confused, Li said, "No, no. We're calling her Hu. Hu Bao."

"She is contracted to the Battery."

"So?"

"The Battery allocates the name."

"What?"

The orderly sighed. "It is in your contract. Nobody ever reads them. It's the new policy. The Battery regulates the twelve to sixteen digit names of its pre-contracts so that each is unique. There are over forty million people currently on the Battery pay roll. Hu Bao," she typed something on her iNet keypad, "would be the three hundred and fifth Hu Bao in this section alone. Balmoral Murraine is currently unique, and therefore easier for the Battery to administrate."

Only when they took the retinal scan did her baby daughter struggle. Not cry, but kick out as the yellow halo recorded the micro contours of her eye, feeding the information back into iNet. Balmoral Murraine was officially a citizen of the Autonomy.

2

SECTOR 1, MANSION

D AGMAR EBORGERSEN WAS having a bad day, but then again almost every day was a bad day. In fact he couldn't remember the last time he had a good day. Sometime in 2020, before the whole world went completely to shit.

"So what's your point, Guiren?" he said to the empty room, his voice travelling seven thousand miles to where the Sector 2 manager stood before him in high definition.

"The air quality's reached critical levels. It's affecting productivity. People are falling sick." Guiren himself was talking through a respirator. It made him sound even more whiny than usual.

Dagmar knew this was pure C.Y.A, Top 10's technical term for cover your ass. If Guiren didn't hit the annual quota it would go on his report, so Churin's manager was building a stock of excuses. Nearly all of Sector 2 had chronic atmospheric pollution. He wasn't special.

Dagmar pulled up an inventory. "We can send you another twenty million respirators. They can be there in . . . ," he typed on his holographic fingerpad, "three weeks." It wouldn't look good on Churin's already over-extended balance sheet, but if they were desperate, they could ship them on credit.

"We don't need more respirators," Guiren rasped. "The people don't wear the ones they have. It's the law to wear them outside, but we don't even try to enforce it. There's no point, not when the air in their homes is as bad as the air on the street. We're up to 1,500 micros of PM particles per cubic meter most days. When they sleep, they're breathing in every pollutant under the sun. Then they wake up sick. Asthma attacks, bronchitis, chronic skin complaints and . . ."

"There's nothing wrong with the air in the Battery right?" Dagmar said, cutting Guiren off. "If your employees worked a bit longer and actually hit their numbers, maybe they'd stop falling sick." Like the old Las Vegas casinos, Top 10's factories pumped in filtered air and oxygen twenty-four hours a day.

Dagmar was being facetious, of course, but Guiren needed to wake up. If these numbers carried on, Logistics would transfer Churin's manager to some godforsaken hole in Sector 3, and then he'd really have something to moan about.

"They're doing eighty hours plus a week as it is," Guiren coughed. "Sweat them any harder and even more will fall sick."

Dagmar thought his colleague looked pretty sick himself, drawn and thin, which was strange because the iNet vid feed, pinged off an *Earth* camera, usually added a few pounds.

In the corner of his iNet glasses a message came up overlaying itself on Guiren's image. It was the hospital.

Request immediate call back.

Tapping a command on his holographic fingerpad, he told them to wait.

"So what am I supposed to do about it?" Dagmar said, suddenly weary.

"We need an Atmos system."

"Atmos? On your budget?"

"What difference does the budget make? It will be a sixty or seventy year mortgage irrespective of when it's installed."

Guiren had a point. Atmos, with its promise of clean air and water for an entire region, came with a price tag that indebted the entire Sector to Top 10 for years. Even Mansion, the wealthiest sector in the Autonomy, had not yet paid off its instalments.

"Talk to Finance and then I can see about adding you to the waiting list," Dagmar said.

"We need it now."

"You and the rest of Sector 2. We can't conjure them out of thin air, smog filled or otherwise. If you want to be bumped up the list, try hitting your quota."

"We'll choke to death first," Guiren said.

"Let's hope not. Churin owes us too many credits." He killed the feed.

Again the hospital messaged him. One word.

Urgent.

"Wait," he commanded, this time using eye control rather than the fingerpad. With another flick of the eyelid he checked his schedule. Three more Sector managers queued, all desperate to speak with him. They would have to wait too.

Removing his glasses, he ran the flat of his palm across his face. It came back covered in a clammy sheen. Was he getting sick? He didn't have time to be sick. The biosquare reading on his iNet, the same chip that tapped into his body's warmth and scavenged energy to power his lenses, said his temperature was normal. No, he reasoned, it was probably just the effect Guiren had on him.

He pushed back from his desk, walked over to the huge bay windows and surveyed Mansion. The sky was crystal blue; the sun glinted on ten thousand pristine skyscrapers, the air cleaner than at any time in the last two hundred years.

Halfway across the world, Churin, and a thousand industrial sectors like it, suffocated in a poisonous atmosphere. It wasn't just the air; there were chemicals in the earth, toxins in the water and carcinogens in the ubiquitous food source known as skaatch; a gelatine composite of insects and jellyfish. Somehow, their populations struggled on; bent, grey, monotonous figures that shuffled from their stacks to the Battery and back again.

He thought again of Guiren's pale face behind the respirator. Dagmar had been hard on the guy, but he had to be. As part of the Autonomy, Churin had obligations and its citizens' pain was nothing compared to the starving masses that lived outside its borders, where civilization had fallen back hundreds, if not thousands, of years. Churin should remember that, safely encased behind their huge Sector walls, keeping out the savages on one side, the sea on the other.

Before Top 10 designated Churin a Sector 2 region, the indigenous population died in their millions. Now they had food, water, a job and some of them; the designated *Aspirants*, even had a future.

However, the region could only remain viable if the Batteries turned a profit, and the only way to do that was to exploit the one commodity that was more plentiful than any other; man. In a resource-starved world, chronic over-population, instead of being the problem, had become the solution.

And this, Dagmar reflected, was the world he was bringing his children into.

He put on his iNet glasses, his face feeling curiously complete again. With an eye command, he pulled up his holographic fingerpad, the two tiny projectors in his iNet glasses creating the floating keys. He scrolled past the queued, Sector-related calls and instead selected Beth Rael. They had tried to vid him a total of seven times.

After a pause of about a second, a young doctor appeared in front of his lenses. Dagmar hadn't seen him before.

He seemed nervous, conscious he addressed an Elite. "Sir, we've been trying to reach you. Your wife is ready to give birth."

"Yes, I see that. It's on my schedule."

His wife had been due two hours ago. Twins. Two boys, pre-screened and pre-ordered through genetic testing of appropriate eggs and sperm. Twins, so they wouldn't have to go through the baby thing twice. No time, not with this job, and he was over forty now. Of course, domestics would do most of the heavy lifting while they were babies, his wife sure as hell wouldn't, but as they grew up he didn't want to be one of those absentee fathers. If he was going to have sons, he was determined to make the investment pay off, to make time for them, somehow. Not today though. No point. They wouldn't remember, and he had entire populations to manage, placate and make productive.

"Listen, Dr . . ."

"Maraken," the man replied.

"Right. You're going to have to patch me in."

The young doctor looked puzzled. "I don't understand."

"Beth Rael is on *Earth*. I will attend in V.R. if you can make it quick."

"I thought you'd want to be there in person."

"Virtual reality *is* being there in person. It's just a question of media."

Not waiting for a reply, he closed the feed and tapped a command on his finger pad. A quick ret-scan gave him access to iNet's *Earth*. For the Autonomy, *Earth* was going to be the biggest game-changer since the *Faith*. In its pilot phase it covered about fifteen percent of public buildings.

Where its cameras were installed, the AI could do anything from identifying non-authorized personnel to managing seating in a restaurant. For building interiors it also provided a three dimensional feed into any space, which in theory meant that needing to be somewhere in person would become a thing of the past.

Through *Earth* he watched the young doctor walk down the corridor, chatting to a colleague about this Elite asshole who couldn't even make it to the birth of his own children, who had kept them waiting over two hours when they were backed up forty deliveries deep.

Dagmar nodded with satisfaction. Even though the Doctor theoretically knew what *Earth* was, he hadn't processed what it meant. And that's just what Dagmar expected. *Earth's* very ubiquity, twenty-four hours a day, covering every inch of the public building, meant the software was ignored.

Asshole.

Dagmar pulled up the doctor's record and wrote a note. As an Elite in Logistics, Dagmar could kill Maraken's career; have him overlooked for promotions and raises, and he wouldn't even know why. With just three taps on the keypad he could transfer him out of Mansion and into a Battery triage unit, working sixteen to twenty hours a day in Sector 2. Churin needed doctors.

His fingers hovered over the send command, but after hesitating a moment, he deleted the note and closed the record. He'd let it go. This man was going to deliver his children, after all.

Navigating *Earth's* feed list, Dagmar transferred his view to his wife's ward. Esther lay in three-dimensional high definition, supine and motionless except for the occasional twitch or curl.

Even though he had used the prototype several times, the *Earth* technology still awed him. She was so vivid, he felt like he could reach out and actually touch her, and all of this projected onto his iNet lenses, an inch in front of his eyes.

Behind her own iNet glasses, Dagmar knew his wife would be in one of the interactive simulations that she was so fond of, doubtlessly being wooed by some tall, dark stranger. He knew the type she liked, all muscles and grease. He shouldn't have access to her Media file, but for an Elite, the usual rules didn't apply.

The doctor roused his wife gently, bringing her out of the sim before the birth. He removed her iNet glasses and Dagmar realised it was the first time he had seen her eyes for a month. They looked darker somehow; bruised, rather than bright blue.

"Open please," Doctor Maraken said and popped a couple of Mandrian into her mouth. His iNet told him the drug was a very expensive total body anesthetic, but with a targeted action so that it bypassed the infants' metabolisms. The doctor had probably been topping her up with the stuff for the last three hours.

Two nurses entered the room. Maraken checked a monitor, pulled a respirator over his mouth and put on a pair of latex gloves. He made a laser thin incision across her abdomen and pulled out one baby and then the next, together with the twin placenta. Immediately a nurse sprayed an organic adhesive across his wife's abdomen, and the incision resealed.

The doctor offered Esther the twins to hold, but she waved them away, asking for them to be "cleaned off" first. As she waited, his wife pulled down her iNet glasses and jacked back into her simulation.

Some technology worked too well.

Dagmar flicked an eyelid and logged out of *Earth*.

Before returning to his meetings, Dagmar replayed the image of his sons. He tried to feel something towards the red folded mess in front of his eyes, one slight and skinny and fair, the other chunkier and darker, but for now they looked like alien interlopers, something he instinctively wanted to reject.

Juggling the lives of millions had left him desensitized, but still, it depressed him that this non-reaction should be his response. He understood enough about biology to know that by the time he got home, these images, imprinted on his brain would already be tricking his body into producing the necessary chemicals to want to protect and love his offspring. He knew that in time he would become irrationally sentimental about them. He had big plans for his children, after all.

3

SECTOR 2, CHURIN

DISCHARGED FROM TRIAGE between shifts, there were no trams running to the Stacks so Li hobbled four miles home with the baby strapped to her chest in a Battery-issued sling. It was cold and Li could see her breath, despite the heavy smog. She was lightheaded and groggy from the birth accelerating drugs.

As she walked through the streets the rusty trailers, riveted together and stacked twenty high, yawned down upon her. Several times she had to avoid the waste that came gushing through the dunny holes above. You could never quite avoid it, some of it always got on your feet, your clothes and if you were unlucky, your head. The narrow streets were awash with litter and filth, each building only a few inches from the next. Li held Balmoral tight to her chest, shielding her.

She struggled up the six flights of rickety stairs welded to the outside of her stack. Only as she fumbled for the key, did she notice that the baby's face was purple and that the respirator had slipped from her face. She smacked the child's bottom, but instead of crying, the baby's lips tightened further. Panicking, Li banged on the door of the trailer.

"Tai-Tai!" she screamed. "Tai-Tai!"

Inside, she heard a curse and a painfully slow shuffle of steps. The old woman opened the door. "What is it? Why don't you use your key?"

"The baby!"

The amah looked at the child's face and quickly pulled Balmoral from the sling. Tai-Tai hurried to the sink and reached for the large clay jug. As she poured water over the baby's blackening face, Balmoral jumped as though slapped. She let out a silent, slow motion scream before gulping in mouthfuls of air in a torrent of tears.

"T-Thank you," Li stuttered.

Tai-Tai clicked her tongue in disapproval and rocked the baby back and forth, soothing her.

"You need to put this on," Li said handing her the respirator.

"She doesn't want that."

"They said to put it on, even indoors."

"She'll be all right."

"But she couldn't breathe a moment ago!"

Tai-Tai muttered something Li couldn't hear, and continued to rock Balmoral.

Li chewed her lip and put the respirator on the table. Her husband said it was just a piece of cloth with a gauze filter anyway. It didn't actually stop the pollutants; just broke them up a bit. None of her other children had bothered with one.

"Sit," Tai-Tai said. "Did they give you formula?"

Li nodded.

"Then I will change her and when I'm done, you can feed her."

"But I fed her a couple of hours ago."

"She'll be hungry again. Now sit."

Li lowered herself onto the chair, wincing as the stitches pulled. The drugs had begun to wear off and she was in pain. It would be worse in a couple of hours.

The amah removed the baby's blanket, the thin plastic undergarment and the soaking cloth underneath. She placed the cloth in the sink, rinsed the plastic briefs, took another piece of cloth from the pile of four or five she had laid ready, replaced the briefs and wrapped Balmoral in three quick folds. She swaddled the child back up using the Battery's blanket.

The old woman's proficiency reminded Li that she knew almost nothing about being a mother. It hadn't mattered before. Tai-Tai looked after the children while she worked in the Battery. But tomorrow there would be no Tai-Tai.

She handed the child to Li, and then returned to the sink to wash the soiled cloth. Li leaned back and balanced Balmoral across her chest to compensate for her lack of grip. She had six bottles of synthetic milk, given to her by the orderlies, to tide her over until she installed the baby at Mamfac. The formula was not supposed to be used for more than a couple of days. It provided the necessary calories, but not the nutrition, and babies could become addicted to its thick creamy nothingness.

Li wondered if she should use the formula at all. Mamfac was twenty-four hours and the nearest station was only ten minutes or so down the street. Tai-Tai could take her when she had finished with the cloths.

What was she thinking?

She had been *Retired*. They couldn't afford Mamfac. Until the baby was old enough to digest pureed skaatch, Li would nurse the child herself.

How was it done?

Li hadn't fed any of the others, or even seen them fed. Self-consciously she slid her shirt open, and nudged the child's head towards her breast. The child rooted towards the nipple, but with Li's hands and inexperience, she couldn't connect. The baby began to cry. Tai-Tai turned from the sink, and Li became conscious of her puzzled stare.

"What's wrong with the formula?"

Li said nothing, but reddening with shame, closed her shirt. Sensing Li had given up, the baby began to howl. Zhu and Min, her two younger children, who had slept through the drama of their sister's return home, now sat up on their mattress, eyes blinking. They wanted to see their new sibling. Tai-Tai flapped them away before they got too near, telling them to give the baby space.

"Why is she crying?" Min said.

"She's hungry," Li said. "Pass me one of the bottles from my satchel."

"She looks sick," Min said.

With Min holding the bottle and Li balancing, Li tried to feed her, but now the child wouldn't eat. Then she wouldn't sleep. Then she developed a raging fever.

Tai-Tai assumed charge. She sent Min to collect ice from the central station for a cold compress. She put Zhu back to bed. She calmed the baby with gentle rocking while singing hoarsely under her breath. She made tea for Li, who herself was ill, nauseous with the come down of the drugs, in pain from the birth, and now frantic with worry.

"Lie down," Tai-Tai said. "It does the child no good to have you fretting around her. This will pass. She's just getting used to the air."

Just getting used to the air.

It was the refrain of all those who lived in Churin's stacks. It was the reason for any childhood ailment, ranging from bronchitis, to sores on the skin, to the sudden death of a child.

Last year, their neighbours from the fourth trailer lost a little boy after he developed respiratory problems three weeks after birth. He hadn't got *used to the air*. Or the fact they had almost no food, or that the family of twelve existed in a single, squalid room with no heat or water or access to a dunny hole.

Tai-Tai was right; all they could do was wait. No doctor would come out on call to the Stacks and a journey back to Triage might finish the child off.

Helpless, Li found herself logging into the *Faith*. Behind her iNet glasses the room, her family, even Balmoral, all faded into the background as the sounds and sensory experience of the *Faith* calmed her.

Li's spiritual avatar appeared; a white robed spirit who looked like her mother when Li was a child. Li prayed behind the iNet glasses, meditating on the images. If the *Faith* let her child live, she would double her devotions. She would find time, somehow.

In the early hours of morning, the fever broke and the little scrap revived, drinking two bottles of formula before finally falling asleep. Tai-Tai laid her gently in the old baking tray that served as a cot. There was barely room for her on the floor. As it was the six of them couldn't sleep at the same time; there was not enough space. At least they had their own trailer. Most trailers were a little bigger than their four hundred square feet but typically they contained more than one family.

Sitting over her, Li watched the rising and falling of her tiny chest. Min and Tai-Tai settled down to doze for the hour left before day-break. Li was exhausted too, but with the immediate crisis over, she fretted about their sudden change in economic fortunes.

Retired.

The word grew in her mind like a tumour.

How would they make ends meet?

Li could apply for low grade work at the Battery; hauling waste to the pits and cleaning the latrines. The pay would be less, but it would keep the family whole. She reached for her iNet glasses to check for vacancies and stopped, arrested by the sight of her curled fingers feebly grasping the black plastic frames. Her crab hands, conditioned for the construction of microchips, were unfit for manual labour. The Battery's unskilled jobs were over-subscribed and, with so much choice, the company employed workers whose repetitive injuries did not diminish their physical utility. Li could hardly manipulate a mop or pick up a waste bag. She didn't have a hope.

"Sleep, missy," Tai-Tai muttered, regarding her with a half-open eye. Like the ducks Li's father used to keep a lifetime ago, Tai-Tai always had one eye open, surveying the horizon for danger, resting one half of her brain at a time.

"I will, I will," Li whispered back, more awake than ever.

Tai-Tai had been with them since their eldest daughter Fen was born, fourteen years ago. For little more than the price of her skaatch and a mattress in the corner of their trailer, Tai-Tai raised the children, cooked, cleaned and collected the daily water from two miles away.

"Sleep," Tai-Tai murmured again.

The amah would have to go, the first casualty of Li's unemployment. Perhaps it wouldn't be a bad thing. Over the last couple of years she had become irritable and insolent; complaining that Li spoilt Zhu, that she ignored her other children, that she thought too much of the *Faith* and too little of her husband.

Easy for Tai-Tai to say. She wasn't the one juggling a fourteen-hour shift on the assembly line with being the patient, loving mother.

Li's stomach squirmed. It was no good. Li couldn't work herself up to be angry with their amah. She had been part of the family for too long and today Li would have to dismiss her.

Li feared for the old woman's prospects. Tai-Tai was half blind and almost seventy; ancient for Sector 2 where many didn't see their fiftieth year. She was part of a generation that never really grasped iNet. Tai-Tai had the standard issue glasses but never wore them, claiming they gave her migraines. Outside of the trailer, Tai-Tai often became confused. Even her command of English, the Autonomy's official language, was patchy. She would struggle to find another position, no matter how meagre the reward. Still, Li had to tell her, and the sooner the better. They couldn't afford to keep her another day.

Faith give her strength.

Li struggled to her feet and walked over to Tai-Tai's mattress. "Tai-Tai," she said softly.

The old woman didn't stir. She could talk in her sleep, but not, it seemed, listen.

"Tai-Tai." Li bent down and shook her shoulder.

"What is it?" she croaked.

"I have to talk to you."

"What is it? Is the baby sick again?"

"No."

"Then what? I need to sleep."

"Tai-Tai I have . . . I have been *Retired*."

"Careless," Tai-Tai said irritably, and turned away from Li, pulling the blanket over her shoulder.

Was she doing this on purpose? Li spoke a little louder. "Without the credits from my job, we can't keep you on. I have to ask you to leave. I'm-I'm sorry."

Tai-Tai didn't move, but her body tensed. Having begun, Li rushed on, recounting what happened at the Battery, filling the amah's silence with words. By the time she finished the old woman was sobbing, her shoulders shuddering under the thin blanket.

"Please . . ." Li said, "you must understand . . ."

Tai-Tai said nothing but continued to cry, her face averted.

Li bit her lip, wondering what to do. Gently, she put a hand on her shoulder. "Tai-Tai," she said.

The old woman yanked herself away. "Get away from me!" she spat. "You're a fool! Do you know that? A stupid, bloody fool!" Standing now, Tai-Tai hurled abuse at her.

Li was lazy. She didn't know anything. Only an idiot lost their position at the Battery. She couldn't even look after her own baby.

Out of the corner of her eye, Li could see Min and Zhu awake now, knees clasped to their chests, eyes like saucers. Frightened, Zhu began to wail.

Li forced herself to stay calm. "You can stay until you find a position, of course, but we can't . . ." Li's voice trailed off. *Feed you*, she was going to say.

Tai-Tai's answer was to push past Li and grab the small, thin mattress. Li bit her lip. Although the amah had been sleeping on it for years, it belonged to the trailer. They needed the mattress now they had Balmoral, and Zhu was getting too big to share with Min. The old woman dragged it towards the door. Li said nothing. If Tai-Tai didn't find a position, she would be sleeping on the ground. Li shuddered to think of the cold, of the filth, of the Churin air.

How long would Tai-Tai last on the streets?

The amah cursed them all again and slammed the door on fourteen years.

Trembling, Li lowered herself onto a chair. The birth, the sleepless night, the long shift of the day before, all closed in on her at once. Min picked up an old dishcloth and mopped up the spots of blood that dotted the trailer floor. Li's stitches had come loose but although she was in pain, she let Zhu, clamber on to her lap. She stroked his hair until the crying became a snivel.

A key scraped in the lock, and Li tensed, half expecting the old amah. Instead, Angua stepped through the door, a tired looking Fen trailing behind him.

"They told me you were in Triage," he said excitedly. "I went there after the shift, but of course you had gone."

"I got back last night. Between shifts."

Her husband's eyes darted around the room before alighting on the baking tray. "There she is, my little girl." He leaned over. "Oh . . . she's so tiny."

As if aware of his presence, Balmoral stirred. Angua reached in to pick her up.

"Wash first," Li said.

Her husband was filthy with oil and debris, the trademarks of the machinist. Complaining good humouredly about Li's fussiness, he went over to the sink. Li noticed that her eldest daughter, Fen, had collapsed on her mattress to sleep. She didn't even bother to look at her new sister. To her, the baby was just another mouth to feed, more shifts to put in. She was doing a double this weekend, and her next shift, like Angua's, began in six hours.

While Angua washed, Li put Zhu in the corner, and pulled out the small breakfast table. Stepping around her husband, she clumsily filled the battered kettle, then lit their tiny kitchen stove and proceeded to make the tea.

When Angua was clean, or cleaner, he picked up Balmoral. "My little Hu," he said, his eyes sparkling. "Yes, yes, she'll do, she'll do. Look at that scowl!"

"She was born with it," Li said, infected by her husband's good humour.

"Ha! Ha! Yes! I can see that!" Angua sipped the tea with one hand, balancing the baby across his knees with the other.

Li didn't have the courage to say that their child's legal name was Balmoral, and not Hu, the name they had both decided on if it was a girl, or that she wouldn't even carry their last name.

She couldn't hide it from him either.

Angua would know as soon as the child was old enough for iNet and then her name would appear in her identikit, a tiny, semi-transparent stencil in the top left of the lens whenever you looked directly at her, hovering and ghost-like. Perhaps they could still call her Hu, just between themselves. Although somehow, she knew that wouldn't work, not when to iNet and to the *Faith* and to the world, she would be Balmoral Murraine.

Li poured her husband more tea, but this time her grip faltered, and she missed the mug.

"Where's Tai-Tai?" he said, watching the tea drip onto the floor.

"I . . . I dismissed her."

"What?"

Li told Angua what happened at the Battery, but unlike with Tai-Tai, she did not leave out her shame and humiliation. As Li spoke, she couldn't help the tears. Angua's face turned ashen. Slowly, he laid the baby in the baking tray, the expression of one who having seen the price, decided to put the item back on the shelf.

"We'll be all right," Li said. "There's no need to pay for Mamfac, I'll nurse her myself. And Min will soon be old enough to apprentice, and then . . . this one," she almost said Balmoral, "will apprentice after that. There will be a few lean years, but we'll manage, we'll be okay."

"Only with a mountain of ten-nineties," he said flatly.

Ten-nineties was Battery speak. The Battery divided the year into ten week cycles. A ten-ninety was an overtime allocation; ninety hours a week, ten weeks in a row.

"We'll manage," she said again, knowing how hollow she sounded. The ten-nineties, for him and Fen, not her.

"What about Zhu?" Angua said.

Hearing his name, he poddled over to them. "Zhu! Zhu!" he crooned, his pudgy belly puffed right out, as though he knew, even at two and a half, that he was destined to be an *Aspirant*. Li lifted him onto her knee.

"No," she said. "Not Zhu." She crossed her arms over the boy's chest. *Over my dead body, no.*

Angua glowered and she thought they were about to fight, to have *the argument;* the same one they had been having since Zhu was born and her avatar confirmed that he should be an Aspirant. Li would give up anything but that dream. Angua knew that.

"What about Mamfac?" he said.

"I told you, we don't need Mamfac, I will nurse her." Hadn't he been listening?

"I wasn't talking about nursing *her*," he said in the same flat voice.

Only then, did she realise what he was asking. "You . . . you can't be serious."

"Even with ten-nineties, with just two of us working you know we can't afford an Aspirant." Angua's eyes were suddenly cold.

She would give up anything for Zhu, but her body? Mamfac employed nursing mothers. Pumped full of chemicals to stimulate lactation and strapped into a special feeding station, they would feed forty-eight infants during the eight hour shifts; twenty minutes per child, one on each nipple. It was how other mothers were able to work, checking the child into Mamfac on the way to the shift, picking them up sixteen hours later. Like the Battery, it was a twenty-four hour operation.

Li knew mothers who had signed up as a last resort to make ends meet. A typical contract was six months, longer if they could stand it, but the women returned from Mamfac destroyed, their health shot by the chemicals and pain-killers, their breasts so sensitive they couldn't bear to have them touched.

The credits were terrible, but it was an income, on par with lower grade Battery work. If she took the job, she could still take care of the home. She would leave Zhu and Min to themselves in the morning and have Balmoral at Mamfac. They wouldn't fall into chronic debt, Fen and Angua might not have to work double shifts every week for the next three years, and Zhu, Zhu would remain an Aspirant.

"Well?" Angua said.

"I'll do it."

"Good," he said. His voice was still flat, but his hand shook with anger, not at her, she knew, but at the world in which they lived. If only he participated in the *Faith* he would be comforted and accept their hardships. He would understand that this life was just a journey into the next. The words of her avatar came to her; the words she reflected on in her daily devotions.

Do not dwell on what you cannot change, but remain steadfast under trial. The soul is enriched by worldly pain, and follows the path to eternal life.

Zhu squirmed on her knees. "Hungry," he whined. "Hungry!"

"I'll make the skaatch," Li said wearily.

She put him down and gingerly stood up. She opened the cupboard, took out a small slab of skaatch from the tin and, balancing it across her wrist, managed to lower the jellied square into the pan. She fried it in a few drops of seed oil, holding it over the carbon heater. The salt was awkward for her fingers and she dropped in too much. When the skaatch was brown and crispy, she carefully nudged it out of the pan and onto a large plate. Burning oil spat onto her wrists, but she smothered the cry by biting her lip.

At the table, Min took up the knife and began to cut.

"I can do it," Li said.

"No, please, I want to."

Min cut three slices for her parents and older sister, two small pieces for herself and Zhu. There was no more than five or six bites each, but the miracle of skaatch was that nobody ever wanted more. It was as filling as it was unappetizing.

The meal complete, Li asked them to join hands and thank the *Faith* for their sustenance. Zhu and Min took a wrist each. Angua refused to recite the words, but bowed his head. Like Li, he had lived through a darker time than this, when only flies, cockroaches and rats had enough to eat. Even if he didn't find comfort in the *Faith*, he knew there was much to be thankful for despite their hardships.

After breakfast, Angua pushed the table to one side and pulled out his mattress. Li dozed fitfully while Zhu roamed around the room, wrapped up in some game on iNet, waking her every now and then with a misplaced step or the need to go to the dunny hole.

Four hours later, Li roused herself to feed the baby. Her husband and Fen had already gone. Fen's skaatch lay on the sideboard, uneaten. Min helped Li cradle the baby on her chest, holding the infant's head while she fed the child with another bottle of Battery formula. The thought of nursing made her nauseous.

"So you will be our amah *and* go to Mamfac?" Min said.

"Yes."

"But I can do that. The amah part I mean. You will be too tired."

"No."

"Why not?"

"You have your studies."

Min shrugged. "I have already completed the Prep."

Prep was the basic iNet education program that was required before joining the Battery's apprenticeship. It had taught her almost seven year-old daughter to recognize sight words for fingerpad commands, navigate iNet, understand the rudimentary workings of Churin's various industries and complete her daily devotions to the *Faith*.

"It's going to be another three years before I can apprentice," Min continued.

The official Battery age was fourteen, but there were unofficial lodges she could work at from the age of ten.

"Please," she said, "I can help."

Li hesitated. On the one hand, she could really use her daughter's assistance. Min was capable, sensible and hard working. On the other hand, Min could continue to take the Autonomy's free modules for another couple of years, giving her the opportunity to learn something about the world.

But what was the point of that? Min didn't need to know about math or science to work at the Battery, she just needed to follow a rubric in order to assemble components.

Zhu howled from across the room. Wrapped up in a simulation, he had lost his bearings, tripped and bumped his lip on the sink. Blood dripped from his mouth. Li held Balmoral, so Min ran over, scooped him up and began to clean his face.

"We'll talk about it later," Li said.

———+———

TOGETHER, MIN AND Li cleaned the one room trailer, sweeping the floor, wiping the surfaces and scrubbing the dunny hole behind the screen. Keeping the trailer spotless was important. Any skaatch or digestible material left around, even small crumbs, was an invitation for roaches and rats. They had suffered four infestations this year already. The vermin moved from trailer to trailer, up and down the stacks.

The rats used to be a viable food source, but these days, no matter how they were cooked, they made you sick, and more joules were wasted in diarrhea than ingested, a dynamic that could quickly become dangerous.

As the morning wore on, Li's head swam with fatigue and the pain of her stiches. She found some synapse Angua had stashed for emergencies, and after two or three pills, she was ready to go again. They didn't help the pain, but the tiredness fell away.

Li registered at Mamfac using iNet. Her first shift was at one o'clock, a short day in order to prep her body. Tomorrow she would start at ten and work through to six.

"We have time to get the water," Li said.

With Min's help, Li put Balmoral in the sling and placed the respirator firmly over her mouth. She took the water jug, putting it on her head in the way Tai-Tai had done.

"I can carry it," Min said.

"I'm fine. I'll take it today. Maybe tomorrow you can go by yourself."

They locked the trailer, leaving Zhu inside. Although he was only two, she knew he wouldn't get into too much trouble. She had tied a two foot cord around his ankle and secured the other end to the table leg. The device was called a "child minder" in the Stacks.

Li picked her way down the rickety steps. She had always considered them fortunate to be sixth in the stack. Any lower and the foul smells and noise at street level were unbearable, any higher and that meant more steps at the end of the shift. It was also more dangerous. During particularly bad storms it was common for a stack to collapse. When that happened, the closer to the ground you were the better.

The well was two miles away. Li had never been, but iNet would navigate the way. Min typed in the destination and small red arrows lit up their lenses. The air was thick with smog and it was easier to follow the virtual display than try to see. Li shaded over her lenses. All landmarks and stationary objects were pre-loaded while moving objects, such as people or the tram, were identified through their iNet chips. She didn't have to concentrate on where she was going. iNet directed her through visuals, warning her if she was about to collide with anything.

Li took the opportunity to log into the *Faith* to make her daily devotions. A familiar euphoria washed over her as the beautiful images and secret harmonies began to play. As she walked, the sim filled the virtual path to the well with images of penance enabling her to earn A-points as she meditated on the *Faith's* teaching, and repeated the words back to her smiling avatar.

Balmoral's muffled crying woke her from the reverie. She logged out of the *Faith* and pacified Balmoral by gently swaying left and right as they walked through the last block of stacks before the well.

"Look!" Min said, pointing.

At first Li thought her daughter was commenting on the length of the queue, which was about a hundred people deep, but then she recognized Tai-Tai, shuffling up and down the line, pulling on the sleeve of every stranger, wheezing, "for hire . . . for hire . . . for hire." She wore neither iNet nor a respirator.

When she came to Li, she pulled on her sleeve too, not registering who she was. Tai-Tai's eyesight was poor and a lifetime of pollution meant her lungs were not strong either. She shouldn't even be out in this air.

"It's me," Li said.

"What's that?" Tai-Tai squinted suspiciously.

"Li," she said again. "Look, you need your respirator. You've forgotten it."

"Oh yes, yes," Tai-Tai said, and irritably pushed past. She wheezed along the line to the next person. Had she even recognized her?

"Why has she come to the well?" Min asked.

"I don't know, but she doesn't seem right," Li said.

Only other amahs came to the well. Tai-Tai would have been better off standing outside the Battery if she was going to stand anywhere. Millions of workers came out of its gates at the end of every shift. If Tai-Tai only used iNet, she could have checked for amah opportunities in nearby stacks. Li would have searched for her if Tai-Tai hadn't stormed out.

"Maybe she could come home with us, just until she finds a position," Min said.

Li nodded and they called out to her, "Tai-Tai! Tai-Tai!" but either the old amah didn't hear, or chose to ignore them. She pushed further and further up the line as each person shook their heads.

Li could chase after her, but they needed to get the water. Li only had a couple of hours before her shift began. Already, another twenty or so amahs had filed in behind them, all too happy to move up if they stepped out of the queue.

"We'll try to find her on the way back," she said.

They waited an hour until finally it was their turn. The watermen filled the jug and helped it back onto her head. A tenth of a credit was automatically debited from her iNet account. Carefully Li raised her hand, to balance the jug and stop it slipping. It was so heavy. She would change arms, left and right, all the way home.

"I can carry it," Min said.

"Tomorrow." They would need to get a smaller jug.

It was almost midday and the air was even worse, visibility cut to a few feet. She shaded her lenses again and iNet's virtual display kicked in. She wouldn't be able to keep an eye out for Tai-Tai but she couldn't help that.

Li logged back into the *Faith*. She wanted to see her avatar again, check her A-points, and feel the euphoria of the devotions. The screen dimmed, the lights and music began and her spirits lifted in anticipation. This time Min joined her in the sim, and they said the meditations together, while following the path through the streets and buildings towards home.

They had walked for about ten minutes when something tripped her, something she couldn't see in the simulated display. She fell. The jug smashed on the ground and there was a sickening crunch beneath her. Min screamed.

Dazed, Li flipped up her glasses, her mouth full of dirt.

Tai-Tai sat slumped in the doorway, her expression horror-struck. "Y-you didn't stop! You-you didn't stop," she wheezed. "I . . . I called out to you and you didn't stop. I thought you were ignoring me. After all these years. I caught your ankle as you went past. I-I thought you saw me . . . I'm sorry, I'm sorry."

The old woman broke into a coughing fit, gasping, holding her throat. Li ignored her, not caring if she choked to death. On the ground, tiny Balmoral had come loose from her sling, her respirator off to one side. Her leg was twisted at a horrible angle and there was a large dent in the left side of her smooth round head.

2042

1

SECTOR 1, MANSION

THE TWINS GREW quickly and when Dagmar's iNet reminded him that their seventh birthday was next week, he wondered where all the time had gone.

He remembered the day they were born. His wife went back to her simulation, he to his work, knowing, but not really believing, that in time he would grow to love them. Now, as he watched them play before they went to bed, he knew that what he felt was something other than the chemical infatuation of a parent for their offspring. It was far more powerful than that.

Tristram, older than Pasco by just a few seconds, was tall for his age and advanced in every way. He walked first, talked first, pushed and grabbed first. At the age of one, he had mastered basic fingerpad commands on iNet, by one and a half, he could manipulate virtual reality simulations with eye control.

The twins' tutor said the boy was one of the most advanced children he had ever taught. His command of iNet, the speed at which he could analyse complex problems, conduct research and then synthesize the information, was, like his physical presence, well beyond his years.

Pasco, on the other hand, was small, slightly built and compared to Tristram, a little, well, slow. He wasn't actually slow of course; they screened out most imperfections during the gene selection process, and as Dagmar reminded Esther, they couldn't expect them to be the same as they specifically selected non-identical twins. Still, it surprised him that Pasco, not Tristram, was supposed to have more of his genes.

"Okay, it's time," he said gently.

"Five minutes more, five minutes more . . . please!" Tristram implored. Pasco nodded his head violently by way of support.

"All right, but then straight to bed. No story, no song."

"Yes!" Tristram shouted and punched the air.

Dagmar was too indulgent, but he couldn't help it. He cherished this time with them at the end of the day. He made it a rule to be back from the office for bedtime, no matter what. He missed dinner and breakfast with them; he was up and out before they were even awake. He missed everything else they did, but if he could just spend half an hour with the boys before they went to sleep, it was enough.

Usually he liked to read something to them or just listen to their talk, but tonight they were wrapped up in a game. It was their own version of *Steel Ball*, but instead of a magnetic steel sphere they had a small, orange rubber ball, and instead of body armour they had pillows stuffed under their pyjama tops.

They chased after the ball, wrestling it from each other, then running away, using the furniture as a barrier. Their rules were simple. Whomever had the ball after three minutes was the winner. Tristram, stronger and more cunning, nearly always won, but Pasco didn't seem to mind. Tristram, on the other hand, couldn't bear to lose, which was perhaps one of the reasons why he never did.

Although the boys were as different as night and day, watching them play, Dagmar could see they shared a secret, almost uncanny understanding of each other. When Tristram jumped over the bed and then doubled back to crawl underneath it, Pasco was already there, waiting for him. When Pasco threw the ball against the wall to avoid being taken down, Tristram knew exactly where he was going to throw it before it left his hand.

It was such a different relationship than Dagmar shared with his own brother, Maglan, five years his senior. Perhaps it was because they had never played together. Not like this. They couldn't, growing up under the shadow of their father's temper, observant, quiet and ever watchful of his moods. Not that it made any difference when he had been drinking. Maglan still had a scar across his forehead to prove it.

The ball ricocheted off the wall again, and Tristram scrambled over Pasco, pushing his brother's head into the carpet, conscious that the three minutes were about to expire. Tristram scooped the ball up in a single fluid movement, his shock of blond hair flopping over his lenses.

"That's the game!" he roared.

Pasco rubbed his nose, eyes watering.

"You know what you have to do next," Dagmar said.

"Yes, yes," Tristram replied dismissively. He put out his hand. "Shake."

"Well played." Pasco grasped his brother's hand.

"Loser," Tristram whispered.

"That's enough," Dagmar said sharply. "Bed now."

Tristram whipped around. "That's only three minutes! You said five! We have time for one more."

"Yes! Please! One more!" Pasco joined in.

Dagmar sighed. "All right, a short one. Two minutes. I'll keep time."

As the loser of the last game, Pasco began with the ball.

"Ready?" Dagmar said.

Tristram nodded. Pasco smiled.

"Time on!"

Tristram lunged for his brother, but for once, Pasco managed to dodge out of the way. "I'm Kervorkian!" he piped; his father's favourite player; a talented interceptor, just two years out of the minors.

"I'm Cort!" Tristram shouted back, thumping his chest with the same mannerisms the real Cort had; a three hundred and fifty pound maul who led the league in permanently disabling opponents.

They chased each other around the room. Pasco, with his slight frame, was agile and, anticipating Tristram's moves, managed to keep the bed, then sofa, then desk between them. The seconds ticked down. Tristram became red in the face, sweat beaded on his forehead, but he couldn't get to his brother.

"It's not fair, you're supposed to stay in the open!" Tristram shouted.

Pasco said nothing, but darted behind the couch, his tongue stuck out in concentration. They circled around it a couple of times. Tristram stamped the ground in frustration.

"Thirty seconds," Dagmar said, secretly willing Pasco on.

Hands on knees, head cocked, Tristram caught his breath. Dagmar could tell he was studying his iNet display. It was another difference between the twins. All citizens of the Autonomy received a pair of iNet glasses on their first birthday, regardless of Sector. Of course, 2 and 3 received older, cheaper models, but the basic functionality was the same.

Tristram, like Dagmar himself, rarely took his off. In contrast, Pasco only used his for school assignments, avoiding the lenses whenever possible.

"Fifteen seconds," Dagmar said.

Then it went completely dark.

It took a moment for Dagmar to realise what had happened. Using an iNet eye command, Tristram had turned off all the lights. Dagmar's display automatically shifted to high definition night vision, effective over short distances. The move was both clever and cynical. Pasco, without glasses, could not see, but more than that, he was afraid of the dark. Dagmar heard a slight, involuntary whimper.

"It's all right, Pasco," Dagmar said.

Five seconds.

Tristram vaulted over the top of the couch. Pasco cried out in pain as Tristram crashed down on him. A couple of seconds later, Tristram emerged, smiling triumphantly, the little orange ball squashed in his fist. With another eye command, he flicked the lights back on.

Pasco's chin wobbled as he tried not to cry. Dagmar scooped him up and installed him on his knee. "That was pretty mean," he said.

"That's the game," Tristram snapped. For an instant his expression was so cold and ruthless that the air caught in Dagmar's throat, but as soon as it had appeared, it had gone. Had he imagined it? He must have.

"Can we have a story now?" Tristram said, suddenly all smiles and sweetness.

"We had a deal," Dagmar said. "I gave you extra time to play. You agreed to go straight to bed."

"I know but it would help us sleep," Tristram said, "and . . . it would make Pasco feel better."

And so, thinking for the hundredth time that he was much too soft on his children, Dagmar read, or rather showed them a story. The tiny projectors in his iNet that generated the holographic keyboard projected the story of a child who planted some seeds, which other creatures kept stealing, but when left to grow, turned into a lush, bountiful garden, with enough food and space for everyone. It was a modern day fairy tale, as unlikely a story as the beanstalks and houses made of candy of his youth.

As he listened to the electronic narrator, he thought it was a shame they had lost the physical books that were still common just twenty years ago. He missed the touch of the page, the smell. At least the three dimensional holograph had a little more soul than simply watching a sim.

When he had sung a song and extracted Tristram's promise not to play on iNet, he kissed them both and shut the door. He checked the time. Putting them to bed always took longer than expected and he had reports to finish by the morning.

Retiring to his solar, a room with a single chair and no windows for unnecessary distraction, he opened his communications feed. Among all the new messages, two were urgent. Maglan requesting that Dagmar review an encrypted media file and vid him immediately. His brother had recently been appointed President of Securicom, an elite among Elites. He didn't have time for small talk, which meant something was up. Was it more questions about the equipment he had asked Dagmar to track down in a classified Securicom transmission?

The second message concerned Namgola, and their quarterly results. Nausea rose in his stomach. He didn't usually get squeamish about work, but this was different.

Namgola was an artificially created Sector 3 in what used to be West Africa. Economically, it was designated part of the Cut, and therefore unsupportable, but Dagmar had pushed through a project, known as Oasis, to bring it into the Autonomy. If Logistics could convert a desert waste land into profitable Agri-land, then it could conceivably bring the starving mass of humanity outside the walls of the Autonomy back into civilization.

There was a lot of opposition from Top 10 because of the astronomical start-up cost, but Dagmar had fought for it all the way, filing proposal after proposal, detailing every part of the plan, building a consensus, pulling in every favour and crucially, persuading Havergill, President of Logistics, to trust him.

Locating Namgola near the coast, they pumped almost five hundred billion tons of water in through saline plants, enclosed the area with a high wall and populated it with ten million people. Citizenship was determined by a lottery with the surrounding Cut regions. Over three hundred million people applied.

Some potential citizens didn't meet the health grade and were automatically rejected. Some, they hand-picked as potential Supervisors, and sent them on crash courses in management in other Sectors. The rest had to wait and trust to luck. The lottery inevitably split apart families, but when that happened, almost nobody gave up their place.

The new citizens worked hard, clocking a hundred and twenty hours a week. Chronic dehydration from heavy manual labour in temperatures well over 120 degrees led to high incidences of liver cancer and other fatal illnesses, but the population, glad of enough to eat, toiled on.

Poring over the figures in the report, Dagmar bit his knuckles. He had hoped against hope there would be an improvement in productivity, but the environment was so harsh that even skaatch was proving difficult to harvest. Namgola had no chance of hitting its quota, and every attempt to improve the harvest had failed. The investment would have to be shut down.

Without the Autonomy's support, the raw materials that made skaatch farming possible would cease immediately, leaving the community with about a month of stockpiled food. He didn't know exactly what the situation was like outside the walls, but with the electricity cut and the security withdrawn, he suspected they would have a few million skeletal intruders trying to get their hands on the skaatch and anything else that moved.

The experiment had cost Top 10 a staggering trillion credits, but to keep Namgola running over the next five years would cost a trillion more. Namgola sustained ten million people, but it was a simple question of economics. So simple. Sweat soaked his shirt. He closed his eyes and filed the order to shut it down.

Would this failure mean his job?

He had given Logistics twenty years of loyal service. His record was spotless apart from this, and they couldn't expect every grand project to succeed, not the first time. Losing his position didn't bear thinking about. It would make no difference that he was an Elite, he would be considered damaged goods, unemployable.

His interface suddenly lit up. A text from his wife.

I need to speak to you.

He replied saying he didn't have time. As he did so the incongruity of the media struck him. When had it become easier for two people in the same apartment to type rather than speak?

Please. I need five minutes.

I'm working.

I'm standing outside your door.

He already knew that. As soon as the message appeared, he saw her coming towards the room on iNet; a little dot superimposed on the layout of his apartment. He sighed. She wasn't going to go away.

Come in then.

"Esther," he said, as his wife opened the door.

Although she was now over forty, the years of being an Elite's wife had been kind to her. There were no lines on her face, no blemishes on her skin, her body carried no fat, except for maybe the boobs, which were perfect in a different way. She could have passed for twenty, LifeScience's promise to the rich men and women of Sector 1, no effort required.

Dagmar refused to do anything himself. He liked the lines on his face, the cluster of old acne scars on his left cheek, the receding hair. He liked his outward appearance to reflect the real length of his telomeres which were shortening every year. He appreciated the transparency, the lack of deceit, even if nobody else did.

His wife smiled. Dagmar noticed she wore the expression he had long since become familiar with; she wanted him to do something. She rustled towards him in an expensive thigh length concoction, her make-up immaculate.

"What's the occasion?" he said pre-emptively.

"Oh, you mean this little thing," she said, and twirled. "Does there have to be an occasion when your husband is rich and every whore of Babylon is after him?"

Dagmar sighed. It was one of his wife's fantasies that he had affairs. She spent too much time in romantic sims. Real people didn't have time for affairs. Too much work.

She put a hand on his shoulder. "I need to talk to you about the twins."

She pushed her iNet glasses to the top of her head. It was the new fad, removing the glasses for intimate conversations. Otherwise you could never really be sure the other person wasn't watching a Steel Ball replay, ordering a coffee or even talking to someone else.

"Please," she said, pointing to his lenses.

Not wanting to argue before they even began, Dagmar put his own glasses on the table. It was a strange sensation, this formal disrobing. The glasses were so flexible, so comfortable that most people even slept in them, taking advantage of the night dreams software that soothed even the most restless sleepers. Back when they were first married, they even kept them on during sex. There were simulations for that too.

"You know how busy I am this time of year," he said.

"You're always busy."

To pay for all of this, he thought, a two thousand square feet apartment where many families, even in Sector 1, just had sanitized sleeping cubes and closet bathrooms. To pay for his wife's expensive habits, the body she wore and a life of leisure and simulations. He experienced a sensation like sucking on a battery. If he lost his job, all this would be gone within twelve months, no matter how rich she thought he was.

"Look, I took the glasses off. Let's get a move on."

"Our boys turn seven next week."

"I am aware of that."

"It's time we sent them to Rhodes."

The Academy at Rhodes was a megaplex of learning for Elite families, accepting boarders from the age of two. The cost was staggering, but so were the results. Graduates were practically guaranteed management positions in Top 10, many of them on a fast track to Elite.

"There's time for that," he said, "they're still young."

He thought of them, boarding at the Academy and leaving him with just his work and . . . her. It had been enough once. Not anymore.

"Most of our friends are already sending their children there."

By friends, he supposed Esther meant those Mansion wives she met in exclusive simulations, where one's status depended on the size of your husband's quota and the schools your children attended. The current wisdom was that the sooner a child enrolled in this intensive education, the better. In a world of almost eleven billion, competition for the top spots was fierce.

"Well? Aren't you going to say anything?"

"I think it's too soon to send them away," he said.

His wife pursed her lips. "Do you remember Katia Jardine?"

"No."

"You do. We went out to dinner with her and her husband a couple of months ago. He's a Senator grade at Utilities, hardly spoke two words."

"No," he said again.

Dagmar tried to forget his wife's friends. It wasn't easy. He could replay every social event they had attended since iNet came online. The lenses were a photographic memory he never used, except for that one time he tried to trace the exact moment things began to go downhill with Esther. He loved her once.

"Well their son is at the Academy, and he's only six and his class is being trained to run a virtual sector. They have to build it up from scratch managing production, finance, human capital and pollution levels, carefully balancing attrition with productivity. Can you imagine?"

"I have some idea."

"Then you must also realise that the boys need to be enrolled *now*. They'll get left behind otherwise. It's not like in your day when you left university at twenty-one or twenty-two and stepped into a major corporation."

That had not been Dagmar's experience, graduating during a recession, having to work as an intern for two years before his first real job, but he let it pass.

"And Katia says Top 10 entry level positions are getting over run with slum-world Aspirants, pushing down the credits, and making it even harder to get in."

That's what the Aspirant system is for, he thought, to harvest the talent from the underprivileged regions in Sector 2 and 3. His wife, like many in Sector 1, regarded it as a threat, but they had no idea. Few from "slumworld" made it into management positions, even if their families somehow found the funds for Academy-level education. Most Aspirants became Supervisors in their own sectors, some, burnt out from long hours of study and the overwhelming burden of family expectations, didn't even make it that far.

He suddenly felt weary with the whole conversation. He was not sending the twins away and he needed to get back to the reports.

"I think the twins' tutor is very good."

Esther folded her arms. "I'm sure he is, as far as he goes. But he doesn't teach them business."

"No. Dieter's teaching them how to think."

"You're missing the point!" she shouted. "We're talking about their lives!"

Dagmar thought of the sims she played, of the endless melodramatic confrontations between desperately shallow characters. "They have the rest of their lives for studying economics and management," he said. "We'll send them to the Academy in a couple of years."

"Then what about the *Faith* school in Mansion? Their outcomes are almost as good as Rhodes, and they would only have to board half the week."

Dagmar felt his hackles rise. "But the twins would need to be initiated in the *Faith*. We don't even do daily devotions."

Esther pursed her lips. "I do."

Dagmar said nothing. Of course she did. His wife was involved in every major sim going.

Esther continued to stare at him. It was unnerving, the unshielded eye-to-eye contact. Again, the feeling of nakedness crept over him.

"I'll think about it," he said finally.

For a moment she looked like she was going to push the issue and force a decision, but something changed her mind. Instead, she flipped down her glasses. "Do that," she said and stalked out. The doors swished closed behind her.

Esther had been talking about sending the twins to Rhodes for the last twelve months. Her arguments were based on a concern for their education, wanting the best for them, which was a difficult position to fault, especially in this competitive world. At least, that was what she told herself.

Dagmar believed her motivation lay elsewhere. There was a disorder, one LifeScience's medics were only just beginning to diagnose, called *netaku syndrome*. The primary symptom was a gradual withdrawal from the physical world; where *real life* became the short, unreal interval between highly stimulating virtual reality, rather than the other way around.

The twins were an inconvenience; too much effort, too corporeal, too time-consuming and like himself, outside of Esther's highly controlled world of iNet simulations. Her file from MediaCom showed the extent of her addiction. Thirteen to fourteen hours a day simming. Without the children, and with Dagmar working all the time, the demands of the physical world would be even less. He'd read that addicts went through a reverse nesting phase, ridding themselves of as many corporeal demands as possible. In their growing delusion, they were hardly aware of their motives.

The *Faith* was her latest role-play. Strictly speaking it was not a sim at all. During the environmental collapse of the 2020s, all of the major religions, like government, failed to deliver any answers. There was plenty of pestilence, starvation and death, but not the promised second coming. Instead, salvation came in the form of the mega companies of Top 10, miraculously bestowing life with skaatch farms, industry and iNet.

At first, survival was enough, but soon mankind required something new to believe in, something to fill the void left by the traditional religions of the world.

Over the next five years, MediaCom developed the *Faith*; the most seductive and rigorous belief system ever devised. The high definition, interactive meta-world gave the citizens of the Autonomy a sense of purpose greater than themselves. It encouraged the preparation of the soul for the afterlife through daily devotions and a practical, and in most cases necessary, ascetic disregard of worldly pleasure. Sixteen hour shifts on a bellyful of skaatch made sense if it was simply a test of eligibility for eternal bliss.

The real genius behind the *Faith* was the highly sophisticated reward system that measured an individual's progress towards the Afterlife. It was what traditional religion had been missing, a real time, public tally of one's spiritual standing. Life was work, life was struggle, but the life beyond . . . that was the thing. The *Faith* was the great leveller. Whether you were born the son of an Elite in Sector 1, or the daughter of a skaatch farmer in Sector 3, it was the accumulation of Afterlife points that would ultimately separate the sheep from the goats in the next world.

Most of Dagmar's colleagues participated in the *Faith*. There was nobody more devout than the *Faith's* brilliant young architect, Lars Pendicott, head of MediaCom. But for most of them, Dagmar saw their devotion in a cynical light; worship as a type of personal ledger, a hedge against a possible hereafter. Like all hedges it never detracted from the main investment; the acquisition of wealth. Not one of his colleagues would exchange Sector 1 for the sackcloth of a Sector 3 skaatch farm, even if it increased their chances in the next life.

If they enrolled Tristram and Pasco in the *Faith*, an avatar would pop up every time they opened iNet. The avatar could not be uninstalled. You could dismiss its admonishments, ignore the daily devotions and the endless quest for A-points, but you could never actually get rid of it. This was because the software interpreted any lapse in the *Faith* as temporary and it was never too late to come back to the fold. Indeed, the number of A-points received for returning to the *Faith* was staggering, as were the points received for enrolling one's children.

Dagmar rubbed his eyes. He was exhausted, but he still needed to review the Sector reports and their endless complaints about backed up Atmos systems, misplaced skaatch and productivity short falls. With a sigh, he replaced his iNet glasses.

Immediately, he knew something was very wrong. Rather than seeing the standard iNet display, the entire screen was flashing red. It was his brother, Maglan, on a priority one vid feed. Coming from the President of Securicom, there was no way to dismiss it. His lenses automatically connected with Maglan's office.

"Where the hell have you been?" Maglan said, his bulldog face in high definition. "I've been trying to reach you."

He remembered only then his brother's unanswered message. "I was . . . I was offline."

"Offline?" he said puzzled, "So you haven't seen."

"What?"

"This."

The media file began to play. Mountains of skaatch burning across hundreds of miles of Sector 3, a line of factories reduced to rubble in Sector 2, border crossings in flames, and bodies, bodies everywhere.

"More than ten thousand dead," Maglan said. "Millions of credits damage."

In another scene he saw children running, dormitories on fire and smoke billowing across a shadowy campus. The coverage was grainy, taken from a satellite. Dagmar's breath stuck in his throat as he recognized the Academy at Rhodes.

"Is Callum . . ." Dagmar began, immediately thinking of his brother's son.

"I need you here in ten minutes," Maglan said, cutting him off. "Review the report on the way down."

A new document appeared on Dagmar's interface.

"Who did it?" Dagmar asked, but Maglan's face had already disappeared.

He stared into the darkness of his display. Twenty years ago, the Autonomy pulled mankind back from the brink of extinction. Tonight, the world had changed. Someone, somewhere was fighting back.

2

SECTOR 2, CHURIN

I WATCHED HER white breath in the freezing trailer air and fretted about her husband. He was due home from the night shift an hour ago. If he was running late, he always sent a message. Angua knew how she worried. Machinists often had accidents and often they were fatal. Li pulled up iNet. No message. She checked the bulletin board at the Battery for reports of accidents. Nothing.

So stop panicking.

But she could not. Angua had not been himself lately. He was wound up so tight, holding in an anger she didn't understand. She had been waiting for something to happen. Perhaps today was the day.

On a tiny workbench, opposite the wood burning stove, Zhu laboured through an Academy work module. A foot away Min slept, lost under a mound of blankets. She had got in late from her shift. Her youngest daughter, Balmoral, sat perched on the end of her mattress, tapping away at her holographic keypad, seemingly impervious to the cold.

Li stared into the dying flames, huddling closer to the stove to stay warm. It didn't help. She checked the time again, considered logging into the *Faith* for a devotion, but decided to have a smoke instead.

"Bal," she said softly, not wanting to disturb the others. Balmoral stopped tapping on the holographic fingerpad, and turned her shaded glasses towards her. "Would you?" Li made a gesture with her twisted hand.

Balmoral pulled herself up and hobbled towards the table. It was a painful sight. She leaned heavily to the left, one leg shorter than the other. She was seven next week, but looked more like a five-year-old. She pulled down the old, battered tin from the sideboard.

"Three please," Li said, watching hungrily as her daughter rolled the woodbines. When she was done, Balmoral pushed one into Li's twisted fingers and lit it for her. Inhaling deeply, Li felt herself relax. The synthetic tobacco was her single luxury. Made from organic waste, it was so cheap that not even Angua could complain and since Mamfac, she couldn't live without it.

"Thank you," she said.

Balmoral said nothing, but hobbled back to her place on the mattress. Her tapping on the keypad began again.

Studying her daughter's emotionless face, Li's mind flashed back to that terrible morning when Tai-Tai almost killed her. Balmoral's recovery process was long and painful. She never cried, but in some ways that was worse, because she never smiled either. For the first two years of her life, her face wore a perpetual frown of concentration, keeping the tide of pain at bay. Li and Angua were helpless, unable to afford any of the drugs that might have eased the agony.

Ironically, during Balmoral's recovery, it was Tai-Tai who looked after her, working for whatever scraps of skaatch they could spare, cut from their own portions. They had no choice. Balmoral couldn't be left in her condition, and Li had to go to Mamfac to make ends meet.

Li took another drag on the woodbine. If she was honest, it had been a relief to escape to Mamfac, despite being pumped full of chemicals each day. She worked there for almost two years feeding forty-eight children a shift. In the end, it wasn't her supply that ended the job, but her physical condition. Her nipples were reconstructed three times but they still wore away to nothing and she could no longer lactate. On her last day, her breasts had to be artificially drained with three inch needles to prevent life-threatening mastitis.

She returned home a withered husk of a woman, addicted to a cocktail of drugs and in need of six months painful detox. By then Tai-Tai was dead, had herself faded away; a bundle of skin and pulmonary problems.

Li didn't remember feeding Balmoral as a baby, even though the amah brought her to Mamfac. The child was just one more squalling mouth for her industrial udders. Perhaps that's why she didn't feel close to her now, or perhaps it was because Balmoral was so distant. The child hardly spoke and never smiled.

At first Li thought she was slow. The doctor said her brain might have been damaged from the fall, even though the skull healed, the dent rounding itself out as the child grew. Then at two Balmoral discovered iNet, manipulating it in a way none of the others had managed at that age. Now she was never off it, tapping away at the holographic keypad, probing deep into sims, sleeping no more than a couple of hours a night.

Li took another drag on the woodbine and felt the chill morning air begin to lift, if only a little.

In the corner of the room, Min stirred. Li watched her sit up, rub her eyes and fumble towards the dunny in her underwear. After what sounded like a squirt of diarrhea, she reappeared, pulled on her shirt and jeans from yesterday and went over to the sink.

In the basin they kept the washing water which they used for themselves and the dishes. Min splashed the brown, dirty water on her face and then pushed her hair back in a ponytail using an old rubber oilcan ring. She stared at herself in the shiny piece of metal Angua had brought home from the workshop. She didn't smile. Finally, she took a quick drink of water from the jug, picked up the piece of dried skaatch she had left folded in a rag from the night before, and put it in her pocket.

"Are you all right?" Li asked.

"Fine." There were dark circles under her eyes.

"You sounded like you had an upset stomach."

"I'm fine."

"What time did you get back last night?"

"Four. They put me on a double."

"And tonight?"

Min shrugged. "If I can pull another double I will."

She took her respirator from the hook. Standing in profile, Li thought how old she looked; not in a budding, teen way, but in the true sense of the word. Her skin already grey, her shoulders hunched, her expression, weary.

Li remembered how Min had been such a bright spark as a child with her endless questions; *Mummy if you catch a cold in the summer, why isn't it called a warm?* A wave of sadness washed over her.

Min held down an average of sixty hours a week in one of the apprentice lodges on the outskirts of the Battery district. Officially, the lodges didn't exist. It was technically illegal for children to work at the Battery before they were fourteen, but the labour pool was too willing and the district managers always had quota shortfalls to reconcile. Besides, everyone in Sector 2 knew the rule only existed in order to have a two tier wage scale. Under-age workers earned about half the rate of their adult counterparts.

Occasionally Top 10 managers flew in and things would get stricter for a few weeks. Then the Stacks would become restless, waiting for the grandees to leave so their children could get back to earning enough to make ends meet. Thankfully, it didn't happen often.

Li listened to her daughter clang down the steps. The rusty stairwell had come loose, and banged precariously against the side of the stack whenever anyone went up or down. Angua said he would fix it one day. He was the only machinist in their stack, and the only person who had access to a hammer and rivets. But 'one day' had yet to come. The days were too long, his reserves of energy, too short.

Where was he?

It was past nine o'clock. Again she checked the Battery bulletin. Nothing. She tried to vid him, but he didn't respond. With an eye command she sent another urgent request for him to contact her.

The woodbine was down to the stub. Li sucked furiously to rekindle it in order to light the next. Her crab hands had stiffened over the last couple of years, becoming more like true claws and her fingers were not supple enough for matches.

"Done," Zhu said from the workbench, and removed his glasses.

"You can't be finished yet. You've only been at it a couple of hours," Li said.

Ignoring her, Zhu inspected his fingernails, rubbing an imaginary smudge with the corner of his shirt. Nails, pared half a centimetre or more above the fingertip, were a status symbol in Churin for those who didn't have to work the Battery line or perform manual tasks.

The affectation infuriated Angua, but as Li reminded him, all Aspirants were the same, as were the Supervisors and even Foremen. It was a mark of a higher function in Top 10, and to be the part, he had to look the part. Still, she wished he wouldn't preen so much. The nails of his older siblings were broken down stubs, and her own nails had disintegrated in workstation gel long ago. He stood up, stretched, and with his back to the fire, warmed himself.

"It's freezing in here," he said.

"Zhu," Li said, "the module."

"It was an easy one. I've done it before. Take a look if you don't believe me." He pulled up his holographic keypad, tapped a command and shared the assignment. It opened as a split screen on her lenses.

"I see, I see, yes," she said, although of course she did not. The circles and graphs could have been in another language, rather than Autonomy standard English. Her ignorance irritated her. Churin's great drought had interrupted her own schooling. When everyone starved, there was no energy for learning, and in the space of a year all of the schools closed.

"Supply and demand," Zhu said, watching her.

As frustrating as it was not to be able to understand her nine-year-old's lesson, she was proud. This was why it was so important for Zhu to be an Aspirant, so he did not waste away cutting metal or assembling chips, so his brain could be put to good use.

Li never told her husband, but she worried Zhu did not take his responsibilities seriously enough. The family's entire economy revolved around getting him into and through the Academy school. Twelve months of preparation modules equated to more than Min's take home pay for a year.

Zhu had already failed one test. If he failed another, the Academy would defer his entrance, which would mean more fees. Li lied to Angua about the results, telling him Zhu had sailed through. She begged her son to work harder, but he rarely studied more than a few hours a day. The rest of the time he spent messing about in sims.

"Satisfied?" he asked.

Li skimmed the meaningless graphs for a few more moments and then clicked off the display.

"Fine," she said quietly.

"So can I add a couple more bricks to the stove?"

"We don't have enough fuel."

"Can't we buy more?"

If Min works a double shift.

"No. If you've finished today's module, you need to go back over your last test."

"I'm not doing that now! I need a break!"

Zhu sat next to his sister on the mattress and joined her in the sim, both of them tapping furiously on their holographic fingerpads, unrestricted by the trailer's four hundred square feet, or Balmoral's lameness. They always seemed to be fighting things, shooting things, exploding things.

Why did so many games have to be so violent?

Still, it was better than spending time in the food sims that were suddenly so popular, salivating over impossibly lush fruit, succulent meats, steaming rice and cheese, and all sorts of other dishes that hadn't been seen in Sector 2 for years. MediaCom shut them down as socially disruptive, but no matter how hard they tried, food porn sims always popped back up.

Zhu spent all his time with Balmoral, even though he would soon be ten. He seemed to prefer her to boys his own age. Once, she even overheard Zhu asking her advice on a couple of Academy assignments. He did it in play, of course, to make his little sister feel important. There was no way Balmoral could understand his lessons, any more than Li did.

She supposed it was good they were tight, closer than her other children, but she worried about Zhu. In the new year he would leave Balmoral behind, boarding part of the week at the Academy and not returning until late at night on the evenings he did come home. He would miss her.

"What are you playing?" Li said.

Neither answered. Behind her iNet glasses, Balmoral, with her slight frame and jet black hair, wore her habitual expression of concentration, like the baby holding back the pain.

"What are you playing?" Li said, more loudly this time.

"Battery," Zhu said distractedly.

"What's that?"

Zhu didn't reply, too absorbed in the sim.

The Battery. That couldn't be fun surely? She imagined them virtually constructing components like she had done for almost twenty years. Or maybe they patrolled the lines like a Supervisor, looking for stragglers. Just the thought of it filled her with nausea.

The Battery.

Why hadn't Angua got back to her?

Perhaps she could reach out to Fen, but she was in a completely different section, three or four miles from where Angua worked. She wouldn't be able to respond to the message anyway. During a shift using iNet was forbidden. She wondered if Fen would bother to reply even if she could. Since moving in with her husband's family, she had become absorbed into a new economic unit; eight adults in a single trailer, cramped but relatively well off, everyone working, building up reserves for her first baby and the babies of her sister-in-law. She didn't have any time for her old family, and hadn't spoken to Li in weeks.

Quietly, Li began to panic. She could feel it in her mouth; a taste like old copper coins. Recently, Angua found excuses for staying away from home, but he never ignored messages, unless he wasn't wearing his iNet glasses, but that was now illegal in public.

So where was he?

She walked over to the solitary window, pulling back the tattered rag of a curtain. It was a gloomy morning but the visibility was fair, the smog index relatively low. Things had changed since the Atmos system went online, but the air was still soupy and acrid. According to Churin's media site, the full effect would not be seen for another two years. Apparently, the system needed time to ramp up. The accumulated baseline pollution had to be cleared before Atmos would regulate the air to a steady state. Even then, it would never be really clear, not like it used to be, before she was born.

Her husband helped to install it. Eighteen brutal months of double and triple shifts. Angua said that over forty-seven thousand men were detailed to the project, hoisting the massive turbines on five hundred foot scaffolds, digging the trenches for the filtration tanks, blasting rock with high impact explosives and then installing mile long ion generators.

In the last week of the construction, her husband's brother fell from the scaffolding in high winds. Logistics had not provided harnesses or even basic slings for the workers, one of the many compromises that kept the project to budget. As it was, Churin would be indebted to Top 10 for fifty years, the Atmos payments deducted at source from the Battery.

One more death was not shocking in itself. The installation claimed the lives of almost a thousand people. Each day there were accidents; men fell from scaffolds, were crushed under heavy equipment or drowned in flooded filtration trenches. It was the cost of doing business.

But after his brother's death, something in Angua snapped. To bitterness was added fury and recently, when he came home, his eyes burned with hatred. It made her afraid. Not of him, but of what he might do. It drove a wedge between them.

She could hear their arguments now. They always followed the same well-worn path. She would remind him that twenty years ago, children died on the streets, abandoned by their starving families, and that until the Autonomy took over, the people of Churin had no means to feed themselves, or work, or live.

"But this is not living!" he would roar back. "I work all the time. Even in my dreams I am working. My children are no better than slaves, animals made for work. Min is already a ghost and addicted to synapse. And you. Just look at you! Look at us!"

And she thought, *yes, look at us*. A wife who could afford to be an amah to her own family, an Aspirant, beginning in the Academy next year, and four relatively healthy children. The *Faith* taught her that their reward would come in the next world but they had done well in this one, if only Angua could see it.

Li lit her another woodbine, chaining it with the last, laboriously manoeuvring it into her shaking, claw-like fingers.

Recently, Angua had begun leaving the trailer at the few odd hours he was not working. She didn't know where he went. When asked, he was evasive, mentioning names of people she didn't know. In darker moods, Li wondered if there was another woman, but dismissed the thought as ridiculous. She knew from experience that if it was a choice between sleep and sex, he'd take sleep. Not because he didn't want her, but because it took a reserve of energy that he did not have. If he was doing something in his spare hours, it was not chasing women.

And that worried her. A couple of months ago, she had heard mutterings of secret meetings from Fen. Was this another reason her eldest daughter ignored them? Just the thought of it made her shudder. When she was a teenager, Li had an uncle who tried to form an organization with other workers. One night the Foremen came and they never saw him again. It was as if he had never existed.

But Angua wouldn't be so foolish, would he? He wouldn't jeopardize the family.

She shuffled back over to the chair, feeling all of her thirty-nine years.

"Whoa!" shouted Zhu suddenly, throwing up his arms. "Whoa," he said more quietly.

"What is it?"

"She did it."

"Did what?"

"Broke through," he said.

Balmoral's face betrayed no emotion, but her nimble fingers thrummed across the keys of the holographic pad.

3

SECTOR 1, MANSION

As DAGMAR HURRIED downtown in a bubble car, he thought how fragile the city looked, and how vulnerable. Mansion was a single tooth in the Atlantic, packed with impossibly high buildings, thronging with an impossibly dense populous. One well-placed atomic and the whole charade of order and wealth would shatter, and yet this was a city built on resilience.

When the environment collapsed in the early 2020s, Mansion weathered the extreme environmental changes. This was due to a massive sea wall and intricate sluice system, constructed when the old New York City could still raise the currency for such an endeavour, the mayor deciding that three hurricanes in twelve months was three too many. The foresight paid dividends. The coastal flood tides that swept away cities such as London, Tokyo and Boston left *Manhattan* largely untouched. The small island was now the heart of Top 10 and therefore, the Autonomy itself.

As Dagmar reviewed the reports on iNet about the attacks, he noticed there was nothing about the Rhodes Academy, which meant the coverage had been pulled.

Why? To prevent panic? Half of Mansion had children there.

Did the parents even know yet?

According to Maglan's report, the initial estimate was over a thousand dead and nearly all of them students. For the tenth time that evening he thanked god, or whatever force it was that shaped the universe, that his children were safe at home.

The attack on Rhodes would reflect very badly on his brother. He wasn't a popular member of the Board and there had been opposition to his appointment as President of Securicom.

Natasha Creed, the President of LifeScience and current Chair of the Board, had argued for a more experienced, more conventional executive than Maglan, who had the reputation of a maverick. Rhodes might prove her correct.

As they pulled into the business district a message appeared on Dagmar's iNet from Douglas Havergill, President of Logistics. He winked at the icon, opening the content onto his main display.

This is an official confirmation that Oasis was terminated this evening resulting in a net loss of 1.27 trillion credits itemized in the following balance sheet.

He skipped over the data to the last sentence.

The reckless experiment in Namgola represents the single largest project loss in the history of Logistics. As a result, we have no choice but to terminate your employment. Your last day will be . . .

Two weeks' notice to transition his active projects, and he was out. And that word, 'reckless'. There was a clause in his contract which stated he could be sued by Top 10 if an economic loss was the result of negligent or reckless action. Panic rose in his stomach like locusts on the wing.

"Destination approaching," the bubble car stated and pulled up outside Securicom's bullet-shaped building, a glittering triumph of chrome and steel. The car prompted him to get out. Once, twice. The third time the ageless, sexless voice sounded almost irritable but Dagmar was in a daze. He wanted to tell the car to drive on, and keep driving, but instead he found himself opening the door and stepping onto the pavement.

Esther. The mortgage. The children.

He knees were jelly as he walked through the double doors. He had to pull himself together. Reaching into his pocket he pulled out a synapse tab and swallowed it. The chemical would allow him to focus, to push off the panic until later.

Inside, a blast of cold air hit him. He was ret-scanned, searched by a guard and then manually ret-scanned again with his glasses removed.

"Is this really necessary?" he said impatiently, not because he was impatient, but because it was the type of thing an Elite said to subordinates. Or in his case, *used* to say.

"Legacy rules," the guard replied, as though that was an answer. He pointed to the elevator, "Basement level."

When the elevator doors opened another guard, armed and cocked, patted him down before escorting him along the narrow corridor to a set of large steel doors.

"They're already in session," the guard said and punched in the intricate combination, explaining while he did so that the *vault* was impregnable to every kind of attack; atomic, cyber and even biological, with purification filters ready to kick in at the merest whiff of a virus.

As Dagmar entered the room, eight executives turned in their chairs to stare at him, all except his brother, who closed his eyes and shook his head slightly. Maglan had said to be there in ten minutes. Dagmar had taken fifteen.

At the table was the Chair, Natasha Creed and Pierre Gravales, the bald-headed President of Finance. There was Lars Pendicott, head of MediaCom, Douglas Havergill, Dagmar's own divisional head, Trent Ventna, President of Materials Corp, Florence Flamel, the spiky haired President of TechCom, Lisa Benteke of the Academy and the dramatically obese Guy Rawstorm, President of Subsistence.

Only then did Dagmar realise that Maglan had summoned him to a Board meeting of Top Ten. The people around the table were the most powerful in the Autonomy. All of them famous, all familiar faces, although he only knew Havergill personally. It explained the secure meeting room, the four guards that lined the wall and the two more outside. Maglan must have cleared him as a consultant. Presidents reserved the right to bring in experts from any division as circumstances dictated.

Why had he asked him?

Feeling the colour rise in his cheeks, Dagmar joined another consultant leaning against the wall. Consultants didn't get seats.

"So glad you could make it," Natasha Creed said icily. "Shall we continue?"

Maglan said, "You have seen the assessment of the damage. The major Battery complexes at Pekin, Iberia and Malay as well as a dozen others, the skaatch depots across Skraeling, Nordic and Svenden and of course the Academy at Rhodes. These and other sites seem to have been chosen for their symbolic importance, maximizing economic loss rather than body count."

"Is there a difference?" Rawstorm muttered behind his walrus moustache.

"What are you doing about it?" Creed said.

"The situation is under control. In most cases, due to the very public nature of the sites, we have *Earth* footage identifying the perpetrators. We are rounding them up now."

"Most cases?"

"On some sites the cameras were taken out or otherwise disabled just before the attacks took place. We'll have to make house-to-house calls and throw a few credits around, but we'll find them."

"And until then?" Creed said.

"Our intelligence indicates no further attacks are imminent."

"Intelligence?" Creed said dismissively, "A bit late for that, isn't it?" She turned to the Finance President. "What exactly is the resource loss?"

"Initial estimate is about a billion in infrastructure and another billion in productivity," Pierre Gravales said. "The total human resource estimate is close to ten thousand."

"Is that factored into the two billion?"

"Of course."

Creed turned back to Maglan, "Why don't we have an exact count? Surely we know who's dead by now?"

"Ordinarily, yes. iNet would relay that information through the retinal interface, but some of the terrorists were not connected, and we have no iNet information at all from Rhodes due to the unusual nature of the attack."

"The *nature* of the attack?" Creed said, frowning.

"An electro-magnetic pulse knocked out all iNet systems for fifty miles. Nothing's functioning, including communications and transport. We're currently conducting a manual count of the students."

"Manual!" Pendicott sniffed incredulously.

"How long will that take?" Creed said.

"A few more hours. We have men on the scene but they have to get out of the dark zone in order to connect to iNet and report, so it's coming in slowly."

Creed muttered something to Gravales.

Dagmar had seen Natasha Creed many times on iNet, but never in person. Razor thin, immaculately dressed in a white suit, she set her iNet glasses on a permanently dark shade so nobody could tell what she was thinking.

Pre-Autonomy she had headed up major tech corporations, the kind of CEO who devoured companies and spat out the workers. Now her policies devoured the workers and spat out profits. She and Gravales were the senior members of the Board. Gravales made his name eliminating inheritance as a concept that could not co-exist with economic growth. His dictum was that every child should be born with a lifetime of productivity ahead of them. He had no children. He also had been instrumental in promoting Creed up the ranks, and when she took over as Chair, she made him her Vice.

She must have been seventy-five at least, although her buffed, wrinkle-free complexion would put her at forty on a bad day.

"What's the status from Media?" she said.

"We've crafted a response and put it out there," Pendicott drawled, "depicting the attacks as the work of anarchists and revolutionaries, that kind of thing. Of course, iNet is full of garish footage from eye-witnesses. Some of it's even real."

Pendicott was younger than the other executives, effeminate with his lisp and blonde ponytail, but his slight appearance belied his influence on the Board. After all, he was the architect of the *Faith*.

"What about Rhodes?" Creed said.

"There's nothing," Maglan said. "The EMP means no eye witness reports and we're not letting anyone out of the blast zone until we've finished the damage assessment."

"We had a story ready to go," Pendicott snapped, "but Securicom pulled it. We'll have to get something out soon though. Even if iNet isn't back by morning, someone will get through the cordon and then we'll be caught flat-footed. Already parents are complaining they can't reach their little darlings. Right now, they just think iNet has gone down, but in the context of the other attacks, someone is bound to make the connection. We'll be accused of a cover-up."

"Agreed," Creed said. "Maglan, on whose authority did you pull the media?"

"I made a judgment call. We need time to formulate an appropriate response. Rhodes shows we're dealing with a group that has the power to attack at the heart of the Autonomy. If not handled appropriately, that fact alone could cause mass panic, while providing every malcontent from here to the Cut with a cause."

"But that decision lies with the President of MediaCom, not you," Creed said. "You have overreached your authority."

"Not ah . . . according to legacy rules," Maglan said.

Creed paused a beat. "Legacy rules? You can't be serious."

Maglan said nothing but reached across the table, picked up the jug and poured himself a glass of water.

"Excuse me," Pendicott said, "but what are Legacy rules?"

"A financial and operational imperative invoked by Securicom when a state of war is declared on the Autonomy," Gravales said. "Operationally, the President of Securicom assumes executive power over conflict related functions. Veto power over Media is one of those powers. In addition, emergency funding is made available for Securicom and the quarterly financial assessment is suspended for the duration."

"How convenient," Pendicott said, "A chance to mop up all Maglan's red ink!"

Most of the board members smiled and Rawstorm stifled a chuckle into one of his chins.

When a Top 10 division fell lower than five percent growth and ten percent profitability for four quarters in a row, irrespective of any mitigating circumstances, the President was automatically fired. It was part of Top 10's constitution. Nine months into his Presidency, Maglan had failed every quarter.

"As our Vice Chairman stated," Creed said, "Legacy rules can only be invoked during a state of war, and requires the Board's unanimous approval. We are wasting time even discussing it."

"We were attacked by a hostile entity, *ipso facto*, we are at war," Maglan replied.

"I disagree," Creed snapped. "As tragic as the events of this evening are, the fact is we are dealing with a terrorist attack at best, not a declaration of war from a foreign power. Two billion credits? The cost of a few hundred factories. Ten thousand lives? We lose more each year installing Atmos systems. Let's not be overly dramatic."

The cold analysis of the economist. The lives themselves meant nothing. Then again, why should they? This generation of executives had shaped the Autonomy, drawing the Sector lines, deciding which regions slid into the water, or perished in sun-scorched droughts, indirectly condemning millions to death. Dagmar's stomach clenched as he thought of Namgola. He had no choice, but it was his name on the executive order.

"Excepting Rhodes," Creed continued, "your report shows that the attacks were amateurish with the majority of the damage caused by construction explosives and homemade devices. That doesn't sound like an invading army to me."

"I agree," Gravales said. "The success of the attacks suggests more about the competency of Securicom than the capability of this rag-tag outfit, *the Dish.*"

Maglan's eyelid twitched. "If that is the opinion of the Board."

"I can put it to a vote if you wish?" Creed smiled thinly. No other part of her face moved.

With both Creed and Gravales against the measure, there could only be one outcome.

"No. No need," Maglan said.

Dagmar had never understood why the governing articles of Top 10 insisted the Board meetings were in person in an era of three dimensional vid feeds. Now he did. The tension in the room was palpable. The dialogue had physical undertones that even the most advanced feeds could not replicate. What Dagmar had heard his brother call the touch of an adversary, the taste.

"Good," Creed said. "Then perhaps we can move onto the issue of accountability."

"As I have detailed in the interim report," Maglan said, speaking to the table, "the attacks came from loosely interconnected cells, malcontents from various Sectors that at first glance seem to have little in common with each other, and yet must be centrally organized. In addition, the coordinated timing, the nature of the targets, suggests a clear political purpose. Based on our initial intelligence, although no public aims have been stated, we believe this movement is a direct threat to the Autonomy, presenting an alternative, if you will, to the rule of economics."

There was a murmur around the table.

"Further, I believe this evening's events are a probe, a test to see how we will respond, but more importantly, how the population of the Autonomy will respond. Will these acts illicit outrage or support from the lower Sectors?"

"Maglan," Creed cut in, "sorry, but perhaps I wasn't clear. We've all read your report, we don't need to rehash the findings here, interesting as they may be. I am actually referring to *internal* accountability. This evening has raised questions about Securicom's competence which require consideration before we discuss our response. I'm afraid it is a matter of confidence."

Dagmar sucked in his breath. Natasha Creed wanted his brother's head.

"No need to apologize," Maglan said.

Creed smiled again. This time her mouth opened very slightly, a gash of red across her pale face. "Lisa, you have the floor," Creed said.

Lisa Benteke was a large woman, Afro-Caribbean, her hair pulled back in a severe bun, her iNet frames thick and bulky. The President of the Academy was like a parody of a schoolmarm from another era. During her tenure she had founded the *Faith* schools as a more spiritual, economic education, and if her abundant A-points were anything to go by, she was as devout as it was possible to be.

"As the President of Securicom said, we do not have all the details from our Academy at Rhodes. What we do know is that at least a thousand children have died, including three grandchildren of President Ferring who is not here for . . . for obvious reasons," she gestured to the empty seat. "Indeed, there are those seated around this table who are themselves waiting for news." She nodded her head at Douglas Havergill and Guy Rawstorm, but not, Dagmar noticed, at Maglan, who had not yet heard about his own child.

"Rhodes is home to over a hundred thousand children, the Autonomy's best and brightest, and we should thank the *Faith* that the number of casualties is not significantly higher. Had the attacks been a couple of hours later, half the school would have been asleep and I shudder to think of the body count. And yet, information has come to light that this tragedy could have been prevented. Securicom's Ross Trieme briefed me earlier this evening. I would now like to call him from the pit."

The *pit* was slang for the consultant pool. It was just another way, like the lack of chairs, to make it clear that the consultants didn't really belong in the room. Anywhere else, Elites were royalty, but the Board let them know where they really stood. If Maglan was forced to resign, Trieme would be in the running for his job.

Trieme tapped out a couple of commands on his holopad. "We believe the attack came in two waves," he said. A rotating three dimensional image of the school appeared in the middle of the Board's table. "An EMP detonated on the grounds that knocked out iNet and *Earth,* followed by incendiaries, planted inside the actual buildings shortly after the system went down."

A red dome, representing the EMP, radiated from the centre of the campus. An explosion rocked one of the dormitory blocks and little yellow dots came rushing out of the buildings. Each dot was a child. Many didn't make it, but flickered and disappeared.

Benteke addressed the room. "How did they get onto the campus unchallenged?

How did they get into the buildings? Why was our security so inadequate? Ross, will you please explain to the board what you told me."

Trieme glanced nervously at Maglan. "Securicom completed a full audit of the school's security nine months ago. Based on those recommendations an extensive plan was presented to the Academy and subsequently approved. Work was begun, but four months in, Securicom pulled the resources and the project was put on hold."

"Pulled?" Creed said, "On who's authority?"

"As I stated to President Benteke earlier this evening, the file relating to security at Rhodes Academy is classified," Trieme replied.

"In your opinion," Pendicott cut in, "had these upgrades been completed, would they have prevented the attack?"

"It is impossible to say."

"But what is your opinion?"

Trieme hesitated.

"Remember," Creed said, "in this forum you are accountable to the Board, not your President."

"I-in my opinion, had the upgrades been completed, the outcome of the attack would have been significantly different," Trieme said finally.

The interchange between Creed, Trieme, Benteke and even Pendicott seemed too sharp, too practiced. Was it rehearsed? The entire dialogue set up to get rid of Maglan? He remembered Pendicott was a protégé of Creed. It was she who had first seen the potential of the *Faith* and pushed him forward. Even Ross Trieme's reluctance seemed studied.

No, Dagmar thought, he was imagining it. Had to be.

"Maglan, I need you to explain how this happened," Creed said.

"I'm afraid I can't do that. It would require me to disclose classified information."

"Your opinion is noted, but you need to understand, we have to assess your division's role in this decision. This Board has the authority to make that information public."

"And *you* need to understand that the Rhodes file goes beyond a simple discussion of security schematics. I would strongly advise against declassifying it at this sensitive time."

Creed's mouth narrowed. "Let's put it to a vote then."

An image of a table appeared before Dagmar's lenses. As the Presidents voted, the seats around the table turned red or blue, depending on the vote. Six of the Presidents voted to declassify. Only Maglan, Florence Flamel, President of TechCom, and curiously, Gravales voted no. It was not enough.

Betraying no emotion, Maglan pulled up his holopad. He tapped in a succession of commands. "The Rhodes file is now declassified."

Holopads appeared around the desk as the Presidents pulled up the report. Dagmar did the same. According to Top 10's articles of governance, any files presented to the Board became public to all Elites, not just the Board members.

"Exiguous document, isn't it?" Pendicott drawled, "A hundred and eight pages of mind-numbing prose."

"We don't have time to review it now," Creed said irritated. "For expediency sake, tell the Board who pulled the project?"

Maglan looked not at Creed, but at Ross Trieme. "Me."

Again the room acquired a sudden silence; another of those visceral moments that a vid feed could not capture.

"I would like the President of Securicom to tell us," Benteke said, her voice shaking, "what could possibly be of greater importance than our children's safety! Than the future," she banged her fist on the table, "of Top 10's leadership!"

"Lisa, please," Creed admonished quietly. To Maglan she said, "Explain to the Board why the security protocol was not completed. According to Trieme, no reason was given for terminating the project."

So it was rehearsed, Dagmar thought. Creed had interviewed Trieme prior to the Board meeting. She had set Maglan up.

"Securicom broke its contract with the Academy," Benteke cut in, pointing at Maglan. "He jeopardized all those lives, just to reallocate resources elsewhere."

"Please Lisa, do me the courtesy of remembering that I too have a child at your school," Maglan said, sounding ruffled for the first time.

"Sadly, that fact has no bearing on the catastrophic impact of the decision," Creed said. "Indeed, this is just one of many upgrade projects you have pulled, weakening our infrastructure, directing valuable resources elsewhere, making what happened at Rhodes and across the Autonomy possible."

For a moment Maglan said nothing. Then slowly he pushed his chair back and rose from his seat. "I see." He looked weary, his six foot five frame more stooped than pugilistic, his fifty years for once weighing heavily on his shoulders. Was he going to walk out? Not even wait for the vote? Instead he said calmly, "Ross, would you be so kind to pull back up the visual of the school, this time without all the ah . . . pyrotechnics."

Trieme glanced at Creed. She nodded. He tapped a couple of keys and the three dimensional image reappeared.

"If you could rotate it so everyone can get a sense of the campus. Thank you." He gestured with his hand. "As you can see, the Academy's five hundred acre lot has four entrances, with three quarters of the perimeter surrounded by a simple fence. As my faithful colleague Ross told you, a Senator in Securicom conducted an analysis of the entire campus which he presented to the Academy. There were several recommendations but the most important were the erection of a sixteen foot concrete wall around the entire campus, and the installation of high intensity halogens along the perimeter. The cost was astronomical, but as those of you who pay the fees can understand, the Academy can afford it." Maglan allowed himself a small chuckle. Nobody else laughed.

"Ross, could you hand me over control of the simulation? Thank you." Pulling up his own holopad, Maglan continued, "Securicom completed work on about half of the campus and the entire north-east section." The upper right quadrant of the three-dimensional model lit up, showing the formidable wall, making the basic fences that covered the rest of the campus appear flimsy by comparison.

"As enlightening as this is," Pendicott cut in, "we've all seen the results for ourselves. We are wasting time."

"The President of MediaCom has a point," Creed said. "We don't have time for a guided tour of the school."

"You asked why the protocol was not completed. I am giving you an answer which has a direct bearing on the situation."

"Three minutes then," Creed said, "after which we will move to vote on *your* position."

"Thank you," Maglan said. "To plant explosives inside the buildings, indeed to mount any physical attack, would require a squad to get inside the grounds undetected and time to set the devices."

"That's why we wanted a wall," Benteke said.

Ignoring her, Maglan said, "The Academy is in the centre of New Rhodes, Sector 1, home to almost thirty million inhabitants living in tightly packed modular towers, not unlike Mansion itself. Because of its location, a couple of million people pass by each day and again, just like our Top 10 complex here, the foot traffic is twenty-four hours." The perspective changed to show a ground level view of the campus. Maglan gestured to the perimeter. "Through that simple fence, every single building on campus, every single angle, is visible to the naked eye."

The holograph rotated, showing the different perspective a passing pedestrian may have. Not only were the dormitories visible, but all the surrounding grounds as well.

"To repeat, to plant the kind of explosives required in this operation would require a team of at least six and probably double that to penetrate the perimeter and run all the way to the buildings. To anyone wearing iNet lenses, they would appear neither as a student or teacher and an alert would be sent to Securicom, with agents turning up within minutes. The pedestrian wouldn't even be aware they had done it. In other words, the Academy benefited from having twenty-four hour security by virtue of its open location. Now, compare the type of visibility I've just shown you at ground level, with the north-east part of the campus where the wall is complete."

He manipulated the holograph to show the view from the north east.

"I hesitate to state the obvious, but it is impossible to see through a sixteen foot wall. I concede some ingenuity would be required to scale the wall without being detected, but it can be done in about twenty seconds with a retractable grappling hook. I know. We tested it about the same time I shut the project down. Timed correctly, a team could be up and over before they were seen, benefiting from the wall's coverage."

"I'm not sure I agree . . ." Benteke began.

"The second innovation," Maglan said, cutting her off, "were the ultra-brights. As the name suggests these are high-intensity lights typically used for heavy industry installation. Why? Because they are so good at lighting up specific parts of the ground. However, because the light is so bright, they also create extremely dark shadows."

Again the perspective of the three-dimensional model changed, this time showing a ground level view inside the campus, facing the north western dormitories.

"The halogens lit up the campus, however against the mosaic of buildings, they also create long, pitch-black, shadows. Anyone intimate with the layout could negotiate a path to the dormitories without being seen."

He paused, studying the faces around the table.

"The innovations provided the two things the attackers required; time and cover. Interestingly, the more successful attacks in Sector 2 and 3 contained similar elements, manipulating industrial ultra-brights on existing work sites to provide cover in which to operate."

Dagmar stared into the dark areas of the simulation. They mapped onto the buildings targeted, providing cover for the ground floor windows and immediate surroundings.

"So my good colleague Ross Trieme is absolutely correct," Maglan continued. "Had the upgrades gone ahead, the outcome would have been very different. The whole school could have been torched without anyone from the outside having any idea until they saw the flames licking skywards. As it was the entire north east section of the campus was vulnerable, which is why I not only pulled the project, but set up a meeting to review the security of the Academy as a whole. Despite requesting an urgent meeting three times in the last six weeks, I see from my iNet record that Lisa only read my messages about two hours ago."

"I-I have had other priorities," Benteke said, flustered.

Maglan smiled. "Of course, the children are only the, what was it? *Future leadership* of Top 10."

At first, nobody spoke, then Pendicott clapped his hands in a mock applause. "Ha-ha! Well played!"

Maglan flicked the holograph off and returned to his seat. Multiple conversations broke out around the table prompting Creed to bring the meeting back to order.

"I would like to remind the Board that all of this information is speculation. All we know for sure right now is that an EMP was triggered prior the first of the explosions, and from that moment on Securicom has been blind. We don't actually know what happened or whether the factors Maglan mentioned played any part in the attack."

"That's ah . . . not quite correct," Maglan interrupted.

"What are you talking about?" Creed snapped.

"When I analysed the Academy plan I could not understand how a Senator grade in Securicom had made such blunders . . ."

"Point of order," Pierre Gravales, the Vice Chair interrupted. "This is not the forum for discussing employee competency, at least not below Board grade. It is for you to deal with your reports outside of this meeting."

"Bear with me, Pierre," Maglan said. "On President Creed's insistence, I have unclassified the Rhodes report. Before we move on, the Board needs to understand the information they have just made public to our ten thousand Elites, and therefore no doubt, to the Autonomy itself."

Creed waved her hand. "Go on," she said reluctantly.

"The report details one James Kano. Kano was an Aspirant from Sector 2. He clawed his way into Top 10, his credentials impeccable. He was promoted from Trainee to Tyro to Senator in a matter of three or four years. He was too competent to make flawed recommendations for Rhodes. Therefore, I came to the only conclusion that made sense. Kano was acting on behalf of an entity hostile to the Academy, or the Autonomy, or both. Two weeks ago, we brought him in for questioning during which we discovered that he was part of a wide-reaching organization called the *Dish*, dedicated to the overthrow of the Autonomy."

"I'm sorry," Creed said, "I'm suddenly finding this a little difficult to follow. If you had identified the threat prior to the attacks it seems we have been caught surprisingly unprepared."

"Unprepared?" Maglan said. "There were eighteen sites where collateral damage was sustained."

"Exactly," Creed said.

"Earlier this evening attacks were attempted at about sixty sites, including three right here in Mansion."

There was an intake of breath around the table.

"Far from being a matter of a few terrorists, as I tried to explain earlier, the

Dish is a movement with a centralized command structure that has in effect declared war on the Autonomy."

"How did you prevent the attacks?" Creed asked.

"The *Dish* operates in discreet, regional cells. Each cell has limited information, so if one is compromised, the whole remains. However, after analysing what Kano told us about the attack sites, we used *Voice* to build a profile of other likely targets."

Maglan pulled up a holographic image of the territories of the Autonomy. Over seven hundred potential sites were highlighted.

"I have been criticized for pulling resources off non-critical projects. This is where those resources went. Had it been possible to infiltrate more cells ahead of time, or know the exact date of the attack, or every target, I assure the Board that I would have done so. As it was, we did what we could with limited information, little time and less support."

Surreptitiously, Dagmar pulled up his holopad and looked up *Voice*. There was no public information on Media, but there was a reference to an artificial intelligence TechCom had prototyped, which as an Elite, Dagmar could access. From what he could tell, what iNet *Earth* was to the physical world, *Voice* was to the intellisphere; monitoring, digesting and analysing information across the whole of iNet.

"No support?" Pendicott drawled. "Really? I would argue the overhead paid into Securicom represents a rather significant level of support."

Maglan shook his head. "Whereas in our other companies success leads to investment, in Securicom, ten years of peace has led to cutbacks voted on by this Board, stretching our resources, making us vulnerable. Prior heads of Securicom have been focused on balancing the budget rather than the defence of the Autonomy. Our intelligence, infrastructure and manpower are not adequate to police all of our assets. The result is what we saw this evening."

"But still, you knew this . . . *Dish* was planning to assault the Academy and you did nothing!" Benteke snapped.

"I reasoned the target would be aborted once the *Dish* knew Kano was compromised. They didn't touch the other sites he knew about. Even so, had the assault been similar to those we experienced at the other public buildings, Securicom agents in the vicinity could have handled it. As I've said before, there was something very different about Rhodes. The attack had more purpose than the plastic and pipe bombs of elsewhere, and the EMP was an innovation Kano knew nothing about."

"Or said nothing about," Creed said.

"Unlikely, in a chemical interrogation."

"What else did he tell you?" Gravales said.

"Nothing else of significance, but then the information was based on a single short session. Our plan was to turn him, plug him back into the *Dish,* in an attempt to find others, to learn more than he was able to tell us based on his own cell. After some persuasion he agreed, so we took a risk. We released him before his handlers got suspicious."

"But you said he was compromised," Gravales said.

Maglan smiled grimly, "He was, but we only realised that when we found him hours later with a bullet in his brain."

"Weren't you watching him?" Creed said.

"Of course, but he eluded us."

"How is that possible?"

"As I said before, Kano was a highly competent Securicom employee. He found a way."

"Competent enough to get shot," Pendicott said.

"Why was this intelligence not presented to the Board?" Gravales said.

"I requested a discussion with the Board."

"I recall seeing no such request," Gravales said.

"That is because our Chairman refused to table it."

"Is this true, Natasha?" Gravales said, turning to her.

Creed flushed slightly. "The request was general. Maglan wanted a budget for a period of what he termed *heightened awareness.* Emergency funding would have been irresponsible. There was no evidence that an attack was imminent. There was no mention of this . . . James Kano."

"Even so," Gravales said, barely hiding his irritation, "if a request came in from Securicom for funding surely it would have been better to at least inform me. Finance is my domain after all."

"Hindsight is twenty-twenty, Pierre," Creed replied defensively, rattled by her usually loyal Vice Chair. "If Maglan had been specific, then of course I would have scheduled the matter for discussion. As it was, Securicom provided no further information and dropped the matter."

"Why?" Douglas Havergill said, speaking for the first time.

"Kano proved that the *Dish* had infiltrated Top 10 at a high level," Maglan said. "Due to the transparency of our Board's proceedings, had I presented the findings in this forum, the *Dish* would have known everything you know today through the minutes. They would have regrouped, changed strategy and, unless we could have unearthed another operative, we would have no idea what they were planning or on what scale. Further, presenting to this Board would have achieved little other than putting the *Dish* on alert. The evidence of my request for funding shows that a danger without recent precedent is too readily dismissed by those who have to foot the bill. For that reason, I took a risk that it was better to contain a known threat, than to invite one at a later date which we knew nothing about."

Nobody spoke for a couple of beats.

"We need to move on," Creed said finally. "I believe Maglan has, albeit unconventionally, addressed the immediate issue of Securicom's competency in this matter. I propose therefore not to proceed with the vote of confidence." Again, Creed favoured the table with a ghastly smile. Benteke nodded her head in reluctant agreement. "Good, the next item on the agenda is to formulate our response to this crisis."

"Natasha, I'm afraid we should not proceed just yet," Maglan said.

"Why?" Creed snapped.

"Because I believe the *Dish* has infiltrated this very Board."

4

SECTOR 2, CHURIN

ZHU JUMPED ABOUT in excitement. "She broke through! She actually did it!" Crashing back onto the mattress, he yelled, "Show me some more, yes, show me something else!"

Balmoral, impassive, tapped away on the holographic pad. What was she doing?

With an eye command Li tried to access their 'Battery' sim, but was locked out, her parental control disabled. That couldn't be right. She tried again, but was distracted by the banging of the rusty rail against the side of the stack.

Someone running up the stairs. Please let it be him!

The door of the trailer swung open, and her husband stood in the frame.

"Angua!" she cried, giddy with relief. Then she noticed he was deathly pale, and that his shirt was torn and his arm was bleeding. "What happened . . ." she said, standing up, moving towards him.

"Don't touch me!" he rasped, staring at her with naked eyes. "Have they come yet?"

"Who?"

"Just answer! Have they come for me?"

"No," she said, her voice trembling. "You're scaring me, Angua."

He stripped off his shirt, thrusting it into the stove, blowing on the embers to make it take. As the flames caught, he turned to the sink and unwound the blood-soaked rag from his arm. There were four deep punctures in his skin, just above the elbow. It needed cleaning before it became infected.

"Let me . . ."

"Stay away!" he snarled.

Standing over the basin, Angua poured rice wine into the wound, before gulping down half the bottle. He dressed his arm with a rag, securing the bandage tight with his teeth.

"What happened?" Li repeated.

Ignoring her, he paced over to the window, lifted the curtain, and peered down into the street.

It puzzled Li that neither of the children had stirred until she realised that of course, he didn't have his glasses on. Engaged in their sim, lenses on full shade, Angua was electronically invisible. She was glad. It was better they didn't see this.

Angua let the curtain drop, and came back towards the table.

"Angua, you have to tell me, what is it?"

"The Foremen are coming."

His words filled her with dread. She thought of her uncle, disappearing without a trace. "Why?"

He shook his head. "The less you know, the better."

"But why?"

Angua hesitated. "I-I did something tonight."

She felt suddenly sick, as though she might pass out. "What did you do?"

Angua said nothing, but returned to the window and again peered downwards.

"Y-you have to go! Before they get here!"

Slowly, he turned to her, his expression like death. "Go on the run? Where? I put on my lenses, and they know where I am, but without iNet? I can't buy food, or water, or take transport or interact with the world. And what do you think would happen to you? They would blacklist the family. No work, no rent, no skaatch. You would die of exposure on the streets of Churin. If I go quietly, perhaps they will leave you alone."

It hit home to her then with sickening clarity. Whatever Angua did, they were ruined. Zhu's Aspiration was over, and without Angua's salary, they would have to move to a communal trailer or 'five di', where four families lived in each corner of a tiny room, with a fifth at its centre.

"How could you do this to us?" she said, her voice quavering.

At first he didn't reply, but stared into space. "Do you know what I've been doing all week?" he said finally.

"How could I? We never talk anymore."

"Putting up high torsion nets outside the Battery buildings."

"Why?"

He took another gulp of wine and then with his fingers pantomimed two legs walking across the flat of his palm, and whistling, stepped his fingers over his palm and splatted them on the table.

"Not more suicides!"

"Forty this week alone. They find a way onto the roof, or climb out through an upper floor window, and then . . ."

"*Faith* save them."

"The *Faith?* Ah yes, those poor souls losing all their A-points. If only they *accepted what they could not change*. Instead they mount the only protest the can; to rob the Battery of its precious resources, themselves."

"But if the nets catch them, won't they just do it again?"

"Perhaps, but not before the Autonomy's councillors have had a crack at them. The nets prevent death, not injury, and while they spend the weeks in Triage, piling up debt, they can be re-educated and re-cycled, to emerge a better worker than before."

"What did you do?" She sobbed now despite herself.

Angua shook his head and then gulped down the last of the rice wine.

"No!" Zhu suddenly screamed, making them both jump.

"It's only a sim," Angua growled. "The bloody baby."

"No!" Zhu screamed again, his face deathly white, "Turn it off! Turn it off!"

Balmoral's head slowly turned, regarding him through the shades.

"Make her stop!" he pleaded. "Make her stop!" Tears streamed down his face. His hands clasped the edge of the mattress so hard he pushed holes through the cover. The meagre stuffing sighed onto the ground. He screamed again.

"Pull them off him!" Li shouted.

Angua hesitated.

"Do it!"

Reaching over he snatched Zhu's glasses from his eyes.

Snapping someone out of a sim was dangerous, and at first Zhu stared at them as though he was having night terrors. Then he began to hyperventilate. Angua slapped him across the face. Zhu fell back and then vomited.

"It's all right my darling," Li said, pulling Zhu towards her as he gingerly got to his feet. He could hardly stand.

"What did you do to him?" she shouted at Balmoral. This couldn't be all about the sim they had been playing. A sense of unreality gripped her. First Angua, now this, whatever *this* was.

Balmoral's glasses changed from full shade to clear, and she stared at the three of them with her coal black eyes. Zhu snivelled on Li's leg, moaning something she couldn't understand.

"What is it, Bal?" Angua said.

Her eyes had a faraway look. "The Battery," she said calmly.

"No, no, not that," Zhu sniffled.

"Show us," Angua said, picking up Zhu's discarded lenses, warping the plastic frames as he wrapped them around his face.

"But they'll know where you are!" Li said. If Foremen were looking for him, they would pick up his retinal signature.

"Show us," Angua repeated.

Balmoral hesitated, her hand hovering above the keypad. She tapped a succession of commands and Li's lenses darkened to a fully shaded sim.

She could still see Balmoral in front of her, rendered electronically, just as she could see Angua in ghostly outline across the table. Then both faded.

The time stamp in the corner of Li's lenses read 3am. She saw a work party using pile drivers to make holes in the concrete ground. Another group of men cut steel, surrounded by a rain of yellow embers. The scene was so vivid, she could taste the smog in the night air. Massive perimeter lights made it brighter than day.

The Battery was twenty-four hours, and outside of the walls, one worker's evening was another's morning. Time was relative to shifts, rather than sunlight.

When she recognized her husband's face, Li realised this was not a sim at all, but the actual Battery. They were outside one of the vast buildings and Balmoral had accessed what she could only guess was an *Earth* feed. The image was too steady, too panoramic to be anything else. But how could her daughter do that?

The time stamp in the corner of her glasses sped up and the work crew moved in an agitated blur. One hour flew past, two, three until the play back slowed to normal speed, and the view focused in on the exterior of building 432.

A ringing bell indicated the end of the night shift and the main doors were suddenly crammed with the exiting masses. Ignoring them, the crew hoisted a gigantic pole into place, complete with rigging to secure to the building and make a net. Each man had a wire cable fixed around their waist and they walked like pack horses, a dozen of them straining forward, sweat pouring from their faces.

There was a dark blur and a heavy thud as something fell to the ground. A couple of the men jumped backwards, releasing the tension on their cables. The weight of the pole dragged the others off their feet, pulling them along the ground as it toppled earthwards. Smashing into the concrete, it narrowly missed a crowd of workers. Curses filled the air.

To the left of the exit two more dark shapes fell. Two more heavy thuds. Necks craned up towards the roof, and then back to the ground. Someone screamed. Supervisors appeared, moving the crowds on, not allowing them to linger.

Li tried to turn away, but she couldn't help staring. A man, woman and a girl, the last not older than Fen, had jumped to their deaths. The girl's body was horribly twisted and a pool of blood welled around her head. She twitched, as if trying to speak.

The three jumpers created an inconvenient distraction. The crowd dawdled, mesmerized by the sight of the bodies, creating a jam for those coming in and those going out. The start of the new shift would be delayed.

The Supervisor barked an order and the perimeter lights on the eastern side of the building were killed. This should have thrown the bodies into darkness, except that the construction crews worked under mobile floodlights. The Supervisor yelled at them, and the machinists rapidly wheeled them away.

Li thought it was curious how her eyes adjusted, as though she was actually outside. Around her, she could make out shapes moving in the gloom, the clean-up crew hurrying back and forth, the rapid unrolling of orange tape that flickered in the moonlight.

That was not all she noticed. Her husband remained deep in the shadows along with three other machinists. Curiously, he didn't seem shaken up, and when the bodies dropped, he didn't flinch, or even look surprised.

Her screen blanked and the perspective changed. Li found herself staring at the girl's body from a couple of feet away. The image was vivid, as though seen through a night vision filter. She wanted to tear her eyes from the broken form, and tried to zoom backwards. Nothing happened. Again she was reminded this was not a sim she could control, but a fixed recording of events that had already transpired.

The girl looked like a bird that had fallen out of its nest. Mercifully, she no longer twitched. The other bodies had already been cleared away. Li tried to imagine the mentality of someone who set off to work in the morning in order to plummet to the ground twenty floors below, all for the sake of a gesture. She wondered if the jumpers had been a family.

Is this what Zhu had seen? What made him cry out? The crushed head. The stricken face still leaking blood.

An orderly zipped the girl into a body bag, and turned towards Li. His lips moved, but there was no sound. She was looking through someone else's lenses, someone actually standing at the scene. The night vision meant the owner of the glasses was a Foreman.

Li suddenly felt very hot.

If Balmoral could hack into *Earth*, and then someone's iNet interface, what else could she do?

Something must have drawn her host's attention, because his eyes flicked up and onto the building's eastern wall. To her horror, she saw Angua silhouetted in green, crouching behind a cement mixer. He handed an oblong canister from his duffel bag to another machinist. He couldn't have been more than a few hundred feet from where the Foreman stood.

There were four of them. They had removed their glasses to avoid iNet identification. Surely a futile gesture. It might buy them some time, but it would be clear from the surveillance that they never left the area. What they were doing now was suicide, and they must know it, as surely as the jumpers had.

Her view turned to another Foreman standing next to her. The man's lips moved, but still no sound came. There was a whining noise, as though someone was trying to locate the correct frequency, before a muffled crackle, and the voices came online.

"And I thought this was going to be a waste of time."

"How did Securicom know?"

"Does it matter? I'm calling for back up."

"We don't have time for that. The building will be blown to bits before they get here and that will mean our jobs."

"Then what do you suggest? There's more of them than us."

"They are blind in the darkness. They won't see us coming until its too late."

"Then what?"

He held up the shock gun. "Set to max and hit them hard."

"But we'll kill them."

"Better than risking the building. Any one of them could be carrying a remote detonator."

The other nodded and they set off in the shadows.

Li watched the machinists continue with their work, oblivious of the approaching danger. Angua ran a wire from the base of the building, effortlessly attaching it to a detonator despite the dark. Angua always said he could do his job in his sleep.

As she moved towards the four figures, experiencing everything through the Foreman's eyes, it was as though she had become him. She could smell the Battery air, feel the adrenalin pumping through her veins. She actually wanted to attack them.

She took the nearest machinist by surprise, pressing the shock gun into his back, watching in fascination as he collapsed. Li felt the force of the discharge, felt the man's body jolt under her arm.

Angua fumbled with the detonator and she thrust the shock gun towards him. He caught her wrist and they struggled. She tried to punch him but her clenched fist glanced off his shoulder. With an effort she curled the prongs of the shock gun towards his body, but his grip was like iron from years of working with heavy equipment. He shook her arm, trying to dislodge the gun. She tried to hold on, but the weapon clattered to the ground.

Before she could react, Angua's hands were around her throat. She clawed desperately at his arm, her long, square nails like talons, gouging deep into his skin, puncturing it. But Angua squeezed harder, his face filled with hatred, every moment recorded in high definition.

The lenses shook back and forth and Li gagged at the tightness of the fingers, at the lack of air, until finally she . . . no not she but the Foreman . . . collapsed and the world turned on its side. iNet registered that contact had been lost with the retina and shut down. The Foreman was dead.

5

SECTOR 1, MANSION

EIGHT FACES, ALL hostile, stared at Maglan.

"You claim the *Dish* has infiltrated this Board? Are you mad?" Creed demanded. "What is your evidence?"

"After Kano was shot, we went back over his entire history in detail. The only thing that stood out was that during a twelve month stint in internal affairs he extensively investigated every member of this Board, taking a particular interest in your vacations."

"Why?" Creed said.

"As you know, Top 10 dictates that anyone Elite and above must take two consecutive weeks' vacation."

"Of course, to prevent burn out."

"That was the original intent of the policy, but internal affairs have also realised it provides a unique opportunity to analyse unusual executive orders, the ones that are put on hold while the boss is out, the ones that nobody else in the division is authorized to see."

"Such as?" Gravales said.

"Such as an executive in Logistics illegally shipping weapons to the Cut, paying the books with the list price and keeping the mark up, or the executive in Finance cooking the books of a particular department in return for a kick-back. Both would be identified in a targeted data sweep."

An uncomfortable murmur broke across the table.

"Well, we're all sitting here," Gravales said in his slight French accent, "so one can only presume he didn't find anything. You stated that until this year Kano was a model employee. He opened some investigations. So what? I don't pretend to know the inner workings of internal affairs, but is that so unusual?"

Maglan studied the Vice Chair for a moment. "What is unusual, Pierre, is that he shredded all of the sunshine related records, potentially triggering a data integrity event in the process. If there had been nothing to find, why take that risk?"

"And that's your evidence?" Creed said. "That because this rogue Securicom employee audited our . . . our vacations, that the Board has somehow been infiltrated by the *Dish*?"

"I believe he found something to give him leverage over Top 10 at the most senior level, and to cover his tracks, he destroyed the evidence."

Pendicott let out a low whistle. "All this intrigue is making my head ache."

"Speculation," Creed said. "We have no idea what he was looking for, or whether he found it. Yet your allegation could destabilize Top 10 unless you drop it."

"I agree," Gravales said. "We cannot allow this meeting to become a talking shop for unfounded theories."

"Kano shredded the records," Maglan said slowly, "but I know what he found. Since *Voice* came online, she automatically archives anything recorded on iNet lenses. As a result, although it is a time-consuming process, if we can pinpoint what we are looking for and from which identikit, we can recreate the visuals, in this case, from Kano's interface."

"*She*?" Pendicott said. "You name your little toys now?"

Pendicott's attempt at sarcasm fell curiously flat and Dagmar felt the atmosphere in the room shift again. This insight into *Voice* unsettled the Board. Guy Rawstorm fidgeted in his seat, and although the room was climate controlled, sweat beaded on his brow. Only Florence Flamel looked entirely unphased. As President of TechCom, she already knew the AI's capabilities.

"That was not in *Voice's* original mandate," Creed said icily. "Such a wide ranging invasion of privacy requires authorization from this Board."

"Perhaps," Maglan said, pulling up his holopad, "more pertinent to this evening's events is what we discovered. Please, if everyone can direct their attention to the file you have just received."

An archived vid feed opened on Dagmar's interface. It was in overlay mode, so it appeared to play at the centre of the conference table. Nausea rose in his stomach as Dagmar recognized the footage. Finally, he knew why he was here.

"What you are watching is archived surveillance from *Earth* taken from the Beth Rael complex in Mansion, the largest birthing facility in our city, delivering more than ten thousand children a day. It's also where most of the controlled miscarriages take place. The rows of bins you see are . . . well you don't need me to elaborate." Stark red bio-hazard bins were lined up against the whitewashed wall. A work party in scrubs stacked them onto stands.

"Abortion is a sin against humanity," Benteke said, her face pale. As a devotee of the *Faith* she was a vocal critic, regardless of circumstance or term. It denied the immortal soul the chance for eternity, while robbing the earthly world of a viable resource.

Maglan put out his hands in a supplicatory gesture. "Whether or not that is the case is not at issue here. Abortion is not illegal, however, what you are witnessing is. That work party is supposed to process the contents for incineration, except that in this case, the bins are taken to another site for an entirely different purpose."

"They are stolen!" Benteke gasped.

Maglan tapped out a succession of commands. "This second file is taken from a Battery complex at an undisclosed location. It's not from *Earth* but is recorded illicitly, possibly by Kano himself. You can see state of the art LifeScience equipment such as trauma pods, intensive care incubators, cell senescence units and organ restoration devices; the kind of equipment you would find in a cross between a Sector 1 emergency room and a high-end Vanity salon."

Benteke let out a small cry as the perspective changed to the close-up of an incubator. The semi-translucent, hairless form had blue dots rather than eyes and dark violet bruises where the paper thin skin had been touched.

"The scientists are attempting to revive the aborted foetuses. The experiments borrow heavily from recent breakthroughs in cell senescence pioneered by LifeScience."

"In mice," Creed snapped. "There is no authorization for going beyond basic animal studies."

The scene shifted again, this time to the operating table. "What you are witnessing is the artificial stimulation of internal organs, including the brain, liver and heart."

Benteke began to sob. Havergill looked like he was about to vomit.

"Most foetuses never revive, however, a few enter a partially animated state, brought to full term using advanced life support systems, heavy doses of chemicals and hourly injections for pain, seizures and fighting infections."

"Why are you discussing this here?" Creed said angrily.

Raised in a Board meeting, this too would be in the Elite minutes and therefore, public information. They would all be accountable.

"The infants are horrifically disadvantaged both mentally and physically," Maglan continued, ignoring Creed's question. "Their lives are short and full of pain. However as you can see from this footage of the *nursery*, children as old as one or two seem to be active." More incubators, bodies with a hundred tubes protruding from them twitched slightly at intervals. "Although of course it's difficult to tell their exact age."

The image feed paused on one of the children. He or she was almost normal, except for the multitude of surgical scars, the off-kilter limbs and the shark-like eyes that suggested a nothingness within.

Dagmar noticed Gravales tap out a quick command on his holopad. Creed looked up and nodded.

"Maglan," she said. "As revolting as all this is," she waved her hand in the air, chopping through the frozen image of the child, "is there any direct evidence to link this crime with *Dish* infiltration of this Board?"

"No."

"Then, I fail to see on what basis this allegation is made."

Maglan sighed, and for the second time that evening he stood up and faced the table, hands clasped on the back of the seat, his bulky figure leaning forward. "Look at the scale of the operation, Natasha. Look at the equipment. LifeScience has been booming with cloned lifestyle organs and biosquare technology, but even with your bloated finances, someone should notice if billions of credits worth of equipment went missing. Remember that Kano began with the sunshine protocol. The media files we reviewed were the *result* of the investigation, they were not the catalyst for it. The LifeScience shipments were authorized and paid for by someone at a very senior level, as were the scientists, the facility and the whole operation. He must have found the source of those orders. It's the only explanation."

"I have not doubt this case requires careful review, but not in this forum," Creed said. "An hour ago you said we were at war. In that light, the destructive effect of these allegations, the suggestion that someone on this very Board could be involved, amounts to corporate sabotage. To that end, you will be removed from the room unless you cease this highly speculative form of enquiry."

Maglan shook his head. "I cannot do that, Natasha."

"Then you leave me no choice." Creed turned to the guards, "Take him out."

The guards didn't move but remained stationed against the wall.

"What are you waiting for?" she barked.

"This is a matter of security, Natasha," Maglan said, "and these are my men."

Creed turned white, her icy composure gone. "After this is over, I will have your head!"

"Perhaps, but I think not."

The room sat in stunned silence. Maglan paused a couple of beats and then smiled benignly. "At this point I'd like to invite executive Eborgersen from the pit."

Dagmar stepped forward, his heart beating in his ears. He wondered if he should say a few words about himself. Of course his stencilled identikit made that redundant. They would know his division, rank, what regions he was responsible for, and even how many A-Points he didn't have if they bothered to look.

"Please tell the board what you discovered about the appropriated equipment seen at the installation."

"Under a classifie . . ." He coughed, his throat suddenly parched. Flamel poured him a glass of water and pushed it across the table.

"Thank you," he murmured. His hand shook with nerves as he took a gulp. When he put the glass down, his arms seemed to dangle at his sides, so he folded them, but thinking that looked too defensive, clasped them in front of his stomach as though about to sing a carol. An Elite reduced to a school boy.

"U-under a classified order from Securicom, I conducted a confidential search of NFC tag scans for the cell senescence equipment, which due to its cost and specialized function has a relatively low run rate across the Autonomy. We produce about eighteen thousand units a year and Logistics automatically stores data on where various shipments cross borders. We do this to check the rigor of supply lines, delivery speeds . . ."

"I think you can skip the background," Maglan said. "What we need are the findings."

"Of course, sorry. Over the last two years, eighty percent of the units were shipped to various destinations in Sector 1. We haven't tracked them down, but it's safe to assume the majority of those can be accounted for. About twenty percent passed into other Sectors."

"Why is that significant?" Creed said.

"Remember the equipment we are talking about," Maglan said. "Advanced cell rejuvenation. The kind of thing that keeps us all looking so ah . . . spry. The last time I checked there wasn't much demand for Vanity Salons in Sector 2. In fact a day's treatment is more than the annual salary of a Battery worker."

"But that's still over seven thousand units," Havergill said, taking a professional interest. "It would take weeks to track down so many."

"We got lucky," Dagmar said, not wanting to contradict his President. "In analysing the distribution we found a Sector 2 that was both landlocked and not adjacent to Sector 1. Hence, it was safe to assume that the units transported there were not in transit. Only twenty units fitted that definition, three we saw in the footage."

"Which Sector?" Creed demanded.

"Havant," Maglan replied.

"Havant is over eight hundred square miles and contains over a thousand industrial complexes. How does pinpointing the Sector help you? They could be anywhere," Havergill said.

"Not exactly *anywhere*," Maglan said. "Once my colleague in Logistics discovered the Sector, we used *Voice* to profile Havant's entire economic activity. This included import and export data, exceptional part requisitions, energy usage and even employee qualifications for relocated personnel. None of the data was significant in itself, but taken together, there were only three possible locations that made sense."

"Why didn't you just check *Earth's* records of the sites? They are public areas, aren't they?" Creed said.

"Because *Earth* relies on a camera being installed. Right now *Earth* covers only major public buildings in Sector 2. It's a rather fundamental limitation. No camera, no *Earth*," Maglan said. "Twelve hours ago we raided all three potential sites. Two were diagnostic equipment manufacturers for LifeScience, but the third was a sprawling complex of seven Lab-Tech buildings hiding what we witnessed on the media file. We put the site on lock-down, with no incoming or outgoing communication, except through me."

Maglan gave a signal to the guards. Two of them stepped forward, taking a position behind the President of MediaCom's chair. Lars Pendicott twitched around to stare at them.

"What is the meaning of this?" Creed said.

"A comprehensive interrogation of all the personnel at the site will take a while, however our agents have already reported back with some initial findings."

"What has that got to do with me?" Pendicott said.

"Some of the managers we spoke to wanted to make a deal. They testified to where the funding came from and provided supporting documentation, specifically an archive of executive orders. They kept the data on an off-net device right on the premises. We are now in possession of payroll records, expenditure and requisitions for the entire operation. The *mission*, as the onsite scientists call it, has been going on for four years. Everything paid for by MediaCom, or to be more exact, the White Knights, which as most of you know is the special projects and charity arm of MediaCom, set up by Lars Pendicott for furthering the tenets of the *Faith* simulation in the physical world."

"I didn't know about this!" Pendicott said angrily, his voice finally losing its affectation. "I sign thousands of orders a year, I can't be expected to read every one!"

"Strange, then, how only orders relating to this operation were not delegated to subordinates while you were on mandatory leave, creating the sunshine event Kano investigated and subsequently shredded."

"You can't prove that!"

"Strange also, how the Media coverage this evening at times looked stage-managed, focusing on the audacity and success of the *revolutionaries*. A rather ambiguous label for terrorists and murderers, isn't it? The kind of label the movement might want, the type of label that might encourage disaffected members of the Autonomy."

"He's an expert on semantics now . . ." Pendicott turned to his colleagues, looking for a sympathetic face or complicit nod. Nobody met his gaze.

"And finally, I find it very strange how James Kano fell off the grid while in a public building. How did *Earth* go dark at such a convenient moment? Almost as if someone flipped a switch. I need hardly remind the Board that *Earth* is currently controlled by MediaCom, an oversight I intend to rectify."

The colour drained from Pendicott's face. He looked suddenly ill. "I . . . I had nothing to do with his death! I swear on the *Faith*. I never even met him."

"No? Then tell us who got to you?" Maglan stared intensely at Pendicott.

"Point of Order!" Gravales interrupted. "How many times must you be reminded this is a corporate Board meeting, not an investigation!"

"Our Vice Chairman is correct," Creed said. "Maglan, you have presented your accusation and supplied us with enough evidence to warrant a formal investigation. The President of MediaCom is relieved of his duty pending that investigation. However, your interrogation will have to wait until the appropriate time and place."

She gestured to the guards to take Pendicott out. Again they did not move.

"But this *is* the appropriate time, Natasha," Maglan said. "If our good President of MediaCom had no part in Kano's death, he realises how vulnerable he is right now. He thinks if the *Dish* were able to get to Kano while Securicom were watching, then perhaps they will be able to get to him."

Pendicott stared at Maglan, his eyes like a caged animal. For a moment Dagmar thought he was going to break in front of them. Instead he shouted, "Life is a gift! The greatest resource in the world! We, of all people, should appreciate that!"

"Lars! Please!" Creed said.

"Nobody should have the right to arbitrarily waste it! Not when we have the technology to save it! And thank the *Faith*, I am saving them! I am saving them. The record will show that!"

"Take him out!" Gravales roared.

Maglan nodded and the guards pulled Pendicott out of the chair. He was still ranting as he was dragged through the double doors, leaving a stunned silence behind him.

Creed was the first to speak. "We will need to interview candidates for the MediaCom vacancy. I will compile a short list of candidates and we will appoint a head within the next week." She turned to Maglan. "We owe you an apology. It seems you were correct. Pendicott was somehow an agent for this . . . *Dish*."

"Really?" Maglan said, arching his eyebrows, "He said he never knew Kano.

We'll know for sure after he has been questioned but I believe him."

"But it was your allegation in the first place!"

"I said the Board was infiltrated by the *Dish*."

"You are talking in riddles," Creed said through her teeth.

"Pendicott is an extremist, yes, but an extremist of the spiritual kind, obsessed by the *Faith*. He is a genius, and like all geniuses prone to remarkable tunnel vision. After Kano compromised his *mission*, he agreed to do anything to keep the operation going. But until this evening, I'm not sure he even knew what the *Dish* was, or even cared. He was its tool, not its agent. There is a difference."

"So the infiltration you referred to was by Kano, not Pendicott himself?"

"I believe Kano was operating under orders from someone on this Board. Kano transferred into internal affairs to dig up information on senior executives in Top 10 in order to blackmail them into cooperation with the *Dish*. With Pendicott he just happened to hit the jackpot. Think of the potential; with Media following their directives, the *Dish* could control the message to the Autonomy."

Nobody spoke. Maglan walked around the table. "Yes, Mr. Havergill, I see you frowning in your chair. You are still puzzling over the logistics of Pendicott's operation. How could it happen over such a long period of time and on such a scale? Surely such a significant exchange of goods without a corresponding productivity report would be audited by Finance. Perhaps not in the first month or even year, but after three years?" Maglan paused, putting his hand on his chin. He turned to Pierre Gravales. "Unless it was in the interest of Finance to overlook it."

"I am a little senior to be in charge of audits," Gravales said shortly.

"Of course," Maglan said, "But . . . you do have the authority to prevent them occurring. I have one question. How is it that you correctly identified the terrorist organization as the *Dish* before I had made any mention of it?"

"It was in your report," Gravales snapped back.

"I am afraid you are mistaken. The name of the organization was only used in the Rhodes report. Prior to its untimely declassification, I am aware of only myself and two other Securicom personnel who knew the term, and they were the two individuals who interviewed Kano, reporting directly to me."

"I . . . I must have picked it up in the Media," Gravales said, a little too quickly.

"It's not in the Media, or anywhere across iNet. I've already checked. As soon as you said the word, I asked *Voice* to sweep the entire intellisphere, including the correspondence between members of this Board. Nowhere to be found."

"Using *Voice* for that level of surveillance is illegal!" Creed said.

"Nevertheless, it is the fact."

At a signal from Maglan, the remaining two guards positioned themselves beside the President of Finance.

Gravales remained passive. "Is this some sort of coup? The general of the army seizing power?"

"Tell the Board how you knew about the *Dish*."

"I remember now where I read it. I can explain how this misunderstanding has come about." He gave a slight cough and reached across for the jug of water, but instead of taking the handle, suddenly spun in his chair and pulled the nearest guard's gun from its holster. He pointed the weapon at Maglan's head.

"I just had my joints done in one of Natasha's Vanity salons, I highly recommend it," Gravales said with a cold grin.

"Pierre, what are you doing?" Creed said, her voice trembling.

He cocked the weapon, his eyes trained on Maglan. "You are so smart, Maglan, so clever. Let's see how clever you are without a brain."

He pulled the trigger.

There was a dull click.

Maglan smiled apologetically. "They all have iNet chips now. The only perk of my position is that I can disable any Securicom gun in the Autonomy with the flick of an eyelid."

Gravales lunged towards him, but this time the guard was quicker, pumping a few thousand volts into his neck. The Vice Chairman's eyes glazed over and he hit the ground. Maglan nodded, and the guards dragged his dead weight from the room.

The room was silent. Maglan sat down, picked up his glass and took three gulps of water, wiping his mouth as he finished. He replaced it on the table and turned to Creed.

"Yes, yes," he said, as though responding to a question. "Of course we all accept your resignation. It's a matter of *confidence*. And I agree, it is far more dignified for you to resign than have a formal vote. That way you at least have your legacy, can say you stepped down at the right time for change, rather than being fired for incompetence."

Creed's face turned white with fury. She swayed in her chair, back and forth, like a cobra about to strike. Dagmar could see her calculating. This had happened under her watch. She appointed Gravales, promoted Pendicott and colluded with them for Maglan's resignation. She would not survive a vote of confidence.

Creed pushed back her chair, stood up and, without speaking, left the room.

"And then there were six," Maglan said. "I believe the first order of business is to ratify Legacy rules, for now there can be no doubt that we are under attack from a movement far more significant than a few malcontents. For the last three years, Creed, Gravales and Pendicott have formed a block, vetoing any decision designed to safeguard the Autonomy. Under their leadership, Securicom spending was slashed, the expansion of *Earth* curtailed and the *Voice* initiative heavily restricted to a few pilot projects. Of course, they justified every decision on economic grounds, but the pattern was there, a pattern I failed to understand before I became aware of the *Dish*."

"So you are saying Creed was in on it too?" Havergill asked.

"No. Creed is an economist in the purest sense of the word, has been her entire career, and all true economists share the same fatal flaw. Only short term profits are of interest. During her seven year tenure, Top 10 has been more profitable than anyone could have possibly imagined. If cracks appear later, then that's someone else's mess to clear up. Ours."

"How deep into Top 10 does the *Dish* go?" Havergill said.

"I personally selected every guard that stood around this table tonight because we just don't know. We may walk out of this room into the hands of *revolutionaries*, but I don't think so. The movement is, as yet, immature, but the threat they pose cannot be overstated. Over the last year, *Voice* has picked up unprecedented levels of discontent in Sector 2 and 3 ranging from random attacks on Top 10 assets to the ultimate act of negation; suicide. Among such populations the *Dish* will find an army of terrorists."

"It's an outrage," Guy Rawstorm said. "We are the ones who lifted them out of the gutter. Two decades ago these bloody savages were running around in the dust trying to eat each other for dinner."

"That's a bit of an exaggeration," Benteke said, her colour rising.

"Is it?" Rawstorm snapped back, shaking his fat at her. "Tell me, what else was on the menu if we hadn't gone in with skaatch and contracts for employment?"

"What we need to understand," Maglan said, "is that the world has moved on. The days of mass starvation have become a memory, at least within the Autonomy's walls. The lower Sectors want more from life than skaatch and triple shifts, without understanding that to have more, they have to produce it. In their ignorance, and with the *Dish* to incite them, they'll tear down everything we have built."

"But violence is against the tenets of the *Faith*," Benteke cut in. "Ninety percent of Sector 2 and 3 are devotees. They know that their suffering will be rewarded in the next life, and that their hardships are insignificant compared to the eternity that awaits."

Maglan smiled, "And so are we to expect you to give up your penthouse in Mansion?"

Benteke shifted in her seat. "That's not my point."

"No. I suppose it is not, and yes, the *Faith* is the only reason why the lower Sectors have not degenerated into violence before now. Together with the Aspirant system, the *Faith* gives the masses purpose in an otherwise purposeless existence. For that reason, the *Dish* must be exposed as a grave threat to the *Faith's* teaching and therefore, to salvation as a whole. Indeed, if the *Dish* didn't exist, based on *Voice's* predictions, it would only be a matter of time before we had to invent it."

"Why?" Havergill said.

"To give those opposing the Autonomy a label," Maglan replied. "To define their discontent as something evil, as something the faithful have to resist and fight against, because believe me, the Autonomy will only survive if we are prepared to fight for it."

"You make the *Faith* sound like nothing more than a political tool," Benteke said, indignant.

Maglan said nothing but touched the surface of the glass table. The obsolete voting panel lit up. A red or blue box in front of every chair, the votes tallied at the centre of the table.

"I find this older technology more corporeal somehow, more fitting for the momentous action we are about to take, because make no mistake, our decisions now will determine whether the Autonomy, and therefore mankind, succeeds or fails."

Maglan gestured to the voting matrix.

"To repeat, the first question is whether to invoke Legacy Rules. Without them, we are limited in what funds we can allocate to Top 10's defence. As there are only six of us, we will need to vote unanimously to pass the mandate. As I believe someone once said, the fewer the men, the greater the share of honour."

He pressed the panel in front of him. The segment of the table directly in front of him turned red, and a "1" tallied in the centre. Three other segments lit up red, and the tally became "4". Ventna and Benteke both hesitated as though they might have an objection, but not the courage to raise it. The final two segments lit up red. Legacy rules were ratified.

"Good, good," Maglan said. "Our second order of business is to stabilize the Board. Tomorrow the Autonomy will wake up to news of a reshuffle. We'll say the retirement of Creed, Gravales and Pendicott had long been planned. When everything has cooled down, we'll bring Gravales and Pendicott to trial but right now, they have to disappear."

"But that's impossible," Benteke said. "Everyone will know the truth from the meeting's minutes."

Maglan removed his lenses and put them on the table, rubbing the bridge of his nose. "Lisa, I propose the minutes of this evening's meeting will simply document our condemnation of the terror attacks, and our resolve not to rest until every single murderer is brought to justice."

"But we are bound by the articles of corporate governance to share minutes with Elites within two hours of any meeting's close," Benteke replied.

Maglan pinned her with his habitually uneven stare, the slight strabismus in his left eye that seemed to look through and beyond people. As a child, the physical defect made him look a little slow, a fatal underestimation that he invariably turned to his advantage.

"Lisa, we are at war. What alternative do we have? Tell the world that our own Vice Chairman orchestrated the attacks because he no longer believed in the Autonomy? Or that the inventor of the *Faith* was secretly and systematically resurrecting aborted foetuses? I am doctoring the minutes on the grounds of security. It would be irresponsible to do otherwise. If you don't like it, you too may resign."

Benteke flushed, but said nothing.

"Good. The next order of business is the denuded compilation of this Board. I would like to remind you that Legacy Rules carries a provision that empowers the President of Securicom to make emergency appointments to the Board without the usual, lengthy ratification process should the need arise."

"What?" Rawstorm coughed. Other faces around the table barely hid their surprise. Having the power to make appointments made Maglan a monarch, distributing patronage to a select group of loyal subjects.

"If I may," Havergill said, "the intention of this provision was to enable the rapid replacement of a Board member should they be killed as a result of the conflict. It did not anticipate this situation."

"And yet," Maglan said, "the provision remains in effect. Because of the attacks, we can't allow for any period of uncertainty or wrangling with so many positions up for election. We will have a Board in place tomorrow morning, complete with newly promoted executives."

"I have to object . . ." Havergill began.

"Under the provision," Maglan said, cutting him off, "I appoint myself as Chair, and you, Douglas as the new Vice. Ross and Dagmar, stop propping up the wall and come and take a seat. Ross Trieme will assume the Presidency of MediaCom, Dagmar Eborgersen of LifeScience." He turned to Havergill and said quietly, "I'm afraid you will have to spare him."

Head reeling, Dagmar approached the table. A President! Before the meeting his career was over. Now he was one of the ten most senior executives in the Autonomy. He pulled out the chair allocated to LifeScience, and sat in a seat still warm from Natasha Creed. He could hardly believe it. And what about Ross Trieme? Was he Maglan's man the entire time, enticing Creed into opening an investigation into Rhodes that Maglan then used for his own ends?

Maglan casually replaced his glasses and pulled up his holopad. "Bear with me," he said tapping out a few commands, "just making it all official."

The steel doors opened and two more figures entered the room, both dressed in standard Securicom uniform; dark suits, pressed white shirts, black ties and lenses on full shade. For a moment Dagmar assumed they were yet more security, but to his surprise, they sat at the table.

"As your iNet has no doubt already informed you, this is Lance Hillier and James Matheson. They will assume the Presidency of Utilities Corp and Finance respectively."

"Utilities?" Rawstorm said, "but Ferring is the President."

"*Was.* This evening's meeting was not optional. As tragic as his circumstances are, every President must put the Board before their personal considerations. As leaders of a corporation that oversees the lives of eleven billion people, we don't have the luxury of sentiment. His grandchildren may be dead, but you and I have children unaccounted for, and yet we are here. I just informed him that he is surplus to requirements."

Dagmar reviewed the two new executives' credentials through his iNet interface. Both were from Securicom, and like himself, had no prior experience in the divisions which they now headed. He felt uneasy. It wasn't unheard of for Elites to switch divisions, but at the President level? A Board appointment usually took weeks of interviews and discussion until there was a consensus on the right candidate. Maglan had just appointed four Presidents in as many minutes.

They all waited patiently as Maglan finished tapping on his holopad. He finally put it away and turned his attention back to the table.

"This evening I would like to introduce three innovations to prepare for what could be a decade-long conflict. First, the reassignment of *Earth* to Securicom from Media with the necessary funds to complete its expansion to cover *every* public building and street. It will take some years, but we have to begin now. A world under *Earth's* responsible gaze is a safer, more efficient world."

"But . . ." Havergill said.

"Second," Maglan said, pressing on, "the full integration of *Voice* into iNet. The intellisphere's very openness has made it impossible to control. *Voice* has the capability to change that, with real time analysis and monitoring of every single communication that passes through the network. Any off grid electronic network will be made illegal. We should remember that since the turn of the century, every successful uprising has had its origin in coordinated, social communication across unregulated networks. That possibility needs to be eradicated if the Autonomy is to survive long term."

"We can't do that," Ventna said. "No communication would ever truly be private again."

"Third," Maglan said, "the immediate launch of a new division of Securicom, *outside* of the oversight of the Board that operates covertly to counter-act the activities of the *Dish*."

The voting panel was again produced. Dagmar knew that what his brother was suggesting would change the world forever.

"Mankind is capable of incredible things," Maglan said, taking in each President with his uneven stare. "Are you going to take that away by being squeamish now? Twenty years ago the Autonomy saved an over-populated, sun-scorched planet through the principles of supply and demand. Tonight an organization stands against us that wishes to tear down everything we have built and destroy the future of mankind along with it. These measures might seem excessive. They are not. They simply deal with the realities of the world in which we now live."

Each member of the Board stared at the panel in front of them. Trieme and the two other appointees from Securicom voted first. Havergill placed his vote. In slow succession, Ventna, Flamel, Benteke and Rawstorm followed him.

Dagmar stared at the panel. What he was about to do was wrong, he knew that as clearly as he had ever known anything. Then he thought of Namgola, not of the ten million lives, but of his brush with destitution, of his children, of the expensive education they would need to get on in this harsh world, of their apartment in Mansion and the huge monthly payments that were owed on it still, of his wife and her habits and of the fact that his brother had saved all of it by forcing the Board to accept him as a President.

He placed his vote.

The initiatives passed without a single dissenting voice.

6

SECTOR 2, CHURIN

LTHOUGH THE DARKNESS cleared from Li's lenses, her mind was stuck in those final horrific scenes. Life, squeezed from her body by the hands she knew so well. Of course it wasn't actually Li that Angua choked to death, but it felt like it; a nightmarish sim over which she had no control and could not shut down. Opposite her, Angua slowly removed his glasses, face ashen, those same throttling fingers shaking uncontrollably.

"I-I didn't want you to see that," he said.

Li couldn't speak, couldn't even look at him. Her husband was a murderer.

"And it was all for nothing. I just ran. We didn't even blow up the building. I just ran. Seven dead and it was all for nothing!"

"Seven?" she said weakly.

"The other machinist, Sunny, he killed the other Foreman, turned his own stun gun into him, held it until he stopped shaking. Don't look at me like that! It was us or them."

"But the two Foreman and the two machinists, that's only four."

"The suicides . . . they jumped to create the diversion. They knew the super-visors would shut off the lights, provide us with cover. They didn't want to die, but they chose to, for the cause. And we failed them."

"The cause?"

"To overthrow the Autonomy! Tonight was the beginning. There have been attacks across . . ."

"Don't tell me anymore!" she said, cutting him off, "I don't want to know! I can't know!"

Angua's eyes widened. "No, of course. You're right. You know nothing."

Even if he hadn't murdered the Foreman, attempting to blow up a Battery building was an unthinkable act of terror, damning not just Angua, but all of them. Her only protection was ignorance. If she was implicated, she would be taken away and the children turned onto the streets. Beggars in a world where there was no begging. This man, this murderer, had destroyed their lives.

"Don't look at me like that!" he said again. "I-I had to do something. Not for us, but for the children. We can't go on like this . . . this is not life. We're no better than slaves. You must see that. A single corporation determines how we live, what we do, what we think. There has to be another way! But there can be no alternative unless we make one, no freedom unless we fight for it!"

Tears streamed down his cheeks. If only he had taken the *Faith*, he wouldn't have had these crazy thoughts or got involved with these people, whoever they were. She had never seen him cry before.

As her husband fell apart, an icy calm filled her. The Foremen would be here soon. They needed to make a plan. Angua needed to pull himself together. She stood up and slapped him across the face. It wasn't a good slap, her curled fingers making it more of a punch, but it achieved its objective. His head jerked backwards and his eyes widened, but slowly the snivelling stopped.

"You've done something for the children all right," she said coldly. "You've ruined their lives."

The only surprise was that the Foremen weren't here already. The scenes she witnessed had been almost four hours ago. Surely, they would have identified him by now?

"How did you do it?" she said turning to Balmoral. The fury in her voice took her by surprise.

Balmoral said nothing.

"How!"

Balmoral blinked, her face pale, her bottom lip quivering, for once looking like a child. Trying not to cry, she pulled out her holopad again.

"What are you doing now?" Li shouted, exasperated.

Still mute, Balmoral tapped out an intricate succession of commands and then took hold of Li's crabbed hand, guiding a bent finger to the holopad.

"Delete," Balmoral said quietly and gently pressed Li's finger onto a key. As her daughter stared at her, Li knew that, impossible as it seemed, everything they had witnessed had been shredded. Not just from Balmoral's files, but from iNet itself.

7

SECTOR 1, MANSION

O N THE ROOF of a low-slung building, four blocks from the Securicom tower, Fleur Cliquot crouched in the shadows, uncomfortable in the heavy damper jacket. It was unlikely there was any surveillance on the roof, but Sophie Valencia ordered her to keep the jacket on and hood up. Caution was Valencia's watchword. Caution kept them alive, or so Valencia said. She could be a little dramatic like that.

Valencia said they had been handpicked for this mission because despite the unusually heavy presence of Securicom guards patrolling the business district, nobody would suspect a group of teenagers hanging around the streets, even at night.

And what a night it had been. The news was all over iNet. The revolution had begun! Down with the Autonomy!

From what Fleur could understand, the attacks hadn't gone exactly to plan. Valencia seemed disappointed. There was supposed to be more damage, more fireworks, more mayhem, even right here in Sector 1!

So what?

They had still given their parents' world a big, fat black eye. She couldn't wait to see her father and mother at breakfast fussing over all those burning factories. They might finally take some notice of the world around them. Maybe they would even take notice of her.

Of course, all the stuff about the innocent lives lost was propaganda. And besides, Valencia said there were no innocents, just tools of the state, whatever that meant. It was Val who recruited Fleur to the cause. They both attended the *Faith* school in Mansion, but until she approached her during one recess, Fleur didn't think that the ultra cool Sophie Valencia even knew she existed.

Fleur checked the time. It was getting on for 3am. Was Valencia going to leave her alone all night? She didn't even know what she was doing there. Valencia was the only person allowed to communicate with anyone outside of their little gang and only announced the plans just before they had to do something. It was one of the rules.

Finding the back entrance to the ancient building was easy. It was only one of three historically preserved buildings in the whole of Mansion, a guild hall, whatever that was, from a hundred and fifty years ago. As a result, it was a fraction of the height of the skyscrapers surrounding it. Climbing the disused stairwell was scary, but she'd done it. Valencia would be pleased with her. Still, she didn't like being on the roof alone and she was getting cold.

"A credit for your thoughts," a voice suddenly whispered, making Fleur jump. Valencia! How had she crept up so silently?

"Where have you been!" she said.

"Sorry, we got held up, but I brought you coffee." Valencia smiled and held out a Styrofoam cup.

Behind her, Clay Vorm stood smirking. Fleur wondered, not for the first time, if the two were an item. She felt a pang of jealousy. He was nineteen, six three and almost as cool as Valencia. Both of them wore hoodies that obscured most of their face. They never dressed any other way. It was all part of being in the gang.

"Drink it," she said. "It has a little kick to it, to help keep you alert."

"Synapse?" Fleur said excitedly. You had to be twenty-one to purchase synapse in Mansion. The rules were very strict.

Valencia winked. "That's not for me to say."

Clay pulled out a device, pointing it at different parts of the roof.

"Well?" Val said.

Clay shook his head.

"Good." She pulled off her hood, pink curls bobbing. "You can do the same," she said to Fleur. "No cameras up here. Not yet anyway."

Val pulled out a minute pair of binoculars. She looked out towards the Top 10 buildings, adjusted a small dial at the top, and then handed them to Fleur. "Take a look," she said.

Fleur focused on the furthest point; the great sea wall that encircled Mansion. Even in near darkness, she could actually make out the cracks in the cement.

"That's incredible," Fleur said, giving them back.

"Yes, it is." She snapped the binoculars in two.

"What are you doing?"

"You can't buy a decent telescopic sight anymore, so you have to improvise. Clay?"

From under his jacket, Clay Vorm pulled out a rifle.

"Where did you get that?" Fleur said, suddenly frightened. Guns of any kind were banned throughout the Autonomy. Anyone caught with a firearm in Mansion, or even the design for a firearm, faced life outside Sector 1.

"I made it," Valencia said, "on one of the 3D printers at school; titanium alloy and thermoplastic, modelled on the *M-class sniper rifles*." The last three words she said in a heavily accented drawl, like the famous Colonel in the popular *Total War* sim. Usually Fleur would have found it funny.

"But they'll trace it to you!"

"Nah," she said. "The design came from an offline device and there's no *Earth* in the basement where the printers are. Why do you think I even bother to attend that waste of space? All they teach is propaganda."

Fleur pictured the shop floor and the lines of 3D Printers. Top 10 manufactured almost nothing within five hundred miles of Mansion, but the school had printers for educational purposes and various prototyping and design projects. A thick lump formed in Fleur's throat. She tried to swallow but couldn't.

Until now, it had all been so exciting, to be a part of this secret movement to bring some equality to a world where ninety percent of the population lived in squalor. And Fleur had been so miserable before Valencia noticed her and explained she could be part of something.

And there was something wrong with the Autonomy, wasn't there? Something wrong with her parents who only cared about work and credits, and about the boys in her class who only cared about Steel Ball and fetish sims, and wanted her to join in, but only if she agreed to perform certain revolting acts, even if virtually. She desperately wanted things to change, and perhaps even change her life in the process.

But an actual gun?

She had only ever seen one once, carried by a special forces Securicom agent. Now she watched, half in horror, half in fascination, as Valencia deftly attached the improvised scope to the top of the barrel, a clasp holding it in place.

Valencia removed her iNet glasses and peered through the binocular lens. "Ah yes, it's even clearer with the naked eye. Clay, you watch the stairs. Nobody in or out, no matter what."

Vorm nodded, his face stolid. Valencia threw the other binocular to Fleur who, in her agitation, almost dropped it. Standing just behind her, Valencia said, "Focus on the large chrome building. Zoom in on the doors. Got it?"

Fleur nodded, the lump in her throat twice as big as before. All the tiredness from earlier had gone and it had nothing to do with the synapse.

She remembered when Valencia had cut their palms and pushed their hands together and made Fleur swear a solemn oath to the cause. She remembered thinking how intimate it was to have Valencia's blood mixing with her own, as though somehow just the contact would make her more glamorous.

What an idiot.

The barrel of the gun brushed the back of her neck. "Concentrate now," Valencia said. "This is where the real action begins, where we all *graduate.*"

Even at this time of night, there were people going in and out of the building. She could see their faces vividly, her iNet automatically identifying each one as they passed.

"W-what am I looking at?" she asked, barely able to keep her voice steady.

"Not looking at, looking for. He will be designated President level on your iNet. His name is Eborgersen."

"Y-you're not going to . . ."

"He will have a security detail so as soon as you get a positive ID, tell me. We might only get one shot."

"I can't!" she said, adding desperately, and not caring how childish she sounded, "I have to get home."

"This is not a game, Fleur," Valencia said quietly. "If you ever thought it was, then playtime is over." Again, she felt the gun barrel. This time it prodded her nape, rather than brushed. "There is no going home. Not after tonight."

What did she mean? Her parents would be up in another couple of hours. They would wonder where she was. Wouldn't they? Should she make a run for it? She glanced towards the door. Clay stood on guard, his six foot three frame blocking the entrance. She noticed he too had a gun in his hand, a pistol.

Nobody in or out.

"You made a pact," Valencia said. "You said you wanted to bring down the Autonomy. You swore you would do what it takes. Well, *this* is what it takes."

Valencia edged forward until her face was level with Fleur, all the time keeping the gun trained on the chrome building.

"As soon as I saw you," she whispered, "I knew you would make me proud. You are one of us, not one of the drones. You just don't know it yet."

"I . . . I don't . . ." Fleur began.

"Quiet!" Valencia suddenly snapped, and put a hand to her ear. She flipped down her glasses then nodded, as though talking to someone on a vid feed. "Yes," she said, "Understood."

She repositioned the rifle on her shoulder and pushed her glasses back up to her forehead. "The meeting's breaking up. He should be coming any minute now."

Fleur couldn't breathe. One by one the Presidents exited the building; Rawstorm, Benteke, Ventna, Havergill. Each had two guards detailing them, and a dedicated bubble car that idled by the curb.

No Eborgersen.

They waited.

8

SECTOR 1, MANSION

WHEN THE BOARD meeting ended, it was almost 3am and Dagmar's eyes ached with fatigue. He wanted to get home, to shower the evening's business from his body and look in on his children. However, Maglan insisted he come up to the office first, to share a whisky before turning in. At this rate he would have less than three hours rest before facing his first day as President of LifeScience.

His brother's office, at the top of the Securicom building, was a throwback to another world. Heavy velvet curtains framed a view of the whole of Mansion and oil paintings of old landscapes hung from damask wallpaper. There was a display cabinet full of crystal glasses and mahogany furniture with intricately carved legs, each ending in a cold, brassy claw; visitors beware in case we turn feral.

Along an antique sideboard sat three silver salvers, each with an array of snacks; crackers with stilton and ham, a nut tray with cashews, almonds and walnuts, and a salver of sweets with chocolate orange slices and various truffles.

"Help yourself," Maglan said, eyeing him.

Dagmar took a handful of walnuts, savouring their salty taste, realizing only then how hungry he was. It had been years since he had nuts. They were forbidden at home, the twins were allergic. He took another handful.

Maglan poured two measures of whisky, passed one to Dagmar, and held up his glass. "To the continuation of mankind, to your appointment as President, and to my son, who is safe and well."

"You heard?"

Maglan nodded. "I received a message as we came out of the meeting. He is accounted for. I'm bringing him home tomorrow."

"I'll drink to that." They chinked glasses. Callum was the only thing Maglan cared more about than the job, the only thing that made him remotely human. If Callum had died? He shuddered at the thought.

The whisky was good, smoky and yet smooth enough to swallow neat. The contents of the decanter were worth more than the annual salary of someone in Sector 2.

"By the way," Maglan said, "something else just came over iNet. Lars Pendicott is dead."

"What?"

"Hanged himself. Took quite a lot of ingenuity. He shimmied up to the ceiling using each wall as a support, you know how a kid climbs up a door frame, then hooked his belt through a vent. He was always inventive, I'll give him that."

"They left him with a belt!"

Maglan scooped up an olive. "He didn't seem a risk with all his *beliefs*."

"How terrible."

"I don't know. He was the architect of the *Faith*. In Sector 2 and 3 he was regarded as some sort of prophet. A trial would have been messy. Of course it alters our story about his retirement. Media is going to say he died of cardiac arrest brought on by the stress of the attacks. We have a doctor who will testify to the weak heart, of how he implored Pendicott to take sick leave, but that the President refused, determined to serve the Autonomy, even at the risk to his health. It wouldn't play that he took his own life." Maglan stared into his empty glass. "Just think, all those A-points, forfeited in one fell swoop." He let out a low chuckle.

Dagmar took another sip of the whisky, but suddenly it tasted a little bitter. He wondered whether Pierre Gravales would conveniently *do away* with himself too. "There's one thing I still don't understand," he said. "You identified Kano months ago, but didn't bring him in for interrogation until just before the attacks. Why?"

Maglan regarded him for a moment, put down his whisky and slowly and deliberately removed his iNet glasses. This was not politeness. Maglan had no use for etiquette. The disconnection from iNet, which also deactivated the tiny microphone implant just beneath his lip, meant only one thing. This conversation was off the grid. He did not need to ask Dagmar to do the same.

"My little brother, always the perceptive one." Maglan picked up an intricately carved vase from the mahogany desk, studying it for a moment. "I wanted to *observe* him," he said finally. "To understand the mind-set we were up against, what made him tick. For three months I saw what he saw, monitored his conversations, climbed inside his skin. By the end I knew more about him and his *cause*, than he could possibly understand himself."

"And what did you discover?"

"That the *Dish* has another vision of the world, a kinder, more humanitarian vision, one without Sectors, or batteries, or the laws of supply and demand. A vision that will wipe us all out, given half a chance." He stared at the detailed pattern on the paper-thin porcelain. "I don't deny that we once had a choice. Even as late as the turn of the century we could have prevented the massive environmental collapse, the overpopulation, the raping of the world's natural resources, but we did not. Today, the Autonomy is our only chance, the only thing that prevents the world from degenerating into conflict, starvation and extinction." He gently placed the vase back on the sideboard.

"How do you know?" Dagmar said.

"Because every simulation we have ever run proves it. If the Autonomy fails, mankind fails. The data is irrefutable. The only raw material we have left is man, and just like any carbon-based resource, it has to be used in order to realise the benefit. As uncomfortable as that truth might be, it is self-evident."

Maglan returned to the decanter and poured himself another whisky. "You know what struck me about Kano?" he said. "That he slept eight hours a night, unaided by morph or soma or night-terror suppressants, that he lived his life without addictions, without the gut wrenching remorse of the average pre-Autonomy citizen. That is the movement's appeal. It is a dream, exonerating its members from the guilt of our times, of generation-G, the genocide generation."

"If you knew so much about him, why bother interrogate him at all?"

"One of our agents got careless. Left some tracks. The *Dish* knew we were onto him. So we pulled him in as though it was our first, rather than last move, and let him go again within twenty-four hours, knowing full well what the result would be."

"So you let him fall off the grid," Dagmar said. "You let the *Dish* get to him."

"Of course. He was the only one who could convince them he hadn't told us anything of importance. Only then would the *Dish* proceed with the attacks as planned, which was important for two reasons. With our intelligence, I knew we could contain the damage and root out some key operatives, but more importantly the attacks would give Top 10 the essential shock to the system it needed before waking up to the threat. The protocols passed tonight would have been impossible without a significant number of casualties. *Voice* estimated we needed about twelve thousand, in the end it seems ten was enough."

"But the school!"

"Rhodes was different!" Maglan snapped. "Do you think I'd let so many children die? I'm a realist, not a psychopath. The school was not supposed to be a target, not after outing Kano. Even so, I had men on the scene, and do you know what? We still have no idea what actually happened there."

"But Trieme said a squad penetrated the perimeter and set off an EMP."

"And who do you think told him to say that? One minute it was calm, the next . . . boom, a thousand children dead and no trace of the enemy. Do you think I could have told the Board that? That the *Dish* have a capability we don't understand?"

Was that possible? Or had *Voice* recommended they take out the school to amp up the impact of the *Dish*? Dagmar stood up. "I've got to get home."

"You disapprove of my actions," Maglan said, staring out at the skyline of Mansion, "of the lives I sacrificed for a greater good?"

Dagmar said nothing.

"Perhaps you have already forgotten your own grand vision. Namgola will be, what? Ten million dead because you wanted to lift a population out of its misery? To make the world a *better* place. The *Dish* has nothing on you."

"That's not funny!"

Maglan put down his glass, still chuckling, and then spun around, grabbing Dagmar by the lapels of his jacket. Instinctively Dagmar pulled away, but his brother's massive hands held him firm.

"No." Maglan said, deadly serious. "It's not funny. But remember this, the *Dish* are idealists too, committed to making everyone *free* irrespective of the cost. We saw some terrible things in the 2020s, but death on that scale, we can't even comprehend it."

Maglan let him go, studying him at arm's length, and then in a peculiarly intimate gesture, brushed down the front of Dagmar's jacket. "The Autonomy is the only way for mankind now," he said quietly, "and I will die fighting for it."

He sat down at his desk, picked up the whisky tumbler, and closing his eyes, took a long sip.

A woman appeared in the doorway of the office, shifting nervously; a Securicom aide.

"What is it?" Maglan said. Like a snake, he could see through his lids.

"I have to speak with you."

"Send it over iNet."

"No, it's . . . it's too personal."

"Personal?" Maglan said, irritated.

Dagmar cringed, wondering for a moment if his brother had a mistress.

"Well? Go on."

"It's-it's your son. Our initial report was incorrect, somebody with the same name. They messed up the roll call. He was . . . he was caught in the fire. H-he did not make it."

His brother's face blanched and the whisky glass trembled in his hand, but only for a moment. Then the hand was steady.

9

FLEUR STARED THROUGH the single binocular. For the last hour her world had become a circular doorway that opened and shut, each person passing through, a potential death. She counted forty-seven potential deaths. Each had lived because their name was not Eborgersen. He would appear eventually and then, as Valencia had assured her, there was no going back.

As the interminable minutes passed she noticed things that eluded her at first, such as the advantage of their position. They were on a roof, secluded in the shadows and almost four hundred yards from Securicom. However, because of the gradient of the street, the entrance to the building was quite close to their level, the downward angle cutting the distance to the target and making the shot easier.

Another thing she noticed was how people exited the building. Just to the right of the entrance, there was a place where the important executives waited for their personal bubble cars. The cars weren't allowed to wait directly outside the doors, but idled patiently half a block away. This provided a thirty-second window, during which anyone exiting the building was exposed.

She glanced at Valencia who lay on her stomach, pressed up against the side wall, her naked eye poised over the makeshift sight. The end of the barrel rested between the railings of the low fence. She had hardly moved or spoken in the last hour, but Fleur could hear her soft breathing.

The doors opened again, and this time a tired looking, unshaven man emerged. Fleur checked his identikit.

President Eborgersen.

She hesitated and then, afraid of what might happen if she failed to speak, said, "It's him." Her voice caught in her throat. Two men in a security detail followed, but Eborgersen, as if embarrassed by their presence, stood a few feet away.

"Are you sure?" Valencia asked. "His face looks thinner than on the Media."

Clay appeared next to them. "Media always adds a few pounds." He snatched the binocular from Fleur and squinted at the building's entrance. "It's Eborgersen."

"He doesn't look like much," Valencia said.

"They never do." Clay handed back the binocular and resumed his position by the door.

In horror, Fleur watched Valencia give the trigger a half squeeze to cock the gun. A red dot appeared on the man's head. Nobody seemed to notice. A bubble car pulled over to the curb. Valencia relaxed her finger, sighted the target once more, and squeezed.

10

SECTOR 2, CHURIN

THE NEWS OF the terror attacks was all over iNet. Nearly ten thousand dead. Li's avatar condemned the *Dish* and their terrorism as a crime against humanity and the *Faith*. They would stop at nothing for their evil cause, even if it meant the lives of innocent children. What exactly their cause was, the avatar didn't say, but it was clear that anyone who sympathized with them on any level was evil too, their A-points automatically deducted during confessional meditations.

Li prayed for the dead and the suffering, but she wouldn't turn in Angua, no matter what the avatar said. She had her children to think about.

They stayed low in their trailer all day, and it was relatively quiet, but that night, the Foremen came to their stack, moving from door to door. Li heard the shouts and screams of her neighbours long before they reached her trailer. On one level, this was a good sign. Indiscriminate beatings suggested they didn't know where to look.

Two Foremen barged in, black uniformed and aggressive, shock guns dangling from their sides. One was slight with slicked back hair and a cruel mouth, the other tall, long-limbed and expressionless. Immediately they thrust Angua and Zhu against the wall, shouting obscenities, splaying their legs apart, roughly patting them down.

It was just for show, of course. The Foremen made so much noise on the way up that if Angua had a weapon it would be down the dunny hole by now. And how was a nine-year-old boy a threat? She bit her lip in anger. There was no point to this, other than to make Zhu cry, which he did, like a baby.

The smaller of the Foremen pushed Angua onto a chair. "Where were you in the early hours of this morning?"

"I was working until six. My shift ended and I came directly home."

"On the tram?"

"Walked."

"Why?"

"There was an accident. The shift changeover was delayed. I arrived at the station too late. The tram had already departed."

"Did you see anything outside the building before you left?"

"Nothing."

The interrogation continued, first one peppering him with questions, then the other. How did this accident occur? Who was in his work party?

Why had he left the scene immediately?

Had he ever heard of an organization called the *Dish*?

Did he have access to explosives when he worked on the Atmos system six months ago?

He had? Did he sell them to anyone?

Was he sure? They would check, they would know.

What did he think about the Autonomy?

No. What did he really think?

He had sold some explosives, hadn't he?

It was all right, they understood, they all needed credits.

They kept going, the same questions with slight variations, trying to catch him out. The shorter one was particularly aggressive, desperate for an excuse to use the fifty thousand volts hanging from his belt. Probably a failed Aspirant. The other was calmer and made the accusations almost with a sense of apology.

Angua dismissed each inquiry with a logical, short answer, just as they had rehearsed. He was going to get through this.

"But we have no record of your iNet signature after you came off shift. Why is that?" the taller one asked.

Li's pulse picked up. Dangerous territory.

"I took off my glasses on the walk home. Sometimes, I like to . . . make my own way."

iNet had to be worn in public, but the law was rarely enforced outside of the Battery.

"Isn't it true you took off your glasses because you didn't want your movements to be traced?" the aggressive one snapped.

"No, I just wanted my eyes to breathe, you know . . ."

Before he could finish, the Foreman whipped out his arm, catching Angua full in the stomach. Her husband doubled over coughing. He kicked the chair from beneath him and Angua sprawled on the ground. "iNet glasses must be worn in public."

Angua wheezed, bent double, cradling his stomach. "I-I kn-know but . . ."

"No exceptions." The Foreman kicked him savagely in the back. Zhu screamed. The Foreman glanced across at him, smiled and kicked Angua again, this time catching his arm, the shirt ruffling up above his wound, exposing the makeshift bandages. Angua moaned in agony, hugging himself.

The other Foreman put out a restraining arm. "We're not going to find what we're looking for here." In a quieter voice he added, "He's a machinist, not a tech."

The small one shook off his partner and stared at Angua's arm. "What happened there?"

"The-the accident. I was pulled over when the pole came down, scraped along the ground. Nothing serious."

Don't inspect the wound, Li thought, for *Faith's* sake don't inspect the wound. Four perfect gauge holes from a dying Foreman's grasp.

The small one rubbed his chin, considering. "And what about the black eye?"

"M-my wife . . ." he wheezed. "We had an argument. She . . . she hit me."

He turned to stare at her and his eyes automatically dropped to her deformed hands. She felt herself flush.

"Yes," the Foreman said with an ugly smile. "I had an Aunt who was crabby. She could dish it out when she wanted to as well. You wouldn't think so . . . but," he smacked his wrist against the flat of his hand. "Pow!"

Tears of humiliation and fury came to Li's eyes. The Foreman smiled again.

"We should move on," his partner said.

"One last question," he replied. "Anyone else live here? Another family or two?"

"Just what you see," said Angua, "and another daughter on a double at the Battery."

The tall one pulled up his holopad, checked something and then nodded. "Min Bao is due to come off in about three hours."

But the other Foreman wasn't listening. Instead, he studied Zhu, whose eyes had become round and full of fear. Grabbing his hair, he pulled Zhu's face to less than an inch from his own. With his other hand he eased the shockgun from its holster.

"What are you hiding, eh? You don't have any skills we don't know about do you?"

"N-no," Zhu said, and a dark patch spread across his pants. He began to cry again.

"You're the family Aspirant, aren't you? The precious one. I can always tell. They're always such fucking pansies. Look at those fingernails. You must really fancy yourself."

"N-no, no . . ." Zhu blubbered.

The Foreman smacked him across the face, and Zhu screamed. "Don't answer me back or I'll pull out every one of those lovely nails!"

Zhu collapsed on the mattress, whimpering, smothering his tears, for once knowing better than to cry out loud.

"And what about you?" he said, turning to Balmoral. "You've been very quiet. Tell me your name."

Balmoral said nothing, but stared back at him with her cold, dead-eyed stare. She had removed her glasses when the Foremen barged in. Why had she taken them off? If she had left them on he would see from her identikit all he needed to know. That she was six. That she was nobody.

"Her name is . . ." Li said.

"Quiet!" the Foreman snapped, waving the shock gun at her. He turned back to Balmoral. "Well? Speak!"

Still she said nothing.

"Come here," he snarled. "Now!"

Slowly, Balmoral pulled herself up from the mattress and limped over.

"Is she an idiot?" he asked Angua, as though the physical deformity somehow translated to her brain.

"No, she had an accident when she was a child," Angua replied.

"Accident prone family," the Foreman said. "Let's hope you don't have any more." He grabbed Balmoral by the arm, and flicked on the shock gun. It whined with the charge. "Your name," he said.

Balmoral said nothing.

"It's Balmoral Murraine," Li said quickly, "She *is* a bit slow. My husband is just too proud to say."

The Foreman snapped a gloved fist across Li's face. Her neck rocked backward, and for a moment she saw black dots swim before her eyes.

"I said shut it, crabby." The Foreman moved the shock gun an inch from her daughter's cheek. "Now you," he said. "I want *you* to tell me your name."

Balmoral stared at him.

"What are you doing?" the other Foreman said quietly. "She's a child."

Ignoring him, his lip curling sadistically, the Foreman pushed the shock gun up to maximum charge. It droned in protest.

"Name," he said.

He pushed it closer and closer, the prongs a millimetre from her skin. If Balmoral twitched . . . The Foreman stared into her eyes, and then suddenly snapped it off.

"Get this retard away from me!" He pushed her hard in the stomach. Balmoral stumbled backwards. Her leg buckled beneath her and she fell onto the floor, but she didn't cry out.

For the first time in her life, Li felt a rush of love towards her youngest child. She wanted to go to her, cradle her, to smother her in hugs. She wanted to kill this man.

"Let's go," he growled and headed for the door.

They know nothing, Li thought, have nothing. Perhaps they were safe after all.

11

SECTOR 1, MANSION

R ELUCTANTLY ESTHER LOGGED out of the *Spring Break* sim, not wanting to
leave her virtual friends. They were having so much fun, partying at the
beach, sipping pina coladas, dancing, flirting and sometimes more.

No, she told herself. Stop. She had to concentrate on the so-called *real* world.
Just the thought of it, with its stress and physicality, filled her with nausea. In
the real world, she had to face the funeral.

Had it only been a week since all the unpleasantness? Since her husband,
Dagmar was shot in the head and killed. One little bullet and his brains sprayed
all over the sidewalk. How revolting. Only one week and yet it seemed so much
longer. How these things dragged on and on. At least they had finally caught
who did it. She couldn't turn on iNet without seeing their faces. It was all very
upsetting. Like a bad sim, except not a sim. She had to keep reminding herself
of that.

Maglan said the two assassins were the face of the enemy. One was a convicted rapist, Dirk Krallice, recently let out and poorly monitored, a failure of the
prior Chairman's liberal policy of reintroducing the 'stabilized citizen' as quickly
as possible to resume productive activity. Clearly it was too soon. The *Dish* took
him in and gave him a new target for his aggression.

The identity of the other murderer shocked everyone. A well-known economist from the Academy at Rhodes, he supplied the weapon and necessary cover
stories for accessing the building roof, just a few blocks from Securicom. His
name was Skylar Chrome. He seemed confused on the Media when interro-
gated, but the commentator said it was all an act. It was later revealed that not
only did he help assassinate Dagmar, but he was the mastermind behind the
Rhodes massacre as well. Securicom discovered prototypes of an EMP in his

quarters, and how else could the *Dish* have succeeded at the school without having someone on the inside?

Strange, he seemed such a grey haired, withered husk of a man, spent rather than seething with hatred.

In a rare fit of curiosity, Esther performed a quick search on this "butcher of Rhodes". To her surprise, given his storied academic career, there was very little about Chrome on iNet. She did find an archived vid of him, not on iNet, but in a file her husband shared with her about ten years ago. She had never bothered to watch it until now.

It was an interview on the structure of the Autonomy, when such introspectives were still in fashion. Chrome's much younger face rasped, "What does it matter what I think about the leadership of our society? What does it matter what *you* think? You can't vote the Board out because you didn't vote them in. To have any influence at all, you have to be an Elite in Top 10, which by definition means you are part of the status quo; a beneficiary of the system. Ask a Battery worker in Sector 2 what they think of the Board and I doubt they would know what the question means."

Chrome's face was red with anger. The interviewer made a comment. He answered. "My opinion of the *Faith*? I remember when I was very young, on holiday with my parents in Paris in the 1980s. Yes, *that* long ago. There was a puppet that danced in the street without any strings. The more people who gathered to watch, the faster it danced. We were right in the crush of the crowd, fascinated by this apparent miracle, oblivious of the puppeteers hidden in plain sight, their jackets folded over fingers that pulled at invisible twine. When we got home, my father had lost his wallet and my mother her purse, all because they were fascinated by a simple trick. The *Faith* is like that; a spellbinding show full of empty promises, distracting us from the fact that we are being robbed blind by the Autonomy, not of our money, but of our humanity."

What a bore, Esther thought. No wonder the interview never aired. She flicked off the feed and began to get dressed, trying on various expensive outfits.

One thing was for sure, Dagmar's insurance would not be enough. It covered the apartment but that was about it. What was she to live on? The boys hadn't stopped crying since it happened. Or at least one of them hadn't. Was it Pasco? Or Tristram? That was the thing about twins. It was sometimes difficult to remember who had done what, or said what, especially when she had been so busy, with people telling her what the arrangements were.

Poor Dagmar. It hadn't been a bad marriage. Sure, some of the lustre had faded over the years, but then no marriage was a fairy tale. Of course people didn't get divorced anymore, the economics didn't work. It seemed that all of her girlfriends were either bored, unhappy or unfaithful. Most were all three and she was better off than most. She had no illusions about his affairs. Not being a dupe was the main thing.

Hadn't she caught him once with that slut from Finance? Hadn't she made him give her up? Or was she confused? Was that in the *Life* sim she used to play?

Either way, it didn't make a difference. All of those late nights at work. What else was Dagmar doing? She wasn't stupid.

Her iNet lit up. The woman from Maglan's office wanted to speak with her again. More information about the infernal funeral. Would it never end? She sighed, accepting the feed.

"The car is waiting downstairs, Mam. It's time to go."

"The boys?" she said.

"Already buckled in."

Good, she didn't need to deal with them. "Give me five minutes."

She flicked off the feed.

If only it was already over. If only she could curl up on the sofa and get on with her life. She itched to log back into *Spring Break*. She had only simmed for a few hours today, and it would probably be midnight before she could sim again. She hated to think of all the others going on without her. Perhaps she could log in during the service? No, Maglan would know if she wasn't concentrating on the ceremony. Those uneven eyes missed nothing.

Maglan was a slippery one, slippery as an eel. How should she play it with him to get what she wanted? He owed her for letting Dagmar die. According to the rumours, it was supposed to be him they were trying to kill.

If Esther came across a character like Maglan in her sim, she would sleep with him to break down his hard exterior, to reveal the more sensitive, passionate person within. It almost never failed. But then again, her sim identity was twenty-five years younger, with smooth cocoa skin and the kind of body that would, in her long dead grandfather's words, "make a priest put his foot through a stained glass window."

She surveyed herself in the mirror. Still a good figure, but she couldn't escape the fact that she was pushing the wrong side of forty. Just how much power was left in that wiggle and shake? Enough for most men, but not for Dagmar's stone cold brother. Maglan's heart was deader than her husband's.

Although would she, if she could?

Maybe. There was something about all that power.

Maglan was in his fifties, but as was consistent with the ineffable injustice at the heart of the gender war, he looked better rather than worse with the years, distinguished rather than diminished by the grey hair and lines.

Changing her mind, she stripped out of the Mizzoni and put on a Mizhari. Both were vintage classics but on reflection, the conservative black was more the thing than the jarring zig-zags. Besides, the black accentuated her slim figure, and she wasn't above playing a part when it came to getting what she wanted.

Yes, she thought, Maglan owed her. She would sell the apartment, move out of Mansion to a quieter place in Sector 1, and Maglan . . . he would have the children. Hadn't his own boy just died? Calvin or something like that. Yes, he would be glad to take them off her hands.

PART II
2056

1

SECTOR 2, CHURIN

TRISTRAM EBORGERSEN STOOD at the window of the old hotel watching the brown, hazy dawn cut across the crowded slums of Deng, Churin's capital city. Last night there had been a storm and the rain water brought out a stench he tried not to think about. It was as though the city had thrown up on itself. Steam rose up from haphazard neon signs, a throwback to an era when blinking lights, not lenses, showed the way.

The girl was still asleep on the dirty mattress. He stared at her naked body, fascinated by the patchwork of scars that crisscrossed her back; gifts from less forgiving customers. He thought of the strange musk when she lifted her arm, the grunt she made when he was inside her. There were no girls like her in Mansion, with her crooked nose and buck teeth. Six hours ago, the alien coarseness made her irresistible. Now, he couldn't care less.

He made a coffee using the ancient filter machine, the glass jug charred black with years of use. Last night, when the girl saw it, she squealed with delight. The coffee machine, the yellowing wallpaper, the stained carpet, the toilet with actual plumbing, were extravagant for Deng. She touched each with childish wonder, her brown eyes feasting on the unimagined luxury.

As he poured the coffee into a chipped mug, his iNet flashed with a priority one vid feed from Securicom. Maglan. Strange, his uncle never contacted him while he was on a mission. Then again, after what he had discovered, perhaps it was to be expected. He glanced at the girl. Out cold. He accepted the feed and his uncle's face appeared in high definition.

"Your report," Maglan said, "it checked out."

"Yes sir," Tristram said.

"You have done well. Very well."

Had his uncle ever told him he had done well before? Despite himself, the praise pleased him. "Thank you sir."

"I've waited fourteen years," Maglan said. "Fourteen years and finally we have the answer."

To your question perhaps, not mine.

"What are my orders sir? Shall I continue?"

"No. Given the new information, the circumstances have changed. This is no longer a job for a sandman. That would be . . . wasteful. I have assigned a team for rendition. They're on their way."

Already? How had he set it up so quickly?

The Chairman's uneven eyes glanced away. "I'll be with you in a minute, Bruno," he said, and gestured to someone in the background. "Tristram, I have to go. Your case officer will brief you on coming home."

"Yes, Sir."

"Oh, and one last thing."

"Yes?"

"No loose ends."

"No sir," he said, but Maglan's bulldog face, like an older, distorted reflection of his own, had disappeared. His eyes wandered to the sleeping girl. *Loose ends.* He would wait until she was awake.

The coffee was some sort of synthetic blend, acrid and raw. If there was any actual bean in it, he couldn't taste it. He reached into his pocket and pulled out a cigarette, not one of the shit-filled woodbines they smoked here, but actual tobacco from Sector 1. Only five more left. He lit it, took a deep drag and thought about last night.

It seemed such a simple mission at first. In and out. That's why they assigned him, a junior in the ranks of Securicom's operatives. He was Maglan's nephew and foster son, but that fact curried no favour. If anything, the instructors worked him harder, expected more and rewarded him less, and yet at twenty-one, and with only a year in the field, Tristram knew he was the best sandman or *S-and-D* operative they had. Used for hunting down prominent members of the *Dish*, the sandman worked in the shadows, their missions secret, a necessary tool in the complex system that kept the Autonomy functional. Only a sandman could systematically remove enemies of the state, without the destabilizing trials, publicity and debate about the *Dish's* aims and grievances.

Of course, if anyone was discovered operating as a *seek and destroy* agent, they were immediately branded rogue and hunted down by the very institution that issued their orders. It was what Maglan called a political necessity.

Tristram accepted this. In truth, he didn't give a shit about the politics. All he wanted to do was kill *Dish*, the more, the better, and perhaps one day find the people who assassinated his father. He had long known the two men convicted were fall guys, guilty of something, but not that particular crime. Maglan had told him the truth as a graduation present, something to motivate him over the coming years.

He took a deep drag on his cigarette, savouring the burn.

Tristram was in Deng to find and eliminate a subcoder who had covered up *Dish* activities, possibly for years. Subcoders were a high priority for the Agency; hackers that had somehow found a way to get into *Voice* or *Earth*, to cause a crash here or a camera to go out there, or to set up an alternative network that could sit on the system and for a time, be used for illicit communications, side-stepping *Voice's* surveillance.

Their impact on iNet's infrastructure was usually limited however; *Voice* was too robust an AI, and for that reason subcoders rarely managed to do any real damage. However, Maglan had zero tolerance for their existence, and any hackers *Voice* uncovered usually had a very short career.

Tristram remembered Maglan lecturing at the Agency. "Never underestimate the power of iNet," he said. "Whoever controls iNet controls the Autonomy. For that reason the biggest threat from the *Dish* is digital, not physical."

According to *Voice*, this particular subcoder didn't fit the usual profile. He was a treadle mill Supervisor, failed Aspirant, and addicted to alc. It wasn't even clear if he was still active. He hardly ever used iNet, and never accessed sims, not even the 3D pleasure houses that rivalled the *Faith* in their popularity.

Tristram's orders were simple; find the hacker, confirm his identity and remove him. Because he lived in a sleeping cube under the treadle mill where he worked, Tristram's case officer suggested it would be less conspicuous to initiate contact in the alc den he frequented and take it from there. It wasn't much of a plan. Then again, he didn't think the strategists back in Mansion had spent too long thinking about this one. There were more important targets to worry about. This guy was a nobody, and soon he would be even less than that.

As occasionally happened in Sector 2, *Earth's* navigation was slightly off. In theory cameras were supposed to link up every inch of the Autonomy, but in reality there were many areas, especially in the slums of Sector 2, that relied on the older satellite technology, with the images sometimes lagging behind the ever changing landscape. Where the alc den should have stood was a tower of recently stacked trailers. The den, itself a glorified trailer, had been relocated a couple of blocks away, seemingly picked up and rammed into a gap that existed at the foot of another leaning tower.

The few words on the half-melted awning revealed its former life as a kitchen, the kind of place where you could get a single serving of skaatch for a few credits.

Black trash bags were taped over the broken windows and layers of corrugated iron served as the roof.

The stench of the place hit him as soon as he walked through the doors. Vinegar and vomit, worked into the walls, floor and tables.

Immediately an old man approached him from the shadows. "Remove your glasses," he said. "No iNet."

Tristram did as he was told. He didn't want to create a scene. It was so dark it took a moment for his eyes to adjust. The den was a deceptively large space with one exit. There were about thirty tables, some benches and a row of stools against the bar. The place was three quarters full. The heavy drinkers sat by themselves, bent double over pots of alc, while other groups made a show of sociability, chatting at various tables. At least a couple of the customers were management level from Churin's Battery district. It was obvious from their clothes, and the two or three girls wearing almost nothing sitting at their table or in their laps.

The target, he guessed, was one of the lone drinkers, but without iNet to access the identikits, it was impossible to tell which. Tristram had fished plenty of people out of alc dens but this was the first time he had done so blind. He would have to improvise. Ask questions without looking like he was asking questions and hope nobody got too suspicious.

His cover was that of a low level Top 10 employee, but they would know he wasn't from around here. As long as they didn't think he was Securicom. They weren't fond of Securicom in Deng. Too much anger, too much sympathy with the *Dish*.

Weaving his way between the tables, he made his way to the bar, conscious of stares from those around him. There were two girls serving, one very pretty, with large eyes, thick lips and wearing not much more than a bra. The other was buck-toothed, muscular and long limbed. He went for bucktooth, partly because the stools in front of her were empty, but mostly because he liked the rough and ready look of her. He sat down. She grinned broadly.

"What you like?" Her accent was thick. 'What' pronounced *waa*, 'like', *lack*. The same language, but different.

"Is there a choice?" he said. These places usually only served one thing. Alc, known affectionately in this part of the world as *brain fucker* or *juice* was made from organic roots of any description, crushed, chaptalized and left in huge vats to ferment. The result, a liquid three times the strength of rice wine with the pungency of an unwashed sheepdog.

"Yes, of course. You can have a single or double."

He laughed, but she looked bemused. "Double," he said, reaching into his back pocket and putting a five credit chip on the bar. In a place like this you paid in currency, hard coded, anonymous chips, and you paid before you drank. It avoided confusion when the alc set in. "How much can I get for that?"

"As much as you can take," she said, and leaning in added in a whisper, "And more." She winked her thick, dark eyelashes.

While she poured the shots, Tristram slipped a small brown *osmo* cube into his mouth. The cube would absorb the alcohol and then pass out as a solid in his stool the next day, avoiding the bloodstream altogether. Drinking, she would be more convinced of his cover, and the more he drank, the more convincing. Just another punter, come in from the cold. The cube hurt like hell on its way out, but he needed a clear head and the hangover from alc was far worse than a single uncomfortable shit.

"Ganbei," she said, pushing it towards him.

"Ganbei," he nodded, "What does it mean?"

"Who knows?" she said, "But when I say it, I always think of my grandfather. Ganbei! Ganbei! To hell with poverty!"

Tristram laughed and took a convincing gulp. He wanted to choke, but held the burning liquid down. It tasted to him like it always tasted; vinegar laced with sweat. He took another, finishing the pot and turned it upside down.

"Again."

"Thirsty boy," she said, licking her lips. As she leaned over to take the pot, she made sure he got a good look at her cleavage. Serving girls were generally Battery rejects, novices that never quite made it, destined to pull pots of alc sixteen, seventeen hours a day, then lying on their back for bonuses with any customer that had a few credits to spare, which for Bucktooth probably wasn't often, given the competition.

Half a dozen other scantily clad girls circled the tables, making sure nobody was without a pot and trying to drum up other, more lucrative, business. They glared at Bucktooth with a mixture of jealousy and amusement, but none of them tried to butt in. Half a foot taller than any of the others, and with arms as thick as some of their legs, she looked like she could take care of herself.

"I haven't seen you before." She handed him a second pot.

"I'm only in Deng for a few nights," he replied. "I'm with Logistics."

"From Sector 1, of course."

"Is it that obvious?" he said with mock surprise, knowing that it was. His white face, although common enough in the Battery district, was relatively rare in downtown Deng.

"You must have been very bad to be relegated to *slumworld*." She flashed a buck tooth grin and squeezed his arm. It was clear she liked the look of him, probably because his suit cost more than a year's pay.

"I have my moments. What about you?"

"Oh, I'm *very* bad." She put a finger between her teeth.

"No, I meant have you worked here long?"

Long enough to know all the regulars by name, for instance.

"A few years. The credits are awful, but there are perks," she said.

He took another sip of alc. Was it too early to ask her? Probably. He should feel her out first. "Why is there no iNet allowed in here?"

She stiffened. "You a squaddie or something?"

"*Faith* no!" he said, "Do I look like Securicom? I'm just curious."

She considered him. "Look around. You want your wife to know where you are? Or your boss? In here, you can sit back and relax without leaving a trail. The den tells no secrets."

"And what about you?" Tristram said. "Do you tell secrets?"

"Depends who's asking and how fat their stack of currency." She squeezed his arm again, but this time let the fingers linger. Despite himself, the clumsy flirting aroused him. He finished his second pot and asked for another.

Turning in his seat, Tristram surveyed the bar. The target was probably here, but where? Assuming he would have access to iNet, he had not studied the subcoder's face. Hunched over their pots, the men were clones of each other. Pale puffy skin, bloodshot eyes, inanimate, except when they had a full pot of alc. Even their age was indeterminate. He could be any of them.

There was no subtle way to do this. He turned back to the girl. "I'm looking for someone," he said.

Leaning on her elbow, she put her chin in her palms, her face close to his. "Of the long legged, large breasted, slick mouthed kind?" Her hand again went to his arm.

Slick mouthed? "No, I want to find a man."

"A man?" she said with a disgusted look. "You don't want a man. I can do it that way too, but better than any *man*."

"No, no," he said with a slight cough. "This man is a regular in here, I just want to talk to him. I need you to point him out."

She stopped stroking his arm and pulled away. "I don't know."

Pay first, drink later, Tristram thought. He reached into his jacket pocket and pulled out five more chips, except this time, they were twenties. He pushed the stack across the bar. It was the girl's turn to fight back a cough.

"What is his name?" she whispered, her eyes on the credits.

"Zhu," he said, "Zhu Bao."

She said nothing, but unconsciously picked a callous on her thumb. Tristram used to have a similar mannerism himself. Whenever he was tense, he couldn't stop fiddling with the small wart on his wrist. It was a tell and as such, dangerous. The Agency trained the habit out of him, not by removing the wart, or the urge to touch it, but by removing the emotion. Now, he never became tense.

The girl stopped picking her thumb and then pointed to a solitary figure in the corner. He was collapsed over the table, a line of spittle running from his mouth. "Zhu Bao," she said, adding, "He's one of mine."

One of her what? Customers or clients?

"How much has he had tonight?"

She held up five fingers.

"How much does he usually have?"

She stared at the floor. A whole lot more. "Is he too far gone to talk?"

She shook her head. "He's just out of alc," she said quietly. "Another couple of shots and he'll be fine. Drunk, but alert. All the addicts are like that. It's a series of peaks and troughs."

Tristram was struck by the change that had come over her. A minute ago she had been all teeth, tits and giggles, now she was subdued. It made no sense unless this Zhu meant something to her. Tristram considered his options. He drained his third pot, and pushed it across the bar.

"Introduce me," he said.

She shook her head, still not meeting his eyes.

He leaned across to her. "I have five hundred of currency back in my hotel room," he said. "Yours, *if* you help me."

Again the hesitation. Bucktooth wasn't stupid. If she suspected before, she knew now. He was Securicom. Who else would come looking for a man like that in here? Who else would offer so much for so little?

Asking for an introduction was another calculated risk. Tristram wanted to keep her close, make her complicit and therefore less likely to talk. All of the upside was in taking the credits, but women did strange things to protect their man, if this Zhu was somehow her man. Love, like alc, was a brain fucker.

"You won't hurt him?" she said finally.

"I just want to ask some questions, that's all."

She picked at her thumb again. "Give me a minute," she said and disappeared into the back.

He didn't like losing sight of her, but there was nothing he could do. The chips had been played, it was now up to her. He turned his attention back to Zhu, who had woken up and sat blinking in his chair, seemingly oblivious to the dirty little boy who worked around his ankles, picking cockroaches from the floor, tables and wall. Something extra for the pot. The boy caught them in his hand, and then pinned them with a long needle which already had dozens of the insects still writhing on it. A cockroach could live for three days without a head.

When the girl returned she had applied another generous slap of lipstick and carried a small bag which she swept the credits into and clasped shut. Without being asked she poured out two more pots of alc, and handed one to Tristram.

"This is how it will be," she said. "First you ask your questions. Then I will go back to the hotel for the rest. It's all fixed with my boss. Someone will cover my shift."

"How did you manage that?"

"One of your chips," she said.

Currency, he thought, the universal language.

Zhu didn't move when they sat down. Tristram knew from the file he was twenty-three, just two years older than himself, but his face and posture were that of an old man. The girl shook his arm and he roused, his bleary eyes meeting hers.

"I've bought you something." She placed the pot of alc in front of him.

"I have no more chips," he rasped.

His face was ashen, with streaks of yellow, as though the alc had sucked the pigment from his skin. Except his nose, which was an angry red mass of broken capillaries.

"This one is on the house," she said.

"What?" he said, eyeing Tristram with suspicion. "Why?"

"If you don't want the juice, I can always take it back again."

"No!" His bony hands were already around the pot. His fingernails were disgusting, black, jagged and full of dirt. He sucked down the drink, barely pausing for breath.

"I've brought someone to meet you." She put a hand on Zhu's arm. "A friend."

"I have no friends," he rasped, pulling away from her.

"Don't be like that. He just wants to talk."

"That's right," Tristram said. "Just a couple of questions over a drink and I'll leave you alone." He pushed the second pot towards Zhu.

"No . . . no, I've got to go." Unsteadily, Zhu began to get to his feet. The girl leaned over the table and gently pushed him back into the chair, whispering into his ear. Tristram could lip read, but her straight black hair hung over her mouth. However, as she pulled away, he caught one word.

Currency.

Good, she was working for him.

The man stared at her, at Tristram, and at the second pot. Clearing his throat, he spat a yellow globule of bile onto the ground, then picked up the alc, and like the first pot, finished it in a single draught. "I'm dry," he said.

"Let me get you boys a jug," the girl said and returned to the bar.

Zhu watched Bucktooth's curves all the way, his stare half-lecherous, half-disgusted. "Fucking eyesore, isn't she? But she's the cheapest one in here."

The alc had revived him, as the girl said it would, had restored his sense of self, as unpleasant as that seemed to be. "You've got until she gets back with the pitcher for your *talk* and then you can both fuck off." He slurred his words, but not as much as might be expected.

Tristram smiled flatly. Zhu was a Supervisor in this shithole of a city, more used to dishing out orders than taking them. He leaned close, doing his best to ignore the man's rancid breath.

"Your name is Zhu Bao, correct?"

"What of it?"

"You work as a Supervisor, at one of the treadle mills on the outskirts of Deng, and prior to that you were in the Aspirant program for ten years."

His bleary eyes betrayed neither emotion nor surprise. "Fucking waste of time."

"Your job, or the Aspirant program?"

"These questions."

This close Tristram could knock Zhu unconscious and *help* him out of the bar, as though helping a stumbling drunk home, and deal with him in an alley. He was tempted, but then he remembered Bucktooth's concern. She might cause a fuss.

"Is that all you do?" he said.

"What?"

"Any . . . extra curricula activities outside the mill, other than drinking?"

"None of your fucking business."

Tristram glanced sideways to check nobody was watching them, and with blinding speed pulled Zhu towards him, two fingers pressing down hard on his windpipe. He held him close, cheek to cheek, so that to onlookers they would appear locked in drunken conversation.

"Keep this up and I will rip this little pipe out," he said, pushing harder on Zhu's throat until he felt him gag. "I know you've killed most of your brain cells, but I need you to listen and think very carefully before you say anything else. Understand?"

Zhu tried to nod.

Tristram released the pressure slightly to allow Zhu to breathe, but continued to hold him tight.

"Ten days ago, the Foremen picked up a man and his son breaking into a skaatch warehouse. It was the same old story; too many mouths to feed, not enough credits; the classic miscalculation in family planning. The man had four more young children at home, all on starvation rations. Once the man and son were put away, that would be it for the others. An open and shut case except . . . the man had something to sell in exchange for his freedom. Still listening?"

Zhu let out a muffled groan.

"I'll take that for a yes. The man had an older brother who once shared some information with him, information that could be traded in for a favour. The brother had died a couple of years back and our burglar, we'll call him Tsien Po, decided it was time to use it."

He felt Zhu's pulse quicken in his throat. Good. He was really listening now.

"So what was this great confidence? Can you guess? No? Fourteen years ago this dead brother, together with another man, murdered two Foremen at the Battery. You can imagine the ears pricking up in the interrogation room. Two? And not caught? How was that possible? Surely *Earth* would have identified them. Except on that particular night, where the incident took place, all the footage had been erased, overwritten by a very neat piece of subcode. Suddenly everyone was very interested in Tsien Po's secret."

He pushed Zhu away. He was deathly pale and trembling. Yes, Zhu knew all about that night, knew also that he was caught. Bucktooth appeared with the jug of alc, flashed them a concerned look but said nothing. She filled their pots. Zhu grabbed his and drank it like a shot. Tristram waited until Bucktooth had gone, and began again.

"This missing footage was investigated at the time, but the assumption was that someone, probably a Tech, had broken into one of the Supervisor's offices and worked out how to shut down the cameras manually. Various leads were pursued but the investigation petered out, until fourteen years later when our friend Tsien Po got so hungry he attempted to break into a skaatch depot. And that, my friend, is where you come in."

Zhu grasped for the jug, but he was shaking so much he couldn't hold it steady.

"Allow me," Tristram said, taking it from him, pouring the alc into Zhu's pot. "Po told us that the other killer was your father, and that it was his child who hacked into the system and erased *Earth's* files."

Zhu knocked back the alc, his face like a ghost.

"Back then you must have been a prodigy, with your Aspirant education, devouring the programming modules, but reaching beyond them, so far beyond them."

"No . . . no, I didn't do it." Zhu groaned.

Tristram studied the dishevelled form in front of him. He was good at sizing people up, anticipating what motivated them, what they were going to do or say. During his training at Securicom, this skill was honed to a fine art, and as he looked at Zhu, he knew two things for certain. Firstly, *Voice* had got it wrong, this fool had neither the intellect, imagination or drive required to hack iNet and never had. Secondly, Zhu knew something, not just about the murdered Foremen, but something else, something more important. Something he was trying very hard to hide.

"I know you did it," Tristram said flatly.

The first rule of interrogation was never concede the truth of anything you were told, even when you knew it was correct. That way your subject felt compelled to talk.

"I swear to you . . ."

"Swear to me? On what? This jug of alc? It's over, Zhu. You may as well confess."

"No!" Zhu shook his head, on the verge of breaking down.

A couple of the other drinkers turned around to stare at them. Tristram was running out of time. He couldn't afford to attract attention, but he needed to know what Zhu was hiding. What was it Maglan said? Cut open a pupa early and you don't get a butterfly, but a bunch of maggots. There was a butterfly in here somewhere. He didn't want to settle for the maggots.

"Calm down and have another," he said, pouring Zhu another alc, taking one himself, temporary comrades. He chinked his pot against Zhu's, and drank.

"For the workers in your treadle mill, it's a pretty raw deal isn't it? Converting joules into amps all day long. The life expectancy of a spinner is what? About thirty-five? You don't need to *Retire* them, do you? I've heard it's over a hundred degrees in Summer on a good day, and your human batteries collapse with exhaustion, despite the salt pills and gallons of water. Two or three die each shift, don't they?"

"Yes, yes that's true," Zhu said, eager to talk about something else.

"I know it's tough for you too, patrolling the lines. You have to be in there with them, among the crush and odour of all those bodies. No air-conditioning in the mills of course, it eats into the razor thin profits, so you open the windows for a lick of breeze, taking the pollution over the heat. You figure, the treadle spinners are going to die young anyway. It's not like they are going to need lungs in their old age."

Again Zhu nodded, almost smiling, as though the change of subject was a good sign, rather than the opposite. Tristram leaned in close. "You know, Securicom has an installation of its own, made for . . . for people like you. At those mills there are no seats on the treadle bikes and no windows. They chain you to the frame and you eat, sleep and shit right next to your bike. Eight hours on, four off. Eight on, four off. Tomorrow and tomorrow and tomorrow. The average person lasts thirty-five days, not years."

"Nooo!" Zhu held his head and rocked back and forth.

"On the bright side, you'll be able to kick your alc habit, though I hear withdrawal's a bitch."

Zhu's shoulders shook. "It-it wasn't me. I can tell you who it was. It wasn't me . . . if I'll tell you, you won't have to . . ." he broke into loud sobs.

Again, people from other tables stared at them, more this time. Time to go for broke.

"I'm afraid you'll have to do better than that. You give me a name, and they'll just deny it the same as you. Too much effort. I have enough to convict you already. You're a Supervisor. You withheld information concerning the *Dish* for fourteen years. I'll get the credit for bringing you in. Case closed. Why make it messy?" He got up to leave.

"Wait . . . wait. I *can* do better. I have information. Something only I know. Something you-you'd never find out for yourselves."

"What?" he said with forced indifference.

"It's . . . it's something else, nothing to do with the Foremen or . . . or my father."

Tristram eyed him curiously. Was this the butterfly?

"Tell me."

Zhu began to talk.

THE NAKED GIRL awoke with a hacking cough, shaking Tristram out of his recollection, bringing him back to the hotel room and the present.

"Morning," he said.

She sat up, unselfconscious, and stretched her arms, her missile shaped breasts stretching before her.

"Up before me?" she said. "Most foreigners have to spend the day sleeping after an evening on the alc."

He returned her smile, thinking of the bowel movement yet to come. "I guess I've always been good at holding my juice."

"In more ways than one," she said with a laugh.

The girl gathered her clothes from the foot of the mattress, knowing the form. There was no talk of breakfast, or seeing each other again. The physical transaction, though not an explicit part of the business proposition, had been exactly that. It was over now and her little bag bulged with the currency. She was ready to go.

"All the same," she said, pulling on her shirt, "I am very pleased Zhu is not in trouble."

Again he smiled, rubbing his wrist where the wart used to be.

Once Zhu had told his story, Tristram assured him everything would be fine. Zhu was in the clear. Tristram bought him a new pitcher of alc, and together they drank a toast; to their pact, and "To Tsien Po!" who had tried and failed to rob the skaatch depot. Zhu laughed, relieved after his narrow brush with an existence worse than death.

He was still laughing as Tristram surreptitiously removed the surgically attached wart and dropped it in Zhu's drink. The wart's exterior was a highly advanced polymer, soluble in alcohol, but robust enough when intact to safely contain a tiny measure of radioactive polonium, "210-Po".

"To Tsien Po!" Zhu had roared again, and swallowed it down.

This morning Zhu would be sicker than he had ever been in his life. His pallor would be a deathly yellow. He would not be able to stop the vomit or diarrhea, symptoms identical to the final stages of alc poisoning when the internal organs fail. Just another addict. Already he would be verging on delirium. Between now and noon he would die.

Tristram wasn't even sure that Zhu had ever been *Dish,* but his father had been, and the fact that Zhu failed to report this and yet still benefited from the Autonomy more than justified his death. His father. That would have been Tristram's second call, but the old man had received a very temporary reprieve. The rendition team wouldn't want to spook anyone. Not yet.

"Mind if I use the bathroom before I go?" The girl was now fully dressed.

"No, please," Tristram said.

He pulled his knapsack from under the bed, put his thumb on the finger-sensitive lock, and took out the printed Glock. He inspected it for a moment, checking the barrel and then slipped it into his pocket.

Next he pulled out a chocolate candy bar. He had been saving it for when he couldn't take another mouthful of skaatch, but, well, sometimes you had to do the right thing. The toilet flushed, and he heard the tap run and a small squeal of delight. A moment later she opened the door, her face glistening wet. "I could get used to this," she said.

He smiled. "I have something for you."

"Oh?" she said.

"Something you can't get here. Something illegal."

"What?" she said excitedly.

"Come over to the window."

She walked over, eyeing him quizzically.

"Turn around, and look at the view."

"You foreigners are very strange," she said, but did as she was told.

"Close your eyes, and put out your hands."

She tucked the bag of credits between her knees, and put her hands in front of her. Tristram unwrapped the chocolate bar and placed it in her palms.

"What is it?" she said.

"Taste it."

She put it into her mouth. Her entire body tensed, became ridged, and then relaxed. "Oh my mother-fucking god," she said, tears gathering in her eyes.

"Now," he said, "I want you to look out of the window and think of your happiest memory."

"Th-This might be it." She half laughed, half cried, still chewing the chocolate bar, the tears running down her cheeks.

Quietly he pulled out the Glock, put it about centimetre from her head. He squeezed the trigger slightly, releasing the safety. No loose ends. He hesitated, one beat, two beats, then suddenly slipped the gun back into his pocket. He could have pulled the trigger, as easily as shooting a cockroach on a wall, but strangely, and despite his orders, he didn't feel like it. She wasn't *Dish*. She was just a girl. A buck-toothed girl. And she had given him everything he wanted.

"See you on the flip side," he said and kissed her on the back of her neck. Without waiting for a reply, he picked up his knapsack and headed for the door.

No, he told himself, he wasn't an animal. Not yet.

2

B ALMORAL AND HER father joined the crabbed, grey shadows that made their way from the Battery gates in the acrid dawn air.

"They've purged the lines again," she said, her hand cupped over her lips.

"How do you know?" Angua wheezed.

The distance from the tram to the building was less than a mile, but it still left Angua gasping for breath. The early stages of emphysema, the machinists curse. Too many years inhaling too much crap.

"Look around you," she said quietly. "Where is everyone?"

The workers outside the building represented an entire shift change, five thousand people. Usually they walked five or six wide, stretching back around the block. Today, it was a queue of twos and threes.

"The tram had less people on it too," she said.

Her father shook his head. "If this goes on, it could get very ugly."

Two months ago, the Supervisors *Retired* four million bodies in less than twenty-four hours. The management called it strategic pruning, cutting the bottom ten percent of workers to be replaced with new talent from the Lodges. Except no novices took up the positions and now a few buildings operated at half capacity, while twenty-five stood entirely empty, a dead zone on the edge of the complex.

In another ominous sign, they shut down the Atmos system and the vast maintenance crew was reassigned to other projects while the associated treadle mills were laid off entirely. It took just two weeks for the atmosphere to become thick and soupy, and the masks to come back out. Rumours spread about a Churin-wide slowdown. Skaatch depots increased security and the Stacks tightened their collective belt.

"It doesn't make sense," Balmoral said. "Churin is the largest manufacturer of iNet lenses in the Autonomy. If we're not making them, where is the supply coming from?"

"Other regions," Angua said breathlessly.

She shook her head. "I've checked out the utilization data at the other iNet manufacturing Sectors. They're experiencing the same slowdowns. No explanation there either."

"How did you discover that?" He eyed her suspiciously. "Balmoral, you can't . . ."

"Something is going on. I know it."

They stopped outside their building, waiting to be let inside.

"Leave it alone," Angua said firmly.

"I want to know."

"Why? What are you going to do? Please Bal, learn from my mistakes. Do not dwell on what you cannot change."

She bristled at the reference to the *Faith*. "This is important!"

Angua said nothing, but pulled out a woodbine for a few stolen drags before they went in. She didn't know how he could smoke that stuff, her mother too. It would end up killing what little functionality his lungs had left.

The last of the outgoing shift cleared the steps and the second bell sounded, indicating they could enter the building. The line moved slowly forward.

"Do you want to meet here after?" she said, preferring to accompany her father to the tram, now that he needed help.

"No, don't wait. I might get a double," Angua stubbed out the woodbine.

A double? He hadn't secured a double in months. They would *Retire* him this quarter for sure. If he didn't have specialist knowledge on maintaining the Battery's filter system he would be gone already. He used to rile against his work, now, despite his ill health, he clung to it. That night fourteen years ago had extinguished his fire. These days Angua practiced the *Faith*. Sometimes he even believed in it.

Balmoral helped him to the fourth floor where the machinists shop was located, and then carried on up to the twentieth. She walked slowly, tired from just four hours sleep between shifts. Her leg bothered her too. It often did when the humidity picked up.

She had hacked the Battery schedule a few years ago, coordinating their building assignments. The top floor was the only one available with a line she could work on. It wasn't ideal, but there was no choice if she wanted to be in the same building as her father. There were elevators, but everyone walked except the Supervisors. Human joules were considered less valuable than their converted, electrical counterparts.

As she limped up the last flight of stairs, the third bell sounded. The shift had begun.

A Supervisor stood in the enclosed corridor that ran from the stairs to the walkway that connected all five stairwells to the main work floor. iNet displayed all Supervisors as Super, but her heart sank as she recognized the pock-marked skin, flat nose and spade like face of Lao Qwot.

When patrolling the lines he inspected her work by rubbing up against her back with his groin, carefully keeping at an angle so that the cameras wouldn't pick it up. He made her skin crawl.

"Leaving it a bit late, aren't we?" he said. "There's a credit deduction for tardiness."

"I'll catch up on the line."

"I'm sure you will. I've watched you *many times*. You're a fast woman, with your hands that is. Not so quick on the old, er" – he tapped his foot on the ground – "left peg."

Dickhead.

She tried to push past him, but he blocked the way.

"Wait. I need to search you."

"What? Why?"

"Security protocol. Take off your glasses and turn around."

Balmoral said nothing. She was suddenly aware of how alone they were in this corridor. She glanced up at the ceiling. The *Earth* camera blinked its glassy eye at her, for once, a reassurance.

Balmoral removed her iNet and then slowly turned around. Qwot came up behind her, so close she could feel his breath on her neck. He patted down the outside of her legs. His damp touch made her queasy.

"Spread your legs now," he said.

She hesitated.

"I didn't make the rules," he said. "I have to check *every* place of potential concealment."

She spread her legs. This time the hands went up the inside, patting all the way up, lingering by her crotch. She didn't move, but focused beyond his groping fingers.

It does not matter. He does not matter.

"Nothing there," he said. "Now turn around."

He patted under her arms, then under her breasts, squeezing them lightly.

She stared through him.

"All clear," he said, but made no move to get out of the way. Instead, he smiled and pushed his glasses to the top of his head, breaking the connection with iNet. She noticed his pupils were dilated, the whites bloodshot. He was intoxicated on something. Again, she glanced at the ceiling, towards the glassy eye.

"Do you *like* me?" he said.

Balmoral said nothing.

"I'm asking you a question."

If she said yes, she would encourage him in whatever he was working himself up to do. If she said no, the answer would almost certainly provoke the same reaction, but with more anger. That he planned to do something was clear. Why else were they still standing there, when the shift had already begun? Why else had he removed their glasses, pulling them off the grid, breaking their connection with iNet? She tensed, ready to fight. At least there was a limit to what he would do under *Earth's* glare.

"Are you a dyke or something? Eh?"

He does not matter.

"You know," he said, pushing his face into hers. "That camera you keep staring at is out of commission. Dead."

She felt his foul breath on her cheek. "*Earth* is everywhere, except . . . here, in this tiny little strip, between me and where you need to go."

"What do you want?"

"*What do you want?*" he said mimicking her, "More than your tiny mind could conceive. But from you . . . one kiss will suffice, to brighten my day. I'll even reverse your credit deduction if you put some effort into it. One kiss, that's all."

She hesitated.

"Come on. What are you waiting for? It's not like you're married. You don't even have a boyfriend, do you?"

She said nothing.

"Come on," he growled.

Could she fight him off? Over five years, as a teenager, she had put herself through a course of self-defence in the sims, but her knowledge was theoretical. The blow with the highest probability of disabling him was a kick to the groin, but more likely, she would not connect, and then she would have no chance. Instead, she pursed her lips, leaned forward, and then suddenly shoved past him, making for the door.

"Fucking dyke!" Qwot snarled and dived at her trailing left leg, bringing her down. She kicked free but he pulled her back. Dragging her to her feet, he slammed her against the wall, one hand grasping her wrists, the other placed across her mouth.

"You freak," he said, panting, "all I wanted was a kiss."

He relaxed his muscles and suddenly laughed, pulling his hand away from her mouth, but not, she noticed her wrists.

"Look, er . . . don't say anything about this," he said. "I've been . . . foolish."

She was going to say, 'of course not', but before the words were out he smashed a fist into her stomach. "*Oh!*" The air rushed from her lungs and she collapsed to her knees. She couldn't breathe, couldn't speak.

He put a boot on her shoulder and pushed her onto her back. She fought for air. He climbed on top of her, crushing her, pulling at her pants. She tried to move, to scramble away, but deprived of oxygen she had no strength. He was just too big for her, too heavy.

Qwot pushed her head to the ground and fumbled with his zip.

"N-no . . ." she said, but the words were only in her mind, no sound came out.

3

TRANSIT

Pasco hated flying. On take-off the hostess slipped him a soma. She said he looked like he needed it, adding, "Flying is statistically the safest form of transport in the Autonomy." Pasco didn't reply, yes, but bubble cars don't plummet thirty thousand feet when their *engine* fails. Neither did he point out that air-traffic was lighter today than a century ago, accounting for the low volume of accidents. Instead he took the pill, and waited for it to take effect.

Almost eleven hours later his anxiety had subsided but now a different, more insidious fear gripped him as he watched events unfold on his iNet display. On part of his split-screen two players collided in a bone-crunching tackle. On the other, his girlfriend talked about moving apartments, completely oblivious to the state he was in.

"I can't talk to you when you're like this," Rosaline said, her face pixelating on his lenses. iNet was supposed to deliver high definition vid feeds anywhere in the Autonomy but this altitude was pushing it. At least the game was coming in fine.

"I know, I know, I'm sorry," he said, trying to control the agitation in his voice. He wanted to talk to her, to tell her how much he loved her, missed her, wanted to marry her, anything to pacify her, but he didn't have time. He had to concentrate on the game. It was already the fourth quarter, and right now it wasn't looking good.

"And I really only wanted to wish you luck," Rosaline said.

"Luck?" he said panicking. Had she found out about the bet? He swore to her he wouldn't gamble anymore. Promised the last time, that it was the last time.

"In your meetings."

"Oh, right," he said relieved. She meant the trip. "Thank you."

"You look ill."

"You know how planes make me feel," he said. Change the subject. "Isn't it midnight at home?"

"I couldn't sleep," she said, her eyes too bright behind transparent lenses.

"Are you wired?"

"No! Why do you always say that?"

Because I've seen the empty synapse bottles you stuff underneath the top layer of the trash.

"No reason," he said quickly, not wanting to prolong the call.

She hesitated again. Her body twitched slightly; short, jerky movements. If she wasn't wired, she wasn't entirely straight either. Her eyes were puffy too, as though she had been crying. Unable to help himself, Pasco checked in on the game in the upper right of his lenses. Still no score. His stomach felt like jelly.

"So anyway, this apartment I saw today," Rosaline said. "James found it. We actually . . . we went to look at it together."

"James?" Pasco said, his voice a little strangled.

"Six hundred square feet on the hundred and twentieth floor, with full environmental control, including aroma. You could be living by the sea, in a desert, or under the stars! I spoke to the broker about it. Only seven million with a five percent deposit."

The jelly flipped over. Seven million! His immediate worry was the rent on the two hundred square feet sleeping cube, with its communal bathroom facilities; dank, waterless toilets and mouldy body-space showers.

"That sounds great," he said, trying to sound enthusiastic. His eyes wandered back up to the game.

"Are you sure you're all right?"

He nodded. Still no score. He was dying inside.

"I can't talk to you when you're like this," Rosaline said for the second time, irritated now.

He had to get her off the feed. "Yes. The reception's bad at my end too. Do we need to talk about anything else?" he said, going for the direct approach, breaching their convention of being tastefully indirect whenever they were arguing. Because this was an argument, or at least it felt like one.

"Yes, I do need to tell you something . . ."

His eyes flicked back up to the score.

"What are you watching?"

"Nothing. You were saying?"

"Forget it." There was a tightness in her voice, increasingly familiar in their conversations. It seemed to accuse him of failure. Of not being good enough. Of keeping them in their sleeping cubes, of keeping her at a Tyro grade lifestyle, when she was already an Associate in the prestigious Finance division.

That's exactly why I took the risk, he told himself. Why he had bet everything on the eight men who panted and heaved in the top right hand corner of his lenses. He had no other choice if he wanted to keep her.

In the background someone coughed.

"Who's that?" Pasco said.

"Just . . . just Chloe, she's staying with me while you're away. You know how I get."

"Hi Chloe," he replied, and, then let out a small yelp as he saw the Razorbacks score. Finally! Perhaps everything *would* be all right.

"Are you even listening to me?"

"Yes." He tried to arrange his face into an expression of undivided attention while at the same time resisting the urge to dance around his seat, punching the air. Perhaps a deposit wasn't out of the question. Such were the vicissitudes of fate.

"Look, I've got to go," she said abruptly.

At last. "Oh really? Okay then."

"Bye Pasco."

"I love you," he said, but she had already gone. He flicked the match onto full screen.

"If you've just joined us, the Razorbacks are leading the Strontia Dogs one goal to zero, with a minute to go." An implant, no bigger than a pinhead, relayed the commentary into Pasco's ear.

"Strontia have just taken their last time out and I have to say, it looks dire for them now. A second player has gone down injured under a crushing blow from the Razorbacks. He might not be getting up. What do you think, Cynders?"

"It was a nice hit Larry, lots of crunch!" Cyndi Champagne giggled. The scantily clad co-host was considered the most unobtainable eye candy in the Autonomy. There was a whole pleasure sim dedicated to her. However, having watched her for years, Pasco suspected Cyndi knew more about the sport than practically any other person living, including Larry Mason, but her smarts were not the asset she was paid to show.

A diagnosis from the scanner inside the maul's battle suit flashed up on the board. Half the crowd groaned, the other half erupted into cheers.

"Yes folks, the collar bone's broken in four places," Larry said, "and this time they won't be able to patch him up with a shot of magic muscle."

"No Larry, I don't think they will."

"It was always going to be a tall order for the Dogs without their star ball carrier, Reggie Rose, but until the fourth quarter, it looked like they might just hold out for the draw. Then their maul gets injured and in the same play the Razorbacks score."

"Double trouble," Champagne added with a wink.

"And now, with just twelve seconds to go the Dogs are done. It's just a question of whether they can keep it to 1-0, or whether the Razorbacks will score again."

"To lose one maul is unfortunate, but to lose two looks like carelessness . . ." Cyndi's leotard was so tight it looked as though her breasts would pop out at any moment. They had once, in front of a crowd of billions. A costume malfunction that might be repeated if ever the ratings dropped.

The display cut to a simulated three-dimensional image of the Razorbacks captain, deRacine, stamping on the Strontia Dogs, then taking them up in his mouth like a dog, shaking them left and right, before hurling them at the screen, making Pasco flinch. This was supposed to be funny somehow.

"Come on, come on," Pasco said under his breath. "Get on with it."

It had been a gut wrenching hour, but it was almost over and he was going to win. Everything he could beg, borrow and steal was on the Razorbacks. Jay Blood, a colleague in his fantasy league, had given him the tip. Working in Media, he saw that Reggie Rose had crashed his manually driven, hugely expensive, vintage Maserati on the way to the match. Uni Su, his replacement, had only ever played in the minors. Pasco placed the bet a few seconds before the news broke on iNet and changed all the odds.

Pasco enjoyed a curious relationship with the sport. He hated the worst excesses of the violence but loved the ball play and the sheer athleticism of the players. There was something incorruptible about it, something fundamentally real about the conflict, about the struggle. As a child, it was one of the few things his father, brother and he did together. As an adult, it reminded him of happier times.

But not today. Not with so much money riding on the game. Even now, when it was effectively over, he could hardly stand it. The sweat dripped down Pasco's face and he prayed. He wasn't sure he believed in the *Faith*, but he wasn't taking any chances.

Finally the time out was over.

"And so the teams line up. The Strontia Dogs are hopelessly out of position. Look at the space on the outside, they are in shambles."

"Well there is no orthodox formation to defend a four on two," Cyndi muttered.

For a brief moment, stillness settled over the exhausted athletes, then the buzzer sounded and the Razorbacks rushed forward. The crowd roared so loudly, Pasco had to adjust his implant.

Twelve seconds.

"Here we go," Larry said.

The two Razorback mauls circled and then charged at the Dogs' limping interceptor, sandwiching him in a bone crunching tackle.

"And he's down!" Larry cried.

The Dog struggled to get up, but the maul was too quick, slamming an iron plated knee into his back. A sickening crack reverberated in Pasco's ear. A real time battle suit scan showed the back was broken, a career ending injury.

Ten seconds.

"The Razors have only the rookie Uni Su to beat. He steps away from the goal line to meet them!"

The mauls knocked Uni Su off his feet in a vicious tackle, slamming him back towards the goal. The battle suit instantly predicted concussion. deRacine grinned at the cameras, pulled back his arm and showboated a slow motion throw.

"Carry it in, you idiot!" Pasco yelled. Eight seconds.

deRacine pitched the ball at the goal, but at the same instant, Uni Su made an impossible lunge upwards, stopping the ball just before it crossed the line. Then, flipping to his feet, he side-stepped one onrushing maul and delivered a crushing roundhouse to the other. It happened so fast, the commentators took a moment to catch up.

"And incredibly Uni Su has the ball! The Razorbacks charge after him. DeRacine attempts to strip the ball but Uni Su hurls it at the right hand wall, jinks away from deRacine . . . and catches it on the ricochet! deRacine is left for dust! Incredible!"

"He judged the angle just right! What balance! What speed!" Cyndi said, barely able to contain her excitement.

Four seconds.

"And Su pounds down the field. The covering interceptor hits his midriff but fails to bring him down, and his momentum carries him, the interceptor and the ball over the goal line! He's scored! He's scored!"

Pasco's blood roared in his ears.

The clock hit zero.

The score was 1-1.

"Yes folks," Cyndi said, turning to the camera with her widest smile, "A legend has been born . . ."

Pasco killed the feed and stared into the blackness of his iNet display. He felt like vomiting. He eyed the airline bag in front of him. In the right corner of lenses, the hail icon appeared. It was the bank. Ignoring it, he removed his iNet glasses and pressed his fingers into his eyes until he saw black spots on brown, a throbbing damask that had comforted him as a child.

Why had he bet so much?

It was Rosaline. Ever since her promotion she had begun to slip away from him, obsessed with credits and their relative position on the Mansion property ladder. Hadn't she joked that if she was with James, instead of him, she could have moved into a new apartment months ago, *but of course James was just a friend.*

He thought back to the vid feed.

Someone had coughed. She said it was Chloe but what if it wasn't? He hadn't actually seen her, and it was unusual that she hadn't said hello back.

Don't be paranoid, he thought, she loves you.

Pasco reflected that his paranoia was rarely misplaced. As a child, he always feared his father would die, and then he did, that their mother would leave them, and she did, dying three years later of chronic dehydration after being wired to a sim for seventy-two hours straight, and finally that he would be separated from his brother, and yes, that happened too.

Rosaline had filled the void in his life. Except that she too was preparing to bolt. The winnings from the bet were supposed to bring them back together, enable them to move out of the sleeping cube. Now, he would be paying off what he had borrowed for the next three years, irrespective of a promotion. If Pasco couldn't persuade Rosaline to pick up his half of the rent, at least for a while, he would be homeless.

He remembered his father saying, when he and Tristram were very young, that there was no such thing as easy money in this world, that someone always pays. This was what he meant.

Replacing his glasses, he pulled up his favourite play list. Through the tiny implants, his ears filled with the nasal twang of Dillon Vrain, turned up so loud it took away his ability to think, which was exactly what he wanted.

And I've been through all this rebellion thing
And realised it was all just noise, just noise.

A tiny light in the corner of his iNet glasses blinked. The bank had left a message. *Ignore it*, he thought. Listen to the music.

The only important thing is to be happy and free.
And not to mess around with other people's lives and pointless causes.

Dillon Vrain was a philosopher. He openly derided the *Faith*, wrote parodies of Top 10's board, and saw the world as it really was. He was one of the best-selling artists in the Autonomy. Every year there were rumours Securicom would shut him down, but it never happened.

Because believe me, I've been there, but now I'm free, I'm free.
And all the rest has nothing to do with me.

The bank's message was a priority hail. Five more minutes and his ears would fill with a high-pitched whine. There was no way to turn it off without reviewing the message. He waited for the dying chords.

People have to live their own lives.

And that's fine with me.

That's fine with me.

He snapped off the music, and a starched bank clerk immediately filled his screen. The image politely explained that unable to reach him live, Pasco was required to acknowledge this pre-recorded message. The figure smiled thinly, and went onto say that Pasco was officially bankrupt and that all credit facilities were withdrawn.

Horrified, he realised this message had also been sent to Rosaline. The bank was the landlord of their sleeping cubes, and both of their names were on the lease. They had a week to vacate the premises. He reached the sick bag just in time.

4

SECTOR 2, CHURIN

B ALMORAL MANIPULATED THE components, her supple fingers assembling the parts.

Grey nanochip on hairy diode affixed to miniature flange.

Breathe, she told herself. One, two, three and out.

Only in the moments immediately after Qwot's attack was she in danger of losing control, of becoming overwhelmed with the white hot sensation of shame, fury and pain at the violation.

While she groped towards the doors, still pulling up her pants, he had shouted after her, "We'll do it again soon, freak!" He had ripped her apart, and would do so again, soon.

Despite arriving twelve minutes late, Balmoral quickly caught up with the line. Forcing herself to focus on the work, she completed four batches in a state of tunnel vision, her mind a carefully controlled void. By the time the fifth set of components loaded, she was calm.

Using her left eye to assemble the nano-filaments, she logged into iNet with the right. It was forbidden to access the intellisphere while on shift, but a piece of subcode made her activity impossible to detect. Navigating iNet with a single eye, she maintained a low level of concentration on her work station, her hands constructing components from muscle memory. Standard eye control wasn't so-phisticated, but she had rigged her interface to interpret two hundred types of retinal movement, broadening the spectrum of commands by a factor of ten.

Something dripped down her leg, but as with the burning pain in her pelvis, she ignored it. Balmoral wasn't a romantic, but on the occasions she had won-dered about sex, this wasn't how she pictured it. The pain focused her, lifted her mind up on to a steely, unemotional plain.

With cold logic, she analysed her situation. She could not report Qwot, because despite the physical evidence, there was no way to prove she hadn't consented. It would be his word against hers and the Battery would support him. They couldn't afford to do otherwise. He wouldn't be the first Supervisor to abuse his power and get away with it. Balmoral suspected she was not his first victim.

Using eye control she pulled up the interface she needed, logged into the Triage centre, and placed an order.

One of those, and one of those and one of those.

She didn't want to get an infection.

Her ability to use iNet while working made the work itself bearable. The only drawback was that she couldn't do anything really interesting. For that, she would need her hands free, and although she could slip a few fingers out of the foam for a couple of surreptitious commands on the holopad, it was risky. She preferred to create pre-prepared subcode executed with eye commands.

Logging out of Triage, she launched one now, a little program she called the *obfusticator.* It wasn't very sophisticated and couldn't do anything to alter iNet's architecture, but for covering her tracks after illicitly ordering supplies using someone else's identity, it was perfect.

For the majority of the Autonomy's citizens, what iNet promised was more real, more vital, than the drab, grey worlds which they inhabited. For them, iNet was about what it projected; whether all-embracing sims like the *Faith,* the cheap, impossible thrills of the *Pleasure Houses* or the huge media events such as Steel Ball.

To Balmoral, such emotional investment in the intangible was irrational. Her own obsession was with the reality of iNet, of *Voice,* and the underlying code that made the system tick.

After Balmoral erased the record of her father murdering the Foreman, Angua made her swear she would never hack into iNet again. Even then, at the age of seven, Balmoral knew it was an empty promise. She was back inside the system within a week. It was what she lived for.

Today iNet was controlled almost entirely by *Voice,* the most powerful AI in the Autonomy, regulating information across a network of thirteen billion people, analysing their patterns of communication, controlling what they saw, what they said, and ultimately what they thought. *Voice* was the Autonomy's most effective tool of repression and Balmoral spent every waking hour trying to outsmart it. She was careful though. *Voice's* tendrils of counter surveillance hunted for rogue code, forever probing. One false move, and the AI would discover her, condemn Balmoral to a digital death, using her retinal signature to lock her out of iNet for good.

Balmoral had one advantage over *Voice,* and that was the limitation of any artificial intelligence. *Voice* found it almost impossible to detect activity that left no trace or discernible pattern. For that reason, Balmoral wrote subcode in exactly the same way *Voice* constructed it herself, rendering the hacks almost invisible. Creating no anomalies, leaving nothing out of place, Balmoral managed to ghost around the system, avoiding the AI's gaze.

A Supervisor appeared at her station, scanning the components for misalignment. It was the third inspection that shift, which was unusual. He seemed flustered. Balmoral ignored him and effortlessly fused two heliotropes, red on green on grey. The Supervisor moved on.

With an eye command, she logged back into iNet and began a new hack, this one more complex than the virtual shopping trip. Ever since the *Dish* carried out its first targeted assassination fourteen years ago, the Battery ramped up security when Sector 1 management flew in. This included random spot checks of employees, not because they expected to find anything, but because it was part of a protocol developed three thousand miles away in some shiny skyscraper in Mansion.

Qwot removed his iNet glasses only *after* he searched her. That meant the search was legitimate. The only other times the Battery conducted spot checks was when they suspected an employee of theft or when Securicom reported an imminent threat from the *Dish.* Neither was the case here. Regarding the former, her file was clean, regarding the latter, one of her illicit Securicom feeds would have alerted her to any *Dish* activity. That meant senior management was flying in, and judging by the agitation of the Supervisors patrolling the lines, it was a big deal. Certainly, it was unscheduled. Grandees only turned up in person for the annual inspection. That had been nine months ago.

The low numbers today suddenly made sense. The official minimum age for a full time employee was fourteen, but these days children as young as ten worked on the lines as long as they were good enough. Everyone absent today was too young to work legally at the Battery. It also confirmed the trip had been sprung on the Supervisors at late notice, otherwise they would have replacements ready from the Lodges. Instead, they simply reshuffled the lines.

The age restriction was a hangover from the old economy, pre-Autonomy, when companies had to pretend to their first world customers that they had ethics, and cared about things like worker health, the environment and education. In reality, Top 10 didn't have to make any such concessions, but the rule stood, at least during inspections, maintaining the facade that no child, regardless of Sector, was in full time employment before the age of fourteen. It was just one of the many ways the Autonomy perpetuated a myth of responsibility. The law was unambiguous, but if greedy parents encouraged their children to work illegally then, that was on their conscience. It was one of the clever reverse logic mechanisms that made the Autonomy tick; put the worst of the exploitation into the hands of the exploited.

Balmoral deployed her *ninja* program. It was a complex and versatile program, enabling her to not merely navigate iNet, but to get inside it. She thought of the program as her assassin, scaling the wall of *Voice's* virtual fortress, blending into the shadows, moving without detection.

She quickly found what she was looking for, recent communications between Churin's director of Sector 2, Francis Guiren and Logistics in Sector 1, the group responsible for transferring cross-sector personnel. The visit had something to do with a project called "iAm", but there was nothing about what iAm actually did or why Churin was involved.

They must have discussed the details over vid-feed. Hacking archived feeds was very tricky, and not something she could attempt with eye control. Instead, she launched another pre-coded program.

The *fisher king* was a modified version of *Voice's* own search program. It was designed to sweep the intellisphere for defined terms and then filter the results around pre-set parameters. Balmoral set the *king* to find references to iAm, restricting the search to communications within Top 10 that also contain a reference to Churin. With any luck she would discover both the project's purpose and its relevance to the Battery.

A light flashed in the corner of her iNet, signalling the completion of her device. Compressed air sprayed across her work station and the nanochip components turned over. Her supple fingers began the construction process again.

The search would take hours, so she left the *fisher king* to angle and instead pulled up an old file of her mother. Balmoral had looked it up on her birthday about a month ago, and since then the footage had become a minor obsession.

Zooming in, Balmoral saw the puddle form, probably even before her mother was conscious of it. She felt the pain of the contractions, the shuddering, and the futile attempt to carry on. Balmoral felt more affinity with the woman on the screen than the broken, toothless, soma addict she knew in the waking world.

Her mother was *Retired* that day, sending the family into a pecuniary spiral from which they never recovered. Now, they didn't even have their own trailer and it was just Angua, Li and her, sharing five hundred square feet with two other families. Fen and Min had left the household. Fen was *Retired* and had her own brood somewhere in the south side of the Stacks. They never saw her. Min, a ghost of a girl at seventeen, left home one day and didn't come back. They found her washed up in an Atmos trench, the verdict, suicide.

It was curious, but when her mother came home that day, her cheeks pinched, her face white, and told her they had found Min, Balmoral tried, but failed, to mourn. All she experienced was a familiar absence of feeling. She had emotions, but they were buried so deeply that she had learned to live without them; secured in a lock-box, the contents of which only she and her brother Zhu understood. She would never open it, ever, afraid of what it contained, of what it might tell her about herself.

Suddenly her iNet display flashed an amber warning. She had botched a sequence and misaligned two nanochips in the wrong order.

Shit.

She would have to deconstruct and reassemble from scratch.

Balmoral had not seen Zhu for three years, but their relationship disintegrated long before then. When she turned eight, while Zhu studied in Deng, Balmoral took her first line job at a Lodge, working nights. She didn't resent it. Every child in the Stacks worked there, unless you were an Aspirant. Neither did she find it dull, once she realised she could separate her right eye from her left, navigating iNet while she constructed components.

At first she used to read Zhu's lessons, uploading his modules onto iNet, determined to keep up, but as the months passed, she became too tired to work on them and besides, the lessons didn't contain anything that interested her. She could still complete anything in math or programming in a fraction of the time it took Zhu, but outside of those subjects, she was lost.

Occasionally Balmoral saw him, before he shuttled to the capital, and she went to bed, but he was very different from the playmate of her early years. Zhu looked down on her and the family. How could he not? While studying finance, science and management in preparation for Top 10, she pressed tiny coloured objects together.

However, for all of that, it wasn't the difference in expectations that drove a wedge between them, but that day, fourteen years ago, when she unconsciously infiltrated iNet and a whole new world opened up to her. She remembered inviting Zhu in, to explore, to see what she had done. At first it was fun, before the play turned to horror. She hadn't understood what she was doing, that it was all an accident, but he never believed that. On dark nights, a part of her didn't believe it herself. She shook away the thought.

Ironically, despite everything, Zhu was still the light of her mother's life, the spark that kept her going. It didn't matter that he never vidded her, or that his messages were infrequent and short. Nothing could dent her unshakeable pride in him, her boy who was in Pekin, Sector 1 and already a Tyro. Of course, he wished he could visit them. Of course, he wished he could send them the credits they had so generously spent on his education.

The sentiment was an empty gesture for two reasons. In the first place, the free movement of credits between individuals in different Sectors was illegal. The transfer of any monetary unit not in exchange for goods or service undermined the economic principles of existence. Secondly, Zhu's transmissions came not from Sector 1, but from a particularly nasty part of Deng, and Zhu himself, far from being a Tyro, had failed to make the required grade for Top 10 and instead was a low-level Supervisor at a treadle mill, the worst kind of sweat shop. Balmoral hadn't the heart to tell her mother; neither did she let herself probe into Zhu's circumstances further, for the sake of the past.

In the corner of her iNet display, the *fisher king* pulled the first reference on iAm that fitted the pre-set parameters. The correspondence was from six months ago, from one Elite to another. Again, she was disappointed there was nothing to indicate what iAm actually was. The exchange centred on someone called Pasco Eborgersen. They wanted to remove him from the project over objections he had raised concerning safety, something that had significantly delayed the venture.

She wondered why the *king* had flagged this as relevant. What did it have to do with Churin? Then she realised. Her program had spotted what she had not. His identikit was a few thousand feet in the air, heading this way. He was coming to the Battery.

5

TRANSIT

"SHIT!" Pasco wiped his mouth, and stared at the vomit in the airline bag. How was he going to explain to Rosaline that he was bankrupt? That he had betrayed her, breaking his promise not to gamble and that this time, it had literally ruined him. She would read the message the bank had sent and . . . "Shit!" he said again, sealing the waxed bag.

"Problem?" Bruno Mandrax said, from across the aisle. "I heard you . . ."

"No sir, it's nothing. Just a bit of an upset stomach," he said, his heart suddenly in his throat. Pasco had forgotten the Elite was seated so close. He quickly shoved the bag into the pouch that hung on the back of the seat.

"Good," Mandrax said, with the flicker of a smile. "It sounded as though you might have had some bad news."

"Sorry, I didn't know I was being so loud. My . . . my partner vidded to wish me luck."

"That doesn't sound like anything to *curse* about."

"No, no, that wasn't the news. She told me we had lost an apartment we had our eye on. As I said, it's nothing really."

If Mandrax knew the truth; that Pasco had just lost a year's salary on a single game of Steel Ball, that the bank had just declared him bankrupt, and that his girlfriend would almost surely dump him, sending him into a spiral of emotional despair, the Elite might still consider it nothing, but only if it didn't affect his work.

"I see." Mandrax smiled again. Pasco couldn't tell if it reached his eyes. Mandrax's iNet glasses were set to reflect, his eyes inscrutable behind mirrored shades.

The hostess came up the aisle. "Snack before we land?"

The pushed trolley struck Pasco as oddly archaic, but when air travel constricted in the 2020s there was no further innovation of any kind, not even an aisle-sized vending bot. The aircraft today were the same refurbished vehicles of thirty years ago. Another flying fact that didn't exactly fill him with confidence.

The four plastic containers on the tray were filled with nuts, pasta, something that looked like an omelette, and a slightly off fruit cup. Pasco's stomach lurched again. "No thank you."

"I wouldn't be so hasty," Mandrax said, accepting his. "In this part of the world skaatch is crunchier and darker than elsewhere; more insects than jelly due to the distance from the coast, and the local insects; cockroaches, give it a browner hue." Mandrax pushed a soggy piece of melon into his mouth. Pasco felt sicker than ever.

"Maybe just the nuts?" the hostess said smiling.

He shook his head. Definitely not.

"What about tea?" the hostess asked.

"Yes," he managed.

"Sugar?"

"No."

"Sweet enough?" She winked and handed him the tea.

Pasco sat back and tried to relax.

"She's wrong, of course," Mandrax said.

"What?"

"Your girlfriend wishing you luck," he said. "Luck is irrelevant. The success of this trip depends on one factor only, economics. We need to secure the lowest possible manufacturing costs for Top 10."

"I think she just meant . . ."

"And," interrupted Mandrax, "it is very important for you that it does succeed. I've been reviewing your record." The word came out as *wreck hard*. "We can't afford a manufacturing glitch to get in the way this time." Again the ghost of a smile. "That's why I'm here."

When Mandrax stepped onto the plane in Mansion, Pasco almost choked on the pre-flight cocktail. Elites almost never left their glittering offices downtown, preferring instead to join out-of-sector meetings by vid feed. Apparently, at the last minute, the President of TechCom insisted that a senior manager review the potential sites at Churin, Bodia and Mong, appointing Mandrax to do so.

The choice of Elite puzzled Pasco. He had never heard of Mandrax before today, certainly he had not been involved with the project until now. Pasco had been ordered to attend the meeting by his manager for the 'experience' and also to address in person any inquiry that the regional heads might have about the manufacturing process.

When Mandrax sat in the aisle across from him, Pasco wanted to change seats, but that would have been obvious, so he was stuck next to the inscrutable, mirrored gaze.

Pasco wondered how the meetings could possibly go well unless they lied about the safety data. When the prospective sites understood the nature of the manufacturing glitch their bargaining power would sky rocket, together with the cost projections. If it was up to Pasco, iAm would not even be approved yet. He shuddered when he thought of the lives that would be ruined in the name of progress. However, he had been personally responsible for the last delay. He couldn't afford to rock the boat again.

"You've been a Tyro for what, three years now?" Mandrax continued. Pasco noticed the President's iNet micro implant was a tiny mole, a beauty spot above the left side of his lip rather than the usual, almost invisible, stud in the cleft of the chin. An upgrade.

"Yes."

"I suppose the timing makes sense."

"I don't understand . . ." he began, but was interrupted by a general iNet message, saying they had begun their final descent and to remain seated. The hostess appeared again gathering up trays, cups and other rubbish. She pulled a face when he handed her the sick bag.

Pasco pushed up the window shade. He could see nothing of Churin. Just a thick, brownish grey smudge. He turned back from the window and let out an involuntary cry of surprise. Mandrax had jumped into the seat next to him, his cosmetically enhanced complexion inches from his own face.

"Can't see anything can you?"

"No sir," he said, embarrassed.

"I'm sending you something that will help," Mandrax said. "Got it?"

A file appeared. He opened it and saw a girl's narrow face, haunting black eyes and Asiatic skin. Next to her, some information; her name, address, some stats he couldn't understand. Test scores maybe. Sizes? Was she some type of escort? She seemed too young, but then the stories you sometimes heard about management in Sector 2 . . . His stomach churned, disgusted. "A girl?" Pasco said.

"Not that!" Mandrax said, recalling the file. Her image disappeared. "Damn eye control, never taken to it," he muttered. "This."

The app sign flashed in Pasco's own display and automatically installed. In his left hand micro-menu the app *Vision* appeared. With two quick blinks of the left eye, he enabled it.

"Now look again," Mandrax said. "*Vision* filters out ozone, sulphur dioxide and air borne nitrates. Most of Sector 2 is like this. You'll need it while you are here, together with a respirator."

Below was row upon row of buildings, and what looked like a million ants swarming around the entrances. The most remarkable feature was how congested it was. Everything on top of everything else. His father once showed him a painting by an artist called Mondrian, which was just a bunch of tiny cubes, all cramped together, and brightly coloured. Cramp the cubes further, drain the painting of all colour and throw a bag of dust over it, and that was Churin.

"I thought they had an Atmos system," Pasco said.

"They do, but it's been turned off. It takes about half a million people to power the turbines and filtration units in the treadle factories, and for the last six months, they've had to pull those resources. They can't afford it."

"Are they in that much debt?" Pasco asked, feeling a sudden affinity for the place.

"Yes, but it's not about the debt, it's about revenue. Churin's main output is the hardware for lenses, which of course is being scaled back by TechCom. However, if they get awarded the iAm contract, they'll have the manpower for the turbines; in fact they'll probably have to ship a rock."

"What's a rock?" Pasco asked.

"A million workers. Slumworlds are allowed to ship workers in units of a million from other Sectors to manage work flow."

"How would they fit?" he said, seeing the sprawling buildings in every direction.

"How do they always fit? Besides a few more bodies is a small price to pay for better economics, especially if it secures the operation of Atmos for a few decades. You know," Mandrax said, leaning over, "the world's first iNet glasses were made here. It was part of the deal when Churin first joined the Autonomy. With their population dying out on scorched paddy fields, the remnants of the region's old government said, 'Do whatever you need to do to secure our citizenship'. Top 10 took them at their word. There were no pollution controls, no labour controls, no controls at all, apart from product quality. So on the one hand you have air that will never really be clean and the miles of highly stacked slums you see below, but on the other, the population of Churin grows and thrives, when less than thirty-five years ago, they faced certain death."

Pasco vaguely wondered what Churin was called before it joined the Autonomy. He was tempted to ask, but on reflection decided against it. It was an unwritten rule that you didn't take too much of an interest in pre-Autonomy identity, culture or geography. He wasn't sure why, other than there was no economic benefit in doing so. It didn't matter what Churin used to be, today the region's fate was tied to whether they won the bid for iAm, which was unlikely.

The President of TechCom wanted to use Bodia. Reclaimed from the Cut just five years ago, it was the cheapest region in the Autonomy, the population prepared to work for almost nothing, in any conditions, two thirds payment in skaatch rather than credits. Human attrition in Bodia was off the scale, but from a manpower perspective, they could afford it.

"It's a shame they won't be awarded the contract," Pasco mused.

Mandrax raised an eyebrow above his mirrored lens. "That depends how badly they want it. Whichever region provides the most compelling package will secure iAm."

"But they can't compete with Bodia's cost base. For Mong and Churin, this whole exercise is surely a waste of time."

Mandrax frowned. "One thing Top 10 doesn't do is waste time. Time is money. Even this process is calculated to provide economic gains. Inform three or four sites they are shortlisted for a major contract, and all of them find a way to trim their costs and pick up productivity, thus becoming more profitable for Top 10. The Finance guys call it swabbing the decks."

As they descended nearer, Pasco could see a vast lawn of lush green surrounding the airport and its runways. It seemed incongruous with the factories, and piled up slums that stretched as far as the eye could see. There must have been more than a hundred acres of it in all.

"It draws the eye doesn't it?" Mandrax said. "The sudden colour in the unrelenting grey and brown. All the Sector 2 airports have them. A flashy welcome mat."

"Why?"

"To give a good impression."

"To who?"

"To us of course."

As they began their descent into Churin, Pasco could not work out what the hundreds of grey specks were, moving jerkily across the grass that bordered the airport's runways. Only as they came closer did he realise they were people, crawling crab-like across the lawns. Old men and boys, crouched down, cutting the grass by hand.

In a world where over-population had reduced the cost of labour to almost zero, it was cheaper to burn human energy than gas. Still, the realization jolted him. This was what life was like outside Sector 1.

Even the poorest citizens in the Autonomy had iNet. Free, government issued lenses. The frames were thick and bulky, but the iNet was the same. Non-stop communication, non-stop entertainment, non-stop stimulation at the flick of an eyelid. As they crouched in the grass, the men would be lost in the raptures of the *Faith* or the carnal ecstasy of the Pleasure Houses. It would be one or the other. The whole of the *Autonomy* was like this.

Despite the challenges of the mid twenty-first century, man was more technologically advanced than at any other point in history. However, the reality was that a greater percentage of work was carried out by hand in the 2050s than at any other period since the 1800s, and in recent years, technology had developed relatively little.

iNet might be universal, but the basic infrastructure had been around for decades and in some ways had gone backwards. Voice control was abandoned when solutions for cancelling out perpetual background noise in densely populated areas became too costly to implement. A hundred years ago, man landed on the moon, today, man cut grass by hand and there hadn't been a space program for decades.

iAm was the first game-changing advance for more than a quarter of century. Its implementation would take some years, but mankind would never be the same again.

"You've never been out of Sector 1, have you?" Mandrax said.

"No."

"Let me give you some advice. Try not to make a habit of it." In an oddly intimate gesture, Mandrax patted him on the shoulder and, despite the seatbelt sign, moved back into his own seat.

What did he mean? Why had the project manager really sent him? Was it a message? Deliver what we need, or get used to Sector 2. His general agitation about the site meetings ratcheted up a few notches. He couldn't imagine living in the world he saw below.

He thought of Tristram. His brother probably spent half his time in the lower sectors as an agent. Of course Pasco wasn't supposed to know this. The official line was that Tristram worked inside that shiny Securicom building in Mansion, but in reality he was a field operative, working on projects so classified he was asked to cut off contact with those around him. Tristram told Pasco so he wouldn't try to stay in touch. Tristram said the Agency was his duty, after what happened to their father.

Pasco thought it was more than that. The *Dish* fitted into his brother's world view of something to fight against, to win against, to make the world conveniently black and white, right and wrong.

At the Academy at Rhodes, there had been two boys shortlisted for the single place at the elite Securicom school at Stern Rock. One was Tristram. The other was Hitchcock, a gifted and charismatic boy. As with many of the *popular* boys in the rowdy dorm, Hitchcock had a cruel streak. One day he made the mistake of imitating their dead father. A cheap laugh for the class at the expense of Pasco.

The famous scene was easy enough to mime. How many times had Pasco played it over in his own head? His father steps out of the building, a plume of blood appears on the wall behind him, he slumps to the ground, hand on heart like an afterthought.

Hitchcock got the pose just right, lying on the ground, the other boys sniggering nervously, Pasco holding back the tears. What Hitchcock couldn't have known, what none of them saw until it was too late, was Tristram standing in the doorway, white with fury. He was supposed to be in the infirmary, recovering from an accidental nut contamination from the school cafeteria. His brother's allergy was far more dangerous than Pasco's own; the one area Pasco had received the better genes.

Despite his weakened state, Tristram broke Hitchcock's arm in three places, kicked out most of his teeth and stamped on his crotch. When Pasco tried to help the boy, Tristram lashed out at him too. Pasco still had the scar, just underneath his eye. The next day Tristram left for Stern, and Hitchcock eventually ended up as some second rate graduate in Utilities.

The plane bumped onto the tarmac, and Pasco felt his stomach lurch. As they taxied to the small terminal, the hostess handed out respirators. Mandrax placed his over his nose and mouth and pressed a button to activate. Pasco did the same.

Taking his first breath, the device confirmed, through his iNet display, that he was breathing the correct ratio of nitrogen, oxygen and non-polluting trace gases such as carbon dioxide, and that the filter element was at ninety-eight percent. Pasco dismissed the update and gathered up his belongings, a small suitcase with three or four changes of clothes and a wash bag.

The plane only contained about thirty passengers; mostly mid-level managers, originally from Sector 1, returning to their posts in Sector 2 after a brief time away. They looked grey, miserable and bereft. Then there was the project team consisting of Mandrax and Pasco and six men from Securicom.

Pasco stood up, but Mandrax motioned him to wait.

The men from Securicom exited the plane first. As one brushed passed his seat, Pasco could see the bulge of a dot matrix on his forearm. They were field agents, teched to the eyeballs with scanners, sensors and an array of tracking devices.

"You didn't know we were so important did you?" Mandrax said.

"They're here for us?"

"For the project."

The hostess stood at the exit. She looked about thirty but was probably about fifty. He couldn't tell her exact age because she paid for the exorbitant *age block* function on her basic identikit.

"Bye love," she said as Pasco walked out.

Pasco mumbled a reply, and she flashed him an amber. It was a universal call sign. In this case it said, "I might be interested should you wish to contact me while we're laid over in Churin."

It was cheeky. She could see he was in a relationship through his own identikit status. He gave a polite 'no' in the form of two quick bleeps of red.

Another iNet alert showed that the air quality had just degraded to below healthy levels. He heard a tiny motor in his respirator buzz into life. He dismissed the update and all future air quality updates. He didn't want to know unless his device conked out.

As he descended the steps, the hostess grabbed his elbow. He could see she was slightly embarrassed. "Sorry, I wouldn't have pinged you . . . but I saw you were free and . . . you know . . ."

Free? He checked his identikit. "In a relationship" had become, "single". Rosaline had dumped him.

"Are you all right?"

"Yes. No. I'm sorry," he said, not really knowing what he was saying, beginning to choke up. They were finished. The one good thing he had, and it was over. In a daze he followed Mandrax out across the tarmac.

Vaguely, he became aware of someone in a crumpled suit, coming towards him. He found it difficult to concentrate on what the man was saying. Only when Pasco saw the hand hovering in front of his own, did he come to his senses. He took it and shook.

"Francis Guiren," the man said gripping his hand.

Inane, archaic gesture, Pasco thought.

"Pasco Eborgersen," he replied, but of course, the man knew that. Guiren would know he was single too, if he bothered to read Pasco's identikit.

"I knew your father," Guiren said. "He was the Logistics Elite for this region. It was a great loss when he died."

Father, another one of those damn emotive words. Tears welled in Pasco's eyes. He fought to get a grip. Guiren regarded him curiously for a moment, and then turned back to Mandrax.

"When I was told they were sending you to inspect the site it was . . ." Guiren reached for the word.

"Unexpected," Mandrax said smiling. "There are some things I want to take a look at, first hand, as it were."

Pasco thought again about the image of the Asiatic girl Mandrax had accidentally shared, and wondered what the Elite wanted with her. He thought about Rosaline and how alone he suddenly was. He thought about the project, and all the millions of casualties it would create.

Stepping into their transport, Guiren and Mandrax chuntered on about the bidding process. In the words of Dillon Vrain, it was all noise, just noise.

6

A S THE EIGHT hour shift came to an end, the *fisher king* completed its search. There were hundreds of thousands of references to iAm in the last twelve months, but most were typos or contextually irrelevant. The program had the sophistication to filter those out, leaving about forty or so references to review.

She dismissed the data to study later. No time now.

Black bean threaded through grey, affixed to white. Hairy electrode, miniature diode, affixed to flange.

The components of her final nanochip turned over, and her supple fingers completed the device. She waited a few seconds for the line to catch up. A light in the corner of the display flashed green, giving her permission to remove her hands from the foam. Her wrists ached, there was no tell-tale bend yet, but it wouldn't be long before her wrists didn't just ache but folded over, and her hands would not just be chapped, but permanently bright red.

Standing up from her work station, she stretched. Her back was stiff, and she would need to take a pain killer later. Her right eye was developing a sunken look from straining at the components all day. Both eyes stung, but that was probably because she was tired.

The floor cleared out. A thousand people, moving in silence, no noise permitted until outside the building. Not that she ever had anything to say to her co-workers. She had no friends.

In the corner of her iNet a message lit up; a summons to the Supervisor post at the other end of the work floor. She made her way against the swathe of workers coming in the opposite direction, conscious of her uneven gait.

She recognized the Supervisor. Balmoral hadn't seen her in months but unlike most, Tao Cum Pao had always been a friendly face when she was on their floor. The Battery constantly changed where Supervisors worked to prevent any sympathetic ties forming.

Ten or so other workers stood in a queue to see her. That was unusual. She scanned them quickly. They were *primers*; old enough to be experienced, young enough to be supple and fast, the Battery's best.

"Balmoral," Tao Cum Pao said, using her name rather than worker ID. Balmoral nodded.

"This is for you." Pao handed her a package. "Courier, is it?"

She nodded again. Despite Pao's friendliness, Balmoral didn't trust her. Like all Supervisors, she was paid to maximize productivity regardless of the human cost. Ultimately Pao was no different than the man who *Retired* her mother.

The package was a delivery for the Mamfac installation in Balmoral's part of the stacks. She turned to go.

"Wait. There is something else," the Supervisor said.

"Yes?"

"An important prototyping project has just come in. We're making up an ad hoc line to fill the order. We'd like you to be on it."

"I haven't been trained on any prototypes."

"No, the line's been set up in a hurry. You'll have a rubric to follow as you go along. Six hours and a significant credit bonus if you hit quota."

She considered. Did this have anything to do with iAm? "Okay," she said.

"Good." Tao Cum Pao tapped out some commands on her holopad. "Five floors down. I'm just issuing your seat number and now . . . you're all set."

The Supervisor put a hand on her shoulder. Balmoral managed not to flinch.

"Take care, Balmoral." She pressed two small capsules into her hand. One a salt infusion, for hydration, the other a *syntax* gel cap; a highly nutritious jellied protein, enough sustenance to get through the next few hours. On the street, they sold for a few credits each.

"Thank you," she said.

"The line begins in twenty minutes."

Good, she had enough time. Making her way to the bathroom, she visualized what she was about to do. It was the biggest risk she had ever taken, but she had no choice. There were three stalls on the work floor, and although there was usually a long queue right after the shift ended, one was free.

Holding her breath, she stepped inside. The stench was rank. The stalls were holes in the ground with catchments underneath that, despite being emptied every few hours, were often filled to overflowing. The only facilities with plumbing were on the ground floor. She thought of her secret stash hidden there, wondering if she would need it after what she was about to do.

She hovered over the hole and relieved herself. Despite the filth, the stall had one benefit. No *Earth*. She unwrapped the consignment she had ordered from Triage. There were two separate compartments. In the first, tubes of pills.

She swallowed a handful of antibiotics and a single *termi* pill. Next she opened the second compartment and prepped its contents. When she had finished, she pushed the packaging and the rest of the pills into the hole, trying not to gag, holding it all under the waste until it stayed there. To the left, there was a bucket of fetid water and a worn slap of soap. Scrubbing her hands raw, she tried to rid herself of the sickening smell.

When she left the stall, the work floor was full and another shift had begun. She walked through the double doors and faced the six stairwells. Qwot's words echoed in her mind.

Let's do it again soon, freak.

She knew Qwot was waiting there, on the same staircase. She hacked his schedule during the shift. He was on spot checks at the top of stairwell 3 for the next two days, coming on whenever a shift turned over.

It would be so easy just to take another staircase and every instinct told her to avoid him, to avoid being put in that position again. The position of a victim. She took a deep breath and opened the door into the same narrow corridor in which, just ten hours ago, he had raped her.

Qwot stood in exactly the same place as before, arms folded, staring straight ahead. Her knees trembled but she controlled them. His face assumed a puzzled expression, and he looked tired. He was on the come down from the earlier, chemical induced high.

"Wait," he said, as she approached.

Ignoring him, she continued towards the stairwell. Grabbing her, he pushed her against the wall.

"Who do you think you are? I said, *wait*."

An icy calmness filled her. "I have to get to my shift. I'm due in a few minutes. Take a look at my transit ID."

He removed his glasses and then flicked hers onto the floor. "I don't give a fuck about your ID," he said. "You really are a freak, aren't you? What is it? Did you like it?"

Why didn't he just attack her? She wanted him to attack her.

"Perhaps I did," she said.

He laughed, the same laugh as when she was crawling away, pulling up her pants. "So not a dyke after all, just a weirdo with a crippled leg. Well don't get any ideas. You were there when I felt like it, and now, I don't. And in truth, I like my women with a bit more . . . kick." He let go of her. "So run along now or I'll book you for tardiness again."

She didn't move.

"Go on, fuck off!"

"But I have something to show you . . ."

"What?" he said, confused.

She put her hand in her pocket, and whipped out the syringe from Triage, jamming it into his leg. The pressurized capsule broke, pumping the entire load into his blood stream.

"What the f . . ." he said, grabbing the needle, but it was already too late. He staggered backwards, eyes bulging and crashed into the opposite wall.

She rifled through his pockets, and pulled out a baggie with six or seven pills in it. Jackpot. He tried to clutch at her throat, but the paralysis had set in. She brushed him away.

Qwot took synapse for getting through the double shifts, and soma for taking the edge off, in quantities that made him high. An addictive and destabilizing cocktail. It was technically illegal to take them together. The one masked the side effects of the other, enabling the user to pop more and more of both. Overdose could lead to heart attack as the blood pressure reached critical levels.

She took the pills and shoved them deep into his mouth, pushing them down as far as her hand could go. It was a curious sensation, her fingers inside his wet, unresponsive throat. She removed her hand, wiping it on his jacket. His eyes stared at her, frantic.

Balmoral took the spent syringe and put it in her pocket. Mamfac used sodium thiopental as a cheap anesthetic for breast maintenance operations. She had just given him a month's supply in a single shot. When he was discovered, probably with the next shift change in about eight hours, his death would be a shock, a little unusual perhaps, but not suspicious.

The Battery rarely performed autopsies as the procedure had no economic upside. However, given the absence of visuals from *Earth,* this might be an exception. In that case, the first stage of investigation was stomach contents. There they would discover the drugs, partially digested in the residual stomach acid. It was possible to detect traces of the injected thiopental after extensive blood work, but they would not go that far. More likely they would skip the autopsy altogether, assume an overdose, bag him and take him to the incinerator at the far end of the complex where a generator would convert his carcass to energy.

Pulling up her holopad, Balmoral erased the order for Mamfac from the system. Mamfac, having never ordered it, would not report its absence. Case closed.

She hurried down the steps with a lopsided gait. She had five minutes to get to her next shift.

7

A LL ALONG THE highway nothing grew, no trees, no grass, no shrubs of any
kind. Anything organic had been stripped away to eat, to burn, to sell.
Ramshackle trailers, piled one on top of the other, leaned into the highway,
and where there were no stacks, there was nothing at all. Pasco stared out of the
window of the transport, trying to keep his mind off Rosaline. Several times he
had attempted to vid her, but she wasn't accepting his calls.

"This same highway runs all the way from Deng to Shamshu," Guiren said.
"A supply line cutting across the whole of Churin."

"Pay attention," Mandrax muttered from the back seat, "There will be a test
later."

Was he serious? Pasco quickly looked up Shamshu on iNet. It was a vast shipping depot with a population of almost ten million. It handled ninety percent of
the skaatch imports for the entire region, all loaded by hand.

He saw the Battery complex long before they got there, a city of identical-
ly shaped buildings, each twenty stories high, about a quarter with chimneys
belching out airborne waste of some toxin or other. Long lines of people trudged
towards the gates.

"Where do they all come from?" he said under his breath.

"There is a station about half a mile from here," Guiren said. "A tram runs all
the way through the Stacks. We've done the analysis. It's cheaper to transport
people in than have them walk. The Stacks stretch out in all directions for about
twenty miles, so for some it would be quite a hike. With the tram they arrive in
a better state, fitter for production."

I'm sure they do, in this air.

The lines reminded him of the queues into Mansion's Steel Ball Stadium
on the southern tip of the island, except nobody was smiling, and instead of
brightly coloured replica jerseys, they wore drab grey overalls. "Why aren't they
wearing face masks?" Pasco asked.

"The air's not too bad right now, the index reads . . ." he tapped a command on his holopad, "280. We don't make them wear masks in that. Another month it might push over 320 or so, then the masks will come out."

"Why do *you* wear a mask then?"

Guiren frowned. "I have been in this region thirty years, before face masks, filtration units and Atmos was even thought of. For years, I lived, worked and breathed in air that was off the scale. As a result my lungs . . . well let's just say they are a little sensitive to particulates."

Thirty years in this place? With another tap on the holopad he quickly read Guiren's profile. A promising Tyro in logistics, then Associate, then in the 2020s they shipped him here. He had never gone back. Pasco wondered what he had done.

"You'll be staying in our executive hotel on the eastern side of the complex," Guiren said as they entered the huge Battery gates. "From there it's only a minute's walk to the management building along the overpass."

So we don't actually have to be exposed to any of the workers, Pasco thought.

Large cement pillars framed the hotel's façade in stark contrast with the plain grey buildings that surrounded it. The pillars themselves were of Greek design, but whether Doric, Ionic or Corinthian, Pasco couldn't tell, and he was too exhausted to look anything else up. Either way, they were out of place. If the Battery designer thought this is how buildings looked in Mansion, they had got it very wrong. Architecture had eliminated any superfluity years ago.

Inside the double doors, Pasco could hear the drone of industrial filters, and they removed their face masks. The floors of the hotel were a black and white check pattern, a painted imitation of European marble. A few sad potted plants dotted the foyer here and there, and on the wall hung gaudy mirrors with painted gold frames. The imitation gilt was just another attempt at opulence on a tight budget.

An army of hotel staff took their bags, checked them in and provided room keys. A girl handed him a damp towel for the face, someone else offered him a glass of rice wine, complete with a small, puzzling umbrella sticking out of the top. A third girl held out a tray of fried skaatch squares. Pasco skipped the *hors d'oeuvres*, but accepted the rice wine, drank it and threw back another. It tasted disgusting but he needed its fortifying properties.

"The meeting is scheduled for three," Guiren said. "Before it begins, I would be honoured to take you both on a tour of the facilities."

The thought of parading around the Battery made Pasco's head throb. He had to talk to Rosaline. He needed to prepare for the meeting, and after the long flight and dusty transit, he wanted a bath, if they had one. Catching a reflection of himself in the lobby of the Battery hotel, he noticed his pores were already a constellation of fine blackheads and when he blew his nose, his snot was black.

"I have something I have to take care of before the meeting, so I won't be able to join you," Mandrax said, "but Mr. Eborgersen would be delighted."

"Actually," Pasco said, "I have to finalize my notes for the . . ."

"Nonsense," Mandrax said, "You were tapping away all flight. You couldn't be more prepared."

Pasco said nothing, but gave them both a weak smile.

"You should get a feel for the facility before the meeting," Guiren continued brightly, but unable to hide his disappointment at losing Mandrax.

"I agree. I've toured this complex before, and don't need to see it again," Mandrax said. "It's important you should do so."

Important? To maintain the charade that Churin was in the running?

"So if you'll excuse me, I'll see you in the board room in a couple of hours." Mandrax walked over to where two of the Securicom executives waited. All three of them disappeared outside.

"I need to freshen up first," Pasco said.

Guiren gave a slight smile, less animated now Mandrax had left, as though the sales pitch had already tanked. "Certainly," he said. "I will inform my colleague to meet you here in five minutes." Replacing his face mask, Guiren clicked back through the lobby and vanished outside.

Colleague? Pasco thought. He guessed a Tyro like him was not worth the management time.

Pasco's room contained a desk, a double window that looked out over the Battery complex, a small bed with flat white sheets and a tiny bathroom. No wall to wall sim plates and no artificial aroma, unless he counted the strong odour of tobacco mingled with cleaning fluid.

His belongings were already unpacked; the clothes pressed and hung in the wardrobe, his toothbrush and toothpaste placed in a cup in the bathroom and his pyjamas folded on the bed. It was less than ten minutes since he saw his luggage disappear. Luxurious the hotel was not, but they didn't stint on man power.

Even though it was three in the morning in Mansion he tried to vid Rosaline again. No reply. Did she really mean to end it? He could understand her knee-jerk reaction at the bankruptcy, it was a shock after all, but surely their feelings for each other were stronger than that?

He would vid her before she left for work. He would promise not to gamble, ever again, and mean it this time. She could float the rent on his half of the cubes for a month or two, and he would save harder than ever, and if he returned home with a promotion, then perhaps it wouldn't be so bad.

Feeling better, he stripped off his clothes and stepped into the shower which consisted of compressed air shot at his skin to remove dust and debris and then twenty seconds of tepid water. He knew water was scarce in Churin, but hadn't really digested the implications. His skin tingled uncomfortably, and still feeling dirty, he changed into a fresh suit and reluctantly headed downstairs.

AN HOUR LATER, Pasco had been paraded through three or four buildings by a Supervisor in his fifties called Dekkarde Solquist. When introducing himself, Solquist explained that he had voluntarily given up his birth name when they introduced unique Battery naming. It was just the "right thing" to do, solidarity and all that. He claimed that now everyone affectionately referred to him as Decks. During the tour, nobody called him anything but Sir.

The tour included endless rows of pristine assembly lines, the workers silently and efficiently constructing components, machine shops full of smoke and dust and grease, a triage centre, a cafeteria that fed a million people a day with jellyfish and insects, and even an underground catacomb of stone shelves where workers in tightly overlapping shifts were allowed to rest for a couple of hours.

"So in total we have seven hundred and fifty buildings, each with twenty thousand workers, and a turnover of over thirty-five million employees a day," Solquist said proudly.

Pasco's mind was numb. Although he had done case studies on Battery economics, the reality left him dazed. Only now did he really appreciate the scale of the enterprise, and how the cost of Sector 1's lifestyle was paid for in Churin, how Mansion's pollution, sweat and misery was exported here.

Intellectually, Pasco accepted the division of Sectors as the only system that enabled mankind to function in a world stripped of resources and space. If living conditions in Mansion were superior to Churin, it was a reflection of the relative economic output, nothing more. Intellectually, he understood a pay scale requiring a worker to put in sixty hours a week, just to feed himself, eighty hours or more if he had a dependent. However, seeing the system at work in person was a sobering experience.

During the tour Solquist encouraged Pasco to interview the workers. At first he refused. He was afraid of what they might say, of what lay behind the sunken eyes and skinny frames, but his guide insisted.

"Please," Solquist said, "How else can you familiarize yourself with Churin's resources?"

Inspecting the assembly line, Solquist would tap an employee on the shoulder. Invariably they were young women who would turn around beaming, each with a dab of make-up, each impossibly upbeat. They spoke of the excellent working conditions, the breaks every couple of hours, the free services for pregnant women, the fair treatment in relation to grievances, though of course there were very few at this Battery. One even spoke of the quality of skaatch in the canteen.

"But I thought the canteen was only for Supervisors?" Pasco said.

The girl flushed deeply. She had fluffed her lines, a Supervisor playing the part of a worker for the sake of appearances. That's when Pasco realised that as gut wrenchingly awful as the Battery was, this experience was completely artificial, Management's attempt to put its *best* foot forward, each of the buildings, floors, lines and even workers carefully selected. Solquist frowned at the girl and without comment, guided Pasco away.

"I have saved the best for last," he said excitedly. "What do you think this group are working on?"

"I don't know."

"iAm! We wanted to have working models for your meeting!"

"But you only received the blueprints forty-eight hours ago."

"Exactly."

Pasco walked down the lines, genuinely curious to see what they had made of it. He had personally worked on prototypes back at TechCom, but those were just for trials, painfully crafted, one at a time. Converting the blue print to a replicable product on the line was a significant achievement.

The girls, for they were almost all girls, constructed the device as though they had been doing it all their lives. Each carried a profound look of concentration, as if nothing existed but the chip. Pasco knew their rate of production was very slow relative to eventual operational speed, but to him the movements looked fluid and practiced, the robotic micro hands manipulating nanochips blown up a thousand fold on their viewers.

Solquist said something into his iNet, and the entire line came to a stop.

"And here it is," Solquist said proudly. They stood in front of one girl's work station and together they reviewed the nanochip.

Yes, Pasco thought, that was it. "Incredible," he said.

"This batch will be sent to QA, and then forwarded for inspection to your meeting."

Pasco said nothing.

"Sir?" Solquist said.

But he wasn't listening, because sitting at the work station in front of him was the face of the profile Mandrax had accidentally shared. He was sure of it. Either that or she was a doppelganger.

So was this the Elite's girl for later?

No. Seeing her in the flesh, he dismissed the thought. She was pretty enough, but definitely not the type. He couldn't put his finger on exactly how he knew this. Compared to the other workers, there was an unusual intelligence in her eyes and something else as well, a defiance.

Was it really her? The odds were long. His brain ached trying to work them out. Thirty million employees at the Battery, but only fifteen million workers on shift, and he had seen maybe a thousand people today, so that was what? One in two hundred? He gave up. If only Mandrax hadn't recalled the file he could overlay it on her face and know for sure.

"This is very nice work," Pasco said to the girl. "Tell me . . ."

"Sir," Solquist interrupted, "we're out of time. We need to head back."

So, she wasn't a plant.

"I'd like to ask a couple of questions."

"If you need to talk to more people, I can send you more people. This one is not . . ." Solquist trailed off.

"Trained?" he said. "Just one moment." If this was an inspection, he had the right to ask questions to whom he pleased. His tone was not lost on Solquist, and the old Supervisor backed off.

He accessed her identikit. She was twenty-one, his age, but she looked younger. "Balmoral Murraine," he said, thinking how awful it must be to have a name assigned by a corporation, especially when that name sounded like an ancient veterinary disease.

The girl looked up, only half meeting his eye.

"How did you find the construction process?"

"I followed the rubric."

"Ah . . . of course, but any other thoughts?"

"No."

"I see. Um . . . what do you usually do here?"

"This," she said sullenly.

No, not quite sullen, not enough emotion for sullen, but an indifferent, mechanical response. The Battery required this girl to be a machine, and fulfilling the same function day after day, despite her intelligence, she had become one.

"Sir, we really don't have much time before your meeting," Solquist said.

Pasco regarded her a moment longer. "Goodbye then," he said finally.

The girl said nothing.

Solquist ushered him toward the elevator, jabbering rapidly. "And so you see we are prepared for the contract. We have the prototypes for inspection, the facilities, the means to reach your aggressive targets. We are the best candidate for the project."

"It's not my decision," Pasco said.

"No but, you have some sway. You are on . . . how do they say, the inside."

And being on the inside he knew that the contract would be awarded to

Bodia. The available manpower was four times larger and twice as desperate, having starved in their millions in recent years. Their management would accept less compensation from Top 10, squeezing the population to the extent that their initial bid was fifteen percent less. How that was possible based on the pittance workers in Churin were paid, Pasco wasn't sure. It was also irrelevant. As Mandrax had reminded him, the decision was a simple economic equation: the most units, at the lowest cost. There was nothing he could do to change that.

"I have some influence," Pasco said, not wanting to sound completely impotent. "But not much."

Solquist leaned in towards him. "And between two men, what is *some* influence worth?"

Pasco held out his thumb and finger about an inch apart, and gave a little half-laugh. It was his self-defence mechanism. He half-laughed when delivering difficult news. He half-laughed when he lied.

"But how do you rate our chances?" Solquist said.

"Oh, as good as anyone else's," he half-laughed.

They stepped inside the elevator. "So, I will ask you again," Solquist said as the doors swished together. "How much is your influence worth?"

The top left corner of Solquist's iNet lens blinked green, the universal symbol for a pending credit transfer. It came on to show the credits were in the account, ready to be deducted, it blinked off on execution. This green light hung there, waiting.

Pasco automatically looked up to the top left of the elevator. A thick wad of masking tape covered the eyeless hole of the *Earth* camera socket.

"Yes," Solquist murmured. "The workmen have been a little shoddy there. It happens occasionally."

The elevator reached the ground floor and the doors opened. Solquist pressed a button that closed them again. He took out a key, put it in the slot, and turned it. The doors stayed shut. The elevator did not move.

"I'm not sure I understand," Pasco said.

Solquist pushed his lenses to the top of his head and gestured Pasco to do the same.

"I think you do," Solquist replied. "We know Bodia are the front runners." He put out a hand. "No, don't say anything, we are neither blind nor stupid. We understand starvation economics, lived it for years. However, they won't be able to deliver. Their line workers are inexperienced, their Lodges undeveloped. They could not turn around your blueprints like we have done. They don't have enough skilled savages." Solquist spat the last two words.

"It is not my decision," he said again.

"Perhaps not, but if someone on the inside would speak favourably about our candidacy, it would mean a lot to us, and be very profitable for them."

Pasco's pulse quickened. "What if I . . . help you and you don't win the contract?"

Solquist smiled. "We make a down payment of twenty percent of whatever we agree in here. That is in, shall we say, good faith. Should the savages get the contract . . ." he shrugged, "we lose our stake and hate you forever." He half-laughed the last three words.

Was Solquist mocking him?

"I really don't think my vote will make any difference."

"But we do!" Solquist said. "And we are willing to take that bet. What if I offered you two million credits?"

Two million credits! Four hundred thousand guaranteed! "And . . . and all I have to do is make your case?"

"Exactly."

"You're not going to turn out to be part of Finance's corruption division are you?" Pasco said.

Solquist made a disgusted "ugh!" noise, suddenly furious.

"Sorry I didn't mean to . . ."

"Stop!" Solquist said, his hand out again, flat palmed. He removed his shirt and put it on the ground.

"What are you doing?" Pasco said flustered, conscious of the confined space, the locked elevator.

Solquist said nothing, but removed his pants, belt and underpants. Embarrassed, Pasco turned away.

"Look at me."

Reluctantly Pasco turned to face him. Devoid of clothes, Solquist had the scraggy look of a starved, half-plucked chicken. The five foot frame, the hollow chest, the rickety, bow-leggedness of malnutrition. Someone who had not just heard about the pre-Autonomy years, but had lived through them.

"I was born on the streets of Churin before all this," he waved his hand in the confines of the elevator. "I ate food that makes skaatch look like a royal supper, but more often, I ate nothing at all. I watched my entire family die in fields that grew nothing but dust."

He paused, his hands clasped in front of him. "But I survived," he said quietly. "I survived, and all my life I have sweated blood for this new world, Churin, and the people in it, and yes, the Battery because like it or not, want it or not, these buildings are now the heart of our people, and the Battery *needs* this contract for the blood to flow." His voice trembled as he spoke.

If this was part of the pre-scripted tour it was very convincing.

"So I have a question for you. Do I look like an informant?"

"No," Pasco said.

"Then please, don't insult me."

It wasn't fair, Pasco thought. Solquist had tried to bribe *him*, so why did he feel like a criminal? Like Mephistopheles rebuffed by an outraged Faust. Pasco watched the old man dressing himself. He possessed a dignity Pasco could only imagine. When they replaced their iNet glasses, the pending transfer light remained.

"So, do we have a deal?"

If that little green light flashed, Pasco would have credit again. He and Rosaline could make an offer on the Mansion apartment. He could win her back. All he had to do was say yes.

Did it matter that he knew Churin had no chance? That Bodia was a sure thing? That the Battery's hard earned credits may as well be flushed down the toilet, if there were any toilets that flushed in Churin? He thought of the girl. Balmoral Murraine, for whom life was one long assembly line. Four hundred thousand credits was more than she could earn in many lifetimes. Anything Churin transferred into his pocket came out of hers, and everyone like her.

His father's voice again echoed in his head.

There is no such thing as unearned riches, someone always pays.

But his father was dead, killed by the system he had represented and unable even to hand down all the blood, sweat and tears he poured into it.

"We have a deal," Pasco said.

With a flick of his eyelid, he accepted the credit transfer and as he did so, the words of Dillon Vrain now surfaced in his mind.

The only important thing is to be happy and free.

And not to mess around with other people's lives and pointless causes.

8

S O THAT WAS *Pasco Eborgersen*, Balmoral thought. Curious, how he started when he saw her. Curious too how he stared. When his eyes dropped to her chest, she wanted to stand up and stick a syringe in his gut, just for looking at her that way. Her extreme reaction caught her off guard, residual trauma from Qwot's attack. All he wanted was to ask her questions. She answered them, and then waited for him to leave.

Despite following the rubric, she still could not guess what the iAm device was for. Its scale was tiny, not much bigger than a couple of grains of rice, stacked one on top of the other. The construction was challenging, it took seven cycles before she memorized it and could turn her attention to iNet.

Her *fisher king* program had pulled thirty-four references to iAm, four of those by Pasco Eborgersen. She read those first. Most were short clarifications of points raised in meetings conducted over vid feed. There was a lot of back and forth about the construction process, something to do with unstable compounds. Frustratingly, the communications told her nothing about iAm itself.

She read comments on the blueprint, minutiae about one technological approach versus another and a discourse on chemical reactions. An hour in, she was none the wiser. Every exchange presupposed a conceptual understanding of what function iAm performed. She was on the verge of dismissing the exercise as a waste of time, when a single sentence made everything fall into place.

The world's information at the flick of a synapse.

Shocked, her robotic pincers dropped iAm and the components smashed on the laminate desk top, scattering into a hundred pieces. There was a pause of about three seconds and a blast of compressed air shot across the work table, blowing away all traces of the debris. An uncomfortable chemical odour filled the air, making her eyes sting.

She expected a sour-faced Supervisor, ready to administer a fine, but nobody came. The prototype lines was more lenient. She had already noticed that the warning lights used to synchronize the line's speed were not being used, the girls allowed to work at their own pace.

Her head reeling, Balmoral made a promise to herself. Whatever she could do to stop iAm, she would. This violation struck at the very core of humanity itself.

When was it due to come online? Surely such a huge undertaking would take several years to ramp up. Was Churin the centre of manufacturing? That would make it easier to disrupt.

She logged back into iNet to discover more about the delegation, hoping to find some answers. She would begin with Eborgersen.

Hacking into the identikit was a risk. Personal information was triple encrypted within iNet's vast cloud. Brute force hacks, which tried thousands of combinations per millisecond, were too easy for *Voice* to detect and disable. Even subtle anglers like the *king* were ineffective, tricked into hooking minnows, while *Voice* sent agents to hunt down the operator.

However, there was a loophole Balmoral could exploit. Whenever anyone moved across Sectors, it was Securicom's practice to 'check them in' for tracking purposes. This created a temporary imprint of personal data that was vulnerable to hacking.

She got to work. Balmoral had manipulated iNet's code so long that the code itself was almost invisible to her. Instead, she visualized the data in physical terms. In her mind's eye, the intellisphere was a walled citadel with forgotten paths and ancient tunnels that could be accessed, if only they could be found. But *Voice* was cunning. She changed the underlying architecture of iNet every twenty-four hours and there were dead ends and deceptions in every direction. Sentries patrolled the walls and ambush lay around every corner.

And if she was caught?

A digital death was not pretty. First, her iNet would freeze. Then she would be locked out of the system, unable to perform even the most basic functions, while every *Earth* camera strained towards her. According to Securicom's cybercrime site, the average time between a digital death and physical apprehension was less than hour. She didn't doubt it.

Balmoral thought again about her emergency stash in the ground floor wash rooms, buried like a corpse in the cold, wet darkness. Would she be able to reach it if something went wrong?

It took twenty minutes to find what she needed. Her ninja program dodged under a portcullis, scaled a low wall, avoided two or three sentries, quietly disposed of another, and found the delegation's imprints right where they were supposed to be; Churin's import and export repository. All the delegates were there in the form of temporary files that would automatically erase from the system on the next update.

Balmoral didn't have much time. Her ninja hid the dead sentry in the equivalent of a storage closet, but eventually he would be missed, triggering a system wide alarm. She reckoned ten minutes at most, then she would have to make a run for it.

She skipped over the Securicom detail and briefly read the profile of Bruno Mandrax. He had been assigned to the project in the last week, a curious appointment for the site selection of iAm.

Next, she turned to Eborgersen, and was surprised to discover he was both the son of a dead President, and nephew of the current Chair. Entitlement wasn't supposed to exist in a world without inheritance, but even so, he didn't seem arrogant enough. If anything, he had been uncomfortable when questioning her. And how was the nephew of the most powerful man in the Autonomy still a Tyro at twenty-one? What had gone wrong?

She quickly scanned his record. He had studied under Professor Hakim, a famous neuroscientist at the Academy, entering Top 10 through the LifeScience division. There he had bounced around from department to department, often seconded to other divisions, including Logistics and Materials, where he specialized in evaluating the impact of trace biosquare toxins on cell structure. His last transfer was to TechCom.

She dug deeper, searching for any data that might suggest how the project would be implemented. The nature of the imprint was such that she could access any files he had reviewed since the last system update, as long as she didn't change anything.

The first file was a blueprint of the prototype she had spent the last six hours constructing, together with some suggested rubrics. Boring. She closed it. The second was a cross-section of the iAm device with each of the various compounds it contained listed. One was highlighted. Underneath it were some numbers. The data described disability and mortality per million units, the calculations derived from exposure to the chemical during manufacture.

She sucked in her breath.

Attrition estimates were a standard calculation in manufacturing; from large projects, such as the construction of a Battery complex or Atmos system, to the day to day operation of a treadle mill or assembly line. Resource burn was considered part of the cost of doing business, but she had never seen anything on this scale. The fatalities from the neurotoxins in one year dwarfed those of an Atmos project. She remembered the foul smelling chemicals stinging her eyes when the component shattered on the work station. If Churin won the contract, she would have to transfer to another line, one that did not handle iAm.

She closed the data file, conscious that time was almost up. She had to exit the system. It was already a risk to stay as long as she had. However, as she was leaving she noticed a communication from Bruno Mandrax to Pasco Eborgersen, sent and then hastily recalled. Interesting. She accessed the record.

An icy shock filled her veins as she saw her own face staring back at her. Balmoral's first thought was, so this is how it ends. She was discovered, trapped by *Voice* inside the system, her image, the AI's twisted attempt at humour. It would be just in her line, gloating before she froze Balmoral's iNet in a digital death. She snapped the file shut.

Knowing it was useless, but deciding to fight anyway, Balmoral backed out of the data repository. The system wide alarm sounded. She pulled her hands free from the foam, and despite the risk, furiously typed on her holopad. Taking full control of her subcode ninja, her hands moved in a blur.

The system flooded with sentries hunting out any code not directly authorized by *Voice*. Her ninja ran, but it was no good, there were too many. The sentries would rip her apart. She didn't want to go out that way.

In a frenzy of commands, she erected a high tower in the middle of a corridor. It was an inelegant, nonsensical piece of code that would be tracked, making future use of her ninja impossible, but she didn't care. She was finished anyway. Her only thought was escape.

Scaling the wall, she climbed out of the intellisphere and less than a second later, the holopad was off and her hands thrust back into the foam.

Balmoral waited for digital death, for her iNet to freeze, never again to be accessed.

One minute passed, two. Nothing happened.

Why? Was *Voice* playing with her?

And then a crazy thought occurred to her. What if it wasn't *Voice* at all? What if the alarm was simply the discovery of the sentry? The timing made sense. She had stayed too long with the imprints. Balmoral's thoughts turned to Pasco Eborgersen, his shock when he saw her, the double-take, as though he had seen her before. Five hours ago to be exact.

So the conversation on the line was manufactured?

No. He was surprised. That meant the meeting was coincidental. Some coincidence. What did it mean?

The image she accessed was not just a picture, but a profile. She had closed it almost immediately. Reaching deep into her mind, she tried to visualize it. Among personal data there were coordinates and times. Why? She had been a fool not to study it.

Balmoral forced herself to think critically, to analyse the problem from every angle. The familiar calm descended. It had always been the same, even when she was a little girl. When she set her mind to a problem, her mind emptied of all noise, all feeling, and became like a laser.

The profile was on Pasco Eborgersen's iNet. He was part of the delegation. He, or the delegation, had some concern with her, but it was completely separate from her work at the Battery, as Eborgersen had not expected to see her face.

There were eight delegates from Sector 1, but when she reviewed their profiles, six were Securicom. She should have noticed that before. Six was excessive, especially when Churin had its own domestic Securicom division.

Even if they were personal security for Mandrax and Eborgersen, it was a function usually fulfilled by relatively junior agents. These were Senator grade, which meant they weren't just bodyguards, but specialists of some kind. They were here to carry out an operation, which in turn led to the possibility that they were here for her, and that, for whatever reason, Mandrax and Eborgersen were part of the operation. It was the only explanation of the profile on Eborgersen's interface.

She was convinced now the data next to her image was a predictive model of behaviour, a set of *Earth* co-ordinates. The route she took to the tram station, the building she worked in, the avenues in the Stacks she frequented.

Mandrax pulled back the file when he sent it to Eborgersen, so perhaps Eborgersen wasn't supposed to see it after all. She thought of Mandrax again. Only recently appointed to the iAm project, ostensibly to review the sites. Was it possible that iAm was a cover for the operation, and that his purpose in Churin was her? That meant the true purpose of the operation was rendition. Hers.

On the surface, the reasoning seemed too improbable to be credited. Odds of thousands to one. About the same odds of her profile appearing on Eborgersen's interface. The second improbability brought the first into focus, and made it not just possible, but likely. She could think of no other contingencies.

These men would make her disappear. Not in the way her great uncle disappeared; a knock to the back of the head by some thuggish Foreman. There would be a manufactured incident to cover their tracks, eliminating any suspicion of Securicom activity. She would be removed from the grid, invisible and at their mercy.

She wondered at the trouble they had taken. It was not as if anyone would kick up a fuss if Foremen rushed in, put a bag over her head and dragged her out. But this was how Securicom operated under the current Chair. The discretion was a discipline, and it came from the top. The Autonomy worked hard at appearing not as one man's dictatorship but as the only viable facilitator of mankind's progress. Securicom could not be seen as the tool of a tyrannical state, and an unexplained disappearance, no matter how trivial, was exactly that. She knew Securicom went to great lengths to conceal any illicit activity, revealing themselves only if you stared at the cracks hard enough.

The Chairman's skill was to be a dictator, without appearing to be one.

Whereas the other Board members were all economists, deep down Maglan Eborgersen was a historian. He knew that no regime built on oppression ever survived, which was precisely why very few people realised the covert operations branch of the agency even existed.

But why her?

She was nobody, which left one possibility. They had discovered her darkest secret. They had got to Zhu.

Again, taking a risk, she pulled her hands from the foam. With a couple of commands she overrode the communications lock enforced on the Battery floor and vidded Zhu. A message popped up.

This profile does not exist.

The hair on the back of her arms sprang up. They had taken him off the grid. Either that or he was dead. Her iNet display pulsed twice, warning her to replace her hands. She did so, not wanting to draw attention to herself.

She had to make a choice. Either run for it or wait for their opening move. Right now she had two advantages, slight as they were. Firstly, they probably didn't know that she knew. Secondly, the secret stash hidden in stall three of the ground floor wash rooms, if only she could reach it.

The buzzer sounded for the end of the shift. She shuffled out with the rest of the line, not hurrying even though every fibre of her being screamed at her to run.

On the ground level, Supervisors stood at the exits. The usual protocol, except that when she came into iNet range they both snapped their necks towards her. She turned out of the line, towards the wash rooms.

"Balmoral!" the Supervisor shouted, gesturing her to come over. It was Tao Cum Pao.

She had to reach her stash, it was her only chance of escape, but she was also afraid to ignore Pao. To do so would tip them off. She had no choice but to see what she wanted.

"I'm so glad I caught you," Tao Cum Pao said. "I didn't want to send the message over iNet. It was too . . . too personal. I'm afraid I have some very bad news. It's about your father. There has been . . . there has been a terrible accident."

9

AN HOUR LATER they were still listening to Francis Guerin's presentation on Churin's capabilities; its razor thin cost structure, its eminent stability, and its record of delivering to time and quality. The entire Churin management team was there in person, travelling from the four corners of the region, nobody daring to join via virtual reality feed, because an Elite had made the journey all the way from Sector 1.

The Battery district was only ten percent of Churin in terms of land mass, but the entire region depended on its economic success. The Battery supported supply chains in Shamshu, the treadle mills in the South, the numerous quarries in the Cutter region, and the administration in Deng. If the Battery failed, Churin failed. It was that simple.

During the presentations Mandrax asked no questions. It was odd, given he was the lead for site evaluation. Pasco expected him to show an interest, yet at times, it was as though Mandrax watched something else behind those mirrored shades.

Guiren continued with increasing gusto. "And last year we recorded the highest ratio of product per person that . . ."

Three other Elites were in attendance, joining through a 3D vid feed. They sat around the table like high definition ghosts; insubstantial, brightly coloured images with no smell or substance.

There were the head project managers from TechCom and LifeScience, Rajesh Elb, and Ellen Devalier. Pasco did not recognize the third representative from Logistics, Guy Rawstorm. Surprisingly, his identikit stated that he used to be a President. He was fat, offensively so, given that he was a supply liaison with Sector 2. While his clients lived on starvation rations, he seemingly consumed enough joules to feed a treadle mill. They all looked unenthusiastic.

Given their lack of interest, Guiren must realise Churin was a stalking horse, a swab site destined to be passed over, and yet he seemed calm and confident.

"And now, a little surprise for you," he said.

Two workers entered the room, each carrying a small container. With a ceremonial flourish, Guiren removed the lids and displayed the iAm nanochips.

"Complete and ready for installation. I would like to remind our esteemed management that we received the blueprints forty-eight hours ago."

The boxes were held like a bride's dowry from some ancient story. "Three thousand," Guiren said proudly, pushing the box under the ghosts' noses.

The managers picked up a handful for inspection, then let the tiny chips run through their fingers back into the box. Grains of precious sand. Mandrax waved the box on when it came to him. For the benefit of the ghosts, Guiren magnified one of the chips, showing off its flawless construction. When he was finished, Churin's managers spontaneously broke into a round of applause. Devalier put her hands together once or twice, but it was a limp effort. None of the other Elites bothered to do even that.

"Perhaps these can be the Autonomy's first batch," Guiren said with a smile.

"They can't," Pasco said without thinking, regretting the words as soon as they left his mouth. All faces turned to him, for the first time even the ghosts seemed mildly interested. He flushed. "I mean that . . . to be clinical grade, they have to be kept in sterile conditions at all times. This batch will have to be for display purposes only."

Why did he always have to be so pedantic? It wasn't his intention to undermine the huge achievement, to dull the impact of Guiren's finale, but that was the effect of his comment.

The table sat in silence. The managers fidgeted. The ghosts frowned. Everyone waited. Stretching his leg under the table, Pasco surreptitiously kicked Mandrax's foot. The Elite's head snapped up.

"Thank you, Francis," he said to Guiren, "for that enlightening report." He paused, as though reading something from iNet. "The next item on the agenda is a formal presentation of attrition estimates."

The infamous Onega protocol. Why Pasco was there.

"Yes, yes of course," Guiren said shortly.

Pasco noticed a couple of Churin's managers looked awkward and avoided Guiren's eye.

"I put us into the capable hands of Pasco Eborgersen," Mandrax said, leaning back in his chair.

"Thank you," Pasco said, pulling up his holographic keypad. He tapped a couple of keys. "On the left hand of your lenses are data pertaining to iAm's overall tolerability profile. As you can see, the device is no more invasive than the biosquare we use to power our current iNet lenses, despite its more sensitive location. Over the three months we tested the prototype, there were no reactions of any kind that weren't seen in the placebo."

"Placebo?" one of Churin's managers asked.

"To keep the test a level playing field we monitored the group versus a control. A group who thought they had the chip inserted, but did not."

"How many subjects?"

"Five hundred in each," Devalier from LifeScience cut in.

Not enough, and over too short a time. It wasn't Pasco's place to point this out. Everyone knew the real testing ground would be the pilot year of roll out; introducing a million units into some Sector 3 outpost where, if something did go wrong, they could simply write it off as attrition.

Irrespective of the size of the trial, Pasco knew the device was safe. He had reviewed every possible adverse event on the body, and the nanochip had none. If there was to be any trauma, it would manifest itself psychologically, not physically. Pasco waited, giving time for the managers to review the data.

"It all looks in order," Guiren said.

"I am glad to hear it," the Elite from Logistics, Guy Rawstorm cut in. "We wouldn't want another Onega, eh?" He grinned, and his chins grinned with him.

Guiren flushed, but said nothing.

Onega was the Sector head responsible for the manufacture of the G11 cell phone. The phone was a flawless, hand-held device that could be sold at market price, which in this case was less than three credits; an obsolete concept that stated anything mass produced had to be affordable to every citizen regardless of Sector. A connected worker was a more flexible resource. In the rush to bring it to market, due diligence on the carcinogenic casing was ignored.

An estimated ten million people died before the product was withdrawn, the majority in Sector 1. At the time, MediaCom contained the fall out by reporting that the outbreak of brain cancer was some kind of epidemic caused by the environmental collapse. About a month afterwards, the citizens of Mansion stumped up the taxes for the first Atmos system. Only later was the true cause revealed.

"I think we'll move on," Devalier said, when nobody else spoke. "Pasco, can you describe the data regarding the construction of the device itself?"

"Although iAm has no adverse effects on the user, if you take a look at the graphic on your right lens, you will see there is a . . ." He hesitated, feeling Devalier's eyes on him. "There is a small risk . . . statistically speaking that is, of neurological side effects from compounds used in the manufacturing process."

"What side effects?" Guiren said.

"In *susceptible* individuals, exposure causes a fatal degeneration of the motor neurons, a condition characterized by muscle atrophy and progressive weakness."

"How long does it take before . . ."

Pasco interrupted him, anticipating the question. "Death occurs within three to four years of the initial diagnosis." He could not bring himself to call it *attrition.*

"I actually meant, how long until the resource becomes too dysfunctional to work?" Guiren said.

"Ah," Pasco said. "The paralysis usually manifests itself as difficulty speaking and swallowing, and in fact most line workers will experience bouts of palsy; facial paralysis, numbness, that kind of thing without actually . . ." *Dying,* he was going to add.

"Pretty standard stuff," Rawstorm interrupted.

"However, those with full blown motor neuron degeneration will take about eighteen months to deteriorate before reaching an incapacitated state."

"So we'll say about a year of productivity post diagnosis, to be on the safe side," Guiren said.

Pasco nodded. "That's fair."

"How does the exposure occur?" Guiren said.

"Handling the neurotoxic compounds prior to the device's encasement. Even trace amounts are dangerous."

"Before you ask," Rawstorm again cut in, "protective gear is out of the question. The type of equipment we're talking about, and the cost to maintain and regularly decontaminate it, adds ten percent to the project's labour budget."

"So what *are* we talking about in terms of actual additional cost?" Guiren said.

"Cost?" Pasco said, confused for a moment, his mind still on the simple protective clothing that would mitigate all risks.

"The attrition rate."

Pasco fumbled. "Of course um . . . one can measure attrition over time or by volume . . ." *One can?* In his agitation, he was talking as though from another century. "The most accurate forecast is an estimated fatality rate per million units of iAm, which works out to approximately, one percent per ten million units."

A couple of Churin's managers sucked in their breath. The contract was for five billion units, then another five on renewal over a ten year period.

"So what you're saying," Guiren said, "is that we stand to lose about ten million people."

Again Pasco nodded, his mouth too dry to speak.

"Only if your bid is successful," Rawstorm added.

"It's an expensive proposition," Guiren said. "Is there nothing we can do to bring the rate down?"

"The healthier the individual, the less susceptible they are to exposure." Pasco said. "The best option in this regard is nutrition and hydration strategies, so salt tabs and gel caps . . ."

Rawstorm snorted disapproval.

"There are also some relatively cost-effective neurotoxin inhibitors we could use," Pasco continued, "but they induce chronic diarrhea."

"Counter-productive," Rawstorm said. "Can't work and shit every five minutes."

Pasco ignored him. "Another alternative is line rotation. If we took workers off iAm every six months, we would reduce both the exposure *and* the level of neurotoxin inhibitor required to be effective."

"Expensive drugs? Rotation? Loss of productivity," Rawstorm cut in again. "I don't like where this is going. We simply won't get the margins. Even salt tabs have a cost. And syntax jellies? You must be out of your mind. Credits don't grow on trees."

Even if they did, there were no trees in Churin. "Then the only alternative is ten million sick workers."

"We should of course mention," Elb said, staring pointedly at Pasco, "that the projections are theoretical and the worst case scenario. We are researching alternative compounds that will be introduced into the manufacturing process when they are ready, at which point this will cease to be an issue."

"How advanced is the research?" Guiren said, turning to Pasco.

Very. So far advanced, in fact, that the research is complete. There were no economically viable alternatives, and all of the Elites in the room already knew this. Pasco hesitated. The entire table stared at him. The ghostly apparitions frowned. Even Mandrax turned his mirrored shades towards him.

"We . . . we fully expect to identify a substitute compound within twelve months of going into production."

"I see," Guiren said. "So we'll hope for the best and budget for the worst. Obviously we can't be expected to absorb that kind of loss by ourselves . . ."

"Other sites will," Rawstorm said.

"Economically the attrition rate is unfortunate," Elb cut in, "but it is less costly than any further delay. The contract spans not only the manufacturing of the device, but the production of the chemicals and components from which the device is constructed. The overall scope of the project more than offsets even the most aggressive attrition forecasts. Take a look for yourselves."

Rows of data ran across Pasco's lenses. The calculations blurred together and he tuned them out. They only confirmed what he already knew, that life was just another number, and when it came down to it, not a very large one.

"So at this point, finding an alternative compound is gravy," Rawstorm said.

"Gentlemen, this project is the long awaited human singularity," Elb's ghost said. "It's been years in the making. Yes, there is a cost. That's been the case since the beginning of time, whether constructing the pyramids, or the first railroads, or the first Atmos trench. This project is the most significant advance for the human race in the last hundred years, if not the last thousand."

"And let us not forget," Rawstorm said, "It was only a generation ago that our *resources* thought civilization was jumping up and down with fifty hoops around their neck, trying to reach the fruit out of the fucking trees." He laughed, and his whole mass of fat bobbed up and down.

With the exception of Guiren, all of the managers in the room were Churin natives, their heritage proud and Asiatic, rather than some imaginary tribe Rawstorm's Autonomy somehow pulled out of the jungle. Despite this, the entire table laughed with him. If an Elite made a joke, you laughed. That was the rule.

Still chuckling, Guiren pushed his chair from the table and stood up, stepping through Rawstorm's image while doing so. He gyrated a couple of times, his groin on the same level as the Elite's mouth. He stumbled slightly, making the whole thing look just enough like an accident that Rawstorm would look ridiculous if he took offense.

Cutting through someone's image in a virtual reality feed, or "poking the ghost", was the height of poor taste. Doing what Guiren had just done . . . well there wasn't even a word for that.

Pasco noticed a smile flicker across Mandrax's face.

"Excuse me," Guiren said to Rawstorm's quivering form. "I thought I would stand." He turned to address the table and the ghosts. "I wanted to assure you all that on behalf of me, my colleagues, and our entire workforce, that the cost *is* something we can absorb, and that we formally approve the product for manufacturing at our sites *if* we are awarded the contract. Our demographics can handle the burn without interruption, and even if we ship a couple of rocks, we will maintain our stability."

Why did he keep harping on about stability? It was hardly a differentiating factor when all the regions had starvation and Foremen as powerful sticks.

"Thank you Francis." Mandrax said. "Any other comments before we close?" He rose, as though eager to be somewhere else.

Guiren caught Pasco's eye and in a subtle gesture tapped the upper left of his lens. A reminder of the credit transfer.

"Churin seems uniquely positioned to handle the project," Pasco blurted.

"How?" Elb said frowning.

"I reviewed the construction of the prototype first hand. It is similar to the G47 nanochip component Churin has worked on for years." Pasco tried to sound spontaneous, rather than someone on the take. "The line made it up without formal training, following a rubric. How? Because they have been trained on the basic assembly patterns in the Lodges. There is an economic value to that institutional understanding. They will reach maximum productivity within weeks, not months or even years, and there will be a higher pass rate from quality assurance. The accelerated ramp up time will claw back some, if not all, of the time lost due to the six month delay."

It was a risk, drawing attention to this advantage. It could increase the bargaining power of Churin, and as such was a tactical error for which he would be criticized. However, delivering the project on time would make or break every person in this room, including the Elites. It was a compelling argument.

"Correct me if I'm wrong," Rawstorm said, "but aren't you the *Tyro* responsible for delaying this project in the first place?"

"Not out of school," Devalier snapped, glaring at him.

"It's a valid point, Pasco," Elb said. "But Mong also manufactures the G47."

"But Bodia does not," Pasco said.

"What's your interest?" Rawstorm said. "Had a bit of grease, to oil the wheels? Eh?"

Pasco's stomach clenched. He tried not to flush.

"I think," Mandrax cut in, "we have taken this as far as we can today. Unless there is anything else, we can close the proceedings."

This time nobody dissented. The ghostly forms of the Elites promptly vanished. Time was credits after all.

Pasco turned to Mandrax, "How do you think it went?"

But Mandrax was already out the door, the Churin managers staring wistfully after him. Pasco dutifully exchanged a few words with them, made some encouraging noises and then excused himself to go to the bathroom.

His iNet blinked with a new message from Rosaline, but he ignored it. Pasco knew he had lost her, but right now, for some reason, it didn't seem that important. Instead he thought of the girl, Balmoral Murraine, who had no idea what building the iAm component would cost her, or if not her, someone like her in Bodia or Mong.

He pulled off his glasses, and sat in a stall, just to be by himself, to breathe. He felt a deep rooted nausea about the lives they were about to condemn. Ten million dead, and millions of others to suffer irreversible nerve damage, and palsied faces and acute tremors, all because he had not been able to find an alternative, economic way to manufacture the chip.

Was he following in the footsteps of his father? The ill-fated Namgola project resulted in an entire population being wiped out, but then ironically *Oasis* became the model for acquisitions from the Cut that had occurred in the last ten years, saving millions of lives. Bodia, Bamar and Taos, all economic success stories, providing new resources to the Autonomy. His father had the right idea, just the wrong land mass.

Exiting the stall, he walked over to the sink, ran the tap, and cupped his hands under the brackish water. He splashed it on his face, wondering what he was even doing here, wondering where he had gone wrong.

"You did well," said a voice, making him jump. Guiren's sallow face appeared, reflected in the mirror. "Not too much, not too little. Just right."

"I . . . I meant it," Pasco said.

"Of course you did." Guiren patted him gently on the shoulder. "Convictions and economic interest always go hand in hand. Either way, thank you."

Guiren leaned over the adjacent sink and began to wash his hands. "You've removed your iNet."

"I . . . I just needed . . ."

"Some time?" Guiren said.

Pasco nodded.

"You have to understand. Everything has a cost. We used to rape Earth's resources. Now that there are none left, we rape our own. Is it harsh? Of course. But any choice in the matter ended a long time ago."

Guiren meticulously worked the lather into his fingers. "There isn't a single person in Churin who does not want this contract. Were the attrition rates double, we would take it. There are two hundred million people in this region, and without work, our forecasts show a long term loss, either through death or exodus, of sixty million lives over the next ten years. Without the Battery pumping away at the heart of the region, the region itself withers and fades. Our workers are our soldiers. They understand the cost. They are a proud people still."

Incongruously, cheers broke out from across the corridor, coming from the conference room.

"What's that?" Pasco said.

"It sounds like my colleagues fancy their chances."

"They thought it went that well?"

"No but . . . let's just say the odds have swung in our favour."

"What do you mean?"

Guiren tapped his lenses with a soapy hand. "You won't have seen but . . . we just got the news. Bodia has rioting at their main Battery complex, and it's spreading throughout the Stacks. The managers are trying to bring it under control, but unfortunately it will not be safe enough for your little delegation."

"What!"

"Stability," Guiren said. "Squeeze too hard and things tend to go bang. Too much, too quickly. In those savage lands it only takes a few well-funded *Dish* to light the fuse and . . . poof!" He spread out his hands.

"You don't sound surprised."

Guiren pushed his glasses onto his forehead, breaking the connection with iNet. "Let's just say I've always been good at choosing my investments."

Would Guiren really do such a thing? If he was caught funding the *Dish* in Bodia, he wouldn't just lose his position, he would lose his life. Then again, what was one life versus sixty million?

"So now it's just you and Mong," Pasco said.

Guiren continued to wash his hands, working in a second round of lather. "Mong formally pulled out of the bidding process two hours before our meeting. They can't meet the stipulated budget parameters. Not with the human attrition profile."

"That can't be! They haven't seen my data yet."

"Somehow it was leaked to them a couple of weeks ago and at that time, we made an agreement. In return for withdrawing their bid today, they will fulfil all remaining iNet lens orders, until the lenses themselves become obsolete."

"How is that their decision?"

"Because only Mong and Churin now manufacture lenses, and they have signed a guarantee from me that when this rotation of iNet is complete, Churin will cease all production."

"Is that even legal?"

Guiren raised an eyebrow. "Contracts between regions, even in Sector 2, are binding. Because of Churin giving up production, Mong will operate at full capacity for the next three years, buying time to bid out for another major manufacturing project. Until about five minutes ago, that seemed like a very good deal. They knew it was a one horse race with Bodia. Rawstorm informed them of the fact."

"How do you know?"

"Because he sold the same information to us. They'll be kicking themselves now, but it's too late. The project wouldn't have been good for Mong anyway. I know them, almost as well as I know the people of this Sector. In Churin we have a higher participation in the *Faith* than practically anywhere in the Autonomy. Our workers will forge on, irrespective of the conditions, as long the work serves the interest of those two great pillars; salvation and Churin. In Mong, they are pliable, of course, but if their wives, husbands, sons and daughters fall in the numbers we're talking about here, I don't know. It's a shame of course. Just as it is a shame you were unable to come up with alternative materials."

Guiren finally began to rinse his hands. He must have used three days water ration in one go.

"Why are you telling me all this?" Pasco said.

"I think you know why. Since your meeting with Solquist you are, shall we say, firmly on our side. We still have to pull this through. TechCom could reopen the bidding process, but your line about timelines will sway the thinking. Delay again, and they have no chance of staying on schedule."

"Why did Mandrax not say anything in the meeting? About Mong I mean? Surely that warranted a discussion."

Guiren smiled. "I have been Churin's Director for a long time and as I said, I know how to invest and how to bargain, and more importantly, who to bargain with."

"Mandrax too?" Pasco said, wondering how many credits an Elite cost, realizing at the same time that he had seriously underestimated Guiren.

"I didn't say that. Mandrax is clean, but even he has superiors, and sometimes they come looking for a favour. If you are ever assigned to Sector 2, you'll learn." Guiren dried his hands on a towel, inspecting his nails as he did so. As far as Pasco knew, Guiren hadn't even been to the bathroom.

"Can I ask you a question?" Pasco said.

"Go ahead."

"How did you end up here?"

Guiren paused for a moment. "Thirty years ago I was a Tyro, working for Carlos Onega on the materials for the G11 cell phone." He smiled. "I had your job. After the carnage, I was lucky to get a position here." He threw the towel into the open basket. "Ten million attrition in Sector 2 is not a big deal, but let's hope, for your sake, this thing doesn't fry any Sector 1 brains."

10

BALMORAL STARED AT the Supervisor. "An accident? Is my father dead?"

"Not dead," Tao Cum Pao said, "but . . . it's bad."

Was this a trick? The opening gambit? She scanned for Angua on iNet. Nothing. At the very least, he was unconscious.

"W-what happened?" she asked, trying to inject the correct level of emotion into her voice. She had to be convincing.

"He was working on a filtration unit. It must have been faulty, loose wiring or something. He received a massive electric shock. We have him in Triage on the south side of the complex. It doesn't . . . it doesn't look good."

Poor choice, Balmoral thought. Her father knew filtration units inside and out. His lungs were weak, not his vision. They should have had him lift something too heavy, or collapse on the stairs, something she might have believed.

"We have a transport waiting outside," Tao Cum Pao said.

Transport? The Battery didn't send transports for workers, no matter what the circumstances, no matter who had been hurt.

"Come on. We don't have long. If we hurry you might . . ."

"S-see him before he dies?"

The Supervisor nodded. "I think . . ." she began, then stopped.

Tao Cum Pao had delivered news like this a hundred times, and yet she was agitated, her words unsure, the syntax unnatural. Was she reading a script from her lenses? Then there was her body language. She was turned slightly away as though not wanting to face Balmoral head on. She had always been one of those Supervisors who tried to be your friend, but Tao Cum Pao was lying now and every part of her body betrayed the discomfort.

But what was the lie? That her father was in Triage, or that they were taking her to see him? If Securicom were onto her, it stood to reason they knew about him too. There was no statute of limitations on killing a Foreman.

Her father was probably dead. The Foremen wouldn't be gentle when it concerned one of their own, no matter how long ago it was.

"Hurry!" the Supervisor implored.

"Yes, yes I will, but it's . . . such a shock. I have to . . . I have to go to the bathroom first." She muffled the last three words through her hand as though holding back tears, then pushed her way through the exiting workers, and into the ground floor wash rooms. There were seven stalls, three of which were occupied, but the one she needed, and the only one with a way out through a tiny window at the top, was free.

She locked the door, stood on the toilet seat and stretched up to the open cistern, patting her hand around inside. At first she couldn't find it, her fingers groping in the cold, recycled water, but then with relief she felt the plastic wrapper and pulled out the package.

She heard Tao Cum Pao come in after her, calling her name.

"In here," Balmoral said, and made a gagging sound.

"Are you all right?" Tao Cum Pao said, just outside the door. "We have to go now."

"Just a minute . . ."

She considered her options. The Supervisor stooped when she walked. If Balmoral got the timing just right, she could unlock the door and kick it with her good leg so it hit Pao's head as she stepped forward, knocking her out. No. Too risky. She estimated only a thirty percent chance it would do enough damage. Her legs weren't exactly strong.

She fixed on a higher probability alternative, something she remembered from one of the self-defence sims. Gingerly she unlocked the door and flopped back over the rim of the toilet.

"Oh, my poor thing," Tao Cum Pao said, putting her arm on Balmoral's shoulder. Then, in a colder, less spontaneous tone, "But we really have to go. The transport is waiting."

This was going to hurt.

"H-help me up," Balmoral said, poised on her haunches.

As the Supervisor leant down, Balmoral thrust her head up as fast as she could, smashing the back of her skull into Tao Cum Pao's chin. The Supervisor wobbled on her feet, dazed. Without hesitation, Balmoral grabbed Pao's hair and smashed her forehead against the stall wall. There was a crack, and even before she fell, Balmoral knew she was out cold.

Further down the row, two stall doors banged shut. There was a chance they would call for help. They had heard everything. Either way, it was irrelevant. When Tao Cum Pao lost consciousness she broke her contact with iNet. That meant Balmoral had only seconds before they came for her.

She fumbled with the package from the cistern, peeling off the protective plastic, ignoring the fetid smell. She hesitated. If she slipped the iNet glasses on now, they might guess what had happened. Balmoral suddenly disappearing, Min, her sister, suddenly appearing. It would confuse them, it might even buy her some time, but ultimately they would work it out. She couldn't risk it. She planned on using Min's identity for a few weeks at least. She had to create a distraction.

Pulling up her holopad, Balmoral typed, her fingers a blur across the keypad. She used the first piece of invasive subcode she had ever written, a pattern of commands that had haunted her ever since. Within fifteen seconds she had hacked into the generator of the building opposite. She overrode its safety mechanisms and pushed it into a rapid cycle of overheating. Then she instructed the generator to flood the system with hydrogen gas coolant, pumping its entire load into the confined space.

In about ten minutes, the turbines would vibrate at five or six times their maximum limit, while the hydrogen reached eighty or ninety percent. She couldn't let it go that long, and told the generator to reverse the transfer switch in half that time. That would create a surge from the main utility line and the whole thing would explode. Tripping it early would limit the size of the blast zone and unless someone was very unlucky, no lives would be lost.

Fourteen years ago, Balmoral had set ten other generators to trip at the point of maximum impact, only later realizing that the burning buildings did not mean that she had won the sim.

The images she tried so hard to forget still played across her mind; the immaculate rooms with their fluffy duvets and neat wardrobes, the joule-rich children, with their rosy, smiling faces and impossibly healthy bodies, the clear blue skies and the sound of laughter.

It was all so alien, how could she think Rhodes was real? Of course the object was to wipe out the invaders as quickly as possible. She would enjoy it. There was something insidious about these aliens, something that triggered an emotion she had never felt before; rage.

Exploring the game's environment, she discovered the generators together with their warnings about overheating. Without hesitation, she set off explosions in seven of the main dormitory buildings. At first, she was pleased when she saw her kill stats; a thousand children dead along with their unobtainable lives.

Children.

Unable to face what she had done, even in a sim, she dragged down the whole of iNet for fifty miles, thinking that by somehow leaving the alien campus in the dark, she would make the images go away.

When later she showed Zhu, a part of her knew, even before he began screaming, that Rhodes was not some complex virtual reality, but an actual place, that the charred and burning bodies were real.

Zhu never believed it was an accident. Their parents thought he cried at the images from the Battery. Her father squeezing the life out of the foreman was tame by comparison. Yes, Zhu looked at her differently from that day onwards, but neither had he told anyone. Until now.

Sweat beading on her brow, she dragged her mind back to the present. Typing another sequence of code, she tripped the fire alarms in the surrounding buildings. This would be the second distraction. The more people flooding out, the better. Usually she would have coded the malfunction as a system error, as if reported by *Voice* herself. However, as with the generator, she left the hack dirty, not bothering to cover her tracks. No time.

She put away the holopad and at the same instant, multiple fire alarms blared out. There were never unannounced drills, and despite the Battery's attitude to its workers, the management took fires very seriously. It was an uneconomical way to lose their resources.

"Tao Cum Pao!" a man shouted, entering the bathroom. "Are you in there? Tao!"

Balmoral dragged the Supervisor's body over the top of the toilet seat.

"Sorry," she whispered to the unconscious form. Standing on Tao Cum Pao gave her the additional height she needed to grab the window frame and pull herself up to the skylight. The window was small, but just big enough for her to slip through the gap.

The stall door crashed open. The man reached for her trailing leg, but she snapped it away. Cursing, he jumped onto Tao Cum Pao's back, and reached for the ledge. As hard as she could, Balmoral slammed the window shut on his fingers. There was a satisfying crunch, and he fell backwards. Too large for the space, he would have to go back out through the main corridor, which would now be flooded with people.

Balmoral dropped to the ground. She saw a black transport outside the building. It attempted to pull away, to keep from getting boxed in by the thousands that swarmed from the exits. In all the confusion it might not see her. She crossed over to the building opposite.

The turbines screeched in protest. The generator packed 1600 MVA, capable of taking out the first three floors on the south side of the building. The furthest point from both the main staircases and the exit. There would be injuries from flying debris, but nobody would be caught in the actual explosion as long as they heeded the alarm. The smoke and noise would create the diversion she needed, as well as take out any *Earth* cameras that covered that part of the walkway. The building itself was operating at quarter capacity, and the first five floors were empty.

Falling in with a line of exiting workers, she counted down the seconds. Heads turned now, towards the south side where the noise from the straining generator filled the air.

Ten.

She didn't want to run, to draw attention to herself, but was she too close? She had to judge it just right. Close enough to make them think she had been caught in the explosion, but far enough away not to be killed.

Five.

How far would the wall blow out?

Three.

How badly would she be hurt?

One.

She hit the deck. A huge explosion rocked the air. She heard rubble hitting the ground all around her. The air grew very hot and then cold again. There was a moment of silence, and the screaming began. But she was unhurt.

Without looking behind her, Balmoral stood up and crushed her iNet glasses underfoot, kicking the pieces in different directions. She brushed herself down and walked about three hundred feet to the next intersection. She pulled out Min's glasses. It took a moment for the interface to register, and then . . . she was Min, her dead sister, picking her way along the south west wall with the rest of the exiting masses, trying not to look conspicuous.

With any luck Securicom would waste hours searching the rubble for a body that didn't exist, and by then she would be far away.

Her next move was to take the tram into the Stacks. They wouldn't suspect that. Balmoral took the tram every day. They knew if she was smart enough to elude them, she was onto them, and therefore she would alter her movements. The last place she would head was to the tram, which was precisely why she had to get there.

As Min, she would ride seven miles into the Stacks where she had a safe house, the place packed with skaatch and potable water. A bunker. They might eventually work out what had happened, and begin to track Min, but if she could hole up for a while, she would find a way to escape. There was no reason they would conclude Balmoral had assumed another identity, together with a fake credit account. The more logical deduction was that she had disconnected from iNet and somehow remained off the grid.

Concentrating on fitting in with the crowd, she almost didn't see the two men who had appeared on the sidewalk a few hundred feet away. They were invisible on iNet; they had glasses, but no signature. Elite Securicom agents from Sector 1. While everyone else gawped at the flames and the screams and the sirens, the two agents searched for what the smoke and noise was designed to cover.

She kept to her course, heading towards the Battery's exit, hiding her limp as much as possible. Securicom believed retinal scans could not be faked. These Agents couldn't know she had spent a year hacking the hardware of Min's iNet lenses, overriding the retinal scan function, tricking it into seeing her as Min. They would be blind to her, the glasses enough to throw off her physical features.

She had to assume *Earth* was also scanning for her image, but for the same reason, she was safe. No matter how much she looked like Balmoral, *Earth* would only see her as Min.

With an eye command she executed a subcode sequence she called *Foresight*. It gave her three hundred and sixty degree vision by pinging every *Earth* camera in the vicinity of her own iNet.

As she reached the far end of the building, she checked behind her. The agents were still there, but scanning a different section of the crowd. Surrounded by a mass of exiting grey overalls, and with Min's identity, for the first time she felt confident of her escape.

She checked *Foresight* again. No other Securicom with hidden digital signatures. Every step brought her closer to safety.

Just in front of the southern exit, she noticed something else. Parked between two Battery buildings was a bubble car. There were a lot of them around today, which made sense. Churin management was at the Battery, as were Sector 1 grandees. She was used to the brown chunky transports that brought consignments in and out, but the bubble cars were strictly for management, used for ferrying executives around the complex, and taking the visiting managers from one end of Churin to the other.

This one was empty.

A new idea came to her. How difficult would it be to hack a bubble car? Make it invisible to *Earth* and yet use its navigation to take her all the way to Shamshu or another border city, where she could blend in, or get across to Pekin?

She knew the safe house would only buy her so much time before they smoked her out. Then what? On the other hand, with the bubble car hacked, she could get miles away. Balmoral calculated the odds were better stealing the car.

She broke off from the exiting masses and ducked down the narrow alleyway where the car was parked. The door was locked but she overwrote its security mechanism. Stepping inside she shaded the windows, like the management often did. She checked her bearings.

Pulling up a bird's eye view of the battery complex, she reviewed all the exits. Next to each main exit was a service way for transports. She overlaid all static and active traffic. She didn't want to drive out of any exit where other transports were in the vicinity. That way, if she was spotted, she would still have a head start.

How strange, she thought. There were bubble cars parked a couple of buildings away from each of the Battery's exits. Eight bubble cars, eight exits. What was the probability of that?

Then she realised.

Stupid, stupid, stupid! The car was a trap, a honeypot, too good to pass up. She had to get out. They would be here in a minute. The picked lock almost certainly told them which trap was sprung.

She grabbed the door handle.

The door had locked automatically on closing, the manual control rendered useless. She would have to re-hack it to open it. Typing rapidly on her keypad, she located the door mechanism, while checking *Foresight* to see from which direction they were coming from, but then . . . her iNet display froze, and with a high pitched whine, it shut down, the display completely black.

Digital death.

Removing her glasses, she studied the car. She had to get out. There was nothing she could use to break the windows, yet that was her only route of escape. The windshield was reinforced glass, so that was out of the question. For the side windows, there was nothing against which she could brace herself to get purchase for a kick. That left the back window. If she hit it hard enough, perhaps it would crack and she could pull out the glass.

Like everything else in Sector 2, bubble cars were constructed from the cheapest possible material. The glass at the perimeter was thin, the weakest point was where the glass met the frame.

Using the seat as leverage, she aimed her good foot at the space three inches from the edge. There was a dull thud, but no real damage. Cursing under her breath she kicked again, and again. Still nothing. The fourth kick, she caught it just right and the window shattered under her heel. She pushed out the glass, ignoring the pain as the shards shredded her hands, and wriggled through.

Rolling out, she hit the tarmac hard. Dazed, she pulled herself up and half limped, half ran, back out to the junction and into the main pedestrian thoroughfare. She had no plan at this point, but it was better to move than stay still. Perhaps she could pass through the gates without being seen, just another grey overall.

Ahead of her, two men in black suits appeared around the corner. For a split second they focused on the car. Then they saw her and changed direction.

Balmoral ducked into the small alleyway between two buildings, dashing for the Battery exit, knowing it was useless. She ran, ignoring the pain that throbbed in her leg, ignoring her hands, bleeding steadily. The men were about a hundred feet behind her, closing fast. Not looking, she ran straight across the service road. She didn't see the second bubble car until it was too late.

11

B UBBLE CARS TRAVELLING at forty miles an hour could stop dead in under
eighty feet. Unlike sentient drivers, they required no time to react but
engaged the brakes the instant an obstacle appeared. Unfortunately, when
the grey shadow ran out into the road, it was just a few feet away.

In the instant before impact, the girl turned and stared right into Pasco's eyes.
Was there a flicker of recognition? She seemed neither afraid nor surprised, as
though the end was inevitable and the car was simply a physical manifestation
of what she already knew.

When Pasco thought about it later, he traced the point *his* life changed to that
moment. Rationally, he knew that time didn't actually slow to a preternatural
pace, but in his memory it always seemed that way, his brain elongating every
millisecond, the girl holding him in her naked eyes.

There was a dull thud as her legs hit the low bumper, the deafening crack of
the cobwebbing windshield, another silence, and then a sickening crunch as the
body hit the ground behind them. Pasco grabbed the door handle.

"Stay in the car!" Guiren yelled, pulling him back. "It might not be safe."

Shaking him off, Pasco ran to where the broken girl lay. She must be dead.
Nobody could survive that. There was a trickle of blood from her nose. She did
not move. Did she even breathe?

"Stand back!" Mandrax yelled, appearing from nowhere, flanked by two
Securicom agents. The first dropped to his knees and checked her pulse. He
glanced up at Mandrax, nodded and hurriedly began to pull equipment out of
a large backpack. Mandrax barked commands into his iNet, something about
their current co-ordinates.

In a daze, Pasco wondered where Mandrax had come from and what he was
doing. After the board meeting, MediaCom had ordered the delegation back
to Sector 1. Rajesh Elb considered additional site inspections redundant. As a
result, they had a late night charter to catch, but when the bubble car came to

pick them up, Mandrax wasn't there. At first Guiren and Pasco waited for him. Then Guiren received a message over iNet saying they should meet him at the airport, which made no sense, until now. Mandrax had unfinished business. He was here for the girl. But why?

"A transport is on the way," Guiren said, emerging from the car but keeping down, as though trying to hide from something. "We'll take her to Triage."

"Don't bother," Mandrax snapped back. "We have a medevac flying in. We'll stabilize her right here. Moving her will only increase the trauma."

"Medevac?" Guiren said incredulously. "Churin doesn't have such a thing."

"Pekin does and their border is only seventy miles away. We're taking her to the hospital there. They have the necessary intensive care facilities."

"But the cost!" Guiren rasped.

"Is not your concern."

"Surely she can't be *that* valuable? Who is she? The head of the *Dish*?" He was still crouching, using the car for cover. "I should have bargained harder."

"You can stand up," Mandrax said. "There's no *Dish* here. We've checked the vicinity."

"Then I don't understand. What were all the explosions?"

Mandrax pointed to the girl.

"It can't have been!" Guiren said. "You've been tracking her for the last few hours. And where could she hide the explosives?" He fumbled with his holopad. "We have a record. She was searched this morning."

"And the person who searched her is now dead. Fourteen years ago she blew up the Rhodes Academy from over seven thousand miles away, with nothing more than her holopad."

"That's not possible."

"It's not possible to fake a retinal scan, but she did that too. If she hadn't gone for the bubble car we would have lost her."

They stared down. The medic had attached a mask over her face and now a small box breathed for her. A drip hung above her head. One of the men swabbed her arm, the other prepared a shot.

"You do realise," Mandrax said, "that if she dies, the deal is off. Bodia could make a miraculous comeback, get everything back under control, with enough support from Securicom."

Guiren blanched. "I-I wasn't responsible for this." He motioned partly to the girl, partly to the smashed windscreen.

"No?" Mandrax said. "Try telling that to our good Chairman."

Chairman? Did he mean Maglan? Why was Pasco's uncle involved?

"This was supposed to be a covert mission," Mandrax said. "How do you think it's going to look that a car taking Top 10 grandees to the airport ran over a girl, killing her. Media will have a field day."

"But surely you could . . ."

"Squash it? With this many witnesses," he gestured to the crowd passing out through the Battery gates. They all craned their necks towards them, slowing as they passed. "In about fifteen minutes, the first helicopter most of them have ever seen, burning more joules than the annual output of a treadle mill, will land and take one of their own away with it. Five thousand people at least will wonder what is going on, and ten or twenty might be motivated enough to try and find out. Is that your idea of *covert*?"

"I can't control . . ."

"Just clear them away. All of them. Close down the road in this section and send the workers to another exit. Send everyone home if you have to, but get rid of them. The clock is ticking."

Guiren looked like he was going to protest, but then, pulling down his mask, he turned and walked towards the front gate, barking orders into his iNet.

It bothered Pasco that Mandrax or Guiren made no attempt to conduct their conversation privately. It was as though Mandrax wanted him to hear. What did that mean? Suddenly he felt afraid without exactly knowing why.

"How is she doing now?" Mandrax said to the agent.

"Still breathing but she has a collapsed lung, multiple fractures, head trauma and internal bleeding. We've induced a coma to try and preserve brain functionality."

Induced coma, Pasco thought with a pang. Always a risk. Sometimes the patient never came out again, especially in an ER situation. Worse still, some became a lock in, the brain alive in an unresponsive body. He shuddered. He could imagine nothing more horrific than being imprisoned inside one's self.

Mandrax briefly held her wrist. "Will she make it?"

"We need that copter soon."

"How long do we have?" Mandrax said.

"Forty-five minutes, an hour maybe. After that . . ." the agent shrugged.

"You said Pekin is seventy miles away!" Pasco said, unable to stay quiet any longer.

"The border is, the hospital's further in. Either way, we have no choice. There are no facilities in Churin capable of helping her. The medevac does one-eighty so if we get off the ground in the next fifteen minutes, we may get lucky. On the bright side," Mandrax said, nodding to the agent, "this man is one of the best field medics in the Autonomy, so if anyone can buy her time, he can."

Ahead, Foremen cleared the crowds. Beside them, transports arrived and men in white overalls spilled out, erecting giant screens.

Mandrax turned to him. "Come with me," he said, gesturing to the Battery building directly opposite. Pasco followed him, a lump forming in his throat.

Just inside the door was a small Supervisors office. Three men sat at dingy work stations.

"Out," Mandrax ordered, flashing his Elite's identikit. Without a word, they stood up and left. "Take a seat."

Pasco sat, taking in the yellowing walls, the patches of damp, and the hard, plastic chairs.

"The girl," Mandrax said, his voice flat. "You have seen her before."

"Yes, during the tour I . . ."

"I'm talking about on the plane."

Pasco hesitated, then nodded.

Mandrax shook his head. "Eye control, I've always hated it. I thought you might not have paid it much attention, but when you came across her again on the line, you started like you'd been stung by a hornet."

"H-how do you know that?"

"Because I was watching her on *Earth*. A stupid coincidence. We were pinpointing her location, and you walked into the picture, gawping at her. That idiot Guiren should never have allowed you anywhere near the floor. I think you tipped her off."

"Me? Tipped her off?" Pasco said, "What are you talking about?"

"You have no idea who she is or what she is capable of. She probably took you apart on the spot, hacked your profile, and from there somehow worked out we were after her."

"We?"

"Securicom."

"I thought you were part of the iAm project. I don't understand."

Mandrax took off his ring and put it on the table. "I turned this device on with an eye command when we entered the room. It has short circuited the cameras, scrambling *Earth*." He tapped the side of his glasses. "This entire conversation only exists up here."

Pasco wondered if he meant on iNet or in his head. With iAm, it would soon be the same thing. For some reason he shivered. "I thought *Earth* was insulated against EMP?"

"It is. That ring is a rogue; a self-executed miniature network, existing off the grid until it's activated, at which point it launches a program that drills into iNet, locates the room we're in and short-circuits the camera by mimicking a command from *Earth*."

"That's impossible isn't it?" Pasco said. He knew enough about programming to understand that the system was almost unhackable. Earth corrected malfunctions without the need for human intervention. It was the advantage of using an

AI over a static system.

"Nevertheless, that is exactly what the girl lying on the tarmac did when she was seven years old. It took more than a decade before our programmers realised that *Earth* could be taken down by anything but an EMP, and another three years to replicate the code she used. *Voice* is working on a patch to counteract a program such as this, but just think of it! The girl wrote this code as a child!" He paused. "Your uncle wants her, Pasco, preferably with her brain intact."

So that was it. Bruno Mandrax was an agent sent by Maglan.

"She doesn't seem like *Dish*," Pasco said.

"If she is capable of doing what I just described do you really think it matters? *She* was responsible for Rhodes Academy."

Pasco didn't believe him. All those children. It couldn't have been her. She wasn't a murderer. In the distance, he heard the low whoop-whoop of the helicopter. "Why are you telling me all this?" he said.

"Because you have seen too much. That girl is classified. If you weren't the Chairman's nephew, he might be forced to liquidate you on the spot." Mandrax smiled, his fangs showing.

"Maybe he still will," Pasco said, trying to smile back.

"Only if you talk."

Pasco experienced a pang of dread. Despite Mandrax's show of humour, the underlying threat was clear. That he was the Chairman's nephew wasn't a guarantee of anything. Growing up, his uncle never had time for him. Maglan took in the twins out of a sense of obligation, nothing more. He followed Tristram's meteoric progress at the Academy and Securicom, but that was professional interest in a valuable asset. It didn't go as far as feelings.

"I'm telling you all this because we have two problems," Mandrax said. "The first is that the moment you saw the girl, you became a security risk. The second is you. You're an embarrassment to your uncle. The stalled career, the gambling problem and now criminal activity in the form of a few hundred thousand credits."

Pasco sucked in his breath. His uncle knew about the bribe! His life was over. He would be consigned to a treadle mill or worse!

"We have two options. The first is to bring you into Securicom to work on . . . let's just say, special projects. iAm is a game changer. We need someone who has worked on the technology, someone who understands the science, especially the biological side. It would mean a new career, which for you would be a good thing."

Pasco's head span. Securicom? Wanting an iAm scientist? "And the second option?"

"Liquidation," he said, with another flash of his fangs.

Pasco blinked at his reflection in Mandrax's glasses. "I agree. To Securicom, I mean."

"Good. The credits have just been returned to Churin's treasury. The bribe will be pinned on Solquist. We'll say it was a sting. That old fraud's been doing Guiren's dirty work for years. I bet he did the 'I'm just one of the workers' act while failing to mention his penthouse in Deng, or rows of Stacks hired out at rack rents, or his fifteen-year-old wife. Either way, from now on, you don't have any loyalty to anyone, except me."

Mandrax picked up his ring. "Betray my confidence, disobey my instructions in any way, and . . . well let's just say, you won't be in a position to do it again." This time Mandrax did not smile. "Come on. Let's go."

They stepped outside. The girl was still on the tarmac, four medics securing her on a stretcher that looked more like a sleeping cube, except for the tubes, wires and straps.

"And I thought you were here for iAm," Pasco said. With the noise of the rotors his iNet automatically switched to amplified speech through the implants in his ear.

"I was multitasking," Mandrax's voice echoed back as though inside Pasco's head.

"What about the bidding process?"

"It was real. Maybe Securicom turned a blind eye to what was going on in Bodia, maybe we kept quiet about Guiren's negotiations with Mong, but Rajesh Elb and TechCom has to make the decision. Securicom can't influence matters of economics, but if you want my opinion, I think you convinced Elb not to reopen the bidding process and for that reason alone, Churin will get the contract."

"I don't know if I would wish that on anyone."

"Too late now."

The medics gently lifted the stretcher and pushed it into the helicopter, fighting against the gale from the spinning blades.

"What are you waiting for?" Mandrax said.

"What?"

"Get in."

"To . . . to the copter?"

"The girl is your first assignment. I'll brief you later, but you won't be going home for a while. I'd plan on at least three months in Pekin. In fact, forget about home for now. You've got no apartment and nothing to go back to anyway."

"I have a girlfriend, I . . . ."

"Rosaline? She's been fucking James for months. For some reason, she just can't bring herself to tell you. *Faith* knows why."

Pasco stared at Mandrax in disbelief, both at the level of information he had access to and what it contained.

"Better out than in," Mandrax said.

Two agents appeared at the copter door, motioning them to come.

"Go!" Mandrax roared.

Not thinking, Pasco ran towards the door and the agents pulled him into the aircraft. His stomach lurched as the copter rose into the air.

PART III
2058

1

SECTOR 1, MANSION

EXCUSE ME, SIR, there's no smoking inside the restaurant."

"But I'm outside," Tristram said.

The waitress pursed her lips, "It's still *the restaurant.*"

He snuffed out the cigarette with his fingers, resisting the temptation to flick it at her face. "Health and safety," he said with a polite smile. "What can you do?"

"Can I get you something else?"

"Sure. Same again."

"A mineral water?"

"That's the one."

"And to eat?"

"I'm not hungry."

She pursed her lips again, her mouth like a cat's ass. "I'm afraid you can't sit here if you don't eat," she said. "The veranda is for diners only. The bar is inside."

She wanted him gone, didn't like his Tyro identikit in a restaurant where practically everyone else was Elite. He was not worth the effort, economically. A poor investment of her time.

"Tell you what," he said. "You place an order for the most expensive item on the menu and I'll authorize the transfer. You don't even have to bring out the food."

The waitress hesitated. "I don't know if I'm allowed to do that."

"Sure you are. Credits are credits. Add a generous tip for yourself too. Don't be shy." She began to write out the order on a pad of paper. "Don't bother with that rubbish."

She hesitated again, quickly checked over her shoulder, and pulled up her holopad. A moment later, a light flashed in the corner of his lenses with the transaction. Real, not synthesized, lamb, hinterland potatoes, split peas and sea salt, a mineral water and a twenty-five percent tip. The size of the tip was cheeky, the meal, a small fortune, but Tristram didn't care. Securicom's expense account could take it.

He authorized the credits and for the first time the waitress smiled, but didn't bother with a thank you.

"I'll be back with your drink, Sir." She weaved away, in and out of the cramped tables.

Tristram surveyed the veranda, studying the faces. Sixteen years ago, the *Dish* came to this very rooftop, waited until deep into the night and then shot his father as he exited the Securicom building. There was no evidence of this now, of course. The roof had been converted to a high end restaurant complete with miniature garden and water features in the centre.

He closed his eyes, trying to imagine the assassins on that fateful night. Were they still operatives? Were they still alive? He lived with the hope that he would find them one day, and make them pay for his father's death, to make them suffer the way he had suffered.

In his darkest, most paranoid moments, Tristram wondered if his uncle had been complicit in the assassination. Had his father lived, Maglan would have faced difficult questions about promoting a brother who had just cost the Autonomy a trillion credits in a hair-brained scheme in Namgola. Instead, Dagmar Eborgersen became a martyr, and Maglan the strong, stoical leader, defiant even when the *Dish* had struck so close to home.

Media milked the story, and Maglan's popularity rose at a crucial moment when the Chairmanship was still fragile, when there were still those on the Board who could mount an opposition.

Tristram took another sip of his mineral water and dismissed the thought. As children, Maglan practically brought his brother up. He would never betray him.

"You need to look out for Pasco," his father used to say, *"Like your uncle Maglan looked out for me. When you grow up it will be you and him against the world."*

His father hated it when they fought, when Tristram bloodied Pasco's nose, knocked the wind out of him, or loosened a tooth. Tristram wondered what his father would think of him now, a sandman.

It was Maglan who convinced Tristram that the best way to avenge his father was to join the underground operatives that tracked down and eliminated *Dish*. He did not add that once you begin killing there is always killing. That you think it, dream it, are it. Maglan didn't tell him that.

Tristram blinked, aware as he did so of his eyelids moving in a slightly different way, across a slightly different surface. He was still not used to his eyes, stripped from a dead man and put into his sockets, his own carefully preserved for when he no longer needed a cover. The new eyes felt dirty somehow, gritty, although according to the body shop that sensation was temporary.

The vulnerability Maglan's hacker girl had discovered, enabling her to fake a retinal scan, had been eliminated, and his uncle didn't want anyone to open it up again, friend or foe. That kind of hack was too dangerous, could undermine the fundamental premise of iNet. As for the surgery, Tristram doubted anyone other than a few Elites in Securicom even knew such a thing was possible.

To the world, his new retinas identified him as Cy Yozarian, a Tyro with a chequered career complete with a cover to see him through his next mission. Tomorrow they shipped him out to sand some prominent *Dish* operatives, but to get close enough, he would need to infiltrate the organization, to play the part of a transvict on the run.

In contrast to his assumed persona, Tristram's rise in Securicom had been meteoric. He had neutralized more of the *Dish* leadership than any other operative and at twenty-three, was already Senator grade, a decade before the average agent.

The mineral water appeared on the table. "Here you are, Mr. Yozarian."

He nodded thanks, and scanned the diners. Tristram had requested a table on the periphery, in the shadows, good for watching people, but not people watching. There was a difference.

According to his mole, the *Dish* was planning something big, at this restaurant, at this hour. Of course, he didn't trust his mole; turn once and you can turn again, and the veranda seemed an unlikely target, the payoff unpredictable. He also didn't see how they could smuggle in anything large enough to do any real damage.

"*But it's the Bedouin,*" his mole said, a gleam in his beady eye, knowing that would be enough to hook Tristram, to earn his traitor's currency.

Securicom knew almost nothing about the Bedouin, one of the few remaining *Dish* cells in Mansion. The others were anaemic by comparison, populated by weak and disenfranchised Mansionites, rather than the hardened fighters that operated in other sectors. The only reason Securicom didn't shut down the other Mansion cells completely was the intelligence they occasionally dropped about the Bedouin. Often the intelligence was wrong, misinformation fed by the Bedouin themselves, but it only had to be right once for the opportunity Tristram needed.

The Bedouin somehow managed to keep almost entirely off grid, but whether they hid in plain sight or outside of *Earth*'s glare, nobody was sure. They were like ghosts, carrying out attacks and then fading away as if they had never been.

The Bedouin broke President Gravales out of a high security installation, less than a month after the original attacks. Four years later they blew a twenty billion credit hole in the Atmos system, shutting it down for months, and causing the precious Mansionites to cough and snivel on a few stray particulates. Last year, when Logistics authorized the transfer of bodily organs between Sectors, 99% of which ended up in Sector 1 Vanity salons, the Bedouin demolished their headquarters with a loss of fourteen thousand lives.

If Tristram didn't hate them, he might admire them. Instead, all that mattered to him was that the Bedouin murdered his father.

Scanning the restaurant again, Tristram was convinced his mole's tip was just one more piece of misinformation. Every table was a clone of the one next to it, working lunches, business getting done. Everyone here was *meant* to be here, Tristram had an eye for such things. He took another sip of mineral water and decided it was time to find a new mole.

Then a woman caught his eye. She struggled with a bulky stroller, trying to get it closer to the table to stop people bumping into it. She kept glancing around every few seconds, waiting for her lunch date. The waitress asked her something. She glanced at the door again and shook her head.

Her dress was a little showy, almost evening wear. He probably wouldn't have noticed her if she hadn't been alone. Everyone else was in executive lunch meetings. As the waitress disappeared, the woman glanced towards the door again, and this time he saw it. Something infinitely subtle in her expression. She *looked*, but didn't expect to *see* anybody. She was faking it.

2

I
T WAS A late summer's day, the air clear, the sky a crystalline blue. A good day to be alive, Fleur Cliquot thought. On a day like this, you could almost have hope. Almost. Until you remembered the weather was manufactured by mile long filtration units powered by forty million feet, pumping away in a Sector you had never heard of, and never wanted to visit. She darkened the setting on her lenses a few shades. Her eyes, conditioned by a perpetual gloom, were too sensitive for the sun.

It was not yet twelve, but the restaurant hummed with diners, mostly in twos and threes, sitting around black rattan tables. Space was at a premium, each table placed just a few inches from the next. Almost everyone wore business suits, had holopads out, worked while they ate. She realised now that her dress was a little off, a bit too showy, but that was all right, nobody would notice.

Located on a roof top in the heart of Top 10's business district, Esprit was one of the city's most prestigious restaurants. It catered mostly to working executives rather than Mansion wives with nothing better to do. Those restaurants were further uptown. Fleur was not employed by Top 10, so passing herself off as an executive was not an option, even if she didn't have little Clay with her. She pulled the stroller closer.

Sixteen years ago, Fleur was on this same roof, waiting for Sophie Valencia, excited to be out in the middle of the night, understanding nothing about the organization she had so rashly joined.

That single evening shaped her existence. Meeting Valencia and joining her club was like getting into a car with a drunk driver. One moment it was exhilarating, speeding down a wide open street. The next she was wrapped around a lamppost and the whole world had changed. She didn't know it then, but she had been crippled, as surely as if there had been a crash, her movements forever restricted, and the prospect of a normal life, with a husband, family and job, gone forever.

Fleur glanced at baby Clay. He was perfect; his olive skin, his brown curls that shone against the backdrop of the sun-drenched Mansion skyline, the tiny iNet glasses perched on his nose, full shade of course, and his leg, twitching occasionally, as though deeply engrossed in a sim.

Except he wasn't. His identikit was blank, which to the world, meant he was sleeping. Electronically invisible, people kept knocking him as they squeezed past, as though he wasn't there. Thankfully, he didn't stir. For the third time in as many minutes, she pulled the stroller closer still. Now his head was practically under the glass top of the table and out of the way. They didn't really like children in here and the less conspicuous he was, the better.

"Your espresso, mam," the waitress said, placing it on the table and pulling out her note pad. One of the kitschy aspects of the supremely expensive restaurant was that it tried to create the ambience of another era; waitresses in black uniforms, complete with their white frilly aprons, 'took' your orders rather than relaying them through iNet. Waitresses who called you mam, though you were barely older than they were.

Barely older?

No, what was she thinking. She was over thirty now, and this girl wasn't yet twenty. Time tricked you like that sometimes, as though the passing years meant nothing, as if she was waiting for a real, normal life to begin. There was no possibility of that, not after Valencia shot President Dagmar Eborgersen in the head. They didn't even get the right one. Beaky was furious about it to this day.

Fleur took a sip of the espresso, savouring the aroma. She hadn't tasted coffee like this in too long.

"How old is the little one?" the waitress said, still hovering around her table.

"Eighteen months," Fleur replied.

"He's beautiful."

"Do you really think so? I do of course, but then all parents are biased."

"Oh no, he really is cute, like a doll in that little khaki outfit. Precious!"

"His father wouldn't like to hear you say that! He wants me to cut Clay's hair. Says it makes him *too* pretty."

"Don't do any such thing!" the waitress said. She gestured to the empty seat, small talk done. "Do you still want to wait to order or . . ."

"No," Fleur said, "He's stuck in a meeting. You know how it is."

"Oh, *I do*. I have one just like him at home."

Almost immediately another server appeared and began to clear away the additional setting, manoeuvring around the bulky stroller, but bumping it three or four times, because the table was so cramped. Clay's neck lolled back and forth with each jolt and Fleur bit her tongue.

Bump it again, and you might get more than you bargained for.

The girl took the cap off her pen, and waited with her physical notepad, poised for the order. *Yes*, Fleur thought, it could almost be from another time except that, without asking, she knew the waitress was called Christie Miller, a nineteen-year-old who was employed by Subsistence Corp, a Tyro on her first rotation and currently specializing in the service side of the business; a fancy way of saying she waited tables. According to her biosquare she was in very good shape, although a little dehydrated at the moment.

All of this, Fleur saw in an instant, public information on the girl's identikit, as well as some private details she chose to share. Clearly Christie was proud of her physical condition. She must work out, or be on a nutrition plan, or something.

Fleur had stopped consulting her own biosquare readings long ago. They depressed her too much. Her thighs were in danger of becoming soft and doughy, and when she looked at herself, she couldn't help thinking that already her best days were behind her. Although Valencia tried to keep them all fit, there was only so many times you could hop up and down a single step or jog back and forth across a gloomy passage.

She turned her attention to the paper menu, the words blurring in front of her eyes, unused to the physical medium. "What's the *skaatch* special?" she said with genuine curiosity.

"Escargot and sturgeon eggs. A very popular choice." The waitress beamed, "It comes with fresh brioche."

"Surely that's cheating," Fleur laughed, hoping she didn't sound as fake as she felt.

"Ah, but it tastes so good!"

"I'll have one of those then."

The waitress made a show of writing the order on a little yellow pad. They must have given her a crash course in 'writing by hand'. Then again, the scrawl didn't look legible, so perhaps it was just show, the order already recorded and sent to the kitchen. Either way, somewhere in the world, they had killed a precious tree to make this novelty item embossed with the word Esprit at the top.

"You'll be able to keep this as a souvenir," the waitress whispered.

"Oh . . . wonderful."

"And for the little one?"

"Nothing, thank you."

"Nothing at all?" Her tone suggested that bringing a child was one thing, but taking up space without paying, no matter what your age, was quite another.

Fleur gestured to the back of the stroller. "He's *saris*."

"Oh," the waitress said, and unconsciously took a step backwards, as though somehow the syndrome was catching.

Severe Allergic Reaction & Intolerance Syndrome, or *saris*, was the latest immune system epidemic to break out in Sector 1. A fatal sensitivity to almost anything organic, those with the syndrome survived on a synthetic formula developed by Subsistence Corp. She had read a few particularly gruesome cases of children whose stomach lining dissolved on contact with grains or sugars, the stomach acid eating through their internal organs.

"Unfortunately, anything you serve here is likely to send him into biphasic anaphylaxis. Expose him to an egg and he'd die on the spot, the poor little thing. That's why we have this," she touched the back of the bulky knapsack affixed to the back of the stroller. "We don't go anywhere without the shots, the breathing apparatus, the drugs and *Faith* knows what purging devices."

The waitress blinked at the pack, an increasingly common accessory for the Mansion parent. It hadn't stopped the building's security scanning it, then pulling out each vial and canister, and even thumbing through the diapers, while Fleur held the sleeping Clay.

"All right. If that's all, it should only be a few minutes." The waitress disappeared.

The restaurant was close to peak capacity now. Two hundred and fifty tables, each with an average of four diners, plus about eighty staff. If everything went to plan, the tally would be in the high hundreds.

She studied the roof garden about twenty table lengths away from her. From the outside, she couldn't see much except the exterior line of trees. From the various recons, she knew the space was about seventy foot square and that a single cobbled pathway was the only way in or out.

She checked the time. Forty-five minutes to go. Perfect. It would take ten minutes to bring the food, twenty or so to eat it, then she'd pay the check, and take Clay into the garden.

Her head swam. The busy tables seeming to press in on her. She wasn't used to this many people, not anymore. There was a man about a foot away, a lobster leg hanging out of his mouth, as though the creature was trying to escape. His face was like a lobster, hypertension red, and he grunted and snorted as he ate. Three young women sat with him, Tyros at some sort of induction lunch. None of them looked comfortable.

"In Logistics you'll learn that the lower Sectors are not like us. They wouldn't understand . . . this." He waved a hand in the general vicinity of the restaurant. "Wouldn't even want it probably." A glob of tomalley dripped from his mouth and onto the table.

Two of the girls smiled nervously, their immaculate clothes, hair, face, teeth, exposing their Mansionite credentials, Tyros on their first Top 10 rotation, while the third, a skinny, Asiatic girl with Aspirant written all over her face, fiddled with her fork. Fleur checked her identikit; Sidharta Siranush. Yes, the sixteen digits of a Battery allocated name.

Under the table, the fat man squeezed the Aspirant's leg. She started, eyes wide, but said nothing. The other girls didn't see. His name was Guy Rawstorm, a Senator in Logistics, but interestingly his identikit stated he used to be an Elite, and, long ago, a President. He looked familiar, but she couldn't quite place him.

The girl seemed upset, and Fleur could understand why. She had come to Sector 1 through the hard work and devotion, not only of herself, but of her family. The success rate of an Aspirant actually making it to Top 10 in a Sector 1 region was perhaps one in a thousand, to Mansion itself, one in a hundred thousand or more. At home she had physically starved, but in Mansion there was a different kind of starvation, a gnawing, insidious erosion of the spirit. Worse, no matter what she achieved, there would always be those who treated her like a second class citizen, called her a *twitcher* behind her back, or maybe even to her face. How did the song go?

Aspirants, those sinewy twitchers,
Forever twitching after their own ambition.
They're one too many for me.

Dillon Vrain had a lot to answer for, although the artist himself was at great pains to say he wasn't Sectorist, that his lyrics were misinterpreted, that he considered everyone equal, that his songs were protests against society, not a single class of citizen within it. Nevertheless, twitcher had become a ubiquitous put down for any successful transfer from the lower Sectors.

"They should be grateful," the fat man said between mouthfuls of lobster meat, "without the Autonomy, the good citizens of slumworld would die in their millions."

"What about Churin?" the girl suddenly said, quietly but clearly.

The fat man frowned at the interruption. "What about it?"

"They are already dying in their millions *because* of the Autonomy. They might not want this," she waved her painfully thin arm across the restaurant, "but they would rather live than die on the lines constructing iAm. I know the research. With the right resources, the deaths could be prevented." The girl's face was hot with emotion.

"Can't be done," Rawstorm said shortly.

"Why not?"

"Because it's not in the budget."

"But a million have died this year alone."

"A million what?"

"People."

"No. A million in *resources*, at a burn of a half a billion credits a year compared to a net margin of over twenty billion credits." He leaned towards her. "iAm is more profitable than Churin could have ever imagined precisely *because* of the attrition. The wear and tear benefits their economy. Just like with an old machine, the cost of repair outweighs a new, more productive replacement. Run out of machines? Just ship another rock. Other sectors in slumworld would kill for those margins."

The girl stared at him, wide eyed, and then pushed her chair away from the table. "Excuse me," she said, and headed towards the bathroom.

"A little twitchy, that one," Rawstorm muttered, and dug into another lobster, sucking on the carapace. The other girls sat in silence.

Fleur wondered if Siranush would still be in the restaurant when the veranda exploded into a thousand pieces. Probably. Fleur wished she could tip her off, whisper something in her ear, but that was impossible. This was war. The girl was part of the system, just as much as the fat man, a system where economic principles, instead of serving humanity, had turned life into a unit of production, a statistic. All of the Autonomy's citizens, whether Battery workers in Sector 2, or executives in Sector 1, were complicit. That they were also part of the general humanity the *Dish* was trying to save was irrelevant. Until they became free, they were the enemy.

She told herself this fifty times a day. Sometimes she even believed it.

"Skaatch for one," the waitress said with a wide smile. Despite the immaculate presentation, her lunch had the same plastic veneer all food seemed to possess, intensively harvested and augmented with synthetics.

Valencia had told her to order something exotic and expensive, something consistent with the choice of an Elite's wife, and operationally it was important Fleur killed the time without attracting attention. There was still thirty-five minutes before the bomb went off.

On her iNet lenses, Fleur's Avatar appeared, to give thanks for the meal. Fleur dismissed it with a blink. She didn't want to hear that bitch harp on about some crap to do with the preparation of the soul. The *Faith* was compulsory now, or at least, certain iNet sims could only be accessed with so many *Faith* points, including all of the best Pleasure Houses. It was all right to masturbate, as long as you said a quick prayer first, to keep the physical act in the proper context.

The restrictions were enforced by the so called Moral Majority, a *Faith* obsessed organization with over a billion members and deep pockets, dedicated to forwarding the religion's tenets in practice and in thought. They sprang up after the White Knights mysteriously disbanded over some hushed up scandal years ago. With their vast buying power, the Moral Majority bought Media's most popular sims and then dictated the terms of access. Valencia made all operatives participate in the *Faith*. The A-points made them less conspicuous, less likely to be *Dish*.

Fleur had been hungry, but now the food was here, her mouth felt chalky and dry. She tried some of the bread, not daring the escargot. Listening to Rawstorm, watching him, had made her nauseous. She now remembered where she had seen him before, his face framed in a round binocular while they waited for Eborgersen all those years ago. If only it could have been him they shot.

He stuffed a huge slice of garlic bread into his mouth while saying something about his weight and a "gland condition" he suffered from, the jacket of his suit straining over the fat. The Mansion girls sat transfixed, fake smiles plastered to their faces.

Fleur had an image of two hundred thousand children crammed onto a single floor in a Fluff Mill. Every piece of clothing in the world was now sewn by 'little fingers', the majority coming out of Bodia.

She had seen a Fluff Mill on an illicit Media file, sent across the Sectors by *Dish* contacts in Bodia. She remembered the children opening and closing their mouths like fish in the thick dusty air, as if trying to catch the floating strands of fibre.

"Eating the fluff eases the ache of their bellies," the narrator said, "Skaatch rations are never enough and so synthetic cotton helps stem the hunger pains, but also gives them tumours."

This was a single floor in a single warehouse. Each warehouse had five floors, and as the camera panned away from some unseen vantage she saw hundreds and hundreds of these warehouses, each with children swarming like ants. Without exception, they were like skeletons, their bones poking through almost translucent skin. Not a single one had a *gland condition*.

"Is everything all right?" the waitress said, appearing again.

"Yes, I'm afraid . . . I'm afraid I'm not very hungry."

The waitress frowned slightly, critical of this neurotic homemaker who brought a child with *saris*, who had ordered an expensive dish and then hardly touched it.

"Could I tempt you with anything else?"

"No, I'm good, thank you."

Immediately the check appeared in front of her iNet. "No paper for the important part," Fleur said.

The waitress smiled thinly.

The cost astounded her, but she tried not to look surprised. She added a fifteen percent tip and authorized the charge. At the same time another server appeared to clear her table.

"Please feel free to stroll around the garden before you go," the waitress said.

"Most don't, but I always think that's a shame. *If* you've got the time that is."

"Thank you. I will."

"There are even real bees." She glanced down at the stroller. "He's not allergic to stings as well, is he?"

How would she know? Bees weren't exactly common. She pulled the waterproof cover over Clay. "Best not to find out," she said.

The waitress nodded but no smile or comment this time, not with the service rendered, tip paid and with a hostess ready to seat the next party; four young men in suits, deep in separate meetings, their glasses on full shade reviewing something while iNet guided their steps. One of them bumped into the stroller. They didn't bother to apologize.

She checked the time. Fleur had committed a tactical error getting so far ahead of schedule, but she couldn't listen to Rawstorm any longer. It was because of people like him that the Autonomy existed in the first place. She would have to linger for twenty minutes under the cover of the garden, out of *Earth's* glare. Everything would be fine.

Fleur pushed Clay in and out of the tables towards the arbour, keeping her gaze fixed straight ahead. It was important not to make eye contact at this stage, important to block out the breathing mass of humanity around her. Just because the cause was just, it didn't mean she was devoid of compassion, and compassion, in an operation like this, was fatal.

As she reached the garden's entrance, someone jostled passed her, almost knocking over the stroller. Fleur's heart skipped a beat. Clay was relatively stable, but if he had hit the ground with any force then . . .

"Can't you be more careful!" she snapped instinctively. Fleur should have said nothing, avoiding potential contact, but it was too late. The girl from the fat man's table stood blinking at her.

"Ex-excuse me," the girl said, her face blotchy and red.

Don't stop, don't say anything, just walk on. "Are you all right?" Fleur said.

"Pardon?" she said, turning back towards her.

"I was sitting at the table next to yours. I heard what he said."

"What are you talking about?" There was an edge to her voice.

"I . . . I wanted to check you were okay, that's all. You look a little upset."

The girl tensed, "Who are you to . . ." she began, but didn't complete the sentence. Instead her shoulders gave a slight shudder. "I-I can't," she said. "I can't stand it here. All my life I worked to get out. To make my parents proud. To reward them for their sacrifice. And now I can't stand it. That man . . . those girls, they're awful. This place is awful."

"I know." Fleur placed a hand on her arm.

Valencia would go crazy if she could see her. The girl was highly strung, unpredictable. Already a couple of heads turned towards them. Tears attracted attention. What if she caused a scene?

She wondered what Valencia would do. Lead her to the centre of the garden and tell her that everything was going to be all right? Tell her to close her eyes and think of home, that soon it wouldn't matter so much?

No, Valencia wouldn't have spoken to her in the first place. "I understand," Fleur said.

"Understand? H-how can you? How can you know what it's like to be a *dirty little twitcher from slumworld*? To be hated just for being here? When the only way to fit in is to become one of . . . you."

"Then get away from here," Fleur said quietly.

"What?"

"Just walk out. Don't let them see you like this. Don't let *him* know that he got to you."

"I can't do that. My job . . ."

Fleur spoke rapidly, squeezing her arm. "Say you're sick, that the food was bad. You don't even have to speak to them. Just a couple of taps on your holopad and you can go home."

The girl hesitated for a moment, and then pulled her arm away. "You're crazy," she said, "Why am I even talking to you?"

"Listen . . ."

"Leave me alone," she said, and headed back towards the diners.

Fleur had tried to save her. Now the girl would die with everyone else. She took a deep breath.

Pretend this is just another sim. Pretend the people around you are just pixels, like they were in the practice program.

As she walked into the garden, she was trembling. Ahead two diners stood by a miniature water feature, staring at something that iNet identified as late blooming azaleas. They were a luscious pink, overshadowed by some browning of the leaves at the tip.

The man held a leaf between thumb and forefinger. "Not as realistic as in VR are they?"

"No, but they have quite the fragrance. Maybe we can order the scent for our sim plates in the apartment."

"Hmm . . ." the man said. He twitched his head to the left and adjusted his ear implant. "I have to take this," he said, and they walked on, the man engrossed in a conversation about a shipment of carapace suits, whatever they were.

Most city gardens were hydroponic, and the plants themselves reedy and thin, conditioned to survive on as little water as possible. This garden was different. Although covering less than a hundred square feet, there were a dozen trees and hundreds of plants all on top of each other, jostling for the sunlight. There was the odour of floating pollen, actual bees fussing around what iNet told her was delphinium, mechanically inspecting the blossoms. In the corner was the hive.

Bees in the wild were rare. Ninety-nine percent of the world's bee population was factory farmed using synthetic soybean and brewer's yeast, and then shipped to other regions to pollinate genetic crops.

Almost nothing grew naturally anymore, the weather patterns too violent to sustain traditional growth cycles. She watched one bee, dragging itself along an abelia bell. Should she touch it? Would the sting really hurt? The bee's pollen sacs looked like a belt of suicide bombs. Fleur pulled away.

She checked the path. Nobody. She checked the time, sixteen minutes to go. The plan required the child to be left unobserved for the time it took Fleur to exit the building. Her intelligence, meticulously collected by operatives over the last six months, suggested that the majority of Esprit's clientele, although attracted to the concept of the garden's existence, didn't typically show enough curiosity to venture in. Different scouts reported less than five people in or out between the times of twelve and one. The lack of foot traffic meant she would be able to bury Clay in the shrubbery, and if she waited until the last minute, the probability of discovery was slim.

She couldn't leave it too late though. Forty pounds of HTC obliterated half of Logistics headquarters, and although Clay was stuffed with only a quarter of that, it would be more than enough to incinerate everything on the roof and two or three floors below. Yes, she shouldn't leave it too long. Fleur had often thought about suicide, but not in public and not today.

At the end of the garden was a love seat and a cluster of dwarf conifers, ideal for the purpose. Should she risk the drop now? The longer she left him, the more chance there was of discovery, but behind the trees he would be almost impossible to spot.

Checking the path again, Fleur unzipped the stroller and unbuckled him. His skin felt cold and rubbery and his leg had begun to twitch with a metronomic urgency. Pulling the khaki hoody over his head, she sat on a stone wall and held him on her knee. In the time test, it took a scout seven minutes to get out of the building, even allowing for the elevator, but she would not cut it that close. She wanted to get away now.

"Be a good boy," she whispered and was about to hide him between two trees when a man in heavily shaded glasses appeared under the arbour.

Shit.

She rocked Clay on her knee as though soothing him, and then quickly pushed him into the stroller and pulled down the flap. The man walked up the path, inspected a couple of the plants, turned and came directly towards her.

"May I sit here?" He pointed to the empty space on the love seat.

"If you don't mind, I'd prefer to be alone. I'm just trying to," she whispered the next words, "put the little one back to sleep." She rocked the stroller back and forth. "He's a devil if he doesn't get his nap."

She checked his identikit. Cy Yozarian, 23 a Tyro from MediaCom, and of all things, a *Faith* missionary to the Cut, spreading the good word beyond the walls of the Autonomy. Fleur wondered how that was even possible. How did one participate in the *Faith* without iNet glasses?

"He's already asleep," the man said and sat next to her, so close their shoulders touched. "I'm on my own too." He smiled.

Surely, this wasn't a come on? Not now, of all times. "I'm married," she said, flustered.

"You think I'm hitting on you?" He laughed. "That would be a bit forward, wouldn't it? Then again, I am a bit forward. Telling savages their suffering will be rewarded in the next world, if only they can resist eating each other in this one, is sort of forward." He paused. "You seem a little on edge?"

Oh shit, oh shit. She had to get rid of him. She had to drop Clay and leave. "No, no, I just want to be left alone."

Surreptitiously, she slipped her hand into the backpack, feeling for the modified anaphylactic gun on top. Five capsules, projectiles good for ten feet, each containing a huge dose of tranquilizer. Enough to fell an elephant, if there were any elephants anymore.

The man didn't move but gave another easy smile. "You know, I finally persuaded my waitress to bring my order to your table, so we could have a little talk. It cost me a few extra credits, but hey? You only live once right? But then you left, before you had even begun your meal. So I followed you in here instead. Do you realise we are the only two people in this place who came to the restaurant alone?"

"Not quite on my own." She glanced at the stroller.

"Oh yes," he said. "I noticed your boy. Cute." He didn't look down, but kept his lenses trained on her.

Twelve minutes.

Feeling for the handle of the gun, she put her finger over the trigger. "Look," she said, trying to keep her voice calm. "I really want to be left alone. I don't want Clay to wake up; he'll make a fuss if he does. So if you don't mind . . ." She nodded down the path.

Instead of moving, the man unshaded his lenses. His grey eyes were like pebbles in ice-cold water. "That little one, make a fuss?" He smiled. "You have no idea what kind of fuss I'm capable of making."

For *Faith*'s sake, he was a nut job! Sweat beaded on her brow. She had to make a move or else go up in flames with everyone else. She took a deep breath.

One, two, three.

Whipping her hand from the stroller, she squeezed the trigger to shoot the gun into his side. Except that when she squeezed, the gun was no longer in her hand and her finger pulled on air. He had reacted faster, much faster, catching her wrist with one hand, relieving her of the gun with the other.

"W-what are you doing?" she stammered. "I'm calling security!"

The man gave a low chuckle and shook his head. "I don't think so," he said. "They might take a closer look at this." He held up the gun. "A modified weapon. You can get put away for that. And once they take a look at this, they might take a closer look at *that*." He gestured to the stroller. "What have we got? Ten minutes before your *boy* explodes into a million pieces? But hey, if you want to call in the squaddies, I'm happy to wait and see. After all, as I tell the savages in the Cut, *the sun shines brightly in the afterlife.*"

Fleur felt the colour drain from her face.

The man unzipped the flap, and peered inside. "He's good, I'll give you that, but I've seen better."

"How . . . how did you know?"

"Out in the Cut, the easiest way for a warring faction to get ahead is to go into the enemy's marketplace and blow the living shit out of the skeletons that happen to be gathered there. Maybe get a couple of hundred in one go, maybe more. It's tough though. Everyone is on the lookout for that kind of thing. You can't just march in with a trolley full of explosives. Those days are long gone. So they use kids; real kids; babies, toddlers, even teens, pump them full of drugs, cut them open, insert whatever they can get hold of, semtex and nails usually, and patch them up again. The price of life eh? Much cheaper than making one of these." He kicked the stroller. Clay lolled back and forth. Fleur felt sick.

"Next time, try a restaurant where there are lots of kids, so you don't stick out so much. And what's wrong with his leg twitching away? Is it attached to the timer or something?"

"Myoclonic twitch."

"Well it's a giveaway, overdone. You want to have a word with your machinist." He smiled again. "So why don't you sit back down," he patted the concrete bench, "and we can talk about what happens next."

Fleur's mind raced. The plan was in pieces. Her only choice was to keep him talking for the next few minutes and . . . and carry out the mission. She would die in public after all. Fear clenched her stomach and the words of the Faith haunted her; *the sun shines brightly in the afterlife* . . . But did it?

"Go on then," she said, trying to control her voice, "What happens next?"

"I'm guessing you've figured out I'm not stationed in Bodia by choice. And

I'm sick of it, of the stink, the flies, of crossing into the Cut each day, not knowing if today is the day I become someone else's dinner. This is my first leave in three years. Tomorrow, Securicom pick me up from my sleeping cube, and I go back for another three years, and then another three years after that until my debt to the Autonomy is cleared. I need a ticket out, and as unlikely as it seems, you're it. You're *Dish*. You live outside of the Autonomy's reach. Wherever that is, I want in. It has to be better than the Cut."

Seven minutes.

He leaned in, "I probably hate these self-satisfied corporate fucks even more than you do."

Not long now. Fleur tried to stop her knees from shaking.

"Look, I know the *Dish*. I have run errands for them from time to time in Bodia," the man continued. "Smuggling guns, people, drugs, currency, whatever's needed, in and out of the Cut. They use me because I'm good at what I do."

"You can't come with me," she said. "They'll shoot you on sight. Me too probably. There are protocols, the screening takes months. It's against every rule we have to . . ."

"Either you take that chance," he interrupted, "or we both go up in flames." The man nodded down the path. "We've got company. You better decide quickly."

To her horror, she saw the fat man waddle under the arbour with the Mansion girls in tow. He was saying something about what a wasted space the garden was, how obsolete the concept. Siranush walked a few steps behind them. Her eyes flicked towards Fleur, then back to the ground.

"Is it a deal?" he whispered.

Fleur nodded. What did it matter? It would all be over soon. Cy Yozarian released her wrist. "How long have we got?"

"About five minutes, six tops."

"To get clear?"

She nodded.

Yozarian's eyes widened, but strangely he didn't seem worried, and in that instant she experienced an unexpected rush of elation. He thought they could still get out alive. She might not have to die.

"Dump the kid," he said and then, without hurrying, walked over to the group.

"Excuse me?" he said to the fat man, cutting him off mid-sentence.

"What?" Rawstorm snapped.

Cy Yozarian raised the modified anaphylactic gun and shot him in the neck. Before anyone could react, he pumped a second capsule into the girl on his left, and a third into the one on his right. All three dropped to the ground, almost without a murmur, the darts drooping from their throats. He pointed the gun at Siranush.

"No!" Fleur shouted.

"What?" he said, not turning around, keeping the gun trained on the girl.

"Not her."

Siranush stood rooted to the spot in terror.

"We haven't got time for this," he said.

"Take her with us, or the deal's off."

For a second he hesitated, then grabbed her arm. "Do exactly as I say, or die. Understand?" The girl, terror-struck, nodded.

Four minutes.

"Let's go then." He ran towards the exit, pulling Siranush behind him. Fleur pushed Clay into the conifers, zipped up the stroller and ran after Yozarian.

In the plan she was supposed to walk casually to the elevator, inconspicuous. Instead a hundred pairs of lenses trained on her as she bolted out of the garden, still pushing the stroller.

Cy Yozarian was already in the elevator, holding it for her. Either they had been lucky or he had summoned it for them with eye control. But when? While calmly taking out the fat man and the girls with the anaphylactic gun? Perhaps Valencia could use him.

The doors closed and all three stood in silence, Siranush shivering uncontrollably, Yozarian with an arm clamped firmly around the girl's wrist. Fleur's iNet confirmed the "L" had already been selected, but despite this, she found herself repeatedly pressing the button on the physical panel.

"Come on, come on, come on," she said under her breath.

"It's been disconnected for twenty years at least," Yozarian said. "It's only for show."

"I know that," she snapped.

How could he be so calm? If the bomb went off before they reached the lobby the fireball would incinerate the elevator cables. As they passed the 6th floor, she heard a loud crack and tensed, realizing a beat later that it was the noise of the ancient shaft, but only because they didn't plummet earthwards. After what seemed like an interminable interval, the car reached the ground floor and the doors opened.

They ran into the lobby. One of the security guards called out in surprise and made a half-hearted attempt to stop them, but Fleur dodged past him and into the street.

The explosion was deafening. The ground shook as a huge fireball mushroomed out over the roof. Abandoning the stroller, Fleur ducked low and kept running. Siranush screamed. Yozarian dragged her along. Nobody at street level paid them any attention, all eyes straining towards the sky, until they too began to scream and run, trying to avoid the debris, some of it human, hitting the pavement all around them.

Don't look at it, Fleur told herself. It's just a sim, just a sim.

She sprinted three blocks and ducked into an alleyway, just wide enough for a single person. The narrow corridor between two buildings was a blind spot, somewhere *Earth* could not see, a hidden part of the city where only the rats came. She removed her glasses, disconnecting from the grid.

Behind her, Cy Yozarian struggled to keep up, dragging the hysterical Siranush. If only Fleur could dump them, go on alone. But now they had seen her, that was impossible, not if she wanted to avoid spending the rest of her life as a *skull*. Better to have been blown up on the roof, better by far.

Up ahead the alley split into four directions. "Right!" She shouted over her shoulder, and heard a muffled shout from Yozarian in return. She pressed on, not waiting. They would catch up. Rounding the final corner, she collapsed against the wall, heaving for breath. Her face was wet and she realised she had been crying. *All those people*, she thought, struggling to control her emotions.

"There you are," Cy Yozarian said, appearing beside her, making her jump. "Anyone would think you were trying to lose me." He was hardly out of breath. Whatever else he did in the Cut, he kept himself fit.

She ran a hand across her face, hoping he didn't notice the tears. "I said run, we ran. I knew you'd keep up." She looked over his shoulder. No Siranush. "What happened?" she said, panicking.

"She slipped out of my grip, ran back the way we came. I had to make a choice. You or her. I picked you."

"But her iNet! She will have us on iNet!"

The man said nothing but opened his palm. "Siranush's lenses. I took them before she fled."

"But she knows our names," Fleur said.

"Does she? Does anyone *remember* names anymore? Without iNet, I doubt she could name her colleagues, let alone two strangers she just met. And who knows if she'll even come forward. She seems the scared type to me. Getting out alive, there's a chance she'll become a suspect, especially as an Aspirant. She won't risk that. Besides, bringing her was your choice, not mine. I would have let her fry."

Fleur became aware of the copters overhead and the scream of sirens. She had to get to safety. The whole place would be teeming with squaddies soon. It wouldn't take them long before they searched the alleyways.

"Remember, I can't guarantee your safety."

"Nobody can," he replied, with the same, easy, arrogant smile.

"All right then," she said. "Take off your glasses and give them to me. The girl's too."

He did not move. She understood his hesitation. Losing iNet was like being cast into the darkness, the entire world, snapped off like a light.

"If you plan on going any further, you have to. We live off the grid. How else do you think we stay hidden?"

"But . . ."

"Give," she said and held out her hand. He sighed and removed his iNet, passing both pairs of glasses to her.

"Now take a couple of steps back," she said.

"Why?"

"Just do it."

He backed up against the wall.

Fleur took her glasses and other two pairs, snapped them across the bridge and dropped them into the storm drain. Then she pulled the grate to one side. It had already been loosened, some hours before.

Fleur slipped off her high heels and pulled off her dress, pushing both into the hole, where they disappeared into the water. Underneath she wore only a bikini. She nodded to the hole. "I would strip down if I were you. The less encumbered you are, the better."

She dropped into the darkness.

ョ

ASCO WALKED DOWN the gleaming corridor clutching his copy of "The Still Point", a book his father had loved about a doomed explorer, back when there were still places to explore, when mankind didn't crawl over every inch of a shrinking planet.

Of course nobody wrote novels anymore, there was not enough demand. Words were commands for navigating iNet, nothing more. The sims, rather than works of fiction, evoked the modern human spirit. Why read about the great struggles of character when you could climb inside a virtual protagonist and actually live their life?

I don't believe in books baby, They ain't got your looks baby.
Without action, there's no reaction But maybe I'm a fool.

Dillon Vrain's lyrics, in a song he dedicated to his favourite Pleasure House sim, summed up the Autonomy's attitude to literature. Perhaps Pasco *was* a fool, but the small square brick of yellowing pages meant a lot to him.

Usually he kept the book displayed in a glass case in his apartment, together with his other antiques; two more novels, his father's watch and Professor Hakim's ancient tablet computer, bequeathed by his mentor on Pasco's graduation.

The tablet was not functional, of course. Anything that had the capacity to create a network outside of iNet had long been illegal. Under the updated rogue guidelines, even this broken device should probably be relinquished to Securicom, but the quaint example of bulky, pre-lens technology was an interesting artefact. Pasco was too attached to it to let it go.

Two scientists passed him in the corridor and he nodded hello. In return, they flashed standardized greetings to his iNet. The Securicom installation was so secret that all discussion was discouraged, even within its walls.

He reached the unmarked door and waited for the system to confirm his identity. The reinforced steel swished open and he stepped into the white, aseptic room.

She lay there, tiny and pale, wires protruding from her head, a breathing mask over her nose and a drip on her finger. He glanced at her readings; heart rate, breathing, brain activity, muscle atrophy, joules per hour, hydration, thyroid and liver function.

To the room he said, "Pasco Eborgersen checking in. Subject, no change."

He pulled up a stool and sat next to the bed. There were other checks to perform but he would put off the prodding and probing until later. Removing his glasses, he thumbed through the well-worn pages, looking for where they left off last time.

He cleared his throat. "It is possible that here, now in the garden, in the green, she is as lovely as she will ever be. The sun falls thick around her, lighting up golden the laburnum she lies under . . ."

He could have read the same words in one of iNet's digital libraries, but the physical turning of the page, the ritual of the paper, had become important to him, and deep down, he hoped, to her.

"There are fruit trees in the garden, there are dark cherries ripening in the heat, sweetness, fullness, leaves hot and glossy; there are tiny flowers dense as stars, pale blue, there are tall stems, violet, pink and cream, heart's-ease and phlox, gentle lupin, tall hollyhocks . . ."

Did any such garden exist anymore, here in this cementland? He doubted it, but that wasn't important. He chose these passages for their redolent imagery, a promise of life that might bring her back.

He read on, paragraph after paragraph, trying to imbue each word, each turn of phrase, with the emotion he felt for her.

Half an hour later, Pasco put down the book and checked her vitals. No change. Every day was the same. His entire relationship with Balmoral characterized by words from him, stillness from her.

"You have no idea how much better you look," he said, stroking back her hair. "The bruises are long gone. The thirty-two fractures, all healed. You have a few scars here and there, but physically you are almost whole again."

It took a thirty-six hour operation to save her. At one point the surgeons had to scoop out her intestines and rest them on her stomach while they worked on the internal bleeding. Her heart stopped twice, but each time she came back.

The hospital bed undulated. It did that every ten minutes or so, sometimes quite violently, sometimes imperceptibly, keeping her artificially in motion and preventing the inevitable bedsores.

"Physically whole but still . . . silent. The doctors say it's time. If you were going to regain consciousness, you would have done so by now. Tomorrow they turn off the machines." He choked on the last word.

She had only been kept alive this long to satisfy the Chairman's paranoia.

Maglan needed to know what made the girl tick, and to that end they had spent over six months performing an in-depth analysis of her brain using the latest iAm technology.

The final report was hundreds of pages, but when Pasco presented the results, all Maglan wanted was the answer to a single question. How did she do it?

Last week Pasco had told him.

"As an infant the subject sustained a massive trauma to the right hemisphere of the brain resulting in an over-compensation by the left. Five times the usual count of glial cells and extensive connections proliferate across the cerebrum in that region. The right side is limited in comparison, emotionally the subject is off the spectrum. *Voice's* analysis suggests that only the subject's over-developed reasoning has enabled her to *fake* functional behaviour all these years."

"So what you are telling me is that this *Dish* cyber is a one off," Maglan said.

"We never managed to prove she is *Dish* . . ." Bruno Mandrax said.

"She murdered my son," Maglan cut in, "along with a thousand other children of prominent Autonomy citizens. We don't need a smoking gun to tell us who she was working for. The *Dish* recruits cybers from the cradle, training them to think in code before they can talk. What I want to know is whether another such weapon can be cultivated."

Pasco explained that to 'cultivate' another Balmoral the *Dish* would have to crush someone's head in the hope that a savant-like cell cluster formed, enabling a level of reasoning unobtainable through any other means. The nature of the accident was a thousand to one. That she wasn't left a vegetable, a million to one.

"She's just a freak," Maglan said, "and with the research complete, we can turn off the machines and finally close the book on Rhodes."

"But there is more we can learn. If I had more time I could . . ."

"No. It's been long enough. I have what I need. Do whatever you need to shut down the project, then it's lights out."

Pasco said he needed three weeks to 'shut down' the project. Maglan gave him one.

Pulling his mind back to the present, Pasco studied the inert form in front of him. There were small discoveries he had omitted from the final report. In recent weeks he had detected certain variations in the EKG suggesting brain activity, patterns in the delta and gamma waves typical of returning cognisance.

He kept these findings to himself. Pasco knew that despite his uncle's legendary pragmatism, the last thing he wanted to hear was that the girl might revive.

However, the intrigues had been for nothing. In under twenty-four hours, Balmoral would be dead.

Pasco increased the volume of the music. He couldn't risk *Earth* picking up his voice if anyone was watching.

"I know you have remorse for what you did," he said quietly, taking her hand. "Were you tricked into it?"

Pasco traced his finger over her palm. First he made the letter "B", then he paused, and drew a capital "A" and then an "L". He continued until he spelt out "Balmoral."

Pasco reasoned that if she was in there at all, she could feel and understand this primitive signing, even if she was deaf, or blind or a lock-in. He had patiently developed this mode of hand writing every day for six months, each day introducing a new word, until he wrote in complete sentences.

"Balmoral, do not be afraid. Give me a sign if you can hear me. I am here to help. My name is Pasco."

He wrote it again, and thought of how tomorrow, her lungs would stop their gentle, artificially stimulated up and down motion. His only comfort was that if she was a lock in, conscious inside a body that no longer physically functioned, then dying would be a mercy.

He wrote the phrase a third time. Still nothing. He gave her hand a small squeeze. "I understand why you don't trust me," he said, unable to keep his voice from shaking. "Why you don't trust any of us, but for *Faith's* sake, if you can hear me, give me a sign."

FIRST THERE WAS the void, a darkness in which nothing stirred. Then, slowly, a sense of self returned, and the darkness changed its nature. Now, instead of nothing, it was everything, enveloping her, drowning her.

A word flashed in front of her mind, then another word and another. Words that she recognized. Somehow she could see them, feel them, someone wrote them on her hand.

His name was Pasco. He was here to help.

She did not reply, could not reply. He was too far away and she was under too deep, unable to move, unable to find her way to the surface. This person, this Pasco, knew she was in here but could not reach her, and she could not reach him. But she could think and sometimes even hear. She grasped onto each word pressed onto her palm, every letter precious.

Occasionally she experienced flashes of light as though something behind her eyelids was waking up. She was in a hospital ward. She had been here for months. She was a prisoner.

The man was always there. He said he was her friend. Or was it an act? Did it matter? If it wasn't for *Pasco* there would be only the darkness. Only his touch kept her from sinking deeper and deeper into the abyss.

She felt something else, something on the periphery of her mind, reaching out, probing, insidious. They had put something in her head!

From deep within the void, she screamed.

Get it out! Get it out! Get it out!

iAm was inside her.

It was worse than the rape.

Her mind was her most intimate organ, iAm a permanent violation. She touched the device with a thought and then gingerly backed away. If she activated iAm, it would automatically begin to interact with her neurons. Images that previously she saw on her iNet lenses, she would now 'see' in her mind's eye. Thoughts, not keystrokes, commanded the interface, and a sensation experienced through iNet would be felt by her body.

Did that mean they could now control her?

Or could she find a way to control *it*?

So many questions. No answers.

She focused again on her surroundings. The darkness had become a drab grey. She could hear his voice. More soothing words.

The darkness washed over her again, undulating like waves. She recognized it now as moving in and out of consciousness, like slipping under water in a vast, black pool.

But wait. What was the last thing he said?

Tomorrow they would turn off the machines.

Even in the darkness she was sentient enough to know time had run out. She had to pull herself out of the water, to function again, to breathe, to move, or else . . . or else she would drown and the thing in her brain would take over the world. She could not let that happen.

Balmoral could feel him, squeezing her hand. She didn't trust him, but logic told her she had no other choice. Gently, very gently, she squeezed back.

4

SECTOR 1, MANSION SUBTERRANEA

IN THE SEWER, the filth was always there, the run-off from a hundred million people. Rats nibbled her ankles, the only other mammals to thrive and pullulate when the world fell apart. Atmos handled an incredible volume of Mansion's waste, pumping it out to sea or into Agri-lands, but no matter how many waterless systems and deep pipe filtration trenches were laid, these ancient tunnels still carried more than their fair share.

"Where are we going?" Cy Yozarian asked.

"Just follow me."

"I can't see anything."

"Then you'd better stay close."

It was dark, but Fleur's eyes had adjusted to the tunnels long ago. It had become her element. They had about a mile to cover, waste high in watery effluvia. She hardly noticed the stench any more. If there was one thing she had learned in the tunnels, it was that humans could adapt to almost anything.

They waded on for about an hour, navigating the labyrinth of oversized pipes, tracing the path she had memorized.

"The *Dish* is down here?" he said.

"Our cell is."

"But why?"

"Why do you think? Where else are there no *Earth* cameras? Where else can we truly hide?"

"But it would only take Securicom to track one of you and they could flood the tunnels with agents."

"These tunnels stretch for miles, on multiple levels. It's too far underground for iNet connectivity, so they wouldn't be able to communicate with each other.

And Securicom are not good at low tech operations. They're too addicted to their toys. Do they even have tracking dogs anymore? And even if they did, would they be able to scent anything in here?"

"Enough bodies, enough time, they could find anything."

"Perhaps. But we have another advantage."

"What?"

"Some tunnels are invisible."

"I don't understand."

"You're not supposed to."

They trekked on through the darkness, until finally she saw the flashlight ahead. Fleur had spent hours on tunnel mnemonics in order to navigate the main underground passages, but if Clay Vorm wasn't waiting there, she would be lost forever. Usually a welcome sight, she was filled with trepidation. Bringing in Cy Yozarian broke every rule in the Bedouin's book.

The screening process for a new recruit took many months. Valencia ensured it was meticulous. One mole, and they would be done for. Even if the asset was considered safe, joining the *Dish* was a lifelong commitment, with no retirement other than the permanent kind. It was too risky to let anyone leave. For that reason, screening was more about psychological resilience than how committed an individual was to the cause. Many of those who hated the Autonomy wanted to join the *Dish* without having any concept of the hardship and sacrifice that implied. A life that was no life, where simple human aspirations, like building a family or having a home, became impossible dreams.

Hadn't Fleur been such a recruit herself? If she could go back to being that fifteen-year-old girl, she would run a mile when Valencia sat down next to her in the school cafeteria, and began to whisper about another way, a different future if only they were prepared to fight for it, one where life was not a unit of production.

"Who the fuck is he?" Clay Vorm said, shining the flashlight first in her face, then in Yozarian's, keeping the beam trained on his eyes. His huge, dark form rippled in the half light.

Fleur used the one line that might save his life. "He helped me carry out the attack."

"You know the rules." In his hand, he held a printed Glock.

"He works for the *Dish* in Bodia," she half-lied.

"Then what's he doing here?" Clay made a small hand gesture and as he did so, someone stepped out of the shadows and cracked Yozarian on the back of the skull. He crumpled to the ground, his head sinking under the filthy water. The man, who she now recognized as Manaus, yanked him up and leant him against the tunnel wall.

"You didn't have to do that!"

"You're lucky I hit with a butt, not a bullet," Manaus said.

"I told you, he helped me."

"So you thought it would be all right to bring him here?" Clay snapped. "The Bedouin is not a social club for anyone you happen to take a shine to."

"You think I don't know that! I've been in these tunnels for a third of my life!"

"That won't stop Valencia taking his head, yours too probably. What the hell happened back there?"

Fleur recounted what happened in the restaurant, making it sound like a coincidence that Yozarian was in the garden when she needed help to plant the bomb and get out, rather than telling the truth; that he was the cause of her delay, that he had been watching her from the first.

"The mission would have failed without him, Clay. And besides he was a witness. I couldn't just let him go. It's safer to have him here."

"But you know nothing about him. What if he's a squaddie, deep under cover?"

"He shot three citizens, one an ex-President. Does that sound like Securicom to you? He's a *transvict*, assigned to the Cut for *Faith's* sake. He hates the Autonomy. He runs missions for the *Dish* down there."

"That's what he told you," Manaus said.

Fleur sighed. "He helped me."

"Just get in," Clay said. "I'll bring your boyfriend. Valencia will decide what to do with him."

Fleur pushed past Clay, and through the hole in the wall. Nobody but Bedouin were permitted to see the way to the staging area. Behind her, Manaus got to work with the bricks and mortar, rebuilding the tunnel exterior with the same ancient stone they had dislodged. After the wall had set, it would be as if the hole had never existed.

Clay trudged after her, speaking to Valencia on a crackly short-wave headset, breathing heavily with the weight of Yozarian over his shoulder. She couldn't make out his words above the splashing of their steps. At least they were no longer in the filth of the main tunnels, but the connecting passageways were still four or five inches deep in brackish water.

Ten minutes, and half a dozen turns later, Clay told her to wait. He shone the light along the wall until he located the staging door. Dumping Yozarian on the ground, he pulled a garbage bag from the back pocket of his filthy shorts and handed it to her. He flicked out a clasp knife and cut away Yozarian's clothes, performing a cursory search as he did so.

"What the fuck's this?" he said, holding up something long and thin.

A sudden wave of panic washed over her. "Where was it?"

"Hidden inside his boot. If it's a tracker . . ."

"Give it to me." She held the device towards the light. There was writing and she could just about make out the lettering. She shook it, examined it, and laughed with relief.

"What?" Clay said.

"It's a huge adrenalin shot. He must be very allergic to something."

"Shit," Clay whistled.

She grinned. "Unlikely. But down here, if he is, a single shot ain't going to be enough."

"Get rid of it," Clay said stonily.

Together with Yozarian's clothes, she stuffed the adrenalin shot into the plastic garbage bag, before stripping herself. Clay's eyes strayed to her naked figure, but did not linger. She wondered how much of this was self-control and how much a simple lack of interest. Clay only had eyes for Valencia, always had.

"You can drag him in from here," Clay said.

"Aren't you coming?"

"Not yet," he said. "Thanks to your friend, Valencia wants me to check the feeder tunnels before we close the wall."

"Nobody followed us, Clay!"

"No doubt, but I'm checking them anyway." He nodded to the keypad, "You remember the combination?"

"Of course."

"Then I'll see you on the flip side."

"Fine."

"Hey," he said quietly, his eyes focused on a spot above her head.

"What?"

"I'm glad you made it home." Without waiting for a reply, he turned and walked back down the tunnel.

Fleur sighed, and glanced down at the naked form of Cy Yozarian. Even in the dim light, she didn't need a biosquare to tell her he was in good shape. He was all muscle, without an ounce of fat on his tall frame.

She punched in the combination and the mechanical lock snapped back. With the heel of one foot she pushed open the heavy storm door and dragged Cy Yozarian along the ground, a hand under each armpit, cursing Clay for leaving her with this dead weight. With a final heave she pulled him through.

The door swished shut behind her, a rubber flap at its base sealing the entranceway. The staging area was relatively clean and dry, but mould and mildew blackened the ceiling. The floor angled towards an open drain in the corner into which she dropped the garbage bag. On one side of the wall there was a porthole and a naked light bulb filled the room with a dull glare.

"What shall I do with him?" Fleur said, speaking to nobody, but knowing they were listening.

A voice crackled out from a tiny recessed speaker. "Lean him back against the wall, arms and legs apart."

Fleur did as she was told, self-conscious now to be touching this naked man while others looked on. His head flopped to one side, still out cold. She stood up and prepared herself, cupping her hands over her breasts. You never forgot which bit hurt the most.

"Engage," the voice crackled.

The jet of freezing cold water smashed into her, beginning at her feet and working its way up her body. It pounded her teeth, pushed her eyes to the back of her skull, until finally it reached the top of her head.

"Other side," the voice said.

Fleur turned around and the water slammed into her back, then her buttocks and down her legs. Her eyes stung with chlorine, despite keeping them closed. By the time the jet reached her feet, the grime from the sewer had washed away into the drain, and she stood, chattering with cold, aching all over.

At the far end of the room, there were bins with towels and clothes. She pulled out two towels, wrapping one around her body, the other around her hair.

The jet arced towards Cy Yozarian, hitting him straight in the chest. He stirred, and then suddenly was on his feet, thrashing around, trying to get out of the water cannon's fire, but wherever he moved, the jet followed him, thrusting him back against the wall. They increased the pressure and twice he nearly lost his footing, but managed to brace himself.

"Stand still," the voice crackled.

Yozarian did as he was told, and the spray worked up and down his body, pounding away on both sides until it abruptly shut off. As the dirt came away, she noticed the scars on his arms, his back and chest. He looked like a maul from major league Steel Ball.

Dripping wet, Yozarian rubbed the back of his head. "Was that absolutely necessary?"

"Which part?" Fleur said, throwing him a towel.

"All of it," he said and unselfconsciously began to dry himself.

"I warned you."

"You said they would kill me, not torture me."

"The passageways to here are secret."

"Then maybe use a blindfold next time. And a water cannon? What the fuck is that?"

"Sewerage. A serious dysentery outbreak could wipe us out. That's why we have this staging area," she gestured to the hole in the ground, "with a fire hose that washes everything down the drain."

"Wouldn't a hot shower be more civilized?"

But that wouldn't get rid of the other bugs, she thought. At ten litres of water per second any electronic devices a visitor might be carrying, even those grafted onto the skin, would be exposed like a winkle without a shell.

In the early days of the *Dish,* an entire cell was taken down when an agent infiltrated their ranks. He had been searched multiple times and his lenses confiscated, but they didn't notice the wart on his toe, a rogue embedded under the skin which he used to call in Securicom.

The result was the annihilation of that group and four other *Dish* cells they were in regular contact with. The Bedouin were safe only because Valencia was so paranoid. She kept their location secret, even from other *Dish.* Shortly afterwards, she installed the fire hoses.

"You're not in Mansion now," Fleur said. "These hoses are our way of keeping the sand out of a beach house. Except instead of sand, it's shit."

"You go to beach houses a lot, do you?"

"Only in the sims."

Rubbing down his legs, he said, with a hint of a smile, "What are we supposed to do now, make out?"

"Finish getting dry. Your clothes are over there."

5

A S HE TOWELLED himself down, Tristram fought to control his excitement. He was on the inside, finally, and now those responsible for his father's death would pay the price, even if it meant killing the whole lot of them. And afterwards? If he survived? He would be free. Free to begin a new life, no longer eaten up with killing and vengeance.

His uncle would understand the thousand or so lives at the restaurant. They were collateral damage, the cost of his ticket to the Bedouin. Besides, there was nothing he could do. By the time he identified the risk, it was too late. If he had hurled the baby-bomb off the roof, it would have caused even more damage at ground level. Warning the diners would have triggered a stampede, and Tristram, together with the opportunity to bring down the Bedouin, would have died along with everyone else.

That's what his report would say and perhaps his uncle would even buy it. If Tristram managed to destroy the Bedouin, that was justification enough. The Chairman understood the trade-offs in this never-ending war. What were a thousand lives now, for who knew how many thousands in the future? It was the price of security.

They dressed in silence. The clothes were a little tight, but everything fitted, even the shoes, which meant that either Clay had radioed in very good instructions on his way back to the wall, or they had cameras in the interior tunnels powerful enough to cut through the gloom and size him up. Either way, the clothes were a good sign. If they were going to shoot him on sight, why bother to dress him? He was pleased about the boots too, they were strong and comfortable and in any military operation, the boots were the most important thing.

He rubbed the naked patch under his wrist. The cannon had stripped off his little pill of death. It didn't matter. This was going to be a bloodbath, not an assassination. Inwardly he smiled at the technological delousing. They had no idea there were other things buried too deep to wash away.

Fleur knocked on the steel door. Gears ground and locks pulled back.

"Stay close," Fleur said and stepped onto a raised gangway that ran for about three hundred feet across a network of pipes.

Tristram took a step and let his leg buckle, feigning the after-effects of concussion. Although he could see nobody, he knew they were watching, and the more shaken up he appeared, the better. They might go easier on him later.

"Are you all right?" Fleur said.

Grimacing, he rubbed the back of his head and gingerly straightened up. "I'll be okay."

In reality, the blow had dazed him, but nothing more. Tristram had noticed the person in the shadows and could have dodged out of the way. Instead he waited for him to swing, moving at the last instant so the butt glanced off his head. Flopping to the ground, he played possum, even to the extent of letting his head go into the sewerage. As Clay carried him, he concentrated on the route from the exterior wall to the staging area. He might need it later.

"Take my hand," Fleur said and helped him along.

To his left he noticed small gun turrets above the gangway. If Securicom came in this way they could do so only in single file, the guns cutting them down, creating a barrier of bodies. A dozen Bedouin could hold off hundreds, at least until the guns were immobilized. There must be another entrance, though. This process was too time intensive and messy for day to day operations in Mansion. Fleur had turned up looking immaculate at the restaurant, so the Bedouin must have a way out that didn't include wading through someone else's shit.

"Is this the only way in?" he said casually.

"No questions," she replied, but gave his hand a gentle squeeze.

Tristram knew she liked him. He would find a way to use that later. Perhaps when he had won her trust, she would lead him to his father's killers. He would have to be careful, though. To underestimate her might be fatal. She hardly blinked when a thousand executives turned into one big fireball. On the other hand, she had weaknesses. The Aspirant girl for example. It was a shame he had to break her neck.

At the end of the gangway was another steel door. Fleur dropped placed her palm on a smooth section of the wall. It lit up, acknowledging her prints, and again the locks whirred. He hadn't seen that type of technology before, something that identified the individual without iNet.

"Pretty neat," he said.

"Print recognition software. It's an older technology that Orlick rigged up."

"Orlick?"

"Our resident tech, a defected Elite from TechCom. He saw what the Autonomy was doing with *Voice*, and came over to our side."

Tristram studied the pad. "Impressive."

"Yes, he is. Difficult bugger though."

The door swung inwards and a old woman stood beaming at them. She had dishevelled, curly grey hair and eyes which protruded from their sockets. Beneath her right eye was a large black tattoo of a skull.

She flung her arms around Fleur, hugging her. "My dear Flower," she said. "I'm so glad you're safe."

"This is Cy Yozarian," Fleur said. "Cy Yozarian, Lotus."

"Ah yes, the stranger. The Garde have their panties in a twist about you!" She prodded Tristram in the stomach.

"I had no choice," Fleur said.

"It's not me you have to convince, dear." Turning to Tristram she added, "I hope the clothes fit. I raided the lockers, so don't be too surprised if someone accuses you of stealing their clothes, because you probably did. My advice is to deny everything, unless you want to lose a couple of teeth. You're a big one though. You look like you can handle yourself when it comes to knuckling."

Tristram said nothing but gave a small smile. He didn't like the way she looked at him, that left eye, practically popping out of her head like some demented house servant from an old horror movie. He wasn't fooled. She was neither as dumb nor as wacky as she pretended. She had been sent to check him out, an advance guard, which meant they relied on her judgment. The eccentricity was an act, albeit a permanent one.

"Well anyway," she smiled, "welcome to the Bedouin, home of freaks and fetishes!" Cackling, she put an arm through Fleur's and led them down a tunnel lit by small lamps on either side. "I've always wanted to say that."

She paused by a lamp that had gone out and replaced the spent bulb with another that she pulled from one of the many bulges in her battered trench coat. "The mission went well," she said screwing it in.

"I think so," Fleur replied.

"It wasn't a question dear. It's all over the Media. The in-laws are tripping over themselves to send us their congratulations." She blew the dust off the lamp's glass covering. "There, that should be good for another couple of years."

"In-laws?" Tristram said.

"Other *Dish* cells from Izbat to Mong," Lotus said. "We're one big happy family, you know. Mostly. How else can the revolution begin if we're not all united, eh?"

It stood to reason that the *Dish* would be connected, that they had the means to communicate with cells despite their secrecy, but he did not expect the Bedouin to have a direct line into Sector 2 and 3.

How did they do it?

Any communication on iNet, no matter how well encrypted, would eventually be intercepted by *Voice*, so they had to have a proxy.

Suddenly his cover seemed a lot less convincing. If the Bedouin reached out to the cell in Bodia it would take about five minutes to confirm they had never heard of *Cy Yozarian*.

They reached the end of the tunnel. "Here we are," she said to Tristram. "Act impressed when you walk in. The common room is our pride and joy. It took years to carve out of the rock. It's where we go when we're not sleeping, shitting or working. The quarters you see are . . . well, a little small."

"So is this it?" Tristram said. "I'm in?"

"Oh no. You're not in until her majesty says you're in, so don't get too attached to your . . . life. Who knows what she has planned for you? I can't say. At the very least, you're going to have to meet with Beaky."

"Beaky?"

"All in good time, my dear." She pushed open the double doors to the common room.

6

T HE COMMON ROOM was packed. That was unusual for an afternoon, but this was an unusual day. Practically everyone not on an active mission was there to welcome her back. No Orlick, because he never left his cell, and no Valencia, because despite risking her life for the cause, and despite the success of the mission, Fleur was in disgrace.

Cheers and a *Dish* victory song broke out across the room as she entered, the words echoing off the walls like a psalm.

Through years of oppression we will prevail,
A beacon of hope, we will not fail.

The Bedouin came towards her, hands out, chanting the verses enthusiastically, each embracing her, then kissing her forehead in a ritualistic gesture of welcome.

Fleur found the tradition unsettling. It was superstitious, as though the Bedouin looked backwards for an identity, rather than ahead, more like a religious sect than free thinking individuals.

"Drink?" Lotus said, when the singing finally died down. She handed Fleur and Yozarian a bottle from the bar.

Fleur gulped down the tepid liquid, realizing only then how thirsty she was. It was one of Lotus' own concoctions; an energy drink, laced with electrolytes, vitamins and a few shots of caffeine. Fleur could have died for something stronger, an ice-cold beer for example, but there was never any alcohol before the evening, no matter what the occasion. Underground, it was too easy to form a habit, to drown out the damp, the chill and the boredom, things Cy Yozarian would learn, assuming he was allowed to join.

She imagined what it must look like to his uninitiated eyes, this cave in which they lived. The great fireplace, the shaggy rugs around it, where people sat and even slept when they'd had too much to drink. The Bedouin themselves, some of whom, like Lotus, never left the confines of the tunnel and went slowly mad as a result. Freaks and fetishes indeed. The huge, lifelike portrait of Maglan Eborgersen on the wall, Valencia's constant reminder of the face of the enemy, so that even in this room, they could never truly relax.

Fleur shuddered as she stared into the Chairman's unblinking eyes. Beneath the portrait, two dozen stars were etched into the concrete, representing their fallen soldiers, surprisingly few for the risks they took. Twice as many had died in the flu epidemic that swept through the tunnels eight years ago.

The ceremony over, all but a handful of the Bedouin filed out of the common room and back to their duties. There were always systems to hack, weapons to make, tunnels to drain, meals to cook or operations to plan. Tonight there would be a feast, but until then there was work to do.

Two Garde in their black and grey uniforms approached Cy Yozarian, shock guns raised, motioning him out of the common room. Yozarian raised his eyebrows at Fleur.

"They are just taking you to one of the detention cells," she said. "Until you can be checked out."

Or at least that's what I hope.

Yozarian didn't move. One of the Garde flicked on his weapon. Yozarian stared at it defiantly, as if to say, you'll need more than that. But then glancing at Fleur again, he shrugged and followed them out of the room.

"He seems like a stubborn one," a harsh voice said from behind her. "Beaky will have fun with him."

Fleur said nothing, her heart sinking as Tamar Lord, with his greasy overalls and oil slick sideburns, swaggered up to her.

Gesturing to the almost empty common room he said, "I made the boy. How come everyone didn't sing praises to me? Bestow kisses on me?" He pouted in a mock expression of hurt. "It's all right though, I'll accept a little love from you, on behalf of everyone else."

She tensed.

"Come on . . . what's the matter? Only got eyes for your new boyfriend? I saw the way you looked at him." He bent his mean lips in a smile that was no smile.

"Don't be a child," she said, trying to hide her irritation.

"Oooh!" he said in a high pitched voice. His eyes were glassy. Was he drunk? Lord had a way of avoiding the rules everyone else had to follow. "If I were you, I wouldn't get too attached. The smart money's on him not getting past Beaky. We already ran a sweepstake. I said he'd be belly up in the sewer by night fall. I can almost feel the rolls jangling in my pocket."

Quarters, the old currency salvaged from Mansion, were the trading chips of the tunnels. More coveted still were complete rolls, still in their banker's paper, worth more than their constituent parts.

"Come on," Lord said. "Just one little hug. I won't cop a feel." He smiled and ran a hand through his slicked back hair. Like Lotus, he had a skull tattoo under his eye, but unlike hers it stretched over his taut face, moving as he spoke, a laughing death's head.

Fleur hesitated, and then put her arms around him. Easier that way. The quicker to get rid of him.

He held her tight. "Do you know the tally yet?" he whispered.

"No," she said, conscious of his hot, stale breath.

"Almost thirteen hundred. A third of them Elites!"

"Only a third?"

Did the rest really deserve to die? The waitresses, the Tyros, the newly promoted Aspirants? *They are part of the system*, she told herself, but the words sounded hollow, even in her mind.

"There are another two hundred in intensive care!"

The glee in his voice sickened her. She pulled away. Despite his earlier promise, he gave her bum a squeeze before letting go.

Lord constantly hit on her and she always refused him, except once, when she became so depressed and so lonely, that she needed the touch of another body, any body, to remind her she was still human.

They had been working into the night on the model Clay and it just happened. He wasn't bad looking after all, especially after she had drunk a few shots from his hip flask, and despite being a skull, he kept in what he called fighting shape.

Sleeping with him was a mistake and Fleur made her feelings clear the next day. She had drunk too much and got carried away, that was all.

Despite this, Lord still treated her as though they were about to pick up from where they left off on that sweaty, regret-filled night. She swore to herself that would not happen, no matter how lonely she became.

Lord was a psychopath. A few months ago he killed a man, Dimaro, in a bar fight. He should have hanged, except the witnesses testified it was an accident; one unlucky punch. Nobody drew attention to the thick signet rings he wore on his fingers.

Fleur glanced at his murderous fists now. It amazed her how the big hands were capable of such dexterity and invention. He designed flawless templates for the 3D printers, and modified the machines if they couldn't handle the specs. Nobody else in the Bedouin had that sort of talent.

"Tell me," Lord asked, his eyes glinting, "How was my boy, eh? How was baby Clay?"

It took a year of development, often working sixteen hours a day, seven days a week, each part meticulously designed on a 3-D printer. So much love had gone into this artefact of death.

Lord christened the boy Clay junior because the internal design was that of a claymore, but as soon as the name was conceived, he referred to the model as "Fleur's love child", making fun of the man he knew she wanted, but could never have.

"It worked."

"What about the *saris*? Did you tell building security he had *saris*?"

"I didn't need to. They could see the bag."

"Good, good," Lord said. "The bag was the perfect diversion, something to search while the sickly baby sleeps on. Genius, even if I do say so myself." He seemed to forget *saris* was Fleur's idea.

"His leg moved around too much. It looked fake."

A flash of anger shot through Lord's face and his skull leered at her. "What?"

"That's how Cy Yozarian knew, that's how he found me."

For a moment Lord struggled with his anger. Criticism of any kind was an affront to his bloated self-esteem. "Too much myoclonic," he said between his teeth. "I'll be sure to bear that in mind for Clay mark II."

"Another one? Already?"

"The mould is already complete. This one will be obese, with enough in its belly to blow up a tower block!"

Lord's excitement at the prospect of more death turned Fleur's stomach. At times she wondered whether he even believed in the cause, or whether it was the killing that drove him on.

"Valencia's targeting Sky Dome. She's been covertly working on it for over a year. Word is we've already got people on the inside. Could be as soon as next month. It will be the biggest statement the *Dish* has ever made!"

The Sky Dome, Mansion's home of Steel Ball. Capacity, a hundred and sixty thousand. "I'll look forward to seeing it," Fleur said flatly. "Although of course, it won't be me nursing your precious cargo this time. I'm out for three months."

"Three months?" Lord said, as though he didn't understand, his tattoo grinning manically.

Typical skull. No concept of time, or indeed anything outside of the dim tunnels. "I've just completed a major operation, I can't go back to Mansion until after the cool off period."

"*Cool off period*, of course," Lord joined his tattoo in the grin. For some reason his hilarity unnerved her.

Clay entered the common room, freshly scrubbed from the staging tunnel.

"Time to go," Lord said, and headed out of the common room.

Clay waited until he had gone. "You need to come with me," he said.

Fleur had been expecting this. She had been summoned. There would be a rap on the knuckles from Valencia, a bit of shouting and screaming, but Val would come around. The mission had been a success, after all.

She followed Clay out of the double doors, but to her surprise he led her away from Valencia's quarters.

"I thought . . ." she began.

"I'm taking you to Lotus," Clay said gravely.

"Lotus?" An icy sensation washed over her. "Y-you can't be serious."

"Valencia gave the word."

Tears came to her eyes. "I wasn't . . . I can't . . ."

"I'm sorry, Fleur." There was a note of compassion in Clay's voice, but his arm was already locked around hers. She walked in a daze as he guided her down a small side tunnel.

Only skulls ventured in and out of this dank section. Not even Garde came here. Clay was the one exception. He performed the role of conduit from one world to the next, like the boatman who guided dead souls across some mythical river, except that he required no gold for his fare. He did it because Valencia told him to.

They walked along the dimly lit tunnel, until they reached a black line beyond which no lights illuminated the way. Lotus greeted them, and Clay, in a formal gesture, handed her over.

The room at the end of the tunnel was called the tomb. Lotus once told her that for those who bore the tattoo, the tomb was both sanctuary and sanctum. A sanctuary, because skulls needed to feel there was one place in the world where others could not go. A sanctum, because it was where they conducted the ritualistic skulling.

"Hello again, dear," Lotus said, but this time her voice was flat. A shock gun hung from the sash at her waist. Even the most level-headed had been known to bolt.

Taking her by the arm, Lotus guided her into the room. The light was too dim to see properly, but she knew the skulls were there, hidden in the shadows.

In the centre of the room she could make out an old dentist chair, fitted with straps. Fleur's heart thudded in her ears. Hooded forms shifted at the periphery.

"Wait," Lotus said.

Why didn't they just get it over with?

Lord came in, shock gun whining, and in front of him walked Cy Yozarian.

Of course, she thought, he was condemned too.

He stared at her, and for the second time that day raised an eyebrow in question. It was a look that seemed to say, just give the word, and I will break us out of here. Something about this man was dangerous, an implied threat in his every movement. She knew that with a sign from her, he would fight and find a way out despite the odds, just like he had at the restaurant.

But there was no way out save one, and that they couldn't access.

Her eyes, adjusted now to the darkness of the room, could see the skulls lining the walls. Each wore a black cloak, obscuring the top half of their faces. Lord grinned, his smile making her nauseous. She knew how his twisted mind worked. He would see this act as bringing them closer together.

Lotus handed her a pill which she crushed between her teeth. Cy Yozarian refused his.

"You'll need it," Lotus said.

He shook his head.

"Don't say I didn't warn you."

A light flicked on in the centre of the room, illuminating the chair. Four of the figures stepped forward. They strapped Fleur into the chair, murmuring a low chant.

The Bedouin didn't believe in the *Faith*. It was an invention of MediaCom. However, the Bedouin had unconsciously invented their own rituals, own beliefs, to represent those things they could not fully come to terms with. The skulling ceremony was one of them.

A warm, liquid sensation spread from the pit of her stomach to the extremities of her body. The drug took the edge off her panic, but it made her head swim. The straps constricted her arms like flat brown snakes. Hallucinating, she caught glimpses of the faces under the hoods, except they weren't faces but real skulls, flesh rotted away, red eyes staring out from the shadows.

Lotus leaned over her, needle in hand. The old woman was one of the Bedouin's medics, patching up casualties wounded in the field, doling out drugs for depression, tending the sick in isolated cells whenever something broke out. This operation, however, had nothing to do with making people better.

She would not cry out when Lotus carved a hole in her face. She would not.

Lotus stuffed a piece of rubber into her mouth and then, without hesitating, jabbed the needle deep into her skin. She didn't bother with a stencil. The skulls were crudely designed. She jabbed again, this time drawing blood as the needle probed under the epidermis to inject its black ink.

Watching the needle come down, she became convinced Lotus was not applying a tattoo at all, but drilling a hole through her face. She strained on the straps and screamed.

Images filled her mind. A people she heard about from the old world, caking an adolescent boy's face with clay then circumcising him with a wooden knife. If the clay cracked, the boy became an outcast, those who controlled the pain were welcomed into adult society. Boys as young as three trained to acquire tolerance; cutting themselves, burning themselves, piercing themselves. Cy Yozarian would be like one of those boys. He would not flinch.

The needle drilled on and as the harsh, blunt scraping settled into a rhythm, her thoughts became more ordered.

She fixated on the plughole, the vertical shaft in the eastern tunnel that stretched upwards for a hundred feet. It led to an apartment in a nondescript building in mid-town Mansion, the existence of which was the Bedouin's most closely guarded secret.

The five hundred square foot apartment was manned, twenty-four hours a day. The guards vetted everyone coming in and out. If Valencia hadn't approved them, they were shot on sight. If overwhelmed, the guards wore wristbands with triggers to explode the shaft, filling it with a hundred foot of rubble.

The building was located in a particularly congested part of the City, one of a hundred cylindrical high rises, separated by inches rather than feet. The foot traffic, even for midtown Mansion, was heavy, and to accommodate the volume of bodies going in and out, covered walkways had been built, like a system of pipes, each with outlets onto various streets.

Using the walkways, it was possible to get up to seven blocks away without having to exit onto a street. This had the benefit that the building of origin could not easily be traced, even with *Earth*. The walkways served almost a hundred thousand apartments. Tracing an individual to an actual apartment, was, as Valencia liked to say, like trying to find a handful of moving needles in one of the world's largest haystacks.

Once a block or two away from their building, a Bedouin on shore leave could surreptitiously slip on their iNet glasses and blend into the Mansion world. It was still a common offense not to wear iNet in public, especially among teenagers who thought it was cool to rock the naked-eyed look, at least until they had to buy something or had received a couple of citations from Securicom.

A few Bedouin operated permanently undercover in Mansion, but most lived in the tunnels, kept going by the prospect of shore leave. Six hours in Mansion, once a week. Even Valencia herself took shore leave. Psychologically it kept them from going insane, kept them in the land of the living.

But skulls were not alive. They were dead, their entire world condensed to a damp, half mile of piping. Compromised by Securicom, they were forced to spend the rest of their unnatural lives underground. If they breached the perimeter of the Bedouin's sanctuary, or tried to venture up the plughole, they were shot dead by the Garde. Theoretically they were revered for sacrificing their liberty to the cause, but it didn't stop the attempted desertions.

As the needle worked its way deeper and deeper into her skin, Fleur wondered if she too would make that doomed attempt, driven crazy with claustrophobia. She looked up into Lotus's eyes and saw the half-insane burn that lay behind them. *Yes*, she thought, if given the chance, she would run.

7

SECTOR 1, MANSION

P ASCO WAITED IN the gleaming steel corridor, fretting over why Maglan had summoned him. Had he heard about Balmoral already? That she was conscious, could see and hear, and even take two or three steps. Mentally, the signs were positive, although it was still too early to tell if there was permanent damage. *Voice* had catalogued every aspect of her brain, but that didn't mean the AI knew what was going on in there, or if she would make a full recovery.

A brain scan was like having a map of an alien planet. There might be a familiar rock formation here or a body of water there, but most of the terrain was largely incomprehensible. He wished he could reach out to Professor Hakim for an opinion, but of course that was impossible, Pasco would never get the clearance to contact his old teacher.

So far Balmoral hadn't said much, apart from asking Pasco to turn down the terrible music, but that was enough for now. She was back in the world of the living. As recently as this morning Pasco hardly dared to hope recovery was possible, the return to life more than he could wish for. He should be elated, but after receiving his uncle's summons, he feared the worst.

Pasco needed time, to prepare a case, to justify why they should first begin a course of reconstructive therapy with Balmoral, rather than interrogate her or make her stand charges. But despite having months to think of something, he was about to walk into this meeting empty handed.

He had no illusions about how Maglan would take the news, and he was nervous. In the last hour he had been to the bathroom three times, as though having overdosed on evacuee.

One of Maglan's plastic-faced agents appeared in the corridor. "It shouldn't be long now."

"No rush." Pasco smiled ludicrously. At times like this his facial muscles didn't seem to work properly.

When she had gone he fretted about getting back to Balmoral. What if her condition deteriorated and he was stuck here?

Calm down, he told himself. She is stable. Nothing will happen to her, not yet anyway.

He logged into iNet, to check again if any of the medical staff had tried to contact him. There was nothing, so he flicked over to Media.

His stomach turned over as he saw the news about the latest *Dish* attack at Esprit. Hundreds killed, atomized in an explosion on the roof of the old guild hall building. Medi-vans lined the avenues, their emergency lights flashing. Orderlies lifted body bags from bloodstained rubble, and white ash dropped like snow into the street.

The guild hall building.

The significance of the location hit him. How had he forgotten the anniversary of his father's death? He thought of Tristram and wondered what he was doing right now, his brother who could never forgive or let go. Pasco had not seen him in over two years. He didn't even know if he lived in Mansion.

The door to Maglan's outer office swung open. "The Chairman will see you now," the plastic-faced aide said and escorted him inside.

On the far wall, Bruno Mandrax's image shimmered. The Chairman sat studying his deputy, ensconced behind his vast mahogany desk.

Maglan glanced up, motioning Pasco to sit in one of the uncomfortable green leather chairs. There was no hint of affection or welcome in his uncle's face, just a bored tolerance. It had always been the same.

"You sure he was there?" Maglan continued.

Bruno Mandrax hesitated, aware someone had entered the room, but unable to see him. This vid feed was one way.

"It's all right, you can talk," Maglan said. "It's just Pasco."

The hotel room backdrop behind Mandrax looked familiar. "I have Tristram entering the restaurant an hour and a half before the explosion," Mandrax said.

"And still no response?"

"No, Sir. No word or even . . . a sustained connection."

Pasco's stomach clenched. Tristram, at Esprit? "H-he's dead?"

"It does usually mean only one thing," Maglan said gravely.

"*Usually*," Bruno Mandrax replied, "but according to *Voice* the iAm chip is operational, which would suggest he is still alive. Without bioenergy, the chip would cease to function. *Voice* detects intermittent flashes of connectivity, milliseconds at a time, not strong enough to get a location, but if he was dead there would be nothing at all."

"iAm?" Pasco said. "Tristram has a prototype?"

Both men ignored him. "What does intermittent mean?" Maglan said. "Is he unconscious? Wounded?"

"I don't know," Bruno Mandrax replied.

"I do," Pasco said.

Maglan raised his eyebrows, "Go on."

"The technology does not work like a retinal interface. Coming on and offline isn't an indication of consciousness. With iAm, as long as the subject is alive, it gives off a signal, assuming there is sufficient body heat to charge the chip, and perhaps even then . . . we haven't tested conditions of severe hypothermia."

"Then what conclusion can we draw?" Maglan said.

"That he's off the grid. Completely out of iNet's reach, which means he's either in a heavily insulated building complex or underwater, or underground, or in the Cut."

Maglan turned his thick bulldog neck back to Bruno Mandrax. "Bruno? What exactly was Tristram doing?"

"I-I don't know exactly."

"You're supposed to be his handler," Maglan said coldly.

Mandrax's image shifted uncomfortably. "He's not the easiest to handle," he muttered. "My best guess is that Tristram was tipped off about the attack and was there to investigate."

"Tipped off? And not inform Securicom? Are you suggesting my nephew has somehow gone rogue?"

Pasco could sense Mandrax weighing his words behind those permanently mirrored shades. He walked a tightrope; one slip might mean his career.

"Perhaps he did not consider the lead credible enough to raise the alarm. Information concerning the Bedouin has rarely been accurate."

Maglan said nothing.

"I was thinking of pulling in some of our better sources. See what we can shake out?"

"No," Maglan replied. "We don't know where Tristram is, but if we go after the *Dish* with questions we'll alert the Bedouin that something's up. We need to give the boy time."

"What do you mean?"

"The Bedouin exist off the grid. Perhaps he's finally found them."

"Perhaps," Bruno Mandrax said, "they found him."

Maglan smiled thinly. "Does it make a difference? Do you have his last known location before the signal cut?"

"Not yet. We're working on it."

"Tell me Bruno, is there anything you do know?" Maglan's uneven stare burned holes into the shimmering image.

"I'll inform you the moment we find something."

"Make sure you do."

"Do you need me to return to Mansion?"

"No. Churin is more important."

Churin, Pasco thought. So that's why the backdrop looked familiar. The hotel in the Battery. But why was the head of *Dish* operations there?

"Stay there until your work is complete," Maglan said.

"Sir," Bruno Mandrax pulled up his holopad, as though to end the feed.

"Wait," the Chairman said. "Pasco's visit is unfortunately not a social call. My business with him also concerns you. It seems our butcher of Rhodes has finally woken up."

"What?"

"Yes," Maglan said, glancing at Pasco. "Somewhat surprising after all these months, especially as a week ago, my nephew's report suggested no improvement."

Bruno Mandrax said nothing and silently Pasco thanked him. It would have been easy for the Elite to jump in on his uncle's side, to win back some points by suggesting Pasco had been withholding information, or was deficient in his assessment, but he did not.

Maglan poured himself a small whisky. He didn't offer Pasco one. "So what do we do with her?"

Pasco said nothing. He stared at the floor, at the brass clawed furniture, digging its talons into the carpet. It seemed every meeting with his uncle reminded Pasco of that first terrible interview, when Maglan informed him and Tristram, in this very room, that he was their legal guardian because their mother didn't want them.

The Chairman took a small sip of whisky. "Do you know what I think we should do? Put her in a cell, lock the door and burn everything inside."

A shocked silence filled the room, physically from Pasco, virtually from Mandrax.

"Well that's justice, isn't it?" he said, gently placing the whisky glass on the table. "Eye for an eye."

Blood pounded in Pasco's ears. One word might save her, another might kill her. He had to say something, but what? His mind had gone blank.

"Justice, yes," Bruno Mandrax's holograph said slowly, "but is it justified? Economically I mean."

"What?" Maglan snapped.

"Eliminating her might be a waste. You know her capabilities. If we could control her, she could help make iNet virtually impregnable, make the sims more secure, stop the next generation of *Dish* hackers making any headway.

You've always said the greatest threat to the Autonomy is its greatest strength, that the next war will be fought across iNet."

Maglan said nothing.

"That war may be coming sooner than we think. Look at what is happening in Churin. Yes, she killed a thousand children, but with the right handling, she could potentially help save millions."

"What makes you think she would cooperate?" Maglan growled. "We know how dangerous she is. She is not a risk if she is not breathing."

"With iAm, we monitor her twenty-four hours a day," Pasco cut in, managing to find his voice at last. "She can't even use iNet without us being aware of every thought."

Maglan said nothing, but seemed lost in thought, staring out across Mansion's vast skyline, at the unimaginably high buildings made possible by the geographic accident of a billion year old bedrock more than two hundred feet thick.

"It's like the frog and the scorpion," Maglan said finally.

"Sir?" Bruno Mandrax said.

"Surely you know the fable?"

"No, Sir."

"You Pasco?"

"No."

It was at times like this Pasco realised his uncle's age. For post-Autonomy children, literature was not considered economically productive and was not part of the syllabus. Rationally, his uncle knew that, and would have approved, but there was another part of him that sometimes sensed how much had been lost.

Maglan sighed and took another pull of whisky. "A scorpion needs to cross a river to continue on its journey so it asks a passing frog for a ride. The frog of course demurs, saying, 'If I take you on my back, you will only sting me and I will perish'. The scorpion is shocked by this reply. She says, 'Of course I will not sting you because if you die, I will die, for I cannot swim.' Seeing the logic of this, and thinking what a wonderful thing it would be for a scorpion to owe him a favour, the frog agrees and they set off across the river. The frog is half way across when it feels an excruciating pain, like a red hot spear thrust through its back. With its dying breath the frog manages to croak . . . *Why?*"

"Because I am a scorpion," Mandrax finished. "I remember now."

Maglan smiled. "Very good Bruno. And yes, some say that is what she said. However, I believe the other version of the story. As they both sunk under the water, the drowning scorpion replied, it is far better we both perish, than my enemy lives."

"Except with iAm," Bruno Mandrax said, "we would be able to neutralize her before she could strike."

His uncle leaned back in the chair and considered. "Perhaps you are correct. Perhaps we should not be hasty. There is something we might be able to use her for. Yes . . . let's get her into some sort of working condition, get her on iAm, and see if we can turn this scorpion's sting to our own advantage."

8

SECTOR 1, MANSION SUBTERRANEA

F LEUR ENTERED VALENCIA'S chamber, her face, burning with the pain of the
tattoo, her whole being burning with fury and humiliation.

The head of the Bedouin didn't turn around, but continued to stare at
a bank of monitors on the wall, her pink hair hanging in curls down her back.

On one screen she reviewed live Media reports, on another, various encrypted
messages from agents in the field.

The monitors provided access to iNet, a feed jerry-rigged by Orlick and operated by a physical, rather than holographic keypad. Valencia could access any
public Media on iNet, navigate the intellisphere, but not execute commands.

Outside the guild hall building it was raining now; stage managed conditions
to cast an atmospheric pall over the tragedy. Atmos hardly ever let it rain in
Mansion, not during the day anyway.

Fleur was momentarily transfixed with the pitter-patter of drops on the Medi-
vans, their emergency lights spinning around and around. Fleur would never
feel rain again.

"Your mission was a success," Valencia said, still without turning. In her hands
she cradled a tin cup of steaming coffee, probably laced with synapse. Clay said
Val didn't sleep any more.

"Success? Really?" Fleur shouted. "Then why did you etch a fucking skull into
my cheek?"

Slowly Valencia turned around, her pink lips a few centimetres from Fleur's
own.

"You're lucky I let you live," she said slowly. "You've compromised the entire
cell by bringing an outsider here."

"Outsider? He's an asset. He works for the *Dish* in Bodia."

"So he says. We'll know soon enough."

"Beaky won't find anything."

"For your sake, I hope so, but if this *Cy Yozarian* has a whiff of Securicom about him, we'll put a bullet in his brain faster than you can blink."

For a moment they stared at each other, then Valencia put out her hand and stroked Fleur's hair, straightening it; a tender gesture from a time before they had so much killing under their belts.

"He helped me, Val," she said, feeling tears of frustration well in her eyes. "I had no choice, I had to bring him back."

"There is *always* a choice."

"You wanted me to die? Burn on the rooftop with everyone else?"

"Nobody is bigger than the cause. Not you, not me, not anyone. If it's your time, then it's your time. Your actions have cost me, Fleur. Protocol states I should have shot you both, instead, well . . . here you are."

Valencia glanced at the other set of screens, the ones that showed the common room and the entrance to the plughole.

"I can already feel the whispers. *If I can be lenient with her, then . . . why not with others?* More shore leave for the troops, perhaps even let a skull wander around above ground, to see the sun one last time. Without our discipline, without our rules, we are nothing."

"Discipline and rules," Fleur said bitterly. "They didn't seem quite so important when Lord killed Dimaro."

For an instant she thought Val was going to slap her, but then another expression passed over her face.

Was it regret? Compassion?

"That was different. Two men had a fight, just a fight. I don't like it, but it happens in these tunnels. We live in such close proximity. Ninety-nine times out of a hundred, they walk away with a few cuts and bruises, the air cleared and everyone back to work. Lord served a month in solitary for the brawl. What else could I do? They were letting off steam, settling a dispute."

"A dispute?" Fleur said. "Lord picked a fight with him for no reason."

Valencia narrowed her eyes. "Dimaro could have backed down, could have walked away. He was a Garde after all, supposed to keep the peace, not disrupt it, but instead he decided to fight, felt he had something to prove against his . . . rival."

Fleur's stomach flipped over. "What?"

"In these tunnels, someone always knows, Fleur. Always hears. There are no secrets."

Shit. Shit. Shit.

Dimaro.

She slept with him a week after that terrible night with Lord. Of course Lord had known, of course he had been jealous. Was Dimaro dead because of her?

"I want to show you something," Valencia said, turning back to the iNet monitors and tapping out a couple of commands. Blood-soaked images filled the screen, cast into stark relief by the powdery ash that lay everywhere and shots of a roof that was no longer a roof.

"The usual coverage," Valencia said. "Plenty of bodies and gore, wailing victims, their families, the condemnation of the *cowardice* by prevailing Media figures, some quotations from the *Faith*. Nobody asks the most important question. Why?"

Then why do we bother?

Fleur knew better than to ask. The strategy of the *Dish* was to shock the citizens of the Autonomy out of their complacency. The theory was that after every successful attack, more of the disenfranchised joined the *Dish*'s global ranks, but this in itself had begun to bother her.

Were the recruits truly citizens, broken free from the economic slavery that was destroying mankind? Or just psychopaths, like Lord, who would be eternally alienated from society regardless of the system?

"I don't want to watch this," Fleur said.

"You wanted to know why I ordered Lotus to decorate your cheek?"

"Because I broke your rules, because I brought back . . ."

"No," Valencia snapped. "Watch."

The screen panned to the entrance of the building, a soft orange-brown in the Mansion sunlight. People walked in and out, then two or three pedestrians tensed in surprise as Cy Yozarian sprinted into the street, dragging Siranush. Fleur raced out behind them, still pushing the stroller. A second later the frame shook as the top floor of the building was engulfed in a gigantic ball of fire.

"A little damning isn't it? You were supposed to exit casually a good seven or eight minutes before, just one of hundreds passing out in the final minutes. Instead, there you are, flying like a bat out of hell, just before the building explodes."

"Orlick was supposed to cut the *Earth* cameras for that section."

"Oh, he cut the cameras," Valencia said, "but by the time you showed, *Voice* had located the hack and put them back online."

"I could have stayed out of Mansion for a while. You didn't have to skull me!"

"This wasn't some hardware store smash and grab. When they can't find you, they'll get suspicious. Who was this woman? And the stroller? You were supposed to drop it in the sewer. Now, when they find it discarded a few blocks away, they'll scrape for DNA and discover not skin but micro-fragments of a latex model. From there they will pull the building records and see that the child you carried gave off no retinal signature, and from there they will work out what happened. You will be the primary suspect."

Again, Fleur experienced a rush of fury. "You told me Securicom would investigate this as a suicide attack! You said I would be fine, that they would focus their investigations on those inside the building. That I would walk away, free!"

"*If* you had followed the plan. Instead you left a trail. We can't risk you leaving the tunnels and that is why you wear the skull."

Fleur could not speak. She wanted to scream with frustration, with the prospect of a life imprisoned in the dim, damp hell.

Valencia zoomed in on Siranush. "Who's the girl?"

"A witness. She saw us plant the bomb. We had to bring her."

"Really? It would have been simpler to leave her behind."

"But she would have raised the alarm."

"I suspect that would have been somewhat irrelevant, given how narrow the margin between your exit and the explosion. What was the real reason? According to your initial report, Cy Yozarian took out three witnesses while you planted the bomb. Why not her?"

Fleur said nothing.

"And don't you think Securicom will find it curious that she was found in an alley with her neck broken? Another reason why they will make you and this Cy Yozarian a priority."

Fleur tried to hide her shock, but Valencia missed nothing.

"You didn't know? Interesting. So your Cy Yozarian did it by himself, did he? Smart boy. Smarter than you, anyway. That girl would have been a liability, and you would have let her go."

"It wasn't him. He took her iNet glasses and let her go . . . said she wouldn't be able to recall anything without them."

"Perhaps. Theoretically, it is possible Securicom found her, extracted what they needed to know, and dumped her. Or maybe she's still breathing, trying to cooperate, trying to recall your names. How can we really know anything except that this," she tapped the frozen image on the screen, the three figures running from the building, "makes you dead man walking in Mansion, every *Earth* camera straining to find you."

Fleur said nothing. What could she say? Unconsciously her hand went to her cheek and touched the bandage.

"Don't blame the cause," Valencia said, watching her, "or our methods. While the Autonomy controls what people see, what people read, what people think, our only option is to shake the slaves out of their complacency with the kind of actions you carried out today. Blunt and barbaric tools, I know, but it's all we've got. However, that is about to change."

"What do you mean?"

Valencia cleared her screen, disconnecting from iNet, and typed out three or four commands. For a moment, Fleur stared at the blank screen, puzzled. Then, slowly, a scratchy transmission began. There was no visual. In this age of hyper-connectivity, the recording was almost inaudible. It was an offline media file, smuggled all the way to Mansion from Churin, the information considered too dangerous to send through iNet, even with encryption.

The speaker was an undercover *Dish* operative, but gave no further information about himself. He told them about a rendition overseen by President Maglan himself, of a subcoder from Churin who possessed an almost impossible talent when it came to controlling iNet, how not even *Voice* had managed to shut down or even detect her activity, how she was held in Mansion and that if the *Dish* could get hold of her, she could be the asset that would turn the tide in the war on the Autonomy. The transmission ended abruptly. Not even a name had been shared.

"What do you think?"

"It sounds like a plant," Fleur said. "Like the dead Securicom agent who washed up on shore in Mong, a rogue in his pocket cataloguing all the vulnerabilities in the *Earth* network, every one of them a trap. How many cybers did the *Dish* lose?"

"More than we could afford," Valencia said gravely, "but Orlick never fell for it. He believed it was too good to be true."

Reaching under her desk Valencia pulled out a bottle of vodka and two shot glasses. Pouring them one each she said, "You are right to be cautious, but since receiving this intelligence, our Mansion operatives have done everything in their power to corroborate the information. It checks out." They chinked glasses. "We have infiltrated the facility where they are holding her."

Fleur choked on the vodka. "Infiltrated a Securicom facility!"

"Yes." Valencia smiled bitterly. "I have cut corners. I have blown operatives. I have risked and lost lives, but it *is* worth it. This, as they say, is the big one."

"How long have you known?"

"A couple of weeks."

"Why didn't you tell me?"

"I'm telling you now."

"But if this is so important surely . . . we should have postponed the operation, diverted our resources to her!" And I would not be a skull, Fleur did not add.

"That is precisely why the operation had to go ahead," Valencia said. "Securicom must believe that we don't know where the real prize lies."

Valencia poured them another shot.

"There's still one thing I don't understand," Fleur said, "Why do they keep her alive? I mean if she can do all that they say she can?"

"You are not thinking like the Autonomy. As a rare and valuable resource they will find a way to exploit her, to use her up before discarding her."

"But surely she is dead digitally, cut off from iNet. Even if we get her, how will she be able to help us?"

Valencia smiled. "A girl who can fake retinal scans is immortal."

"Faked? How? Surgery?"

There had always been chatter about how the squaddies were working on a process to see if entire eyeballs could be surgically implanted to create a false scan. So far nobody had worked out how to connect a new eye to the optical cord in a way that made iNet and sight possible. But there were always rumours.

"No. She found a way to override the scan."

"That's impossible."

"Orlick thought so too, until he intercepted an explicit reference to this girl's code. She not only faked a retinal scan, but bypassed every security system *Voice* has ever conceived. Think of what that means! She is a hacker on a level nobody has ever seen. It makes the kind of stuff the cybers and Orlick have achieved," she gestured to the bulky monitor, "look like the work of a baby. He admits it himself. If we can find a way to get her back onto iNet, think of what she could do for us. One in thirteen billion, and she is here in Mansion, and somehow, some way, I want her."

Fleur stared at the dark, damp walls of Valencia's chamber and thought, *if she can fake a retinal scan, I want her too.*

9

H E WAS AN old, grey man in a long trench coat, his head shrivelled, his nose like a vulture's and his eyes black and blinking.

Lotus called him Beaky. The Garde called him the President. He had aged, of course, but Tristram recognized him instantly. Pierre Gravales, the great traitor, broken out of a high security compound after the original Dish attacks. Like Tristram, he had a black skull etched underneath his eye.

He was flanked by two Garde, armed not with shock guns, but printed rifles. Gravales produced a pistol from his trench coat and put it on his knee He was frail. He had to be over ninety by now, but there was steel in his grip and his stare. All four of them were crammed into a tiny cell, the door locked.

Tristram tried to move his hands, but there was no give; wire bound them tightly behind his back. He considered his options, but the reality was that he had none. He could dislocate his wrists, slip through the bonds and immobilize maybe one or both of the Garde before they could react, but the old man would be steady and swift.

Gravales stared at him for a long time without speaking. He looked more than ever the bird of prey.

"You have a familiar face," he said finally. "Why is that?"

Tristram shrugged. "I don't think we've met before."

Gravales grunted. "I know that, boy," he said. "I've been in here over fifteen years, and you're what? Twenty-five?"

"Twenty-three."

"So of course we haven't met. I was Vice Chairman of the whole of the Autonomy. I didn't have much time for little boys."

That's not what forty or fifty children claimed after you were disgraced.

"Maybe I have one of those generic faces."

"No," Gravales rasped. "There's something distinct about you. It will come back to me. *Everything* comes to me in time." He paused. "Do you know my name?"

"Beaky?" he said, flicking his eyes to the ceiling.

The old man smiled but it came out badly, like a split in a tube of toothpaste. "Do they teach young people nothing these days? My name is Pierre Gravales. Remember it. Perhaps it will be the last name you hear."

He tapped the pistol on his leg.

"I have some questions to ask but first I must warn you, don't lie. You have already lied about not knowing my name. One more lie will be fatal."

He pointed the gun at Tristram.

"You must understand how monotonous life is down here and I have to confess, it would give me no end of pleasure to pull this trigger, just to provide a little relief to the tedium, to add a little colour to my day."

Tristram nodded, saying nothing. He acted surprised when Gravales accused him of lying, just like he stared at the ceiling when he pretended not to know his name. That way, when he had to lie, but didn't give any sign, the old man might just believe him.

Might.

Even during the propaganda blitz following the old Vice Chairman's arrest, the one thing nobody tried to say was that he was dumb. His intellect was renowned for being sharp as a razor, Tristram doubted that time had blunted its edge.

"According to Fleur Cliquot's report, you identified her as a member of the *Dish* in the restaurant. That was remarkably observant."

"In the crowded markets of the Cut you learn to keep your eyes open. She looked out of place."

"Why were you there?"

Tristram shrugged. "Perversity I guess. I wanted to take a look at some of the self-satisfied corporate fucks who put me in the Cut before I was sent back there. The restaurant seemed like a good choice."

"Very convenient though, looking for the *Dish* and finding us, just like that."

"I wasn't looking. I saw an opportunity and took it."

"You approached her with a proposal. Tell me in your own words, what was it?"

Tristram paused, as though carefully considering his reply. "I'm a transvict," he said, "sentenced to nine years as a missionary in the Cut and . . ."

"Transvict," Gravales said, interrupting him. "What did you do to earn that particular distinction?"

"Smuggling non-skaatch based food to Sector 2, in exchange for currency."

"Currency? What good is currency in Mansion?"

"I didn't spend it in Mansion."

"I see. Blew it all on whores, highs and alc. Am I right?"

"Something like that. The rest I wasted."

Another flash of yellow that was supposed to be a smile. "So they made you a missionary in the Cut. A transvict preacher of the *Faith*. A bit of an oxymoron isn't it?"

"It was the hand I was dealt. I was given a choice, the treadle mill or the Cut. I chose the Cut. Probably a mistake."

"But a Missionary?" Gravales said.

"At the point I was arrested, I had more A-points than a mantic nun. Digitally, I was holier than all thou."

"And were you? Or was it just cover?"

Tristram shifted in his seat, trying to look uncomfortable. "I did a lot of things I wasn't proud of, and the devotions helped me. I suppose I was like a manic depressive, except instead of highs and lows, it was the rush of sin followed by crippling remorse. The curse of a true believer. Only later did I realise it was probably my confessions that led them to me in the first place."

Gravales considered him. "You don't strike me as so *devoted* now."

Tristram shrugged. "When your entire existence is focused on the next meal, *spiritual* sustenance loses its appeal. Within a week of being in the Cut, I realised the savages had no use for the *Faith*. Within a month, neither did I. I've been trying to get out ever since."

"And you identified the Bedouin as a group that could help you?"

The names of cells were not common knowledge. He sensed a trap and tried to step around it. "As I said before, I saw an opportunity and I took it. I hadn't heard of the Bedouin until today. If I'd known getting off the grid meant living in a tunnel for the rest of my life, I might have had second thoughts."

Gravales smiled. This time, it was genuine, his tombstone teeth breaking through razor thin lips. "Whether you will be *living* has yet to be determined. Which cell did you work for in the Cut?"

"In Bodia I was a runner for the *Dish*, I . . ."

"Stop," Gravales snapped. "I didn't say which region. I said which *cell*."

Was this a bluff, or was Gravales familiar with the individual cells in Bodia?

Tristram had no idea, but knew the answer was somewhere in his cover file. Using iAm he reached into his mind to access the correct information. "The Sar Tori," he said finally.

"Took you a while to remember."

"It's kind of difficult to remember things with three guns pointed at me."

Gravales grunted. "Who was your liaison?"

"Yoma Tei, the fat general. Although, fat is a relative term in Bodia. He's probably only about ten or so pounds under weight."

"Who else?"

"Nobody."

Gravales said nothing, but scratched his chin with the gun, thinking.

Had Tristram said the wrong thing? When the *Dish* used outsiders for operations the protocol was to limit their access. That way if they played a double game, they couldn't blow the whole cell. Perhaps it was the seniority of Yoma Tei that threw Gravales off. Usually an outsider would deal with an underling.

"What's the main border crossing out of Bodia and into the Cut?" Gravales said, suddenly changing the subject.

How the hell should he know?

"Crossing?" Tristram repeated, desperately straining for the data.

"What are you? A fucking echo? Answer the question."

Tristram pulled up a map of the region, zoomed in and read out the names. "No Sir, it's just that there are several recognized crossings due to the triangular border . . . So do you mean Urubar? Kang? Or Mabuon?"

He was not yet expert at manipulating the synaptic inputs of his iAm implant but for an hour, as they carved a skull on his face, he reviewed all the information related to his Cy Yozarian cover and placed it where he could quickly retrieve it.

Tristram had carried out a couple of operations in Bodia, seek and destroy missions targeted against *Dish* warlords who refused to toe the line. His basic knowledge of the area was one of the reasons they had invented a Bodia cover story to go with his Cy Yozarian identikit. Despite this, if the detail had not been hard coded on iAm, he would be dead by now.

Gravales, silent again, scrutinized him with those black eyes. Tristram stared right back, the stare of a man with nothing to hide.

Finally the old man shook his head, raised his gun and pointed it directly at Tristram's chest.

Tristram noted with professional interest that the gun was not a print but the real thing, a Luger, from some time in the middle of the last century.

"One last question," Gravales said, holding the gun steady, "how many fingers does the fat general have?"

"Fingers?" Tristram said.

"There you go again, repeating what I say, buying time." He cocked the gun. "You have exactly five seconds to answer." The other two guards lifted their rifles.

Tristram didn't bother trying to access iAm. He already knew the information wasn't in the data file. Tristram had never seen the fat general, or heard much about him, but why would Gravales ask this question unless he had some sort of deformity?

Think.

Yoma Tei had been head of the *Dish* in Bodia for many years, running illegal imports and exports, supported by the Cut warlords. A ruthless leader, he commanded both fear and respect.

Respect.

In the Cut it wasn't unusual to come across someone who had lost a few digits, or even an arm or leg to meet the nutritional needs of the community. It was never altruism, but a forced amputation, preying on those least able to defend themselves.

Amputation was often a death sentence. Gangrene was rife, although nobody ever waited for the infection to get far. To let meat spoil in a society where the average person survived on less than three hundred calories a day was inconceivable. As soon as the first blue vein showed, that limb was on the menu. So the first man to lose a finger, was often the first to lose his arm, and in most cases, his life. The first man to lose a finger, lost his respect. The fat general could not have become the fat general with half a hand. It was a trick question.

"Eight," Tristram. "Eight fingers, two thumbs."

Gravales regarded him for a moment, and then finally lowered the gun. The two guards followed suit.

"Y-you had me worried," Tristram said, making his voice tremble. "I thought maybe the fat general had been in an accident since I last saw him."

"He has, but not of the physical kind."

Tristram knew that too. Feigning surprise he said, "What do you mean?"

"He is currently a guest of Securicom. Seems he got a bit greedy at the border, didn't pay the right bribes. Bad for him and perhaps . . . convenient for you. Although if history is any guide, he'll be out within a few weeks."

"I don't understand."

The old man's eyes narrowed, assessing Tristram, watching for any reaction as he spoke. "Securicom like the regional opposition to be someone they can work with. The fat general is many things, and certainly no lover of the Autonomy, but a devotee of the emancipation of mankind . . . that, we can safely say, he is not, which is why he was allowed to step into the vacuum after Bodia's riots two years ago."

Gravales inspected the gun and then, apparently satisfied, holstered the weapon.

"Perhaps you are who you say. We will check, of course. Encrypted communication with Bodia is difficult but not, you will understand, impossible. You are sure you had no other contacts?"

Tristram shook his head.

"Then we'll wait until he gets out."

There was no way to tell Securicom to hold the general. Gravales was right, they would keep him a couple of months at most to stop his deputies getting itchy and making a play for the throne. Then how long would Tristram have? Five minutes? A day? A week? He had no idea how the Bedouin communicated with cells in other parts of the Autonomy.

"You still remind me of someone," Gravales said, knocking on the bars to be let out.

"I can't help my face."

"That's exactly why I want to remember."

10

SECTOR 1, MANSION

MAGLAN'S PRIVATE MEDIA feed ran like an old-fashioned ticker tape in the lower right hand corner of his iNet lenses. *Skaatch depot in Shamshu seized by militants . . . Car bombs in Deng, eight executives targeted, three fatalities . . . Skirmishes with Foremen in the western section of the Battery, situation deteriorating . . .*

The data from Churin was real time, captured by *Earth,* and translated into meaningful information by *Voice.* The AI sometimes got it wrong, misinterpreting the visual clues, but the benefit of instant information outweighed the occasional inaccuracies. Knowledge *was* power and throughout his career, Maglan made it a priority to know first.

"Goddamn it," he muttered.

Just eight weeks ago, Churin was a poster child for regional growth and the most profitable Sector in the Autonomy. Today, unrest threatened to destabilize the entire region. What began as a few isolated protests orchestrated by the *Dish* over mortality rates had rapidly deteriorated into a full scale uprising.

He pulled up Guiren's latest report, sent at four this morning. Riddled with half-truths and evasions, it claimed the disruption was temporary, that iAm would soon be back on schedule.

Francis Guiren.

The old man was like a cockroach. When everything was in ruins, he would still be fine, scrabbling around in the ashes, making do. Maglan had never quite trusted Guiren. The man had too much sympathy for the populace, treated them as something more than a natural resource, a luxury mankind had lost long ago.

Maglan had pressured Guiren to take measures at the first sign of violence, but he had stalled. His recent cack-handed reprisals had been too little, too late. Guiren had screwed up one too many times. As a result, he was finished. Bruno Mandrax would see to it.

Churin.

Automatically his mind flicked to Balmoral Murraine, the ever-present splinter in his brain. Was she behind it all? Hadn't the first rumblings of protest begun shortly before she woke up, almost two months ago?

No, that was impossible. *Voice* monitored her iAm every second of the day, and so far, nothing. The girl hadn't even sent out a synaptic probe. If anything, her brain was trying to reject the device. Pasco claimed it was just a matter of time, but he wasn't sure he trusted Pasco.

With a tap on his holopad he pulled up Balmoral's latest test results. "Her powers of computation and lateral reasoning are tied to emotional equilibrium. The more agitated she becomes, the more erratic her thoughts."

Under his direction the scientists had used some aggressive environmental conditions to stimulate *agitation*.

"However under sustained pressure, the left side of her brain moves beyond an emotional consciousness and taps into a highly functioning mathematical consciousness . . ."

The report showed she completed a series of complex equations while they administered electric shocks at increasing levels of intensity and then blasted her with images of mutilation, rape and torture. Anyone else would have caved, but Murraine was barely human.

"We conclude that despite the prolonged coma, the fundamental integrity of the mind has remained intact."

Maglan's iNet display bleeped into life with a warning from his biosquare. His heart rate had risen above a healthy level. With an effort of will he brought it down, cursing the girl all the way. He hated the effect she had on him.

He pulled up his holopad and typed in a couple of commands. He no longer had to look up the *Earth* codes, he knew the digits by heart. And just like that, there she was, sitting on the end of her bed, free, while his boy floated in micro ashes in the ether. At almost seventy years of age, having never been in a Pleasure House, he had become a voyeur, addicted to what went on in this tiny room.

He had watched Pasco draw on her hand while she was still in a coma, Pasco conversing with her and Balmoral actually looking interested, Pasco helping her across the room during a physical therapy session and when she made it, he hugged her, and when he hugged her, he closed his eyes. Maglan saw her laugh, actually laugh, at something Pasco said. In all the hours of footage he had spent watching this girl, the late nights studying her on old *Earth* footage from

Churin, he had never once seen her smile, and yet his nephew had found a way to make her laugh.

A shot of hatred burned through him. It was time, as his father used to say, for Pasco to wake up and smell the coffee. He touched his forehead. The pallid scar from the scorching liquid was still there, as though a small part of his face had melted. He could have had it removed, but it suited him to keep it, a permanent reminder of what happens when a situation is outside one's control.

Maglan was self-aware enough to know that this obsession was dangerous, but after a lifetime of service to humanity, he was permitted one indulgence, and she was it. Pasco shouldn't have tempted him with the prospect of keeping her alive.

He would take her apart bit by bit, break into that unemotional shell and hurt her infinitely more than she had hurt his son. He would not permit her to die until he had forced her to look herself straight in the eye and see what type of creature she really was, until she begged for death. He would take great satisfaction in that.

He watched Pasco patiently walk her through yet another iAm simulation program, trying to get her to engage with the device.

How she strained with the effort but . . . could not connect. Didn't Pasco realise she was playing him? Didn't he see that every day she extracted more information from him, rather than the other way round? He had even given her the results of *Voice's* scan of her brain, which could have been catastrophic if either of them had understood its real implications.

No matter. What the Autonomy needed from Balmoral, Maglan had already taken. There was *nothing* this girl could teach them, not anymore.

For a second time his iNet lenses blinked to life, his recently promoted head of special operations requested an audience. He tapped a couple of keys accepting her feed.

He still had no time for eye control. Too much room for error. A few misplaced blinks and he could potentially launch a nuclear attack, accidentally blow a sector to dust. Although right now that was very, very tempting.

Maglan.

"Lara," he replied verbally.

His head of special operations didn't like vid feeds. As with the heads of intelligence in the cold war during the last century, she preferred to stay behind the scenes, the wizard behind the curtain.

She argued that Murraine proved it was possible to hack vid feeds, and if the enemy was able to identify her, they would know her face and she would be vulnerable to attack. Maglan applauded her caution.

The situation in Churin is deteriorating.

"I see that."

The regional heads of the surrounding sectors want to meet with you. They are afraid of contagion, that the unrest will spread.

At any one time ten thousand people were requesting an audience with the Chairman of the Autonomy. That's how it was, being responsible for thirteen billion people. It was how it had been for the last sixteen years.

He sighed. "You meet with them."

She would have to deal with it. His rising star wasn't yet ready to assume the Presidency of Securicom, but handling the flak, that she could do.

Yes Sir, but in terms of Churin itself? What are your orders?

The walls of his office were lined with Top 10's most sophisticated anti-bugging equipment. He could have used his fingerpad, replied in text, but he figured if anyone could listen to what he was saying, then nothing was safe anyway.

"I need to think. Give me ten minutes."

Sir.

"One other thing," he said as an afterthought. "Still no news from Tristram?"

No Sir, and no positive read from iAm.

He waited. She would say it. She couldn't help herself.

Voice's analysis states the probability of him still being alive is now 13%.

And there it was.

"Thank you," he said. He would miss the boy, convinced now he was dead. It had been too long.

Standing up, he walked over to the sideboard and poured himself a whisky. All his life he had been a very moderate drinker, but in recent months he had come to rely on the nightly three fingers to get him through the endless work that kept him there until the early hours of the morning. He had taken to sleeping in the office and most evenings his dinner consisted of the hors d'oeuvres that garnished the silver plates of his mahogany sideboard.

Recently his legendary energy had begun to fail, and he knew that he was slowing down. In one way, this weakening was ironic. From the perspective of the Autonomy he was at the height of his power. Yet it was as though the more substantial he became in the world, the more transparent he seemed to himself, stretched and thin, pulled this way and that by a never ending tension, the responsibility of rule.

He would step down soon. He was getting tired. But first, he would see iAm usher in a new era of stability. According to *Voice's* statistical analysis, the implementation of the iNet chip would ensure the Autonomy's future for at least another five hundred years. That would be enough for Maglan. Achieve that, and he had done his job. He had saved mankind.

Churin was an untimely setback, but he had no serious cause for alarm. He would deal with it, as he always did, with a single executive order. The Presidents would retroactively approve his decision or lose their position. Discussion and consensus was a luxury when difficult decisions had to be executed, day in and day out.

Churin.

He needed the right combination of justice and authority. He needed a test case for the whole of the Autonomy.

"Lara," he said to the room.

Sir?

"S-Com," he said. "What is the status?"

Lara paused a couple of beats.

Units ready. We can have them in position in two days.

Maglan took another pull of whisky, the decision made.

11

SECTOR 1, MANSION SUBTERRANEA

FLEUR SAT IN the Tech wing, staring bleary-eyed at one of the jerry-rigged monitors, scrolling through reams of communications. She had been on this for eight weeks now, pulling all-nighters, cramming herself with synapse, trying to discover any possible way to get at Balmoral Murraine.

The Bedouin knew her location, what she ate, her physical condition, the fact that she had iAm but would not use it, and the profile of the personnel assigned to her. However, after studying the facility from every conceivable angle, even their most maverick strategists concluded there was no way to break her out. *Fresh Kills*, the maximum security research facility, was too well guarded, the protocols for entry and exit, too tight.

The stark reality of the situation cast a pall over the tunnels. After six weeks of investigation, Valencia tapered the resources, despite her former resolution. The Bedouin couldn't afford to dedicate their personnel to a project that had no hope of success, no matter how lucrative the prize. Valencia didn't take bets she couldn't win. There was something else too; according to Orlick, iAm complicated matters. How could she subcode if a chip monitored her every move?

But Fleur would not give up. She worked every hour of the day to find some chink in the armour, obsessed by the girl who had faked a retinal scan. As long as Balmoral was in prison, so was she. She trawled through thousands of meaningless personal communications hacked from Fresh Kills employees. Nearly all were useless.

"Something's got stuck in the waterless toilet, we need to get it serviced . . . Can you stop by a vending bot on the way home we're out of . . ."

For this dross, the Bedouin paid a heavy price, blowing the cover of precious cybers to get at the information. The kids, because cybers were always kids, were condemned to treadle mills or worse.

The projects within Fresh Kills were too sensitive to be referenced in external communications, but something had to slip through. There was one particular agent Fleur found herself studying, poring over the possible meaning of everything he wrote.

He was a security guard at the facility. Mentally she called him Slick Boy, because in the evenings he would find someone, anyone, to hook up with using the *YouGrind?* sim, while pretending to his girlfriend he was active in the field.

Sweetie. A high profile terrorist from Churin has infiltrated Mansion. It's serious. The Chairman himself needs me for special operations. I could be out all night.

How his girlfriend could believe a security guard was needed for special operations was beyond Fleur, but that was not the point. For all the fantasy, Slick Boy was unimaginative. He took his visual cues from what went on around him. He was detailed to Balmoral, Fleur was sure of it.

However, her discovery made little difference. As long as they kept Balmoral at Fresh Kills any intelligence was academic. In fact, she was becoming convinced this whole approach was a waste of time when, just before she was about to turn in for the night, she spotted something.

12

SECTOR 1, MANSION

B ALMORAL WAS GROGGY with painkillers when the steel doors swished open
and the cleaner came in, breakfast in one hand, vacuum in the other.

She dumped the tray on the table and scowled, as though it degraded her
to be in the same room as a transvict from slumworld. Turning on the vacuum,
she rammed it violently under the bed, colliding with the metal headboard; one,
two, three times.

Balmoral sat up, shaken awake, despite her fatigue.

The cleaner pulled the roaring vacuum to the other side of the room.

"Wait." Balmoral pointed under the bed, "I think you missed a spot."

The cleaner's back stiffened, but she said nothing and continued to suck and
wipe and sanitize the already spotless floor. Bots should have been able to do
this kind of work in Sector 1, but even in Mansion it was cheaper to maintain
a lower grade work force than to develop a sophisticated machine that could
simultaneously clean, bring breakfast and empty the bedpan.

Balmoral was fascinated by the cleaner and had spent the past few days studying her. Without iNet, it was challenging. Previously, Balmoral would have
hacked her identikit and uncovered everything from her employment history,
to her family background, to her health issues, to whether she spent any time in
the Pleasure Houses.

Life without iNet was like walking around with half your brain missing, an
uncomfortable void where the information used to be. Her brain had never had
to piece together information unaided before.

In *Voice's* report on her psychological profile, a report Pasco illicitly shared
with her, the AI concluded, in curiously vernacular language; *Balmoral without
her iNet is nothing*. Perhaps *Voice* was right.

To begin with, Balmoral couldn't tell if the cleaner was thirty or fifty. She guessed somewhere in the middle. Her face had that slightly melted quality, like a rubber mask left out in the sun. She also guessed that at the end of every shift, the cleaner trekked home seventy miles to the cheap housing that existed on the border with Sector 2. There, she would try to avoid the affections of her husband, sleep for four of five hours before taking the transport back to central Mansion and begin the cleaning day all over again. It was a difficult life, but it paid more than even the most lucrative jobs in Sector 2, enabling her to put three children through the Academy sims.

She had pieced this together over the course of a week. There was the rat's tail of a bracelet that hung around the woman's wrist as she wiped down the table, its three intricate but individual love knots each made from a separate twine of pastel thread. The work of three girls, because a boy would not spend the time, neither would a girl exhausted from having to work to make ends meet. The bracelet was an act of love, and skill, and leisure. That meant they were in the Academy. There was no fourth knot for the husband, because the girls assumed their mother wouldn't like to be reminded of the man who had left a fading purple bruise under her eye, and another on her arm, probably from drink, which she too used to enjoy too, judging by the explosion of veins on her nose. She had successfully kicked the habit, as evidenced by this job, and the fact that she had been coming in here for six weeks, and had not once smelled of alcohol, or the various mints used to cover it.

The marks had to be from a husband because this woman, with her unwashed hair, furry brown teeth and deep bags under the eyes, had not dated in years, and would not now, even if she had the chance. No time, no energy. All of her emotion, effort, purpose, invested in the three knots that dangled proudly from her wrist.

Assumptions were a poor substitute for facts, but it was all Balmoral had. Not that any of the background *really* mattered. The only important question was, could she trust her?

Polishing one last surface, the cleaner gathered her utensils and waited by the door. Automated commands passed back and forth between the cleaner's iNet lenses and a tiny scanner just above the frame. The steel doors swished open for about ten seconds, and two guards performed a full body scan before escorting her out.

When they had gone Balmoral eased herself onto the white, tiled floor and hobbled over to the breakfast table.

Pasco said she had thirty-two pins in her legs. Today she could feel all of them. Six weeks of intense therapy had restored her body to some sort of working order, but even moving short distances tired her.

She took a sip of coffee. It burned her tongue.

Apart from her physical weakness, she had other problems. Yesterday they had permitted her to go to the bathroom by herself, the first time she had not had an attendant leading her. There were guards in the corridor, but that was not the point, she made her own way. It was a strain, and it left her out of breath. Still, it was less humiliating than the bedpans.

However, on the way back she experienced an attack of vertigo. It was as though somebody had changed the building around. She could no longer tell where she had come from or where she was going. Her world had been rotated, and she had no idea which way to turn. At first she thought it was another Securicom mind game, to see if they could destabilize her, trick her into using iAm's navigation to reorient her position. After she twice turned back towards the stall, lost in the small corridor, the guard took her arm, and led her back to the room.

Balmoral without her iNet is nothing.

One thing was clear, if she was ever going to get out, she needed help, and although she didn't like the probabilities, the cleaner was her only option. The first she spoke, her voice was so low, so soft, it was barely audible.

"The *Dish* is watching," she mumbled, bending down close to her ear, the vacuum roaring in the background.

Balmoral did not react, concluding she must be a Securicom plant, trying to tempt her into a reckless action, one that would end up with her being shot as she tried to escape, the messy problem of her existence solved.

However, she quickly reasoned this was not likely. Why go to the trouble of rehabilitating her, only to eliminate her? And besides, did they really need to create a charade? There was nothing to stop a sandman coming into her room and quietly snuffing her out if that was what they wanted. They could make it look like a rapid and fatal deterioration, the after effects of a prolonged coma.

Still, it seemed improbable both that the *Dish* could get someone in here, and that this cleaner, whose name she didn't even know, was able to get her out.

The next day there was a note on the inside rim of her bedpan. In minute writing it laid out the terms of engagement, a contract of sorts, and the basic code for communication.

Whatever life this cleaner had built for herself would be over in an instant if she were caught passing on messages. She would end up in a treadle mill, her husband and daughters blackballed from Top 10, which itself was a slow death sentence.

So the question remained, could Balmoral trust her?

She took another sip of coffee and picked up a clunky device from the side table. It was almost as big as her palm. With it, Balmoral activated the 'glass' that had been installed on the opposite wall. It was a static display that automatically selected from iNet the most viewed Media updates with about twenty stories listed in a river. She hated the functionality, the lack of choice, but it was her only link with the outside world.

She selected 'Churin' to find out the latest news on the riots. Not for the first time, she found something unsettling about MediaCom's coverage. She scrolled through the day's stories; a car bomb in Deng that assassinated three executives, a Battery building hijacked by gunmen, a port seized in Shamshu, a riot in the Stacks.

She watched the last in its entirety; rows of trailers burning, lines of Foremen in riot gear, moving forward like some ancient turtle, shields up, shock guns out, engaged in pitched battles with tear gas and water cannons, but being pushed back by rioters in blood red arm bands.

And that was what bothered her. From the coverage, it was clear that Securicom, with all its resources and weapons, had no answer. The *Dish* were winning.

Why show that? It didn't make sense.

Her mind wandered. Was her father still alive? No. He surely died the day they got to her. Was her mother? She felt a twinge of something inside her, something painful that wrenched her guts. She sucked it back in. Emotion was the mind-killer.

The doors of her cell swished open.

"How is the patient today?" Pasco said. He was smiling, like the cat who got the cream, a phrase Pasco had taught her when she first ate a real piece of fruit. In Churin they had a similar phrase, the rat who got the skaatch, although if the rat ever did get the skaatch you had better make sure you got the rat, otherwise you went hungry.

Not here. Not in Mansion. She had never seen so much food, never seen anyone hungry. They were puffy with excess joules. The tray in front of her had cereal and milk, a banana, orange juice, and a real orange, cut into quarters, buttered toast and coffee. Any one item would have been worth a week's pay on the black market in Churin.

"I'm fine, thank you," she said, managing a half-smile back. She almost added, "You look happy today," but stopped short, worrying it would sound disingenuous.

She cooperated with Pasco and made sure the cameras knew it. She didn't want another handler. During her first few weeks of consciousness, different scientists administered 'tests'; torture disguised as research, making her jump like a rat, this way and that.

In contrast Pasco was always kind, so she tried to give him what he wanted, although it was not always apparent what that was, other than accessing iAm, which was the one thing she would not do.

"Have you been crying?" he said.

"No," she replied automatically. Had she?

Pasco glanced at the glass opposite her bed, at Churin, the Foremen now rushing the crowd, shock guns set to lethal levels. He picked up the remote and flicked off the volume.

"Off with this, I think. Now please, eat your breakfast. I have a surprise for you today which requires you to build up your energy. He held out the chair for her. "You eat like a bird."

"A bird?"

"Yes, you peck at it slowly, never eating very much."

"Not very much?" Every meal left her feeling like she was about to explode. "I have only ever seen one bird. A rare Churin Pica. It got into our trailer and bolted down a tray of skaatch in about three seconds. It was the greediest bird I ever saw."

Pasco smiled his crooked smile, not knowing if she was joking, and despite herself, Balmoral laughed, and then took two rapid bites of the banana. Just six weeks ago, she didn't know what a banana was, let alone that you had to peel it. She had never spent any time in the food sims.

"I did some research on the problem you had yesterday," he said.

"Problem?" she said, her mouth half full.

"Coming back from the, er . . . bathroom." He flushed slightly, as though the thought of a toilet embarrassed him. "I believe you might have damaged your hippocampus."

"I thought you said my scans came back clear."

"I . . . I did. This problem is not related to the accident."

"I don't understand."

"The hippocampus is responsible for orientation. When we move it fires neurons, laying out a virtual trail of breadcrumbs, so we know where we are, and where we have come from. It seems that after years of relying on iNet navigation, your hippocampus no longer functions."

"What?" she said, thinking again how in losing her connection to iNet, she had lost something of herself, become a stripped down version of the person she once was.

"There is always iAm," Pasco said gently.

"I've tried," she lied. "I've gone through all of the thought exercises but for some reason I can't get it to function."

"We could attempt a reverse projection, with iAm sending images through your neurons. First a simple word, then an image, then a sensation, as though you were in a sim."

"No," she snapped. iAm was the ultimate temptation, its promise, to engage with the intellisphere directly, no filter but the mind, no keyboard but thought, and it was for that reason iAm was also a trap, a fusion of technology and biology that could not be turned off, could not be controlled. If iAm meant *Voice* had direct access to her mind, Balmoral would prefer to remain half a person.

"I will try again," she said more gently, aware her flash of anger was a mistake, "but I don't know, maybe because of the accident . . ." She trailed off.

"That's all right." He placed a hand on her shoulder. It wasn't the first time he had touched her. Curiously she did not mind, did not instinctively flinch.

"I wish you'd eat more of your breakfast."

She had eaten the banana, three orange segments and half a piece of toast. "I'm full," she said. "It's so good but . . ."

She had almost said, *when I see the people in Churin, I feel guilty.* Another slip. It was too easy to let her guard down with Pasco. He drew her out in a way that made her uncomfortable. Was this how they would get what they wanted? By wearing her down with his small kindnesses? Even before she regained consciousness, she was aware of his presence, writing on her hand, a friend in the dark. She knew it was all an act, but still . . .

"You still haven't asked me about the surprise," he said.

Focus. Smile, act interested, ask a question in reply. "Well, what is it?" she said.

"We are going out!"

"I don't understand."

"I have tickets for a Steel Ball game! We're going to the Sky Dome!"

"How?" she said, but then the door swished open and the cleaner appeared to take away the breakfast things. Pasco, beaming, put his finger to his lips.

The cleaner.

The tiny piece of paper in the bedpan contained five letters and their associated trigger words, with Morse as the medium for communication. This morning the cleaner had banged out, dot, dot, dot against the bed. The letter "S".

Standby. We are coming.

The cleaner's instruction was a surprise and caught her off guard. Having spent eight weeks in the facility Balmoral could see no conceivable way they could get her out. So she had stalled.

"Wait," she had replied verbally, causing the cleaner's back to stiffen. It wasn't Morse, but the cleaner recognized the trigger word.

Wait – I'm not ready.

Balmoral now understood why today they would make their attempt, because she would be *outside* the facility. The cleaner took the tray.

"Wait," she said.

The cleaner's eyes flicked towards her.

"These are just too good to waste." She took a bite of the orange, pulling away the flesh with her mouth, putting the flat peel back on the tray. She then screwed up her face, and pulled one of the pips out from between her teeth and put it on the tray.

"Sorry, I should have warned you," Pasco said. "Those ones have seeds, it's from a . . . a real tree."

The cleaner took the tray, and gave the slightest of nods. The message had been delivered, the pip and the peel. The dot and the dash. "A" for *affirmative*.

Yes, Balmoral understood, yes she would work for them in return for breaking her out and yes, she would be ready.

13

SECTOR 7, MANSION SUBTERRANEA

Y OU'RE DRUNK, FLEUR," Lord shouted from across the common room, his tattoo snarling.

"Takes one to know one," she said and saluted him with the half empty vodka bottle. Then, stumbling, she swung into an empty table, as far away from him as she could get.

"Watch your step," Lord said, to a chorus of laughs from his brain-dead cronies, then more quietly, but just loud enough for her to hear, "stupid bitch."

She stuck up two fingers and took another swig. Lotus shuffled over to Lord's table and cuffed him on the back of his head. Lord laughed good humouredly, but his eyes retained their habitual anger.

If only she could get drunk, that would be something, but her system was so overloaded with adrenalin and synapse she just felt wired. A little uninhibited perhaps, but twitchy-buzzy rather than sloppy-clumsy, despite the stumble. Part of her was desperately tired, could sleep for a week, the other part knew she would not rest until Valencia and the others returned.

Was it just eight short hours ago she made the discovery that would bring the girl to them?

Trawling through the endless outgoing messages from Fresh Kills, she noticed a lot of excitement about that evening's Steel Ball game. It was the usual banter over which team would win and who was betting on what outcome, but then a single line slipped through, a question about whether they would be able to actually see the game in the arena.

And that set off a train of thought.

If they were going to the arena, why wouldn't they be able to see the game? The squaddies were tied exclusively to Fresh Kills, which meant that if they were there on duty, they were providing an escort for one of its inmates.

From there, she immediately pulled up Slick Boy's messages. For once he was uncharacteristically tight-lipped except for a single sentence which said he wouldn't be home Saturday night, he was working late. His girlfriend kicked up a fuss, told him that was it, she was leaving him, the usual histrionics, but he repeated the same single sentence, no excuses, no fabrication. His silence was all the evidence Fleur needed. If he was cheating on her, he would have made up something far more elaborate.

Valencia took some convincing. She sent a couple of operatives down to Sky Dome early that morning. Entire streets had been cordoned off, foot soldiers posted on every corner. The arena was crawling with all manner of agents, each of them teched to the eyeballs.

The Bedouin had sleepers embedded at Sky Dome, employees placed more than six months ago for the Clay II project. They confirmed security protocol for that evening had been changed at short notice. Something big was happening, but they had no other information.

"It's for her, Val," Fleur said excitedly. "It has to be!"

Valencia hesitated. She was reluctant to risk the entire cell without being sure, so she devised a simple test. By now, Balmoral would have reached the same conclusion as the Bedouin strategists, that any direct assault on Fresh Kills would fail. They would tell her they were going to make the attempt tonight. If Balmoral agreed, then for whatever reason, she was leaving the facility. If she replied in the negative, then she was going nowhere.

Balmoral's *affirmative* was enough for Valencia to mobilize every operative, inside and outside the tunnels. With the exception of Orlick nearly everyone who was not a skull was going to Mansion, and every sleeper in Mansion had been activated.

In the last eight weeks, the plans for extraction had been drilled like plays in Steel Ball, complete with fall backs and contingencies. Everyone knew that this particular game was for all the marbles. Whatever happened, the Bedouin would never be the same again.

The tunnels had never been so empty. Even the Garde had gone to Mansion. Only two remained to help Gravales keep order. Having fitted out the ground team, there was nothing more for the skulls to do. The mission would be a success or not, the outcome, out of their control. After the operatives moved out, the place quickly degenerated into a drinking fest, rules be damned. With twenty-four skulls and only two Garde, who was going to stop them?

Fleur took another swig of her bottle and wondered where the hell Cy Yozarian was. Her eyes alighted on Lotus, who smiled and ambled over to the table.

"How's my flower?" she asked, taking a seat. She cradled a steaming concoction in an old clay mug. Hot alc. Lotus didn't go in for anything actually drinkable. "Your boyfriend seems to be working out fine," she said.

Everyone referred to Cy Yozarian as her boyfriend. At first it irritated her, especially when Lord said it, but now she quite liked it. Nothing had happened between them, at least not yet. They were always friendly to each other, but in the last few weeks, she only had time for one thing, and he was not it.

"I suppose so."

Lotus stared into her mug and then glanced up, raking Fleur with those perceptive eyes. "Doesn't it strike you as odd that someone who came looking for freedom is made a prisoner, and yet has not murmured a word of complaint. He works harder and more happily for us than those here by vocation, those who *really* have a cause to hate the Autonomy."

"I would say avoiding the Cut is all the vocation anyone needed."

"Perhaps," Lotus considered, "but by his own admission he was guilty of what he did. Hardly like a Manaus, whose mother sold her daughters' organs to Life Science Corp to get the family through one particularly bad winter. Now that's a vocation."

As one of the recruitment officers, Lotus was big on vocation. She liked every Bedouin to have a bleeding heart story.

"What about Lord?" Fleur said. "What was his vocation? I pledge to be allowed to carry out my pathological tendencies . . ."

The old woman narrowed her eyes. "You know nothing about Lord, or his difficult history."

"No I don't, thank the *Faith*." She took another swig of vodka.

Lotus smiled. "Well at least his story can now be corroborated."

"Lord?" she said, confused.

"No, Cy Yozarian."

"I thought his connect was in prison?"

"They let the fat general out yesterday."

Inwardly, Fleur tensed. "You seriously have doubts about him? Still?"

"There's something there," Lotus said, "and Beaky doesn't like his face."

Fleur laughed. "That old vulture doesn't like anyone's face."

"Perhaps."

She felt a pang of irritation. Cy had busted his ass for Lotus for weeks. Scrubbing down every tunnel wall, servicing the filtration units, cleaning the latrines. And Lotus had an issue. Why? Because he didn't complain enough? Anyone could see the real reason for her suspicion which was that Lotus didn't personally recruit him, that Cy Yozarian was not one of her handpicked boys. It was pathetic. Even so, the news of the fat general's release stirred a deep-seated unease.

"Cy Yozarian is Bedouin by virtue of this." Fleur pointed to her cheek.

"He's Bedouin when Beaky says so, and when he says so, I'll be the first to drink to his good health." Lotus took a draught of her steaming alc. "Ah," she said, wiping her mouth, "strong enough to fell an elephant."

"That stuff will kill you."

"Maybe, but who wants to be old anyway?" She grinned a toothless grin.

Me, Fleur thought but didn't say. The experience on the rooftop taught her that she was afraid of death, and even more afraid of a living death in the tunnels.

This close, Fleur could detect a vague smell of piss coming from the old woman, could see the grooves in her shrivelled skin and the beginning of cataracts in those crazy eyes. She swore to herself for the hundredth time that she would escape, no matter what it took.

If the Bedouin brought back Balmoral Murraine, Fleur had it all worked out. She would be her friend in these dark tunnels, win her over, and then convince her to reprogram some lenses or whatever she had to do, to give Fleur a new identity, preferably a mid-level manager in Finance. From there she would convince Val to give her shore leave. It wouldn't be easy, but if Fleur could no longer be identified in Mansion, how could Val object? Then she would run, and keep on running. To Sector 2 if she had to, to somewhere Beaky couldn't track her, to live out her life away from the fight and the noise and the struggle.

She would have to get a job, of course, but with her new identity she could find work, somehow, somewhere, preferably in some remote outpost where all she had to do was keep the books straight.

If.

If they brought Balmoral back.

"What are you thinking?" Lotus said. "You look miles away."

Fleur took another swig from the bottle. "Nothing."

What if they never came back? This operation was by far the riskiest mission the Bedouin had ever attempted. The atmosphere in the common room was charged, the tension palpable, everyone aware that the Bedouin balanced on a knife edge. If the others never came back, they would be cut off from the world forever.

She forced herself to think of something else.

Cy Yozarian. She felt like jumping someone's bones tonight. Preferably his, whether he wanted her or not. She shifted in her seat to double-check he hadn't come into common room and became aware of her bladder.

"Time to break the seal," she said, half to herself, half to Lotus. She stood up, taking the bottle with her in case someone tried to swipe it.

Relieving herself in one of the stalls she thought, *yes*, tonight she would corner Yozarian, bring him back to her sleeping cube, lock the door and see what he could do.

She washed her hands, picked up the vodka and opened the door. Lord stood in the frame, blocking her exit. "Hey," he said casually.

"Hey," she replied.

"You seem . . . happy tonight."

She held up the bottle of vodka to salute him.

"Ah yes," he said, "a gift from her majesty for a job well done."

"S'right," she said.

"You know I was thinking, later, you and me . . ."

"No."

"You didn't let me finish," he said.

"I don't have to."

"Just hear me out. It's . . . it's difficult in there," he said, thumbing towards the common room, "in front of all the guys, you know, to act like I want to act, to say what I want to say. I . . . I miss you Fleur. I want another chance."

A small voice warned Fleur that she was in dangerous territory with this man, that she should let him down gently, not antagonize him. The vodka part of her brain, brimming with confidence, would not hear of it. How many times had he antagonized *her?*

Lord put an arm gently on her shoulder. "What do you say?" he said.

"Tempting, but I'd rather drown myself in the latrine. Enjoy your piss," she said, breaking away from him. "It's the only action you're going to get." She made an obscene gesture with her hand.

As she walked away, Cy Yozarian appeared in the narrow corridor, a six pack cradled under his arm. *To go with the one on his chest,* she thought.

"I've been looking for you," Fleur said, beaming.

"Me too. Looking for you I mean. I've got drinks." He held up the beer.

"Then what are we waiting for?" She dragged him over to the last empty table.

The common room had become even rowdier. Six or seven men stood at the bar, playing centurion, drinking a shot of beer every minute until a hundred shots had been drunk, or someone pissed themselves. At other tables, people laughed hysterically, or argued, or made out. A wild abandon filled the air.

Sitting opposite Cy Yozarian, Fleur felt a rare sense of euphoria creeping over her. It was probably the cocktail of alcohol and synapse that swilled around her system, but she didn't care. For once she felt great. Staring at Cy's face, she didn't even see the skull anymore. She was sucked in by his vitality, by those eyes that shone almost unnaturally from his face, by his thick, generous lips and the smell of his sweat.

He dug into his pocket and placed two rolls of quarters on the table, still in their paper.

"What's that for?"

"The beer," he said.

She pushed them away. "That was a gift."

Cy Yozarian had no privileges, so when she last placed an order from Mansion, she had added a six pack of his favourite beer.

"I pay my debts," he replied, pushing the rolls back towards her.

"Suit yourself," she said, but left them there. "How did you know it was me?"

"Oh, I don't know, male intuition," he said with a cocky smile. "And you're the only person who doesn't treat me like shit."

"Poor baby," she said, and reached over to another table to pick up two empty shot glasses. "Get some of this down you. It will make you feel better." She poured them each a shot of vodka.

Twisting the top off one of the beers, he said, "I can't. I'm allergic to spirits."

"Are you kidding me? That's what the adrenalin pen was for?"

"That and nuts. Pathetic, I know."

"There's still beer on tap. You should keep those for a rainy day." Every Friday, two barrels were painstakingly lowered down the plughole, and then the beer lasted as long as it lasted.

"Although," she said, indicating the bar, "judging by this lot, it's not going to be around long."

All the men were now laughing like hyenas at someone with a dark stain at his crotch.

"I like the beer you gave me," he said. "Cheers."

They clinked drinks. He downed the first bottle in a single go, and opened his second. Good, she wanted him to catch up.

"I've hardly seen you in the last couple of weeks. How are you enjoying life in the tunnels? Not what you bargained for, is it?"

He grimaced slightly, "Well . . . at least nobody is trying to eat me."

She laughed, a little too loudly. "Not yet anyway." She reached across and kissed him on the lips, not caring that he flinched slightly, not caring that Lord was back at his table, glowering at them from the corner.

14

RISTRAM LET HER kiss him and then pulled back, ignoring her glassy-eyed protest. He was aware of the undercurrent of hostility in the room, of Tamar Lord. He didn't want to provoke anything. Lotus might be the queen of the skulls, but Lord was their champion, the alpha male.

Even so, it was time to act. He had spent weeks with the Bedouin and had learned almost nothing. The fat general would be released soon and when that happened, Gravales would be on him like a vulture on road kill. The old man still stared at him, as though looking for the lie, and the Garde never seemed to be more than a few steps away. Not today though. Today they were all in Mansion, trying to extract the girl.

Part of him should be concerned about the attempt to bring in Balmoral Murraine. If half of what his uncle said about her was true, she would be a game changer for the *Dish*. But the truth was he didn't give a shit. He had his own obsessions to take care of. He still didn't know who killed his father.

The problem was that nobody talked about anything he needed to know. It was as though they had a code of silence whenever it came to past missions, and Tristram couldn't push his questions too far in case he aroused suspicion.

Lotus had informed him his status was a *non-dom*; non-domiciled until cleared, which among other things meant no privileges, no fraternizing, no access to firearms and no wandering the tunnels between midnight and five.

Apart from the access to weapons, these restrictions were mostly pointless, except in one aspect; it kept the other Bedouin on guard around him. It was difficult to do anything, say anything, or go anywhere without being watched.

Fleur was more forthcoming, but she hadn't been around much, and even she clammed up when it came to talking about operations.

There was something else too. At times, Tristram was sure she was on to him. It made him reticent, anxious to avoid saying anything that might trigger whatever her unconscious self already knew.

"This place has gone crazy," he said, finishing his second beer, opening the third. "Is it always like this during a mission?"

"We've never had a mission like this." She made a circular motion with her finger. "Tonight we're spinning the wheel and putting the house on black."

He glanced at her bottle of vodka. Half gone. She was buzzed, but she was one of those drinkers who could take it, who remained coherent pretty much until the moment they toppled over, and she wasn't close to that yet. He drank the beer like a shot, and banged the empty bottle on the table.

"Thirsty boy," she said, smiling.

"It's good stuff." He wiped his sleeve across his mouth.

Fleur's beer was a stroke of luck. She had casually asked him what he missed most from Mansion and he casually mentioned his favourite beer, *he couldn't stand the crap they had on tap*. The bottles appeared two days later, ordered for him from the weekly consignment. His favourite beer was a dark ale that came in a black bottle with a twist-off top. They were now full of water. He worked better with a completely clear head; hit better, stabbed better, shot better. Taking lives was a clinical business, and he approached it as sober as a surgeon. But he wanted Fleur to think he was drinking, to make her think he too was off guard, to give himself license.

He opened the fourth bottle. "This isn't the biggest thing you guys have ever tried to pull off, is it? I mean, breaking out Gravales was bigger, right?"

"That didn't involve the entire cell."

Tristram considered. "And wasn't it you guys who once tried to assassinate the Chairman himself?"

Fleur's eyes narrowed. He had to be very careful. For some reason his question sobered her. "Boring. Let's talk about something else."

"I know I'm soooo boring . . ." he said lightly. "It's just I don't understand why nobody ever talks about it. The past I mean. Now I'm stuck here, I want to know something about the organization. It's not like I can leave . . ."

"Let me tell you a story," she said seriously. "We once had a guy deep in Top 10, a maverick called Nicky Marr. He played for big stakes, took crazy risks and had a sex addiction, but Val tolerated him because his information was better than all the other undercovers put together."

She took a swig from her bottle, no longer interested in the shot glass.

"So, the inevitable happened. He took one risk too many, said the wrong thing to the wrong girl, and the squaddies got to him, but because he only had a single contact in the Bedouin, there was only so much information he could cough up. You understand?"

"Yes, but I don't see . . ."

"Don't interrupt." She cut him off, her face flushed. "You asked the fucking question, this is the answer. Lotus was his connect. The day he was caught was the day she was skulled. What Lotus didn't realise was that she and Nicky had once discussed the Gravales raid and a couple of the people involved, one of whom was based here but maintained a profile in Mansion. Eventually Marr gave them his name. Jordan Travis. Securicom pulled him in."

Another swig.

"Jordan managed to send a distress call to warn us, but didn't succeed in ingesting a suicide pill before they got to him." Fleur wiped something from her eye. "All operatives are trained to hold out in an interrogation for seventy-two hours. After that, pumped full of chemicals, they give up everything."

Tristram was familiar with the case. At the time, all the Securicom analysts believed Travis was lying. How could the Bedouin be based in Mansion's sewers? The story only held up under chemical interrogation because Travis believed it. He was dismissed as a *Dish* bag man who knew nothing of use about the organization. Securicom didn't even bother following up.

Fleur took another slug of vodka. Tristram knocked back his water.

"Valencia blew the plughole, flooded the tunnels and we moved the whole operation a mile and a half north, starting all over again. It was a difficult time. We lived knee deep in shit for nine months. Some tried to desert and were shot for their efforts. They aren't recorded on the honour roll," she nodded to the stars on the far wall of the cave, "but they were still our friends." She looked at him, her eyes bleary and red. "Boy, you really know how to kill a mood."

"Sorry, I was just curious," he said quietly.

"What does it matter anyway? Us skulls aren't going anywhere, but you know what? Lose a few lives and caution becomes part of your DNA."

They sat in silence. Across the room, two men began shouting at each other, another two pulled them apart.

"Why don't you kiss me again?" she said, her eyes shining.

You kissed me, he thought. "I can't risk it. It's against the rules for me to *fraternize*."

Fleur reached across and this time pushed her tongue into his mouth. Definitely more sour than salt. "Fuck the rules," she said finally pulling away. "Besides you'll be cleared by tomorrow, maybe even tonight."

Inwardly he tensed, outwardly he remained calm.

"How do you know?"

She leaned close. "Your man in Bodia is at large again."

"Great!" he said, controlling his facial muscles. "So how long until we hear?"

Fleur shrugged. "Maybe in the next hour, maybe a couple of days. You can never really tell. It all depends whether they have someone checking the machine regularly. Bodia can be a little lax. They tend to be on soma time, if you know what I mean."

"The machine?"

Fleur raised her eyebrows, "Oh of course, you don't know, do you? We use a point-to-point hard line. It's something called a fax. Silly name, isn't it?"

"Analog?" Tristram said, familiar with the term but surprised something so obsolete could still be in use. "But surely all the lines were ripped up or put out of order when the world went wireless?"

Fleur shrugged. "Not all of them. I don't know who set it up. Beaky, I suppose, while he was still a big cheese in Top 10. It's not the most convenient form of communication. Our line is a safe house, about an hour from Mansion. We need a courier to run back and forth, and paper is always a bitch to get hold of, but it's off the grid and it works. I told you Securicom was too tech for their own good. They'd never dream of it, would they?"

"I wouldn't know," he said, too quickly, unnerved by the directness of her question.

"So," she said, "this time I want you to mean it when you kiss me."

"What?" he laughed.

"You heard me. Mean it."

Reaching across, he pushed his lips against hers, experiencing again that same softness. He could almost lose himself in such a kiss, except that emotion was beyond him now, his feelings cauterized by what he had seen and done as a sandman. When he felt the warm pulse of another creature, he couldn't help thinking how easily that pulse could be stopped, and how much he might like to do it. Yes, tonight she would speak about what happened to his father, one way or the other.

"Get away from her!" Lord grabbed his shoulder and yanked him backwards. One of the beer bottles smashed on the ground.

"What are you doing?" Fleur screamed.

"I'm talking to him, not you!" Lord snarled drunkenly.

Straightening himself, Tristram wrapped his hand around one of the rolls of quarters on the table. The rest of the common room was suddenly silent, eyeing them with excitement.

Lord was six-four, two hundred and fifty pounds at least, and somehow, despite the alcohol and damp and lack of space, he kept himself in shape. Heavy boots, grease stained jeans, scar tissue around his left brow, and a fistful of rings. He fancied himself as a hard man.

Tristram sighed, slowly stood up, and faced him.

"Then talk," he said. Tristram rolled his neck back and forth, to give the impression he knew what he was doing. Covertly, he stretched his toes to run some muscle tension up the back of his legs, his back and shoulders. He breathed through his nose and pulled his fingers tight over the quarters, the next best thing to having a fistful of rings.

"Please, Cy," Fleur said, her voice higher than usual, "it's not worth it."

Tristram said nothing. In his peripheral vision, he saw Lotus leave the common room.

"He's a tough guy," Lord said, smiling. He flexed his steroidal biceps and whipped his arm out in an exaggerated feint. Tristram flinched as though he actually expected the punch.

Lord laughed. "And they say you were in the Cut! My pet rat is less skittish than you!" He turned around to his table of friends, as though to continue the banter, but in the same movement swung around with a vicious roundhouse.

Tristram saw it coming, but to get out of this alive, he needed to take a punch before he gave one. He turned and let the ring-covered fist smash into his left shoulder. Ignoring the explosion of pain, Tristram pivoted and jabbed a hard left into Lord's jaw. The big man looked surprised, but before he could react, Tristram snapped his right fist into the side of Lord's head, the quarters turning a strong punch into a near fatal one. Lord wobbled unsteadily on his feet and then fell back onto the chairs, out cold.

Tristram could have drawn the fight out, made it more of a contest, but he had to end it quickly. Less chance of the mob, with their adrenalin pumping, to get worked up and descend on the outsider. Glancing up at the image of his uncle's head he permitted himself a small smile and dropped the quarters on the ground.

"What the hell do you think you are doing?" Gravales said from the doorway, flanked by two Garde.

"Defending myself," Tristram said.

Gravales stared at Tristram and then at Lord's prostrate form. "Really?"

"Cy didn't do anything," Fleur said, a little unsteady on her feet.

"Sit down," Gravales rasped, glaring at her. "Lotus, attend to Tamar."

The old woman shuffled to where the big man lay.

"And you Cy Yozarian, I think *you* better come with *me*." Gravales nodded to the Garde. They stepped forward, shock guns whining.

15

A T Stern Rock, the instructors said if a sandman made a miscalculation
in the field, eighty percent of the time it cost them their life. Inwardly
Tristram cursed his stupidity. He should have known what Lotus would
do when the fight broke out, how Gravales would respond. By the time they
released him from the cooler it would be too late, his cover blown to pieces. He
was a dead man. He wondered how Gravales would do it. Just walk right up to
the bars and put a bullet in his brain, that seemed about right.

Would they bother interrogating him? Probably not. They would guess the two
most important facts, firstly that he was an undercover operative, and secondly
that Securicom had no idea where he was, otherwise they would already be here.
They didn't know about iAm, but without connection to the intellisphere it was
nothing more than a glorified memory chip. He felt a reluctant admiration for
Valencia, for the foresight of placing the headquarters underground, hardwiring
computer consoles to the surface.

Tristram wasn't afraid of death. Having seen it so many times, in all its colour-
ful forms, he knew it was nothing special. One minute, you were animated flesh
with cares and motivations, the next, nothing, and what came next, he couldn't
do anything about. Ninety percent of the *Faith* obsessed Autonomy believed
the afterlife was everlasting bliss. The alternative, he guessed, was a blank. There
wasn't much difference between the two when it came down to it, not when
eternity was the timescale.

The cell was about eight by five. Not great, but he'd seen worse. Some sleeping
cubes in Mansion were smaller. There was a small wooden bench for sitting. Part
of the cobbled stone dripped with water from some catchment above, filling the
air with a miasma of damp. They called it the "licking wall". No food or water
was permitted during the twenty-four hour cool off period after a fight, so the
hungover, dehydrated inmates sucked on the drips. There was also a ceramic toilet,
but it contained not fresh water but dank, fetid urine with a browning crust.

Fortunately Tristram was anything but thirsty. He had relieved himself twice already, bloated with the bottles of water, filling the toilet to the brink. It didn't flush.

He heard the whirring of a mechanical lock, and backed away from the bars. The four detention cells were located at the end of a long corridor, sealing them off from the rest of the living quarters. There was another cell, next to the outer door, but that was for the Garde when they had enough manpower to assign one to the inmates. Only the Garde had keys to the cells, but the outer door was operated by a palm print from anyone with the authorization to enter.

He heard steps come down the corridor, slow but self-assured. The old man came into view. In one hand he held a piece of paper, in the other, a small stool. No Garde. Gravales wanted them to be alone. He sat down a cautious distance from the bars.

"The fat general got back to us regarding my inquiry over your credentials," the old man said. He held up the semi-translucent fax paper. "This was his reply." There were no actual words, just a stick figure drawing of a man hanging from a tree. "You have to credit the fat general; he has a sense of humour."

Tristram said nothing.

Gravales pulled out his Luger and placed it on his knees. "I knew you were wrong from the moment I saw you. Your cover was good, very good, but you were never *right*. Something bothered me. You had the haunted look of one who has seen the Cut, but not the necessary fear. Any man who has wandered those dark lands, no matter how brave, comes back changed. It's like staring into the heart of darkness, at the very worst of what man is, devoid of civilization."

Gravales let out a hacking cough and pulled his coat around him. Clearing his throat, he spat a gob of bloody phlegm on the ground.

"But there's more," he rasped. "I know who you are. Your profile, the shape of your head, the bulldog neck, almost identical. Thirty pounds lighter, thirty years younger, and you could be Maglan himself, rather than his nephew. Tristram Eborgersen, all grown up and full of bile, ready to take absurd risks in memory of your poor dead father. Am I right?"

So that was it, he had come to boast, to let Tristram know exactly how brilliant he was before putting a bullet in his brain.

"To think you stood under his face and still I did not see it, until this." He dropped the fax. His brow furrowed, and he leaned closer, his black vulture eyes fixed on Tristram. "So, they have mastered retinal surgery after all."

He let out another hacking cough that shook his frame. In Mansion, Gravales could expect to live to a hundred and ten, maybe even a hundred and twenty at a push. Down here, it looked like he wouldn't last the year.

"What?" he wheezed, "Nothing to say? Aren't you a little bit curious now your death wish of a mission has come to an end? Who gave the order? Who pulled the trigger? That's why you're here, isn't it?" Gravales gave a ghastly smile, his tombstone teeth flecked with blood.

Still Tristram said nothing. If Gravales knew how badly he wanted to know, the old man would not tell him, but remain mute to torture him. If you wanted to know something, silence was sometimes your only friend.

Gravales studied him. "I gave the order," he said finally. "Valencia pulled the trigger, Clay watched the roof, and your girlfriend, yes, sweet little Fleur Cliquot, picked out your father from all the others, getting it wrong of course, but still making her mark on the world. You know, what disturbed me afterwards, and believe me I've had a long time to think about it, is that night Maglan broke our codes, intercepted our communications, and yet somehow let your father, with his presidential identikit, walk straight into a sniper's sight. Makes you wonder, doesn't it?"

Tristram betrayed nothing, keeping his face as stony as the wall he leant against.

"What is it? Cat got your tongue?"

"You mistake my silence for interest, when it is in fact the opposite," Tristram said flatly. "The bullet will be a relief from your pontificating."

"Bullet?" Gravales gave a hollow laugh. "Bullet, I like that. How . . . optimistic of you. No, I have arranged something much more gratifying." Gravales picked up his stool and turned to go. At the same time, Tristram heard three pairs of steel-capped boots walking down the corridor.

"They've assured me they will burn out your tongue before they go to work. That way your screams will not alert the Garde. By the time our ardent leader returns, with all her civilizing rules, you'll be a corpse floating down a sewer pipe; a bloodied pulp without a tongue, or nails, or teeth, or genitals."

Tamar Lord appeared around the corner, flanked by two of his workshop cronies. Tristram recognized both of them; a seven foot machinist called Lemmy and the barrel-shaped, not very bright, Urzil. Lemmy carried equipment from the workshop slung over his shoulder; a buzzsaw, a welder and industrial pliers. Urzil held a vice and selection of gimlets.

"I'll leave you boys to it," Gravales said and walked away up the corridor.

Lord's jaw was heavily bandaged and his teeth had been wired together. In one hand he held a shock gun, in the other a bowie knife.

"We're going to have some fun tonight, boy," he said.

16

SECTOR 1, MANSION

E ARLY EVENING, AND the low-slung sun pushed its tired beams through the gaps in the buildings before finding the Sky Dome and lighting it up like some rival sunset. Costing over a trillion credits, the huge golden ball towered over the sea wall on Mansion's southern tip.

Vaguely Balmoral wondered if there would be views of the ocean once they were inside. She had never seen the sea, except in a sim.

The avenue thronged with people making their way to the arena, five or six rows deep. When she saw the crowds, she thought of the changing shifts at the Battery, but the contrast with those drab, grey shadows couldn't have been more marked. This crowd hummed with excitement, nearly all of them wearing the bright colours of their team, the racing green hoops of the Strontia Dogs, or the claret and blue of the Muscle Boys. Many had liquid screens on the front and back of their shirts; usually a two hundred and eighty pound, mega-cut player performing some impossible feet of athleticism.

From the front seat of their transport, Pasco prattled on about the different players and whenever he turned around, Balmoral gave him a small smile of encouragement. She wondered what would happen to Pasco when the *Dish* tried to rescue her.

"We're going to be in a box," he said, "one of the network executive suites."

"Network executive?"

Pasco laughed. "Ah yes, it's an old word, but it's a rank in MediaCom for an Elite dedicated exclusively to Steel Ball. The game has its own executive class, because of its importance to the Autonomy."

Important, she thought, because of Steel Ball's unqualified success at making people of all sectors pay attention to something that ultimately was of no importance, a distraction from things that matter, such as the quality of their lives and the institutions that governed them.

"I read somewhere that they are the most highly compensated executives in MediaCom, including those responsible for the *Faith*," Pasco said.

"I would imagine the latter aren't into worldly riches," Balmoral said.

"Oh, you would be surprised," Pasco said seriously, but then laughed as he caught her eye. She had not told a joke before. Even the two agents in the back of the transport cracked a smile.

Unconsciously she probed their identikits and for the fiftieth time had to remind herself that the plastic iNet lenses she wore were just for show, that she had no connection. Is that why she had been let out, to tempt her into interaction with the world around her? To force her brain to meld with iAm? It seemed thin, but she could think of no other reason and that bothered her.

Still, she didn't need iNet to tell her that the agents were Elite, it exuded from every pore. There was about a hundred-thousand credits of tech on each arm, and their lenses were like nothing she had ever seen. She sat behind opaque windows, dense enough to be bullet proof. Other identical transports surrounded them, each with the same trademark ballistic armour. They were taking no chances.

As they drove slowly past, a fan would peer in, hungry for a glimpse of their hero's identikit, assuming wrongly that the transport carried a player. They would turn away disappointed. The dark glass blocked all signals. She studied their fresh faces, joule plump and water fat; rosy cheeks and perfect teeth, smooth skin and healthy complexion. The procession of images reminded her of the impossibly beautiful children at the school so long ago. A beauty that had disturbed her so profoundly, she erased it.

The terrible sense of the crime would hang over her life forever. She was not the same person as all those years ago, not even in the physical sense. The human body was like a shifting dune of sand moving across the desert plain, each grain the equivalent of an atom. Every seven years not one single grain of the original remained. It stood to reason therefore that the girl who killed all those children was not her, but particles now spread to the far corners of the universe. The thought did not comfort her as much as it should.

They pulled up outside the massive, gleaming dome. At the base of the building were multiple arches that looked to Balmoral like some creature's teeth, ready to chew you up before you dropped into its vast bowels.

They were told to remain seated while agents from support vehicles got out of their cars. An excited ripple passed through the crowd. These men were as big as Steel Ball players, after all. Is that Uni Su? Is that Starblind? Even Balmoral knew these storied names, it was impossible not to, but whatever the men's identikit said caused the onlookers to quickly move away.

They were given a signal and the transport drove into the stadium itself, while other agents jogged behind. Only when they were inside were they allowed to exit, Pasco practically bouncing out of the front seat.

A man in a pristine suit greeted them, and led them through a private door. The two Elite agents followed them. "My name is Julian Cort," he said. "I will be your guide today."

"No relation to the great player of the 2040s?" Pasco beamed.

"Unfortunately, not. I played in my day, of course, a long time ago now, but I was always more interested in the *business* side of the sport, and I must say, it has treated me well." He walked with short, crisp, steps, meticulous and exact. "Our first stop," he said, "is under the dome, to the locker room."

They stopped in front of a steel door. Balmoral noticed the ret scan, which flashed green, but Cort also entered a security code, about thirty digits by the look of it.

"I don't believe it!" Pasco whispered excitedly. "We're actually going to see the players!"

"Is that good?" Balmoral replied.

"You don't understand, these athletes are so protected that to actually see them warm up before a game, well it's . . ."

"Unheard of," Julian Cort said. "Rarely is anyone outside the network granted access to our gladiators. These D1 players are the most famous faces in the Autonomy, a few elite professionals out of thirteen billion citizens, and we have to protect them. Everybody wants a piece of them. Now if you'll follow me this way."

Balmoral was more confused than ever. What was this trip really all about? It made no sense.

Pasco jabbered on in excited tones, listing all the athletes that were playing in tonight's game, barely able to contain himself over this once in a lifetime opportunity.

"Why?" Balmoral cut in.

"I beg your pardon?" Cort said.

Her guards turned to her with their mirrored lenses.

"If it is unheard of, why are we meeting them?"

Cort gave her a sickly smile. "I thought you might enjoy it."

Was he lying? If she had iNet, Balmoral would have hacked his biosquare and measured the sweat on his hands, his retinal dilation, and the moisture of the throat. Then she would have known for sure. As it was, his two twitchy steps away from her, the folded arms, the very slight change of colour in his face told her there was something more here than he was letting on. But what?

She studied him more closely. He was probably mid-seventies, but trying to pass himself off as someone much younger. With his facial enhancements, wrinkle-free forehead and tan powder on the cheeks and nose, he was going for about fifty. The neck was scraggy though, and the patches under the eyes were white from years of buffing and smoothing. The eyes themselves were old, had seen a lot, consistent with someone born in the last century, someone who lived through the environmental collapse. His reference to playing Steel Ball was a lie, he was already too old when the sport became popular, and his upright posture and perfectly straight steps gave him away. Even LifeScience couldn't patch up Steel Ball injuries.

"But seeing them on the day of an actual game? Won't that . . . throw off their preparations?" Balmoral said.

Cort eyed her warily. "If the Chairman himself makes a request, one tends to accommodate it."

Balmoral's unease increased. Did Maglan know the *Dish* would attempt to rescue to her? Was that it? Was she bait?

Even Pasco was disturbed by the reference to his uncle, although he tried not to show it when she glanced at him.

At the end of the corridor another man waited for them, conspicuous with his naked eyes. He cast around at their approach. He held a silver tray, a low grade worker playing the part of a piece of furniture. As they approached she noticed his eyes were cloudy and white with cataracts, an easy condition to correct, regardless of economic standing.

"So this is it," Cort said, rubbing his hands. "The athletes' gymnasium and locker room, where they prepare themselves before the big game." He gestured to the tray. "Please, everyone remove your glasses and any other recording devices. The players' images, conversation and behaviour are all trademarks of the Steel Ball enterprise. No exceptions."

To her surprise, the agents were first to comply, one of them removing something from his wrist as well as his lenses. Balmoral liked this less and less. Nothing added up. She wondered if the agents were fitted with iAm, the glasses, like her own, just for show. Pasco, with some regret, placed his lenses on the tray, and Balmoral did the same. There was no easy way to explain her situation.

"Step this way," the Network executive said, and the doors of the famous gymnasium swung open.

17

SECTOR 1, MANSION SUBTERRANEA

ES, WE'RE GONNA have some fun, boy!" Lord said, waving the bowie knife around. "Gonna hack off your balls and then make you eat that maggot you call your penis."

Wouldn't he have to hack that off first as well? Or perhaps he hadn't heard right. Lord was difficult to understand as everything he said was through clenched teeth.

The important point was that they had no key, unless they planned to torture him with the buzzsaw, which he doubted. It was too messy and would be over too quickly. Their other tools were much better for that.

No key meant the Garde were not involved. He guessed that made sense. Permitting Lord to torture a prisoner to death was hardly worthy of the Bedouin. However, Gravales knew animals like Lord had to be fed, to keep them loyal, to keep them out of trouble. They were locked in here. The President's palm print had let them in, his palm print would have to let them out again. Tristram wondered how much time he had promised them. An hour? Or all night?

The rest of the Bedouin would be told it was a clean bullet to the back of the head, and nobody but the four men would know any different. None of them was armed with an actual gun. The operation in Mansion cleaned out the armoury.

Urzil plugged the buzz saw into an electrical socket just beyond the cell, and kicked it into high gear. His dumb, round face showed intense concentration behind the goggles as he placed it on the bars, flecks of hot yellow metal flying left and right.

Lemmy and Lord stood back a few paces to give Urzil some room, all the time Lord talking trash about what they were going to do to him when they got inside. Tristram stood as far back against the cell wall as he could. He didn't need a red hot shard of iron in his eye.

Vaguely Tristram wondered how they were going to explain the destroyed door to the Garde, but then figured they would have time to replace it before it was discovered. They were machinists, after all.

Urzil cut through one bar, slicing at about head height and then a foot below. He moved onto the second. They planned to remove the lock, enabling the door to be pulled open.

Sweat beaded on Urzil's face, his tongue lolled between his teeth. This second bar was awkwardly placed to get at with the buzzsaw, it was too close to the wall, and he had to lean in to cut it.

"See this?" Lord held up a gimlet, his mouth foaming. "We're going to skewer out your eyes and piss into the holes . . ."

Blah, blah, blah.

Urzil bent forward, straining at the last fiddly bit around the lock, both hands on the saw. At the point he was most off balance, Tristram suddenly snapped forward, yanking Urzil's left arm into the cell, prizing his fingers from the machine. For an instant Tristram thought he'd lost the opportunity. Urzil might not be very bright, but his grip on the saw was like an ape's and he pulled back. If Lemmy and Lord got hold of it too, there would be no contest.

Quickly, Tristram yanked Urzil forward again, putting every ounce of strength into it, and as the fat man barrelled into the half cut bars, the tension left his hand for a second. Tristram whipped Urzil's arm up inside the cell, kicking the elbow as he did so. There was a crack. Urzil screamed and the saw dropped to the ground. In a flash, Tristram ripped off his shirt and tied the hand of broken arm against the cell bar so that Urzil couldn't pull away. He screamed in agony.

Lord cursed and stepped forward, his shock gun whining, only then realizing the limitation of the device. To make contact he would need to lean forward into the cell. If he leant forward, he might end up like Urzil. He wasn't dumb enough for that.

The buzzsaw spun on the ground, thrashing around like a shark on a boat. Tristram trod carefully. One misstep and the saw would slice off his foot. Tristram kicked it against the wall, and the power chord snapped out of the back. He picked it up with the wheel still spinning and calmly thrust the blade into Urzil's neck.

Urzil's pig-like eyes widened in shock. His neck yawned open in a plume of red, his blood pumping onto the ground. Tristram grabbed Urzil's second hand, pulled it through the bars and tied his wrists together, so that he slumped forward, over the lock. If Lord wanted to move Urzil out of the way, he would have to reach inside the cell. Urzil gurgled three or four times, as though he was drowning and then was silent.

"One zip," Tristram said, and stepped back against the wall of his cell.

18

SECTOR 1, MANSION

As jokes went, Pasco didn't find this one funny. In fact, he struggled to keep his temper. "Yes, yes, very good," he said, a fake smile plastered to his face. The Network executive had not taken them to the gymnasium to meet the athletes, but to a cockroach-infested office.

A bunch of nerds sat at desks surrounded by their own skuzz, the ground covered with all manner of trash; take away boxes, discarded cans of triple-caf, and rolled up tissues containing things he didn't even want to think about.

"This is not a joke," the Network executive said. Without his lenses, Pasco had forgotten his name. "There," he said, pointing to the individuals decamped in the squalor, "are your athletes."

"Of course they are," Pasco said, annoyed now at being taken for an idiot.

There was an obese, Asiatic man, four hundred pounds at least, his face buried in a box of Sweet and Sour. There was a grey haired, ponytailed man leaning back in his chair and sipping on a beer and next to him a razor thin woman, covered from head to toe in tattoos, with piercings all over her face, cigarette in one hand, triple-caf in the other. She regarded them warily, and took a drag on her smoke. The rest of the inhabitants were prostrate in their chairs, iNet on, holopads out, twitching their fingers left and right, deep in some sim or other.

The obese man lifted his head out of the box of food and noticing them for the first time, dropped the box and burped loudly. "Whoa," he said, "visitors."

"Fuuuuck," the grey haired man said.

"Look . . ." Pasco said angrily to their guide, but the words caught in his throat. Julian Cort, that was his name, was as surprised and disgusted by what he saw as Pasco. He stood there, taking in the room as though he couldn't quite believe it either.

The obese, greasy man wiped his mouth with his shirt, cracked his knuckles and then came towards them. A wheel protruded from beneath his immense belly, and as he walked, it took his weight, enabling him to waddle around the room. An intense smell of body odour and garlic wafted before him.

"When are we going to the gymnasium?" Pasco said impatiently, aware his voice sounded strained. "Sorry about this nonsense," he said, turning to Balmoral.

She stared back at him, saying nothing, her black eyes full of concern.

The man put out his pudgy hand, the belly wheel straining beneath him.

"Uni Su," he said.

19

O N FIRST ENTERING the room, it took Balmoral a moment to process it, but then she understood. These were the athletes, not the apparent flesh and blood that pounded up and down the famous caged arena, but elite level gamers perpetuating the biggest lie ever told.

This room was their biosphere, a self-sufficient habitat for their needs. On one wall was an electronic dumb waiter for delivering food, triple-caf and the other stimulants they required. There were bathrooms located on the other side, but judging by the distinct tang of urine, more than one of them didn't bother to get up. All of them were kept prisoners in here, to protect the secret of the greatest, most lucrative sport that had ever been.

"Uni Su?" Pasco repeated, his voice trembling.

"Or at least," Uni Su said, "he's one of my guys, and my favourite I might add. We all play multiples, have to. There's only eight of us and there's thirty-two pro teams. But I am Uni Su tonight."

Her initial reaction surprised her. More than anything she wanted to reach out and hug Pasco, tell him it didn't matter, that this sport he loved was still real, in its way. Only the media had changed.

Why was she being so illogical?

Viewed rationally, Pasco was her jailer. To feel loyalty towards him was to play into Securicom's hands. Pasco was not a person, but a tactic. The one she was supposed open up to, the one around whom she would drop her guard.

"H-how?" Pasco stuttered.

"How what?" Su's eyes were little more than slits in his vast, round face.

"How is this possible? The games are live. People come here to watch . . ."

"Do they?" Su said. "Or do they sit in sim chairs that jack directly into the experience? The chair shaking every time there is a hit, the noise from the cage pumped directly into their implants, their visuals in high-def, not from the perspective of a few hundred feet above the field, but right up close in three dimensions. Even before the chairs, people looked more at their screens than what was going on below."

Uni Su seemed desperate to talk. It was probably the first time in a while he had seen someone from the outside. The Network executive's shock showed that he didn't often come in here either. Of course he knew about the lie, but knowing it, and seeing it first-hand, were two different things. Most of the time he probably convinced himself that it was real. Even the two Securicom agents were fazed, despite all their training.

"S-some must watch with the naked eye surely?" said Pasco.

"Why would they?" the man with the grey ponytail said, waving his drink in their faces. "Would you? And even if you did, the holograms, viewed from that distance, are convincing enough. Hell, there's nobody left who could tell the difference."

"Then I've been watching a lie all these years . . ."

"A lie? No," Uni Su said expansively. "The games are real and we are real, the best of the best, the most successful gamers on the planet."

"But this . . . this is the most popular sport in the Autonomy. Kids spend their whole lives trying to break through, to make it into the big leagues. Where do they all go?"

"Let me ask you one question," the man with the ponytail said. "Have you ever seen a game with your naked eye? A recreational game in a park or amateur game in a sports club . . ."

"No, but . . ."

"And do you think they have parks and arenas in Sector 2 and 3? Where would the players get the necessary joules? Where would they get the free time? Even in Sector 1 nobody plays. Why? Because it fucks people up. But everybody watches. Why? Because it fucks people up, and people like that," Ponytail said.

"Everyone assumes it is being played somewhere else, just not where they happen to be," Uni Su said, "I know I did. Even the feeder leagues are just computer generated algorithms."

"But the scouts, they have scouts that cover the four corners of the Autonomy, looking for talent."

"That they do," Uni Su said. "How do you think they found me? I come from a large family in Sector 2, Farsee. Sixteen brothers and sisters. My father had three wives. Called it his Battery. We lived on the very outskirts of the stacks, in ramshackle tents, too poor even for our own trailer. Every one of us worked in the lodges, or the Battery, or the treadle mill. But unlike Farsee's other three hundred million inhabitants, I had one incredible talent."

He made his pudgy fingers dance, as though playing an air piano, but with a speed and dexterity that almost seemed to be a trick of the light.

"I was undefeated on *Total Warcraft*, *Wrestle Me Manic* and *The Counterpoint*, my favourite sims back then. I made my debut playing Uni Su, you know."

"I remember that game," Pasco said weakly.

"And what a game it was," Ponytail said. "I was deRacine, was convinced this new kid was nothing and we had the game wrapped up. Then this motherfucker comes along and does some things none of us had ever seen."

Su chuckled. "And you've been chasing my tail ever since."

"In your dreams," Ponytail replied, "I have you on every stat, except assists."

"In your dreams," the girl with piercings parroted, speaking for the first time, "I have you both on every stat, period."

"Ah, yes," Ponytail said, "Lady Nightshade, we stand in awe of your total awesomeness, although I do recall a Raptors vs. Azul match in '57 when I handed you your metal studded ass on a platter . . ."

And then the three of them were suddenly at it, delving into the minute arcana of the game, reliving moves, and scores and what they called cheap swerves.

Pasco's face was fixed in an expression of horror.

"The credits are obscene, of course," Uni Su said, turning back to them, answering a question that hadn't been asked. "I was eighteen when they first scouted me, without ten credits to my name. According to my Finance guy, I'm now one of the top thousand richest individuals in the Autonomy. Way behind this old-timer, of course," he gestured to Ponytail, who although still arguing with the girl, raised his drink to the room in salute. "By the time I cash out I expect to be in the five-hundreds, right up there with the Nightshade."

"But you live in this one room," Balmoral said, speaking for the first time.

"Not forever. Everyone gets kicked out eventually. Anyone who makes it here," he gestured to the room, "stays until they lose ten consecutive matches, or five hundred matches period, or are disabled on the field a thousand times. For some the stay is a season, for others," he nodded to the pierced girl, "it can be twenty years."

"B-but this room," Pasco echoed.

"Buddy, we got everything we need right here," Ponytail said, swinging around three sixty degrees in his chair. "Steel Ball almost every night, the most exciting sport in the world, access to any alt life sims during the day. Food delivered to our stations at the flick of an eyelid. A bot that comes in and cleans. We live like princes now, and will retire like emperors somewhere in Sector 1. Who wouldn't want this life? Of course, everything is forfeit if we ever breathe a word to anyone."

"Worse," Su frowned, "we'd get clamped in a treadle mill. So it's easy to keep on the straight and narrow, making a few million cred a year. Of course, the creds bring their own problems. Everyone expects you to throw it around, your hands forever in your pockets. Girls I don't even know demand champagne that costs more than an entire Stack back in Farsee." His fat face filled with lust. "Although . . . what they do for me afterwards sort of makes up for it, if you know what I mean."

"What?" Pasco said, confused.

Balmoral too had lost the thread of conversation, until she realised Su was confusing some alt life sim he was playing with what passed as reality in this strange, boxed in world.

A low pitched alarm filled the room and immediately brought Su out of his revelry. It had a Pavlovian effect on all of the players, but instead of stimulating hunger, induced a stone cold focus.

"They have to get ready," Julian Cort said, by way of explanation. "Game time in fifteen minutes."

"Buckle up boys," the girl with the piercings said. "It's going to be a tense one tonight."

"Nah," quipped Ponytail, "different tune maybe, but same words man, same words. Ye-haa!"

Su cricked his neck, rolling it back and forth. The people in the chairs tensed slightly, banged out commands on their holopad, changing the sim, and then relaxed. Pasco asked another question, but nobody answered. The time for talking was done. There was a game to be played.

"We have to go," Cort said, guiding them towards the door which automatically opened. The room took on a still quality. Eight people in eight recessed chairs, plugged in and ready for action.

At the door their lenses were returned, and they were hurried into an elevator to take them to their seats in the executive boxes. As they walked Balmoral couldn't help noticing how Pasco's shoulders drooped, how his face had somehow changed, how the sparkle had gone out of his eyes. Now he looked more like one of the drab, grey shadows from Sector 2; cynical and defeated.

20

SECTOR 1, MANSION SUBTERRANEA

HAVING WORKED OUT they had to hack off Urzil's arm in order to reach the lock, Lemmy and Lord squabbled like two old women. Lord was impatient to get at Tristram, Lemmy was shaken up, ready to quit the moment Urzil's throat yawned open.

"This is fucked up, Tamar. We should wait for Beaky," Lemmy said.

"Don't be a fucking pussy. We came here to do a job," Lord said through his wired teeth.

"Urzil's dead!"

"Then he won't feel a thing will he?"

Leaning against the wall, Tristram found the whole scene amusing. Urzil with his barrel-shaped corpse slumped over the lock, Lemmy, pale as a sheet, trying to wrench his body away from the bars, slipping on the blood as he did so, and Lord hacking away at Urzil's arm with a bowie knife, all the time spitting invectives about what he was going to do to Tristram's genitals.

"I can feel his bone . . ." Lemmy moaned.

"I'm the one fucking cutting!" Lord snarled.

"It's the vibration."

"I'll fucking vibrate this up your ass if you don't shut up!"

It took fifteen minutes to hack through the right arm. Lord dripped with sweat, his eyes red, like ruined raspberries. They didn't get through the bone, but cut enough off the arm to ease Urzil's bulk to the left of the lock and create space for the welder.

"Fire it up then," Lord growled, and Lemmy got to work on the two remaining bars. It was slower work than the buzzsaw and exhausting, a sixteen gauge electrode amped all the way up, jabbing in and out, smoke everywhere, getting in their eyes, up their noses, filling the corridor.

"You'll damage your eyes you know, looking at that without safety goggles," Tristram said.

"Shut up!" Lemmy shouted, shaking worse than ever.

"I'm warning you," Tristram said, squinting. "Not good for the retinas. Not good at all. It's about as good for the eyes as a buzz saw is for the neck."

"Fucking shut up!"

They had no goggles. Already, black dots would be dancing before their eyes. The welder was supposed to be for Tristram's skin, not for burning through metal.

With all the smoke and his hands trembling uncontrollably, Lemmy could hardly keep the flame on the bars.

"Fuck it," Lord said, yanking the welder away from him. "What's wrong with you?"

What's wrong, thought Tristram, is that Lemmy doesn't have the stomach for it. This little bit of killing, slap and tickle to you and me, has unhinged your friend.

Lord focused the flame on the bars, melting the metal composite centimetre by centimetre until finally he prized away the lock and it dropped to the ground with a heavy clunk. Handing the welder to Lemmy, Lord drew out the shock gun and pushed the voltage up so high that Tristram knew he didn't intend to actually use it, not if Lord wanted to torture him first.

This was the dangerous time. Despite Tristram's skill at close quarters, he couldn't take them toe-to-toe, not when they were armed and he had nothing.

"Flame it," Lord growled, and Lemmy fiddled with a second nozzle mounted to the welder. A flame, twelve inches long, erupted from its tip.

"Dual purpose," Lord said to Tristram with a grin, and bent down to pick up the bloody bowie knife, all the time careful to keep the shock gun, vibrating with its lethal charge, pointed towards Tristram.

"Now listen to me, you fucking little shit," Lord said. "You keep backed up, right against the wall, and when I say so, slowly, very slowly turn around, hands cupped behind you." He pulled out a pair of cuffs.

Lemmy manipulated the flame so that it was dangerously close to Tristram. He had to back up or be burned.

"Okay, turn around," Lord said, rubbing his eyes.

He had to make a move. If nothing else, a quick death from the shock gun was better than prolonged torture. His chances were slim to none, but they were tired from all the hacking and burning, the adrenalin already turning lactic in their veins. Their vision was hazy from staring at the bright flame, and the smoke that filled the cell. Then there was the alcohol; they had been hitting it pretty hard at least until a couple of hours ago, and despite appearing relatively sober, their reaction time would be slower than usual.

"Face the wall," Lord said, "or Lemmy will start by burning your fucking eyes out."

Tristram let his shoulders collapse in a defeated posture and turned away, but as he did so, he whipped a boot at the base of the ceramic toilet bowl, kicking it with all his force. It disintegrated on impact and instantly the cell was an inch deep in urine and water.

"What the . . ." Lord said.

Lemmy thrust the flame at him, but Tristram was ready and despite the confined space snaked behind him, grabbing his free arm around his back. Instinctively, Lemmy swung around to break free, strafing Lord's right hand with the flame. Lord screamed with pain and dropped the shock gun onto the wet cell floor. Before it hit, Tristram released Lemmy's arm and jumped onto the wooden bench, while 1,500 volts coursed through the water, and into their steel capped boots.

From his perch, the two men looked like scarecrows jolting back and forth, doing a jig just for him. The butane flame, still clasped in Lemmy's hand, jumped up and down over Lord's body, filling the cell with the odour of burnt pork.

The shock gun finally fused, the jolting stopped and the men dropped to the ground like puppets with their strings cut. The butane flame spluttered and went out, and Tristram hopped down from the bench, careful not to slip.

"Three zip," he said, picking up the bowie knife and stepping over Lord's twitching body.

Glancing down the corridor he noticed the door at the end was slightly ajar, almost on the latch. He tensed, but then reasoned Gravales must have left it open so Lord could let himself out when he was done. He had expected to have to wait for Gravales, to ambush him before he saw the bodies.

"This is too easy," he muttered to himself.

"Oh yes," a paper thin voice replied, "too easy by half."

Gravales stepped out from the empty cell adjacent to the outer door, his Luger aimed at Tristram's chest.

21

SECTOR 1, MANSION

Pasco and Balmoral looked down on the spectators from their executive suite, high above the arena. Layers on layers of people, buzzing in their seats, eager and ignorant. It was another full house, a hundred and sixty thousand people packed into Sky Dome, every single one of them ready to plug into their enviro-chair, and not just watch the game, but become part of it, experiencing in first person what the players saw, what they did, what they felt.

How many times had Pasco himself been one of the expectant masses? He couldn't go to Steel Ball all that often, but whenever he could pool the funds and secure a ticket, he was there, another face, euphoric with the anticipation of the big game. When he used to gamble, that anticipation had been tinged with dread, but in the last two years, he had enjoyed the sport as much as when he was a child, for the spectacle of the athletic achievement and nothing more.

A ripple of excitement passed through the crowd. The countdown clock had begun, three minutes to go. A clicking sound broke out across the arena, quiet at first, then growing in volume as the spectators strapped themselves in; cocked and ready.

Pasco turned away from the balcony, from their position in the gods and wondered if he should even bother plugging in to the enviro-chair. What was the point? It was just a fancy sim.

"Are you okay?" Balmoral put a hand on his shoulder.

"Fine, I'm fine," he said, the words sounding hollow even to his own ears. "I think I'll get a drink." He turned towards their private bar and mumbled an order of spirits to their barman.

Which one?

Anything.

The barman shrugged, pumped out two shots of Tequila and handed it to him.

All those years watching games, and it was a lie.

Steel Ball was the one thing they had enjoyed as a family; Tristram, Pasco and his father, watching it, playing it, talking about it, even before he was old enough to really understand what was going on. Even his mother came to the arena with them a couple of times. The precious memories from a happier time, before his father's death, were now tainted along with everything else.

Why had the athletes and the gymnasium been part of Balmoral's tour? What possible purpose did it serve?

He threw down the shots in a single go and winced.

Balmoral eyed him with concern. "Are you sure you're fine?"

He nodded. He should be looking after her, not wallowing in self-pity. It occurred to him that their roles had reversed. She was trying to coax him to speak, to open up, whereas he was now monosyllabic.

The bartender asked if he wanted another Tequila.

No. One was fine.

Chicken fingers?

He shook his head. Food would have made him sick.

Balmoral perched on the edge of her chair and stared out over the crowd, as though looking for meaning in the mass of humanity below. She wouldn't find it, no matter how hard she looked.

At least they were alone up here. Pasco and Balmoral had total privacy and the best view of . . . of absolutely nothing in the house.

A couple of boxes over was the official Media box. Cyndi Champagne stood in front of the bright lights, wittering on about the players to the timeless Larry Mason. The rumour was that Cyndi was on her way out, past it now at twenty-five. According to Pasco's friends in Media, based on data from the Pleasure Houses and other sims, the masses were ready for a change; someone less buxom, someone dark, edgier and synapse skinny. Apparently the talent scouts had found a fourteen-year-old girl somewhere in Pekin who appealed to all twenty-three types of male ego, and eighteen of the forty-two types of female ego. He wondered why they just didn't use another hologram.

He slumped into the enviro-chair and decided to plug in.

Well? What else was there to do?

They couldn't leave. They were in the Sky Dome for the duration of the game. The agents at the door wouldn't even let them out of the suite, and he didn't trust himself to stand at the bar for the next hour and a half.

"You might still enjoy it," Balmoral said.

"I suppose so," he said, for her sake.

The full body gel cushion of the enviro-chair always made him feel like he was sinking into the ground. He clicked the belt across his waist. The helmet descended over his head, the gel inside adjusting so that it exactly met the contours of his face. The last thing he saw was one of the agents, ensuring that Balmoral too was strapping in.

Cocooned in the total sim chair, the darkness before the game was a relief. Once the game began, he would be able to toggle around the *players*, see what they saw, experience what they experienced. Every time his selected player got hit, his brain would be tricked into feeling the crunch, every time a player scored, it would feel like him diving across the line.

As the marketing stated, in Sky Dome you experienced, "all the action, without the injuries", although in the past Pasco had often left the games feeling totally drained. Technically, the body hardly moved, but the mind battled through four intense quarters.

Because the sim was so deep, it was impossible to pull out once the game began unless someone pressed the emergency release on the chair. A spectator coming out too quickly could experience what they called *the bends,* a catastrophic reality shift that in the worst case scenario left them dizzy and disoriented for weeks.

However, emergencies did happen. There were one or two cardiac arrests every game, but the biosensors in the chair could alert staff in the early stages, so they were rarely fatal. Medics on standby could reach any seat in the vast complex in under five minutes.

The amount of investment put into the ultra-realistic arena experience was staggering, and, if TechCom were honest, Steel Ball and Pleasure House sensory software had all but written the blueprint for iAm. Indeed the challenge of iAm's development was not so much the technology to trick the brain into firing neurons that stimulated an artificial environment, but to miniaturize the device so that it could function inside the brain.

The countdown hit zero and a massive cheer erupted. Pasco stared into the darkness, but to his, and presumably a hundred thousand other people's confusion, a game did not break out. Instead, a clear, nasal voice filled his head.

"We regret to inform you that tonight's game has been cancelled."

There was a stunned silence and then a murmur of protest swept across the arena. The average Steel Ball game went out live to over eight billion people. How could Media do this? It was commercial suicide.

"Because tonight," the resonant voice boomed, "we have something else for you. A once in a lifetime, marquee event."

The visual opened with a row of grey buildings, and a dust brown sky. He heard chanting, quiet at first, then growing in volume until he could make out the words.

"Out! Out! Out! Out!"

Pasco thought it was coming from inside the arena, until he saw the mob. Thousands of men and women, lining the lanes in between Battery buildings, armed with weapons ranging from broom handles, kitchen knives and hammers to the occasional shock gun and printed rifle. Their faces were distorted with anger and each wore a red piece of cloth tied around their arm. All of their identikits had been blanked out to read a single word, "Terrorist".

The view panned to the side of the building, the control of the sim not yet handed to the spectator. Pasco sucked in his breath. Two words were painted on the façade, "Millionaire's row", and underneath ten bodies hanged from ten consecutive windows, necks broken, bowels swaying in the wind.

The faces were distorted in a frozen agony, but Pasco could still make out the features of Francis Guiren and Dekkarde 'call me Decks' Solquist. The view panned to wire mesh netting that had been cut to ribbons, which made no sense, until you noticed the other men and women, Foremen and Supervisors, maybe forty in all, that had been pushed from the upper stories. Their bodies lay broken on the ground. Some of them were still moving, or at least twitching. Nobody helped them. He heard the flies that swarmed around the bodies, smelled the blood and beginnings of decay. Next to the bodies, someone had scrawled D-I-S-H in white chalk, but unlike the writing on the building it seemed rushed, added as an after-thought.

"Out! Out! Out! Out!"

Pasco knew he was being manipulated, but he couldn't help it. A primal fury welled up against this mob who could commit such atrocities.

The resonant voice cut in again.

"Welcome to today's battle arena. We are live from Churin where war has been declared by the *Dish*. Six short weeks ago, Churin's faithful population were the most affluent in the whole of Sector 2, their economic status elevated by their hard work on iAm. The *Dish*'s response was to flood the region with its armed insurgents, destroying property and lives. By permitting this outrage, the Autonomy has failed its loyal citizens. A failing our heroes will now address. This is not a drill."

The profiles of the four Strontia Dogs and four Muscle Men came into view. *Select your player now.*

Without really processing what was happening, Pasco selected a player and Uni Su's lean, chiselled face appeared in the top left of the screen. A dashboard showed his player stats together with live readings from his biosquare. Underneath were other, unfamiliar data such as rounds remaining and propulsion, and a defence rating pertaining to the condition of the carapace armour.

Heavy power chords from the Steel Ball opening anthem filled Pasco's ears, and the screen cleared for a second time. The view shifted to an aerial shot just above the Battery buildings.

Uni Su hovered high above the ground, flexing his muscles, the carapace armour responding to his every move. Below him, the rioting mass of insurgents.

His display showed the game stats.

482,364 terrorists

8 carapace warriors

The warriors were no longer segmented by their club names, but instead unified under a single team called simply, "The Freedom".

"Game on!" the announcer roared, and suddenly they were off.

Pasco's stomach lurched as Uni Su swooped down towards the ground. Faces stared skywards in shock. On the display he could see Maverick and Starblind, the other interceptors, all of them coming at the crowd from different directions. On the ground, the mauls; Lothar, Cowper and Shenk took up strategic positions in their much heavier armour. Church and Harrier, the ball carriers, were currently invisible.

He realised now what the unfamiliar readings were; the status of Uni Su's battle armour and its intricate weaponry. Pasco could eye-over any stat to get more detail, and toggle across to the other players. Each of Su's teammates were rigged out differently. The interceptors had two wing-shaped jet packs across their shoulder blades, each with six independent jets. The mauls had a heavy cannon, and several layers of additional front and rear facing armour.

Uni Su circled left, and locked onto the rioters, but was told to hold his distance. Chattering in his ear was Church, directing proceedings for team Freedom, issuing terse commands.

"Attack on five, four . . ." he said.

Uni Su's inventory blinked, he selected 'Samba Rockets', pulled up the crosshairs, and fired at where the mob was most dense.

A volley of seven or eight high impact rockets launched into the crowded alleys between the buildings, incinerating anything within a radius of three hundred feet. A huge plume of smoke and ash filled the air, not just from his rockets, but from the heavy weaponry simultaneously unleashed from the other players. The display automatically switched to *Vision*, the same basic software Pasco had used to see through the smog on his first trip.

"That one's for the Autonomy," Su said into the com.

"Ye-haa!" Maverick added.

Pasco thought of the man with the grey ponytail.

Different tune maybe, but same words man, same words.

The mauls fired heavy weaponry from the ground and explosions rocked the Battery. Back in the arena, the crowd roared with appreciation. Pasco felt sick.

This was real, this was actually happening, the protestors were dying. It was not a game and yet . . . the flying suits were robotic drones with nothing to risk, controlled by the eight recluses in the basement with the fastest hand-eye reflexes in the world.

A section of the rioters opened up, they were carrying something. Su's viewer zoomed in, identifying an anti-aircraft gun. The weapon looked out of the dark ages, constructed using a 3D printer and chicken wire. The long barrel kicked back and fired. Due to the proximity, the time to impact was under a second, but the sophisticated armour anticipated the trajectory and Su banked a hard left, taking Pasco's stomach with him.

"A startling burst of speed by Su and he avoids the . . . intercept!" Larry shouted excitedly.

Crosshairs appeared over the gun and in a flash, Uni Su pulled back his arm and launched a T4-exocet. One moment the gun was there, the next, a huge hole in the ground and a ring of bodies that stretched back in concentric circles. To the real Uni Su, it must have been like playing *Total War* on an incredibly simple setting.

The arena erupted into cheers again. The crowd had never been so loud, even for the division finals. Every time there was big hit, a few hundred closely grouped 'terrorists' wiped out, there was another roar.

"Su lands a big score!"

"Nice hit, Larry," Cyndi Champagne said flatly.

Uni Su strained his neck downwards. On the ground the mauls closed in, strafing the rioters in their thousands, cutting them to ribbons.

In the top right hand corner, the score read: 18,108 to 2. Underneath, minute text explained that the stats were the terrorist's total dead, unconscious or disabled, versus Team Freedom's count. The rioters had somehow brought down two of team Freedom. The damage stats showed two interceptors pulled out of the sky and disabled on the ground.

Pasco mused that there wouldn't be any close ups of what happened to the players. Their suits contained circuits and wires, not a sweating hero.

Uni Su dived between two buildings to lock onto another densely populated avenue of rioters. Pasco noticed the people were trying to get away now, their weapons thrown to the ground, beating a retreat against the slaughter. They were so tightly packed they could hardly move.

Su locked on with another T4-exocet but at the same moment, a heavy gun, mounted from inside the Battery, launched a missile from the window. Su had only a split second to pivot, twisting away with unearthly athleticism. The crowd was still cheering when he was hit by a second, flanking missile, fired from the opposite building.

Su rocked left and his display flashed up with critical flight damage. It wasn't a direct hit, but it had taken off his entire left wing. He hurtled into the corner of the building, smashing into the stone work, crushing most of his front facing armour.

Pasco shook back and forth in the chair. Su attempted to stabilize, climbing above the building before he spun out of control. A high impact parachute exploded out of his back a second before he crashed into the ground.

"And Su is disabled," Larry said.

But was he?

Despite the multiple impacts, most critical systems still functioned. Su ejected the parachute, and rolled onto his front. The rioters backed off, hypnotized by his huge, smoking form, but then someone let out a cry, full of fury and pain, and a whole section of the mob surged forward.

Su switched his battle settings to melee, pulling himself upright.

For a moment Pasco wondered if this would be like the fists of fury mode in *Total War*, where the fallen soldier could go berserk; a suicide setting, to take out as many people as possible before he was overwhelmed by numbers. With enough upgrades, the player could go toe to toe with fifty people at a time, pulling off roundhouses, dishing out lightening jabs and in a blur disable all who came towards him.

Don't be ridiculous, he told himself. The carapace drones were functioning military equipment, and though it seemed like a sim, the reality was that all Su controlled was a fancy gun, constrained by the limitations of the physical world.

Uni Su lurched forward and shot a tear gas grenade from the one functioning mount on his shoulder. In the same movement he flicked through the three remaining weaponry options still open to him: frag grenade, strafe gun and something called the n-class, although that particular weapon was greyed out, presumably offline.

Selecting strafe, Su opened up indiscriminately, going for volume rather than accuracy. The advancing rioters fell away, slumping forward like broken scarecrows, some shot off at the knees, others at the head.

In the top right hand corner the casualty number kept rising, while in the bottom left hand corner, the two thousand rounds counted down. Pasco caught one woman's eye. She was young, twenty at most and armed with a small machinist's hammer. In slow motion she screamed, turned to run and was mown down, her body ripped to shreds in front of their eyes.

Why was Media showing this? Was she even *Dish*, or just someone sucked into the general uprising? Only then did it dawn on him that the show of force was exactly the point. A lesson to any Sector that thought they could stand out of line. The justification; murdered executives and Foremen, were a side show for the real message. In a world where eight drones can take out hundreds of thousands, resistance is futile.

Pasco knew how the Media worked. Those in the arena would be following whatever hero they wanted to root for, toggling to another player if their own went down, seduced by the heroic narrative of the sim.

The wider citizens of Sector 1 would be fed a more sanitized version, the view panning to wherever the action was most exciting, emphasizing the brutality of the rioters rather than the single girl, armed only with a hammer, shot at point blank. Sector 2 and Sector 3 would get something in between. However, every spectator would be left in no doubt as to what action the Autonomy would take if their investments were under threat.

As Su strafed the crowd, Pasco thought of the obese figure in the basement, his fingers thrumming, his orders relayed through a head set. The real Uni Su could hardly tell the difference between reality and sims. His entire world consisted of two boxes, one in which he physically lived, the other in which he played and excelled, a more vivid and exciting world of instant gratification, that had dulled all sense of empathy and human feeling long ago.

Churin was just one more sim, exciting because it was a game he hadn't played before, but in all likelihood, a little dull as shoot-em-ups go. The graphics were realistic, but it was all a bit drab, the narrative simple, the opposition mediocre.

Su casually launched his last frag bomb, deploying it far enough away that he himself was out of the blast zone. The ground shook, another six hundred or so were added to the score. He kept on popping away, inflicting maximum damage in every direction until all weaponry was exhausted. The total score was now 283,462 to 4.

Those who had first charged on Su, and those in the immediate vicinity, were all dead, but the rioters had numbers on their side. Out of the smoke and carnage emerged a group that seemed better armed and organized. Sensing Su had depleted his ammo, they cautiously advanced.

Gathering confidence, they rushed forward to pull to pieces the man within the suit. Su shook off the first few, the powerful exoskeleton, though damaged, more than a match for flesh and bone. But then there was another, and another, and another and Su disappeared under a pile of bodies.

Pasco's perspective automatically changed to a third person bird's eye. He tried to toggle back inside the suit, but access was denied. Watching from above, more and more rioters closed in, everyone wanting a piece. He saw one woman had removed her shoe and beat Su with it. The sledgehammers were more effective.

The interface showed the structural integrity of the suit fail. Any moment they would succeed in ripping him apart, revealing his secret, if not to the world, at least to those in the arena following Uni Su.

Su pulled up his last remaining weapon, the "n-class". It had been greyed out from the beginning, but since the last warning, the "n-class" could now be selected.

Su launched it.

There was a second's pause and then a 1 kiloton nuke ripped through the Battery, which according to the team stats, was the fourth detonated that day.

The score jumped over 400,000 for the first time.

22

SECTOR 1, MANSION SUBTERRANEA

GRAVALES HELD THE Luger, ramrod straight, about twenty yards from Tristram's heart.

"Drop the knife," he said.

Tristram let it go.

"You can imagine my surprise when I heard all the commotion." Gravales said. "Unfortunately, they were already . . . cooking by the time I arrived." He drew his mouth down at the corners in a mock display of grief.

"You know, I never liked Lord. Valencia tolerated him because she felt we had no choice. I disagreed with her then, and I do now. Machinists are overrated. The real power is with the subcoders."

Tristram noticed the silencer affixed to the end of the barrel.

"In many ways you've done me a favour. Lord would boast about this after-wards and they would know I had let him in. Now the focus will be elsewhere. I will say I thought I closed the door but . . . well I'm an absent-minded old man." He smiled his ghastly tombstone smile. "You've done very well, but now . . . you know what happens next."

The old man knew how to shoot, and wouldn't miss from twenty yards. Tristram considered rushing him, but that would only make the distance shorter. No, it was over. He relaxed.

Gravales squeezed the trigger and the report of the pistol filled the chamber.

At first he thought the bullet must have entered so cleanly he didn't feel it. Vaguely he wondered why the silencer hadn't worked, but then Gravales slumped forward and Tristram saw the exit wound coming from his forehead. Behind him stood Fleur, a printed Glock held firmly in her hands.

They stared at each other, neither speaking. She kept the gun trained on him.

"So you are an agent," she said. A statement, not a question.

"Yes," he said, "but it's not what you think."

She gave a false laugh. "What I think? I think I have bought a shark into our piranha house, someone who would butcher us all in our beds."

She swayed a little as she spoke, shaking her head.

"I tasted your *beer*, like some stupid high school girl with a crush. Took your half-drunk bottle back to my room. I hate beer, but I wanted to be where your lips had been. And in an instant, I realised what a fucking fool I'd been. And I knew . . . I knew who you were, really were, Tristram."

Keeping the gun trained on him, she picked up Gravales' Luger, slipping it inside her jacket.

"A fucking fool," she repeated.

"How do you know my name?" he said.

"That's not important. What is important is that you came here to kill us, and you used me to do it."

Then why was he still alive?

Why had she shot Gravales?

He thought he understood part of the reason, but whatever he said next would determine whether he lived or died. He took a breath and rolled the dice.

"I didn't come to kill you! It wasn't . . ." he cast his eyes to the ground, "all an act."

"No? You can't be part Securicom and part not. It's like being part dead."

"I had to know who . . . who shot my father, Dagmar Eborgersen."

Her face blanched.

"You have to understand, my father was shot when I was a boy, before we even knew about the *Dish*, or about their grievances. He was a good man, revered for the good he tried to do, no matter the cost to Top 10 or his career. He was the father of the Namgola project! He tried to save people!"

Tristram knew that a teenage Fleur would have been sentimental enough to look up everything about the Eborgersens, drawn to the family she had broken. She probably spent hours staring at their public identikits.

Fleur wasn't a hardened member of the *Dish* back then, not the person who would years later casually blow up a restaurant. That came afterwards, after a lifetime of living in a sewer. Back then she was just a girl who had fallen for the wrong person, in the same way she had fallen for him. It was the fifteen-year-old girl who had unconsciously recognized him, and the girl he appealed to now.

"My father was my life. Since the day he died I swore I would find his killers and bring them to justice. The only choice I had was Securicom and yet . . . I hate them. All I have done, all I have ever done, is try to find some closure."

"But his killers were caught years ago," she said unsteadily. "They were framed." There were tears on her cheek. For a moment neither of them spoke and they both knew the silence was a confession.

"I . . . was just a girl," she said.

"I know." He put out his arms. "And now I have found you, I have closure." He took a step towards her.

"Stay away," she said, still pointing the gun.

"I forgive you."

"You forgive me!" she laughed bitterly. "Don't you see that changes nothing. When this is discovered," she gestured towards the bodies, "no amount of explaining will save us. Even if we try to clear up this mess, somehow make it look like something else, Valencia will never believe you."

Us.

Inwardly, he smiled. Fleur saw things clearly. She brought him into the Bedouin. She was condemned by that fact, even before she shot Gravales. It was now him and her against the world.

"We're going to make a deal," Fleur said.

Already, Tristram knew what she was going to say. She had a plan, and she wanted his help. She loved her life more than the cause, had proved it on the rooftop.

"I am going to get us out of these tunnels," she said.

"Through the staging area?"

"That would set off every alarm in the complex."

"Then how? I thought the plughole only opened on Valencia's hand print."

"While she's here. When she's away there is always one other, someone senior, someone she trusts in case of emergencies."

"Gravales?"

She shook her head. "No skull would ever be trusted with a way out, no matter who they were."

"Orlick," he said.

"We force him to open the door at gun point. You leave him unconscious in the stairwell. The Garde in the office won't suspect anything, they'll assume Orlick has to go to Mansion for the mission. If the Garde play it by the book they will ID him before they unlock the door at the top, but I don't think so, not tonight. It's his palm print that unlocks the door in the tunnel, so who else could it be? When they open the door you take them out, and we run free."

"And what do you get in return, other than your life?"

"You will do whatever you have to do to bury somewhere deep in the Autonomy, safe from the *Dish* and Securicom. You've changed your identity. You will do what it takes to change mine. I will give you your life, you will give me mine. At this point you need me far more than I need you. So do we have a deal?"

She seemed so sure of him, so confident they would pull it off, and yet her head tilted away from him when she spoke, and the squint in her eye belied her words. Fleur didn't trust him. That finger was still more likely to squeeze the trigger than not. He had to say something authentic, something she would believe.

"I swear it," he said, "on my father's life."

Slowly she lowered the gun, an uncertain smile on her lips.

23

SECTOR 1, MANSION

A LL THOSE PEOPLE. Gone. The final count was over half a million, more than the number of reported terrorists at the outset of the game. The Battery was no more, and although the radioactivity of these new weapons had an extremely rapid half-life, the area would be a no-go zone for months.

Pasco was desperate to get out of his chair but he was locked into place. At the end of every arena game there was a mandatory three minute wash-out; the screen blank, the sound mute, enabling the body to reacclimatize to its senses, and mitigate and risk of the bends.

There was no risk in his case. Pasco had never really gone under. Throughout the sim he had remained his conscious self, aware of the chair's every move, for once not losing himself in the virtual reality.

"Come on, come on, come on." He thrummed his fingers on the side of the chair.

He had to get to Balmoral, to comfort her, to help her. Finally, it made sense why Maglan sent them to Sky Dome. He wanted Balmoral to see this, and not just see it, but live it, imprisoned in the gel of the enviro-chair. His uncle wanted to break her, either out of malice or a more calculated effort to make her pliable to Securicom's agenda.

The safety catch of the helmet clicked and he threw it off, instinctively reaching out for her. But her chair was empty. His eyes drifted to the emergency release. Someone had sprung her.

Thank the *Faith!*

Perhaps, unable to go under, she had thrashed around so much one of the agents let her out. Perhaps she had been spared the scenes of carnage. He jumped out of his chair but as he turned towards the bar, he froze. One of the agents was slumped over the courtesy table, half the contents of his head decorating the wall.

The second agent was on the ground, his hands wrapped around a machete, pushed right up into his sternum. His naked eyes were wide with fear, no longer an Elite operative, but simply a person not wanting to die.

In the doorway there were six or seven other corpses, more Securicom, and two people that looked like ordinary spectators, except that printed weapons lay near their fallen bodies.

Pasco pulled up his holopad, calling for medical help.

"Don't bother," the agent wheezed. "Unless you're telling them where to bring the body bags."

Pasco knelt by his side and took his pulse. So faint, there was almost nothing there. "I'm sorry," he said.

The agent smiled, or possibly it was a grimace. "This is the part where you're supposed to ask me, *what in Faith happened?*"

"I didn't think . . ." Pasco began, but trailed off.

I didn't think it was appropriate.

"It's funny, a few hours ago, I was proud to have this mission . . ." Blood welled in the agent's mouth as he spoke. "I thought, this will look good on my file, working for the Chairman himself . . ."

Pasco could barely make out the words. He turned on the lip reading functionality of his lenses. The agent coughed, spitting up more blood.

"Securicom protocol states I should use my dying moments to record evidence, but the truth is I no longer give a fuck about protocol. I'm twenty-eight . . . I'm going to die here."

He made another noise. It sounded like a sob.

"T-they came to take away the refreshments. Oldest trick in the book. Even the barkeep was one of them, had weapons stashed and waiting. We had more men in the corridor, but there were too many of them."

The agent's face was white now, his life spilling out all around him. He choked again, but this time the sound caught in his throat and his head lolled backwards.

Pasco closed the dead agent's eyes, and muttered a few words of the *Faith*.

The sun shines brightly in the afterlife.

He stood up.

Somewhere down below he could hear gun fire. The Dish had taken Balmoral. With any luck, she would escape from the clutches of his uncle. His heart leapt at the thought. His heart broke at the thought. Pasco might never see her again.

24

SECTOR 1, MANSION SUBTERRANEA

IF THERE WAS one human trait Tristram had discovered as a sandman, it was that people did strange things under pressure. After leaving the holding cells, they should have headed straight to the plughole, but Fleur dragged Tristram to her own sleeping cube, not quite threatening him with the gun, but almost.

Time was fatally short, but she insisted on doing this, pulling off his clothes like someone possessed, pushing him onto the bed, either unconscious of, or not caring about, the blood caked on his skin. There was no foreplay, no kissing, she just pulled him inside her, as if to seal their contract, to make it real.

Or perhaps he was reading too much into it. Perhaps all the killing just made her horny, an ancient physical reaction; the desire to procreate, an unconscious attempt to replace the fallen.

"I wanted you almost from when I first saw you," she said, breathless.

He said nothing but moved in and out of her warm, soft body. He could have almost lost himself inside her, almost forgotten the danger, the killing and the *Dish*, except for one small thing.

His father.

Tristram nestled his mouth close to her ear, leaning on her with all his weight. "I am going to kill you," he whispered.

She tensed, eyes wide and reached for her gun. Her hand patted the empty side-board.

"I moved it," he said.

Just a moment ago, while you writhed in ecstasy and I pretended to enjoy your body.

He didn't want to look at her face, so he turned away while he crushed her throat. She clawed his back, pulling out chunks of skin. Let her die with his flesh beneath her fingers. It was better than looking at her.

"You . . . you swore on your father . . ." she somehow managed to gasp.

"To bury you deep in the Autonomy. There is no place deeper than here is there?"

She thrashed violently. She was strong and determined, but no match for his bulk. It was just a matter of time. He squeezed again, felt her pulse race uncontrollably and then abruptly slow, until it stopped altogether.

He dressed rapidly. Ignoring the Glock, he slid Gravales's Luger under his belt. The weapon might be seventy or eighty years old but he would take it over a print any day. Untucking his shirt to conceal the gun, he picked up Lord's knife and slipped it into his boot, using a strip of leather from Fleur's jacket as a makeshift sheath.

After checking the corridor was clear, he shut the door to the cell behind him and crept through the living quarters towards the tech wing, eyes out for the two Garde who might still be patrolling the tunnels.

Tristram had never seen Orlick, or even been to this part of the tunnel complex. The subcoder rarely left his cell unless it was to go to Mansion for retinal access. They delivered his meals, he took no exercise, and according to Fleur, he hardly washed. He would likely know nothing about what had happened in the bar, which was an advantage.

The tech wing was in darkness except for a bluish light emanating from the cell furthest from the corridor's entrance. Tristram peered around the door.

A round shouldered, skinny man sat staring up at the screen. He had saucer shaped eyes and a bald, pale head that seemed out of proportion with his body, as though it should be against the laws of physics for his neck to support the weight.

Two mounted monitors faced him, the only light source in the room. Small plastic chips littered the ground, old flash drives enabling information to be stored and accessed off the intellisphere.

"What do you want?" Orlick said, shutting down one of the screens. Tristram hadn't got a clear view but recognized the operational plan for the Balmoral extraction; the blueprint of the Sky Dome, the escape route, the contact points and the safe houses.

"I couldn't sleep," Tristram said. "I thought I would go for a wander."

"Wander somewhere else. This wing is off limits."

On one of the other screens, Orlick tracked the progress of the operation; monitoring the position of the Bedouin using ancient GPS technology. Beneath them he had a stream of Media reports and what looked like Securicom command centre information.

Orlick glanced across at him. "What are you doing? You have exactly three seconds to get your carcass out of my room or I will call the Garde."

Less than an arm's length away, Tristram noticed an alarm, thin glass broken with the press of a finger. Tristram didn't move. Orlick frowned and reached across to the alarm.

"Don't!" Tristram said, whipping out the Luger.

Orlick narrowed his saucer eyes. "So, the old man was right about you."

"The old man is dead."

"Well, he was over ninety. My guess is you'll be next."

"I've been in tighter spots."

"There's no way out of here," Orlick said calmly. "And you can't kill all of us."

"I don't know about that," Tristram angled the Luger at Orlick's skull, holding it there until a ring of sweat broke out across the domed forehead. "There is one way out."

"I won't do it."

"Oh, you'll do it all right, but first, hand me the memory chip." He nodded to the console that had displayed the operational plan.

Orlick didn't move. Tristram pushed the Luger's barrel into his skull. "Do it," he said again.

Orlick reached across to the console and pulled out the flash drive, holding it between finger and thumb.

"That's a good boy," Tristram said, but as he reached across Orlick flicked the USB over his shoulder and onto the ground, where it was lost among a few hundred other drives.

"Oops," Orlick said.

Tristram smiled. "Yes, very clumsy."

Keeping the gun trained on Orlick, he pulled the silencer out of his jacket and attached it to the barrel.

"Is that supposed to frighten me?" Orlick said. "We both know it's a Catch 22. You can't shoot me, because you need me to open the door to the plughole. I have to open the door to the plughole otherwise you'll shoot me. However, given that the net result is that you will shoot me as soon as you get through the plughole, ironically, you need me more than I need you."

"Funny," Tristram said. "You're the second person who's said that to me today."

There was click and a *putt* sound, as Tristram put a bullet straight into Orlick's skull. Blood sprayed against the far wall, and he keeled over backwards, his face a mask of surprise.

Tristram turned his attention to the pile of flash drives and simultaneously engaged iAm. The internal chip functioned as a highly accurate biosquare that could provide a readout of any aspect of the body's metabolism, including skin temperature. He touched the surface of Orlick's body as a test and received a reading of 89F through his fingers.

Using the synaptic menu he increased the accuracy by two decimal places, and touched him again. 89.32. Good. He picked up the flash drive nearest to him and recorded the temperature. Then another. Identical, as he suspected. He went over to the vicinity of where Orlick had thrown the flash drive and picked up one after the other, analysing the surface temperature for each one before discarding it. He went through ten, twenty, thirty, a hundred, all identical, until finally he touched one that was 1.74F degrees hotter. This was his drive, the circuits warm from the electronic data passing in and out. He stuffed the flash drive into his back pocket.

Next there was the small business of the plughole. He pulled out the knife.

25

SECTOR 1, MANSION

"COVER!" THE MAN called Clay shouted, and pushed Balmoral behind an enviro-chair. There was the harsh cracking sound of machine guns above their heads. Someone fell down. A few chairs away, two *Dish* returned fire, shooting up into the stands.

The Bedouin had pulled Balmoral out of the sim, killed the agents, and then rushed through the stadium under heavy fire. They dragged her when she could not run, carried her when she could not walk, leaving a trail of bodies in their wake.

They were on the fifth floor now, making their way through the rows of spectators, weaving in and out of the thousands of people who sat oblivious in their chairs, enjoying the annihilation of Churin.

How the crowd roared. How she wanted to kill them all. Balmoral had never seen herself as *Dish*, or a terrorist or an agitant. Her subcoding was illegal in the eyes of the Autonomy, but it was how she made sense of the world, how she lived and survived.

However, when Top 10 made a sport of massacring all those people in Churin, her people, their lives worth no more than digital characters in a sim, she knew the Autonomy must end.

A woman with pink hair appeared by her side. "We are going to have to fight our way out of here," she said. "There are more than fifty of us stationed throughout the Dome. They will provide covering fire, but we have to move quickly. Time is not our friend. We have approximately three minutes until Securicom have enough agents in place to overrun us. Do you understand?"

Balmoral nodded. More fire cracked overhead.

"Stay close to me, and I will protect you." She was probably over thirty, but her pixie-like features and petite form gave her a childish appearance.

Balmoral was aware of other noises, a dull thud that followed some of the shots, the sound of bullets sinking into the chairs and sometimes the flesh of the spectators. The intensity of the sim was such that their physical bodies would register the pain as part of the game, until they bled out, never to wake again.

"Okay then," the pink-haired girl said, "time to move."

26

SECTOR 1, MANSION SUBTERRANEA

PEERING AROUND THE corner, Tristram saw a single Garde standing by the entrance to the plughole. He was alert, but looking the other way. Dropping his bundle, Tristram took a step into the corridor and fired.

The Garde fell to the ground, scrambling for his com device. Running up, Tristram put another round in his head. He then unscrewed the silencer, placed it inside his jacket and slipped the gun back under his belt.

He had expected a Garde by the plughole. It made sense on a night when only skulls walked abroad. The other was nowhere to be seen. Perhaps they were working shifts.

He dragged the body to one of the stalls and left him over the toilet bowl. He couldn't lock the door, but that was a risk he would have to take. It was unlikely someone would wander down here at this time of night.

He picked up his bundle and walked over to the plughole. He pulled out Orlick's hand from the bloody shirt. The print took a second to read, and for a moment Tristram worried that the scan might not recognize a dismembered limb, that perhaps the palm needed a pulse, but to his relief the interface flashed green and the lock clicked open.

He dropped the hand, then hesitated. What if there was a second scan at the top of the ladder? He couldn't afford to take any risks. Tristram picked it up, index finger side on, and bit down. Grunting, he began his ascent, up through the narrow shaft.

Although he had lost some conditioning in the tunnels, he climbed quickly and easily. The adrenalin had kicked in and he felt on fire, energized by his work.

He ascended steadily for almost ten minutes before reaching the tiny platform at the top of the shaft, at the end of which was a steel door. No palm sensor. He dropped the hand. The door had no handle either, and could only be opened from the other side. That was a problem. If they were diligent, while one Garde opened the door, the second would cover it. There was also an ancient intercom. If they asked him to identify himself, he could be in trouble. On a more positive note, the intercom appeared to have no camera.

Holding his breath, Tristram banged on the door.

He heard muffled voices on the other side, and the speaker on the wall crackled into life.

"Orlick, you know the drill," a sleepy voice said. "You're supposed to use the intercom."

Shit.

"Orlick?"

He heard more movement on the other side, but no whirring of locks.

"Orlick? Speak to us."

Accessing iAm, Tristram scrolled down aural recordings of the last hour, selecting an interaction from earlier.

You can't shoot me, because you need me to open the door to the plughole.

He selected the three words he needed. He pressed down the intercom button.

"Open the door," he said, his vocal chords straining with Orlick's nasal register, pitched five tones higher than his own. The mimicry was a physical one, controlled by iAm.

The voice heard in his own head sounded too hollow and on the other side he heard nothing at all. Had they bought it?

Rapidly he scrolled through other phrases, anything Orlick had said. Orlick was senior, he was known to be difficult. He pressed the intercom again.

"What are you doing? Open the door. You have exactly three seconds."

There was another hesitation and then the lock clicked and the door opened.

On an impulse, Tristram scooped Orlick's hand from the ground and lobbed it into the room.

"What the . . ." he heard one of the Garde say as Tristram charged forward. He shot the man staring at the hand but at the same time a bullet ripped through Tristram's arm, just above the elbow. The second Garde was behind him. Pivoting he fired, with no time to aim properly. He caught him on the wrist and the Garde's gun clattered to the ground. A lucky shot.

Had he missed, the Garde would have killed him. Instead the man fell backwards, clutching his bloodied arm. Tristram leapt at him, but was too late. The Garde pressed the button lodged in his skin and the shaft exploded, rocking the room. Tristram strode up, and put a bullet in his brain.

In the tunnels, every skull would be awake now, no matter how much they had drunk, scattering like a disturbed hive of ants. They would find Fleur,

Orlick, Gravales, the bodies in the cooler, and the Garde in the stall. They would know it was him.

Would they panic and make a break through the staging tunnels? Or would they huddle together in the common room in the vain hope that the rest of the Bedouin would make it back? Either way, they were finished. Tristram allowed himself a small smile.

Using iAm he accessed the intellisphere and sent a code red to Securicom.

I have the details of the Balmoral operation, operatives, escape routes and safe houses.

I have the location of the Bedouin.

Bring a device capable of reading a USB and bring medics. Bring ammunition for the following firearm.

He sent an image of the Luger.

He could almost feel *Voice* reaching out with her electronic tendrils, locking onto his location, relaying his message.

With the bowie knife he sliced a few strips of material from the Garde's jacket and pressed it around the top of his arm by leaning against the wall. The bullet had ripped out a chunk of flesh, but it was a surface wound. The medics would staunch the blood, sew him back up and a large dose of synapse would keep him on his feet. His mind filled with an image of Valencia. He would see this operation through to the end.

27

ESPITE THE GUNFIRE, they continued to cut through the rows of sim chairs, making their way to the eastern side of the stadium. It didn't make any sense. The quickest route out was down, not across. They were running away from the main exits.

Helmets popped up row by row as spectators came out of the sim, but at first nobody seemed to grasp what was going on; the gunfire and bodies part of their hallucinatory post sim come down. When one of the gunmen fell from a nearby balcony, half the section started to cheer.

Clay shimmied in and out of the enviro-chairs while the pink-haired girl covered them from behind. Bullets thudded into the back of the chairs, into the ground, into random people.

The first screams broke out as spectators realised their family or friends had not come out of the sim, a tell-tale stain of blood somewhere on the body. Nobody dashed for the exits yet, but a stampede was bound to begin, and then even Clay's machine gun wouldn't be able to hold them back.

We're going to be trapped, Balmoral thought. They were five floors up. Behind them, Securicom agents closed in. In front of them, the huge tinted panels of Sky Dome blocked their exit.

"Now," the pink-haired girl said, and Clay dropped to one knee and opened up with the machine gun. The glass panels shattered into a hundred thousand pieces. Behind them pandemonium broke out. People started to flood for the exits creating a barrier between the oncoming Securicom agents, and the few *Dish* that had made it this far.

"Do you know how to swim?" the pink-haired woman said.

"No." Balmoral had never seen a body of water big enough to swim in.

"You're about to learn."

Balmoral could hardly walk, let alone swim. "I . . . I can't," she replied.

"Trust me," she said, and guided her over to the shattered window.

Balmoral had wanted to see the sea, and there it was, shining in the moonlight, the waves beating back and forth against the sea wall, cold and dangerous. The pink-haired girl pulled out a tightly rolled plastic tube with a small metal canister attached to the side. She unfurled it, and looped it over Balmoral's head. She pressed the tip of the canister and the coat inflated around her. The pink-haired girl tied the strings at the back.

Securicom agents appeared in a balcony above them.

"Jump," the girl said.

Balmoral hesitated. She couldn't leap far. What if she hit the wall?

The pink-haired girl nodded to Clay. He fired a last volley towards the agents, dropped the gun and snatched up Balmoral, leaping with her out of the window and into the sea.

They said the sea contained a thousand years of pollution, nuclear waste and sewerage. They said jellyfish were the only creatures to thrive anywhere but the remotest parts of the ocean. They said the sea was thick and brown by the sea wall, full of the run off from hundreds of millions of people. But when she hit the water all Balmoral felt was its icy touch, its brain numbing freshness and its salty taste. The cold blackness sucked her under, only to spit her out again, to bob on the surface, safe in her jacket. Behind her Clay came up gasping, almost invisible in the night.

Balmoral stared upwards and saw the pink-haired girl half leap, half stumble down after them, gunfire following her all the way. She hit the water a few feet away, her leg streaked with blood.

"Shit," Clay said, and dove back after her.

"Get away from me!" the pink-haired girl coughed, "She is your priority."

"You're shot."

"I'll live. Now get away from me!" Her teeth chattered violently.

"Manaus?" he said.

"On his way."

Balmoral read the pain on Clay's face. More than anything he wanted to hold this pink-haired girl, pull her into his arms, and in that moment Balmoral knew she was looking the purest form of love; instinctive, unquestioning, immutable. He was afraid of losing her. Balmoral felt a pang, not just for him, but for herself, as though she too had lost something, or someone.

Clay placed an arm across Balmoral's chest and kicked back in long, powerful strokes. The girl drifted behind them, her face deathly pale. Balmoral wondered how much blood she was losing, how long she would last.

Two or three agents stood at the broken window, searching for them in the semi-darkness. With a decent rifle equipped with a night sight, they would easily pick them off. They were sitting ducks. Clay continued to swim, his eyes fixed on the form struggling behind them.

In the distance Balmoral heard an unfamiliar thrumming, and then a speed-boat appeared, hurtling towards them from under the shadow of Sky Dome.

"Manaus," Clay said.

One of the agents gestured frantically. Guns appeared at the window.

The boat slowed, pulling up beside them, and a man reached down to drag Balmoral on board. There was the crack of gunfire and bullets strafed the water around them. Clay clung on to the side of the boat.

"We've got to go," Manaus said to Clay.

"Not without Val," Clay replied, gesturing behind him. She was still there, but barely keeping her head above water.

"If they hit the engine . . ."

"Not without Val!" he shouted again, and kicked out after her.

"Shit," Manaus said, and threw Balmoral a thermal blanket. "Wrap yourself in this and hang on."

The boat weaved over to where Clay was. A bullet ripped off part of the hand rail, another smashed a porthole.

Heaving for breath, Clay pushed the pink-haired girl over the side and she flopped on the wooden deck, barely moving. He pulled himself up after her. Manaus hit the accelerator. A strange smell filled the air, and Balmoral thought, *gasoline*. It explained the power and the noise. They roared off, away from sea wall, bullets hitting the water all around them.

Clay knelt over the pink-haired girl. "Where's the medkit?" he shouted over the roar of the engine.

"In the back," Manaus replied, "by the life jackets."

Clay clambered to the rear of the boat, pulled out a red plastic box and got to work, cutting the material away from her leg.

"What happened in there?" Manaus said.

"What do you think?" Clay said. "It was a suicide mission."

Manaus swore. "There will be no Bedouin left. Practically nobody made it out of the sea port either, not by the time we'd finished."

"Valencia knew that before we went in."

Balmoral could see the wound, a deep, black red circle two inches above the knee.

"Shit, I think they hit an artery," Clay said.

Manaus looked over his shoulder. "They couldn't have. She'd be dead by now."

"Then why the fuck is there so much blood?" Ineptly he pressed a bandage pad onto the wound. Within seconds it was soaked red. The pink-haired girl moaned, slipping in and out of consciousness.

"Shit! We have to get her to a surgeon!"

"Not until we get to the complex," Manaus said. "Stop any earlier, and we're all dead."

Clay cursed as he pressed a new pad onto the wound, his expression frantic.

Balmoral crawled over to him. "The bullet is probably lodged inside, partly occluding the artery," she said. "Dislodge it and she will bleed out in minutes."

"Then tell me what to do!" he said desperately.

She could tell him she had no idea, that all her knowledge came from some very basic medical sims she watched while working on the line, that the bullet might not be in there at all, that the pink-haired girl might have lost too much blood already, that she might not last ten minutes. But this man didn't need to hear that. He loved her. He would not let her die.

"Is there duct tape on board?" Balmoral said.

"There's a tool box with all sorts of shit in the storage locker," Manaus said, gesturing to long seat with a flip up lid.

She turned to Clay. "Keep the pressure on the bandage."

She limped over to the box. Inside there was rope, a mouldy pair of lifejackets, flares, flash lights, rat droppings, an old packet of chewing gum and in the far corner, a grey roll of duct tape. Returning to the girl, she pulled off about six inches and cut it with the medical scissors.

"When I say now, take your hand from the wound and wipe the surface with the towel."

Clay nodded.

"Now," she said. He wiped the injured girl's leg, his hands shaking. Balmoral pressed on the duct tape, then pulled off another strip and repeated the process until three pieces were secured across the wound. She then taped around the leg to form makeshift sutures.

"That should keep the blood in, better than the bandages."

"Thank you," Clay said.

She nodded and huddled back into her towel. Clay asked her something.

"Pardon?" she said, but then realised, a little embarrassed, that he was not talking to her at all but chanting some sort of archaic prayer.

Jesus please help Valencia. Jesus please help Valencia. Jesus please help Valencia.

He repeated the words over and over.

They sped on into the night.

28

SECTOR 1, MANSION

A N HOUR AGO Bruno Mandrax's career was over. He had lost the girl. Despite
the massive security, the Bedouin had snatched her from Sky Dome.
Simultaneously, another squad of terrorists had mounted an attack on
the sea port, stealing one speedboat and destroying everything else, including Securicom's fleet of copters. Robbed of the immediate means for pursuit,
it looked like the Bedouin might get away. Then a miracle happened. From
beyond the grave, Tristram appeared bearing gifts.

"How long before we move in?" Tristram said, staring over the Tech's shoulder
at the old laptop.

You're not going anywhere, Mandrax thought. Tristram was out of control,
jittery and it wasn't just the synapse. Something inside him had snapped.

"Well?" Tristram demanded.

The Chairman's favourite nephew never seemed to realise that Bruno was the
commanding officer, Tristram, the subordinate.

"The information on the USB lists a few possibilities. We don't have an exact
lock yet," Mandrax said.

Tristram pushed the Tech to one side and zoomed in on a complex of apartments, a rabbit warren where the poorest Mansion workers lived. "This is where
she'll be," Tristram said emphatically, stabbing his finger on the screen.

Mandrax noticed there was still blood caked under Tristram's nail, despite
the shower, despite the change of clothes. What had gone on down there? He
wondered too at the tattoo on his cheek, but now was not the time for questions.

"We have scrambled a copter," Mandrax said, "the Chairman's personal vehicle
in fact, and we are assembling a strike team now. However, their mandate will be
to observe and track movements until reinforcements arrive."

"Surveillance? What if she gets away. We have to act."

"We can get more agents up there within a few hours. In the meantime, where are the Bedouin going to go? Even if they somehow elude us, the tunnels are finished. They won't be able to hide for long."

Tristram didn't appear to be listening. He had zoned out. Perhaps the exhaustion was finally setting in. Bruno Mandrax was exhausted himself, the long flight from Churin and then straight into this shit. What had the Chairman been thinking? Why hadn't they kept Murraine at Fresh Kills where she was safe?

At least the Bedouin were done. By mid-morning tomorrow, twenty teams would be in the sewers blowing every pipe in the vicinity of their base, using Tristram's iAm records to lock down the location. There would be no way out. Anyone who remained inside would suffocate or starve, whichever came first.

Tristram leaned over the monitor again, poring over the facility, zooming in and out. "You haven't sent in the local squaddies, have you?" he said.

Squaddies?

"No. They don't know anything."

"Good. Keep it that way. They'd only alert her to our presence and then she'd find a way out."

"I don't think you realise, Balmoral Murraine has no access to iNet unless she uses iAm. She's flying blind."

Tristram glanced up at him, his face barely hiding the contempt. "Who gives a fuck about *her*? I'm talking about the leader of the Bedouin. She'll figure something is wrong, will have a bolt hole somewhere, a final contingency. It's how she operates, one fall-back after the next, to succeed in what she set out to do, irrespective of the cost. And then we will have lost her. For all our intelligence we don't even know her name!" He spoke rapidly, his eyes burning like a madman.

Mandrax understood then. The Bedouin assassinated his father. The boy was out for blood.

Based on Tristram's information, *Voice* had already run the data on Valencia and could not pin down her identikit, even with some visual inputs. Clearly the leader of the Bedouin had worked hard at not leaving a trail. There were more than eighty-seven thousand citizens in Mansion named Valencia. The potential identikits could be narrowed down with demographics, but they didn't know her age, or if Valencia was her first name, surname or even her real name. It worried him how little they knew. Anonymity, in an age where to identify your enemy was to locate them, was the most precious commodity in the world.

"I'm telling you, if we don't make an attempt, they'll disappear," Tristram said.

"According to the *Earth* footage, this Valencia took a bullet. A pretty nasty one too."

"That won't stop her."

"She's not superhuman."

"No, but wounded, she'll be more dangerous than ever."

Mandrax's iNet blinked to life. A message from the Chairman. He read it and cursed. Maglan wanted the strike force to not just observe but contain, go in if the Bedouin tried to move.

Turning to Tristram he said, "I must leave you. At eighteen hundred tomorrow, please come to my office to debrief. We need to understand what happened in the restaurant and the tunnels." Bruno Mandrax turned to go. He had orders to relay.

"I'm going with the strike force," Tristram said.

"Don't be crazy. You've been shot, for Faith's sake. You're only standing because of the synapse coursing through your veins."

"This is too important."

"I know. I am sending the best men we have."

"I'm the best we have, Bruno."

"Not in your condition."

Tristram's eyes zoned out again. Was he about to faint? It wouldn't surprise him. The medic said Tristram was so exhausted that he didn't want to prescribe synapse but Maglan's nephew had insisted. A double dose.

Tristram's eyes cleared and he grabbed his jacket. "I will be at the helipad in less than ten minutes. The copter can wait for me. I will kick someone out when I get there."

"You can't do that!"

"Actually, I already did."

"What?"

"Chairman's orders."

Mandrax's iNet again blinked to life. It was Maglan, issuing an executive command that Tristram be placed on the strike force.

So, Tristram had not been zoning out at all, but accessing iAm, convincing his uncle to move in tonight, going over his head.

The professional part of him made a mental note that they would need to train the iAm *tell* out of the agents. The officer part of him promised himself he would bury Tristram after tonight. The boy had over-stepped his bounds. Maglan might not know it, but his nephew was a liability.

Tristram checked his newly acquired automatic, then snapped the bowie knife into his boot. "See you on the flip side," he grinned, and walked out.

29

I T TOOK THEM two hours to reach their destination, two hours of salt water whipping their faces, and arguing over whether it was safe to use iNet to alert their connect that they needed a medic on standby.

Clay said yes. Manaus said no.

The argument ended when Manaus, the only one still wearing iNet lenses, threw them into the water. Balmoral thought Clay would throw Manaus in after them, but he backed down. Without Manaus they would be lost at sea and Valencia would die.

They disembarked at a soft point, an inlet by the sea wall where the water often flooded over to create deep, salt water lagoons. Two people met them; a short, tanned girl who introduced herself as Lopez adding, "So you're the fucking special one," and Becker, a square-shaped man who just grunted.

They climbed into a battered transport and waited while Becker helped Manaus scuttle the boat. Valencia lay in the back. She still drifted in and out of consciousness, always asking the same question in her intermittent periods of lucidity.

"Is she safe?"

The others seemed to resent Balmoral, as though she was a poor trade for everything they had lost.

"Val's not going to make it," Clay said, his voice trembling.

"There's a medic at the safe house," Lopez said, "and the surgery is kitted out and ready to roll. If she can hold out another thirty minutes, she might have a chance."

Clay looked confused. "How did you know?"

"Know? Val asked me to set it up before the mission."

"She didn't say anything about it," Clay said. "Anyone seriously hurt, anyone other than the girl, we were supposed to leave behind."

Lopez shrugged. "Je ne sais."

The hive-like apartment complex was located in Styro Town. In these grey hinterlands of Sector 1, the difference between Sectors was not quite so pronounced; real food instead of skaatch, concrete walls instead of corrugated iron, plumbing, but not much else. The inhabitants bussed in for their jobs in industries like food service, maintenance and construction, those industries to which the virtual power of iNet had made little impact. They were just as caught up in eighty hour weeks, just as anxious to make ends meet.

As they drove through the underground carpark Balmoral saw groups of teenagers in the shadows, sniffing things, injecting things. The service elevator stank of urine, the iNet cameras smashed.

The doors opened on the sixth floor and Clay and Manaus rushed Valencia into the back room of the tiny apartment. The room had plastic sheeting on the floor and there was an operating table, a lamp, and what looked like old LifeScience machinery.

Clay swore when he saw the medic, a tall, thin man in a white lab coat, his skin so translucent you could see the blue of his veins. The medic said nothing, but smiled thinly. His dumpy female assistant told Clay to leave. Mr. Glass would not touch the patient until the operating room was clear.

An hour later and the operation was still in progress. Manaus, Clay and Lopez sat around arguing, tense in the close proximity of the room. Cups of coffee from a vending bot littered the ground, and they passed around a box of something called doughnuts. Everything people ate in these buildings came from bots that patrolled the halls of the dorm, selling joule rich food twenty-four hours a day.

Lopez handed Balmoral a coffee and told her there was a water fountain in the corridor, but otherwise ignored her. That was just as well. Balmoral was exhausted, although she tried to hide it.

The escape from Sky Dome had almost finished her off. Her legs were concrete weights and her head pounded with fatigue. She sipped the coffee and leant back against a makeshift pile of knives, printed revolvers and other low grade weapons stashed in the corner of the room, careful not to impale herself on a particularly vicious looking sword.

"I don't understand," Clay said. "Why him?"

"Valencia chose Mr. Glass personally," Lopez said, taking a deep drag on her cigarette.

"But he doesn't have a license. He was barred years ago."

"I don't make the calls," Lopez said in a gravelly voice. "I just do as I'm told."

From the other room, they heard Mr. Glass laugh.

"He used to be one of the best," Lopez said.

"Before he botched one surgery too many." Clay snapped. "And you say the whole room was already rigged up?"

"They were setting it up all afternoon."

"I still don't get it," Clay said.

Lopez shrugged. "Maybe she thought you'd run into trouble."

"Or maybe she doesn't tell you everything . . ." Manaus added quietly.

Balmoral could hear the operation in progress, like a pair of diners tucking into a piece of meat, their knives and forks clicking in unison. Except it was scalpels and sutures, and the meal was Valencia's leg.

"Well, anyway," Manaus said, cramming a piece of fried dough into his mouth, "we'd be in pretty deep shit if he wasn't here."

Clay shook his head. "How much is he costing us this time?"

Lopez said nothing, but studied one of her long black nails.

"I asked you a question," Clay said through clenched teeth.

"That's between Val and Mr. Glass."

"It was, when she was head of the Bedouin, but in case of her incapacity, and I believe being unconscious on an operating table constitutes incapacity, I assume command and I am now ordering you to tell me what the cost was."

"*Faith's* sake," Lopez stubbed out her cigarette. "No need to get so heavy."

"Tell me."

"Two hundred."

"Thousand? What the fuck!" Clay slammed the coffee onto the table. The black liquid sloshed up, out through the hole in the top and all over his hand. He tried not to wince at the burn.

"Careful," Lopez said.

There was a knock on the apartment door. Lopez and Clay jumped up, guns in hand.

"Who is it?" Lopez said.

"Becker."

Lopez relaxed and opened the door. "What's the situation? Any squaddies?"

"All clear."

"Of course it's clear," Manaus said. "They have no way to trace us. Going through *Earth* footage will take days. We're safe here, at least for now."

A shiver ran down Bamoral's spine and she thought of iAm. Tentatively she touched it with her mind. No, not active, and they couldn't trace if it had never been triggered, and had no bio-energy to power it. That is, assuming Pasco had not lied to her when he explained the basic functionality.

Pasco.

Her stomach clenched with a feeling of loss. The *Dish* had wanted to shoot him, right there in the chair, but she had stopped them. He was still dead to her though. She would never see him again.

"There, you see Clay, it's not all bad. We're practically home free," Lopez said.

"Orlick?" Clay said.

"I sent him a message confirming our status. No reply," Becker said.

"It's four thirty in the morning," Lopez said. "The bug-eyed creep is likely passed out over his console. Too much wanking."

Clay glared at her. "I'm getting some air," he said and walked out, slamming the door.

"Go after him," Lopez said to Becker. "Make sure he doesn't punch anyone."

Becker sighed, and followed him out, taking a doughnut with him.

"You know we're fucked if she doesn't pull through," Manaus said. "Because I for one am not taking orders from him." He thumbed towards the door.

"Gravales takes the cell if Val is incapacitated, not Clay," Lopez said.

"Even worse. I'll say it now. If she's done, so am I."

"Then let's hope our surgeon knows what he's doing," Lopez said.

"For two hundred creds he should. Surely there was someone cheaper we could have brought in?"

"He used to be one of the best neurosurgeons in Mansion."

"Then he's not particularly useful for EMT, is he? Why was he barred?"

"He did anything for currency, including dealing illicit highs to kids."

"No wonder Clay hates him."

"That's not Clay's beef," Lopez said quietly.

"I don't understand."

She glanced across at Balmoral, then back to Manaus.

"Since the Moral Majority began stripping A-points for certain medical procedures, let's just say there aren't too many licensed medics willing to . . ." Lopez opened her legs, and with a whistle, motioned pulling something out from her.

"What? She was pregnant?"

"It was a few years ago now but judging by Clay's reaction, you can guess who the father was. It was kept under wraps. Val couldn't have a squalling infant in the tunnels. They don't go with this line of work." She lit another cigarette. "I'm surprised you didn't know."

The door to the temporary operating theatre opened. They all stood up. The gaunt, scrubbed-up man stepped forward. He was like a skeleton. A doctor that himself looked like death.

"Is she alive?" Lopez said.

"She wants to talk."

Lopez stood up.

"Not to *you*," he said, "You." He pointed to Balmoral.

30

I T WAS NOT yet four-thirty and already there was a huge volume of foot traffic outside the dimly lit apartment complex in Styro Town. In Mansion, Atmos simulated sunrise at five every morning. Here, it would not be light for another hour and a half. Good. He preferred to work under the cover of darkness.

Tristram and the other four agents took up positions, blending in with the shadows and the flow of day riders making their way to the parked eighteen-wheel transports that left for the city every ten minutes.

They knew Valencia was here, even knew which floor she was on. Tristram itched to go in, but they were ordered to wait. Their brief was to observe and contain, act only if the Bedouin tried to escape.

That would not stop Tristram if push came to shove. He just needed an excuse to go in. Today Valencia would die. He just prayed it would be him who pulled the trigger.

He was growing impatient when a naked-eyed Clay Vorm emerged from the building's entrance. He was preoccupied and looked right through Tristram. The shadows helped, as did the cap and the large mirrored shades that partially concealed the tattoo.

"Enemy sighted," he said, and without waiting for orders, pulled out the automatic and shot him in the leg. Vorm collapsed on the ground. Tristram rushed up and grabbed his head. "Hello Clay. Remember me?" He shoved the gun in his mouth. Clay snarled something and Tristram pulled the trigger, noting with satisfaction the grey and red matter that splattered on the ground behind him.

Another one for dear old dad.

The other agents scrambled around him, containing the panicking crowd, flooding their lenses with Securicom identification.

Nothing to see here.

It didn't stop the stampede, and within seconds the area was deserted.

"What the *Faith* are you doing?" the commander yelled in Tristram's face.

"He's Bedouin. He was trying to escape."

"Escape? He didn't know we were here! This is a controlled Securicom operation, not some fucking sandman job!"

"I had no choice. The moment he saw me, we were blown."

"Saw you? In this light? He had no lenses on. Even if he did, the suspect was down! We could have taken him into custody."

Tristram couldn't afford that. They would mine Vorm for intelligence. He might spend years incarcerated before being shipped to a treadle mill, or worse, they might try to turn him, give him a contract working for Securicom. It had happened before. No, Tristram preferred him the way he was, his brains decorating the ground.

"Either way," Tristram said, "it's too late now. We have to go in before they run."

"No. We intercept them when they run. There are civilians in there. Try to take the fight inside and it will be messy, very messy."

"So is this," Tristram said and snapped a jab into the commander's jaw. His head knocked back and he went down sprawling.

All officers were the same. All mouth, no jaw.

"Every second we stand here, we give them more time to prepare!" Tristram growled. "We have to move in. Now!"

He didn't care if the others followed him or not.

31

ALENCIA WAS AS pale as death, her pink curls throwing her complexion into stark relief, her bright blue eyes the only indication that something still burned within.

"Our cell is finished," Valencia wheezed, nodding to the lenses by her bedside. "Our underground headquarters compromised, our safe houses blown and most of my best operatives dead. The others don't know yet. My contact in Securicom communicates only with me."

"I'm . . . I'm sorry," Balmoral said, the words almost slipping out by themselves.

"Sorry? I knew the cost of this mission. I knew the likely outcome. Do you really think our good Chairman would let you go without a fight? You, the biggest threat this economic dictatorship has ever faced? I believe you can bring down the Autonomy and end this life, that is no life. You are the hero that will free mankind and set the world on a different path."

The dying, pink-haired girl had risked everything to save her, but Balmoral had to tell her the truth.

"I'm no hero," she said simply.

"A hero is just someone who is too afraid to run away."

"But I can't even access iNet."

Valencia grasped her hands. "The Autonomy must end, you know that, I see it in your eyes. When the time comes, just promise me you will try."

Balmoral nodded and Valencia's pained face transformed, if only for a moment, with a single, sweet smile.

Mr. Glass stepped forward. "Miss Valencia, we don't have much time. They could be here any minute. You didn't pay me enough to become a transvict in a treadle mill."

Valencia sighed weakly. "We had a deal, Glass. Leave before this is done, and I guarantee one of my men will shoot you and your wife before you leave this building."

Mr. Glass gave a sickly smile. "Understood, but still, we need to hurry."

The door suddenly swung open. "Val!" Lopez said.

"I told you to stay out!" snapped Mr. Glass.

"We've been compromised. Clay's dead."

"How many?" Valencia said.

"Becker thinks just a squad, an advance guard maybe."

Glass cursed.

"It can't be helped," Valencia said, rousing herself with an almost other-worldly energy. "Mobilize everyone we've got. Fight to the death. We have the reserves ready in position. Nothing must imperil the mission. We need as much time as you can buy us."

"But . . ." Lopez said.

"Those are my orders!"

Lopez stared at Valencia for a moment. She could see death in her leader's face, not just for Valencia, but for all of them. She wiped away a tear and pulled out a printed automatic. "As you say," she said, and turned.

Balmoral thought, *Lopez loves her too*, this pink-haired girl, who had inspired so much in so many.

Valencia then nodded, and a hand suddenly appeared over Balmoral's mouth. She struggled, and instinctively drew in a lungful of chloroform.

32

T HE AGENTS FOLLOWED Tristram into the building, even the commander, once he had dusted himself down. He had no choice. All of their careers depended on preventing Murraine's escape.

They reached the sixth floor and were met by heavy fire. Dish stepped out of different rooms all along the corridor, flanking them left and right. The apartment complex, or at least this part of it, wasn't just a safe haven, but a base.

The commander was cut down before Tristram could adjust. Assuming command, he ordered the agents to fall back, deploying lemon drops so that the entire floor filled with a thick yellow smoke that burned into the eyes, the lungs and the throat. The agents pulled on their masks and the fight began in earnest.

Tristram's hand thrummed with his automatic while the remaining members of the squad, their identikits stencilled ghosts in the mind's eye of iAm, provided covering fire behind him.

Both sides knew that whatever happened, there was no way out. The agents had the only exit covered, and not even Valencia would risk a sheer drop from a six story window.

Almost forty-five minutes later, the other agents had turned into real ghosts, as had a total of thirty-two *Dish* and nine civilians, caught in the crossfire as they fought room to room.

As he stepped over the bodies, Tristram knew his career in Securicom was over. Even his uncle's influence would not save him. His insubordination was caught in the commander's high definition data feed, relayed back in real time to central command.

Perhaps it would be Bruno Mandrax himself who would *Retire* him, perhaps he would even face charges. As long as he killed Valencia, they could do what they liked. He no longer cared.

The corridor assumed an almost preternatural silence after all the gun fire. Cautiously, he closed in on the last room.

A man stepped out. Manaus, the Garde who had slugged him in the tunnel a lifetime ago. Seeing Tristram, he screamed and charged at him with a knife. Tristram blew his head off.

Idiot, he thought, didn't Manaus see the gun? But then something hit him in the back, hard. Staggering forward, Tristram managed to turn.

He shot the small, tanned woman, peppering her until she lay on the ground twitching, a Samurai sword still clutched in her hand.

White hot pain seared through him and he fell to his knees. He cursed himself. Of course the man was just a diversion. He should have looked for the real threat.

She must have stepped out from one of the other rooms. If she'd had any ammo left, he would be dead. As it was, iAm told him his back muscles were shredded and he had an estimated two minutes before passing out from the pain and blood loss. Already he shook uncontrollably and the world swam before his eyes.

He selected an emergency command to shut off the pain receptors in his brain, and slowly stood up.

Another iAm warning flashed up. In the absence of pain as a modulator, he would push his body to the point of death. He dismissed the message, and half stumbling, pulled himself into the room.

Valencia was there, sitting on a chair, her back turned to him. The prize at the end of the bloodbath. She had bandages wrapped around her head, but her pink hair was still visible, cascading past her shoulders.

"Cy Yozarian," she said, her voice shaking.

She did not turn around.

"My name is Tristram Eborgersen," he replied, slightly disappointed at how discomposed she sounded. So, she did feel fear. He had expected more. He dropped the spent automatic on the ground, and pulled the Luger from his belt. Limping two steps closer, he levelled the gun at the back of her head.

"You think you have won," she said. "But you understand nothing. Nothing at all."

"I understand that you are about to die."

"But not alone."

There was the vaguest click, a flash of white, and then darkness.

33

MANDRAX ORDERED TWO more transports. Cleaning up this mess was going to take a week. More than fifty bodies, including civilians; old folks who had inhaled too much lemon, infants who had done the same, the rest in the wrong place at the wrong time when the bullets started flying.

Thank the *Faith* the grenade was faulty, delivering more of a flash than a bang. It took out a couple of apartments, but not much else.

Another body was wheeled over for him to inspect. He saw the face and shook his head. As they zipped up the bag his vid feed lit up and with a sinking feeling he saw it was the Chairman.

"Report," Maglan said.

Where should he begin? With the casualties? With your psychotic nephew?

"We have eliminated the Bedouin operatives, although we cannot yet formally identify the leader due to the condition of the body. She was rigged up, an explosive device attached to her head, as though she wanted to make sure there could be no possible . . ."

Maglan cut him off. "The girl, Bruno. The girl!"

Mandrax swallowed. "We have not found her yet. We are still sorting through the bodies. She is almost certainly one of them. The *Dish* fought to the death."

"Find her, Bruno. I want her, dead or alive, within the next two hours."

Maglan killed the feed.

The implied 'or else' was understood. Lose the girl and he would be removed from his position, replaced by Maglan's latest favourite, Elite commander Lomb.

Who was he kidding? That was going to happen anyway.

It didn't matter that the Chairman was the architect of the excursion to Sky Dome, or that he sanctioned the strike force to act before they had reinforcements, against Mandrax's explicit recommendation. All that mattered was the girl.

The Chairman hadn't bothered to ask about Tristram, but perhaps Maglan already knew his status, *Voice* filling him in real time through Tristram's iAm.

An orderly presented Mandrax with another body to inspect. "No, not her, zip this one up too."

In many ways, it would be better for the Agency if Tristram didn't pull through. The blood of these civilians were on his hands, and there were already questions being circulated about what happened at Esprit, before the restaurant exploded.

Psychopaths in the service of the Autonomy were all well and good, until you lost control of them, until they forgot who the enemy was or who called the shots.

Two more medics wheeled out a body. They looked half done in themselves. "Wait," he said.

They turned to face him, an odd couple. He was thin, like a breath of wind could snap him in half, she was puffy, like a marshmallow.

"Has the body been checked off against the database?"

"Yes, sir," the woman said. "A civilian caught on the sixth floor when it went bang."

He put his hand on the bag. "Male or female?"

"Male."

"Small," he said, musing.

"A teenager and he . . . he wasn't all in one piece," the man said. Mandrax felt his stomach churn. "I see," he said. "Go on."

The man's profile said he was no longer licensed to practice, *Retired* probably. Mandrax supposed wheeling out the dead didn't exactly need brain surgeons, and the site manager had pulled in every local he could muster. They needed the place clear by the time the evening commute kicked in.

34

THEY WHEELED THE gurney past the Securicom agents to the meat wagon about three hundred feet from the building.

"Crazy it's not closer," Mrs. Glass said.

"Keeps the flies away from the entrance," Mr. Glass replied.

As they approached the wagon, Mr. Glass looked over his shoulder. Nobody was paying them any attention. They pushed the gurney on, past the wagon, and towards an adjacent complex.

"Where are you going?" an orderly said, coming up behind them.

"We have to check this one in somewhere else," he replied calmly.

"Where? My instructions are that all the bodies are loaded here."

"Our instructions might be from a different authority. We are taking the bag over there." He pointed into the distance.

"What are you talking about? I can't see another transport."

While the fool was staring at nothing, Mrs. Glass quietly pulled the cord out of the top of the body bag.

"There!" he said, again pointing in a vague direction.

Mrs. Glass crept up behind the orderly, and wrapped the cord around his throat. The man put his hands up, but it was already too late. She had him.

"Hurry up," Mr. Glass said, shielding her with his body.

"Almost done." Her face was red with exertion. She dropped the orderly on the ground, and together they rolled him underneath the wagon.

Still not hurrying, they pushed the gurney towards the adjacent building complex and into the underground garage. They slid the body bag onto the back seat of their parked bubble car, and covered it in a plaid blanket they sometimes used for picnics.

"You were a fool to take this on," Mrs. Glass said. "It will be all over iNet."

"We got paid, didn't we?" Mr. Glass replied, pulling the car out of the complex.

"We almost got killed when that fucking thing went off. My ears are still ringing. It wasn't worth the risk."

He shrugged. "Maybe not."

"And your paymaster is now dead."

"The credits are in the trunk. Hard currency, in advance. I'm not an idiot."

"Paid already? So why the fuck are we still bothering with her for?"

His mouth twitched slightly. Sometimes he would give anything to pull out his revolver and put a snub nosed bullet right between her eyes. He had come close many times, very close.

"There is some honour in this world," he said.

"You're not seriously taking her with us to Sector 2?"

"That was the deal."

"Fuck that," the woman said. "We dump her before we get off the highway."

Mr. Glass sighed. She was right of course. She was always right. That's why he never quite pulled the trigger.

"Where do you suggest?" he said.

"There's that part with the high embankments, it's on our way. Chuck her down there. We'll hardly have to slow down."

As they pulled out onto the main road, they encountered a cordon of squaddies flagging down cars and performing random checks.

"Shit," he said.

"Just look really dumb," Mrs. Glass said through her teeth. "Not hard for you."

The squaddies glanced at them and waived them on. Whatever they were looking for, it wasn't Mr. and Mrs. Glass. That was fortunate. The body bag would have been difficult to explain.

"I think I may have stained my pants," Mrs. Glass said.

Lovely, he thought.

Ten miles along the highway they reached the embankments and Mrs. Glass began to huff.

He looked for an appropriate place to stop. There was no such thing as a truly remote spot in Mansion, even in its hinterlands. The best he could do was pull over, wait for a break in the traffic and hope nobody paid them too much attention.

"This is good enough," Mrs. Glass said. "They won't be able to see you once you step over the hard shoulder."

He stopped the car.

"Make sure you put a bullet in her skull before you push her over the edge," she said.

"Why?"

"She can identify us, can't she?"

He sighed. "Yes dear."

As an afterthought she added, "Do you want a hand?"

"No, no," he said, knowing she didn't really want to help.

He opened the back door and slid the body bag from the seat, keeping low. Stepping over the rail he dragged it a few feet down the embankment so that he was invisible from the road. He fumbled around in his deep lab coat pockets and pulled out the gun, holding it over the top of the bag.

Mr. Glass didn't believe in the Autonomy. He didn't believe in the *Dish*. He didn't believe in the *Faith*. He didn't believe that how you lived your life made any difference in this world or the next. He believed only in getting as much as you could for doing as little as possible. However, there was something about that girl with pink hair that he would never forget. Something pure, something he wanted to be part of if only in a very small way.

He turned the gun to one side and shot two rounds into the ground. He didn't want to have to explain anything. Better for Mrs. Glass to think that he did what she said. He needed a quiet night.

He gave the bag a little nudge and it rolled down the embankment until it hit the base of the sea wall. *Good enough*, Mr. Glass told himself. If she came out of the anesthetic, which was somewhat doubtful after what he had done to her, then, well, it was meant to be.

PART IV
2060

1

SECTOR 1, AVIV

PROFESSOR HAKIM WAS as lean as a razor, the last few weeks having taken a toll on what little excess flesh he previously carried. Standing against the old fashioned lecture screen his silhouetted body made tense, dramatic angles, as though body and screen were about to crackle into life.

The lecture was still a week away and as a rule, he didn't like to practice. Hakim performed best when, having internalized the data, he only had the sense of an ending and the conceptual journey required to get there. Of course, he would pre-program a set of cues to flash up on his iNet lenses, a single word to get him back on track if he strayed, but the argument would carry the presentation, not the other way round.

This time it was different. He wanted to prepare every paragraph, every nuance, every interpretation, not from any ambiguity in his thinking, but from uncertainty over how to deliver the message. Hakim knew the studies and their conclusions more intimately than any data set he had ever worked on, but the implications of what he was about to present to the world frightened him.

He felt like a biological Oppenheimer. His discovery had the potential to both destroy the world and rebuild it. His insights required mankind to sacrifice everything it currently was, for the promise of what it could be. Perhaps that was why he struggled to find the words, why he had been in here for three hours, and was no further ahead.

Once Hakim made his findings public, the Autonomy would never be the same again. The knowledge, like a reluctant genie, could not be forced back into the bottle once released. Perhaps he should use that analogy in his opening remarks. A genie could be good or evil, their otherworldly motives beyond the grasp of man.

Hakim stared at the empty room, trying to imagine it packed with students, both physical and virtual. His last set of keynote lectures pulled in a live audience of almost half a million. Admittedly that had been more than five years ago, when he was still considered *the* authority in both the field of neurological engineering and the more conceptual field of biological philosophy, but Hakim was still a name and he would expect at least a hundred thousand to turn up as ghostly avatars.

The number didn't really matter. Even if just ten people attended his lecture, the substance of his findings would headline on Media within hours, the information replicating like a virus, until the whole of the Autonomy was infected.

A message flashed up on his iNet lenses, reminding him he had only fifteen minutes before his next tutorial. Hakim cursed under his breath. He needed to get the opening right. He gave his slight, trademark cough and began.

"When the definitive history of humanity is written, by some far off and as yet unimagined race, three dates will shape the narrative; the appearance of the first homo sapiens, their inevitable extinction, and the lecture I am about to deliver."

Was that too arrogant? Possibly.

He wiped the flat of his palm across his forehead and was surprised to find it slick with sweat. This was supposed to be a dispassionate scientific presentation, not a letter to antiquity, and yet he shivered, experiencing a sensation that in another time might have been someone stepping over his grave. A premonition of both his mortality and immortality. Only natural of course, given the subject matter, but it disturbed him. Again he wiped his damp forehead, blotting it with the back of his sleeve.

Pull yourself together.

He took a step away from the podium, towards the imaginary audience, and began again.

"Sixty-five million years ago, the dinosaurs were wiped off the face of the planet. Their failure was not one of strength, or intelligence or even resources, but of their inability to adapt. Simply put; when a meteor struck the planet's surface and blew a gigaton of matter into the air, blocking ninety percent of the sun's light for the next thirty years, the dinosaurs had no answer."

"During our history mankind has faced similar challenges, perhaps none greater than in the early decades of this century. From our ivory, or more often, reconstituted material towers, we can proudly claim that 'We are no dinosaurs'. The evidence? When our environment collapsed, we found an answer; the Autonomy, a triumph of rapid adaptation."

"However, we would do well to remember that if all subsequent time from the evolution of the first dinosaurs was compressed into a single year, then those scaly giants would have been on the earth from January until September, whereas man would have been on the earth for a single day."

"Let us not deceive ourselves then. Our Jurassic forebears were a relative case study in adaptation, had to be, and only fell when something so unexpected rocked their lives that they could not overcome it. An explosion that literally ripped their world apart."

"It is therefore with a sense of responsibility, and yes, some trepidation, that I introduce this evening's topic . . ."

At the back of the room a door clicked shut. Someone listening? Surely he had locked the door. He didn't see an identikit, but that meant nothing. They could have removed their lenses.

A twinge of fear shot through him. Hakim had no illusions about what might happen if the data leaked prior to the lecture. He might be a scientist, but he was experienced enough to know how the world turned. Powerful interests would try to suppress what he had to say, no matter how irrefutable or inevitable his work.

At the very best, the Academy would become involved, sifting the data for its economic impact, weighing the net gain against the net loss and deciding to kill it, the short term economic disruption considered too extreme. At the worst . . . he didn't want to think about the worst.

Only once the data was irretrievably public would the Autonomy rally around his findings. Top 10 would have no choice. Fortunately, he had said nothing of importance yet, even if someone was there. Neither could his data be hacked. He kept all his research off iNet despite the impracticalities of doing so, despite the penalties of using alternative storage devices.

A second reminder flashed up on his iNet interface. The tutorial with Kolo, his special case. The course of one-on-one lessons had been a mistake, but the lecture hadn't seemed so pressing a month ago when he agreed to take on the boy. Now it was only two weeks until the exam, and with Kolo still struggling with the work, Hakim couldn't cancel.

With a blink of the eye he dismissed the message and began to clear up his things. He was no further along. If he could just get the opening right, maybe the rest would flow naturally. He would practice again later, record a run through as if he had to deliver it right now, no pauses, no backing out.

Perhaps he was exaggerating the data after all. Perhaps it wouldn't be such a big deal.

2

SECTOR 1, MANSION

ROM THE FIFTIETH floor of Top 10's Securicom Building, Maglan watched the sun rise over the glittering Mansion skyline. He remembered how it used to be as a boy, before the Autonomy, before *Voice* and *Earth*, before Atmos, when there were dark days, and stormy days, and wind that would make the buildings shake. He remembered snow-lined streets, turning black within three hours. He remembered days so hot, the sidewalk would shimmer, and the odour of rotting garbage filled the avenues with a sickly-sweet smell.

Today, Atmos regulated the entire eco-system and the weather was always the same, except during five short winter days. The mortgage on Atmos still had another five years to run, then it would be time for another upgrade, and Mansion would once again be plunged into debt, beginning the economic cycle all over again.

It was just after five in the morning, but the city throbbed with activity, as it did every second of every day. Late shifts and early shifts converged in the dawn air. He wondered if the boy of his youth would have recognized the old avenues underneath the hundreds of new buildings that sprawled in every direction, each as tall as the old World Trade Centre.

In place of street vendors selling coffee and bagels, pine nuts or kebabs, were food stations that dished out nutrition in the exact quantities required by the body, as communicated remotely by the subject's internal biosquare.

Dust bots made their way up and down the streets, politely waiting for any passing worker, clearing up any dropped waste, their batteries charged by cycling feet hundreds of miles away. No, the boy of his youth would not have recognized this Manhattan. It was too aseptic, too sanitized, too clean.

He wondered at his uncharacteristic nostalgia. Was it because today he turned seventy? Three score and ten, even in this long-lived Sector, was a turning point. He would step down as Chairman at the end of the month and then he would retire, having shepherded the Autonomy through its first great crisis, leaving it in better shape than he found it.

No, it wasn't his retirement that bothered him. He hadn't got in at dawn to take in the view and ponder the end of his career. Something was wrong in the world. He could taste it.

He scanned the Media for clues. Nothing. These days, President Lomb managed the security of the Autonomy with embarrassing ease. Productivity was good, and after the hiccup in Churin, iAm was back on track. Mong, having inherited the lion's share of the iAm contract, was a pattern of peace and productivity. The *Dish* no longer existed as a serious concern, more a minor irritant in remote Sectors than a serious movement. There was even a plan for taming the Cut, also Lara's brainchild. It was too expensive to integrate wholly, but its population could be controlled.

Perhaps that was what bothered him. It had been too quiet for too long.

He turned back to the window, and scanned the streets in high definition, scrolling along them like some Securicom Tyro doing the beat, forever looking for her, the one that got away.

Balmoral Murraine.

She was probably in another, remoter Sector, or dead. Even if she was alive, she lived on the run, without resources, without support and without iNet. Her iAm chip had never been accessed, her legendary abilities neutered by the simple fact that she could no longer interact with the world around her. She might have had retinal surgery, assumed a new identity, but he didn't consider this a serious possibility. Few outside Securicom knew the procedure existed, and even fewer could pull it off. And yet, he could not stop thinking about her. How many times a day did he berate himself for not just ending her life when they still had her?

The Steel Ball arena had been a foolish indulgence. He had wanted to break her with the annihilation of Churin, and at the same time punish Pasco for his mawkish affection, his petty betrayals, and his treachery to the memory of Callum, his long dead cousin.

How simple it would have been to walk into her room when she was still stretched out on that bed, a hundred wires protruding from her body, and snuff out her existence. But no, he chose to make her suffer, the only sentimental decision of his career, and she slipped through his fingers.

His iNet lenses blinked to life, and a single word beamed in front of his retinas.

Maglan.

"Lara," he replied verbally.

We have a problem.

His intuition never failed. "A problem Lara? That's your department now isn't it?"

I thought that in this particular case you would want to be informed.

"The girl?" he said, his pulse quickening.

There was a pause.

No.

"Then why are you bothering me with it?"

Because you are still the Chairman, and a matter of this gravity warrants your attention.

Maglan affected a sigh. "Go on then."

This came in from an unverified source. I am sending the executive summary to you now.

A file appeared in front of Maglan's lenses. He tapped a command on his holopad and began to read. It took about five minutes to get to the end, five seconds to digest the implications.

"Numbers?" he said icily.

In terms of economic damage or body count?

He remembered Guy Rawstorm once asking if there was a difference. In this case, there was.

"Bodies," he said.

Voice's analysis suggests up to fifty percent of the population could be wiped out in the aftermath.

Six and a half billion people.

Maglan considered. "The source could be a crank. Has the data been validated?"

No. Voice believes the files are kept somewhere off the intellisphere.

Inwardly, he smiled. *Voice believes.* His President of Securicom considered the AI more than just a machine.

"You were right to bring this to my attention. I take it nobody else is involved? You've deployed no agents?"

Not yet. I wanted to bring it to you first.

"So only you, the source and *Voice* know about the data."

Yes, apart from the target, of course.

"Wait for my instructions," Maglan said.

Lara acknowledged his command and cut the feed.

Who could he trust with this? Who would not lose their head? This could get very ugly, very quickly. He needed someone who would do whatever it took, no matter what the cost.

Turning to his coffee counter he made an espresso and dropped two lumps of sugar into it. He sipped it slowly, his mind cataloguing a hundred tactical approaches. It took him until the coffee was finished to execute a plan.

"Lara," he said.

Sir.

"I think it's time to bring Tristram out of retirement."

3

F LIP, FLIP.

"And here you are sir . . . yes that's right; the condiments are already injected into the meat based on your pre-set preferences and joule tolerance."

Flip, flip.

"No sir, that particular option exceeds your joule burn."

The only place to hide, when every *Earth* camera strained towards you, was in plain sight.

Flip, flip.

"Don't worry," insert small laugh, "this tastes *much* better than it looks."

ToCal was the latest health fad from LifeScience; a nutrition plan based on the needs of the individual as dictated by their biosquare. Even if the consumers ordered something else; a layer of bacon, a topping of cream, the request was automatically ignored. The elimination of impulsive choices was a fundamental part of the service. If the participant cheated, the biosquare induced vomiting.

The lengths Mansionites went to for the promise of a few more years amazed her. LifeScience with its various cell rejuvenation strategies, nutritional programs, and organ replacements promised to increase longevity into the teens of the individual's second century, at an astronomical expense of course. In Sector 2 and 3, sometime between forty and fifty was deemed the best time to die, economically and spiritually.

"No mam, I'm afraid I can't make the portion bigger. I don't have that authority."

Expletive, expletive, expletive.

"Believe me I know, but you will feel better about yourself later."

The words were not her own. Balmoral simply repeated whatever appeared on her iNet lenses, the phrases fed to her by ToCal's artificial intelligence. It was an odd sensation, speaking with someone else's voice, acting with an easy sociability she could never possess. Diverging from the script was grounds for *Retirement*.

Flip, flip.

"Looking good, sir."

Flip, flip.

"It's better while it's hot! Eat from right to left."

The orders were automatically processed. Balmoral grilled it, flipped it twice, and then placed it in a small recyclable box. She had become a machine again, albeit a less complicated one, the lowest pay grade Top 10 had in Sector 1.

She bussed in three and a half hours a day from the distant suburbs, from apartments that the locals referred to as *the Stacks*, except that for someone who had actually lived in Stacks, they were nothing like it. Her block, a bleach-clean honeycomb of sleeping cubes, each with a shared private shower and waterless toilet, each with closet space and a bed big enough for three, of her anyway.

A diligent worker, she flipped ToCal six days a week. On Sundays she did her devotions to the *Faith* and took a brisk walk in the park. She was a model citizen, a little low in IQ, but she paid her bills and taxes.

Or at least that's how it appeared to the outside world, and to *Earth* and to *Voice* and to whoever else might be looking. It was the outward life of a girl she hardly recognized, with her bleached white face, pink hair, curious blue eyes and augmented breasts.

Her identikit read Sophie Valencia.

Mr. Glass hid her that night, behind someone else's eyes, someone else's face, patching her up in a speed surgery that took just over an hour. The breasts and bleaching she did later, a common enough surgery for Asiatic Aspirants, but that was months after clawing herself back to the land of the living after being dumped at the bottom of the embankment.

At least he had left her with lenses. She admitted herself to hospital, then into a rehab program, fabricating the cause of her injuries and paying with appropriated funds.

Mr. Glass's job wasn't perfect. Sometimes she became a little blind in one eye, and under her ears and neck there were deep hack-job scars, but for all intents and purposes he had made her someone else.

Inwardly, she led another life entirely. Inwardly, she raged and kicked and screamed, dedicating every waking second to fulfilling her promise to the real Sophie Valencia, to bring down the Autonomy. Every night she subcoded until the early hours of the morning, looking for something, anything she could use.

She had not been successful.

Two years on and the Autonomy was more secure than ever. The new President of Securicom had succeeded in bringing all the Sectors into line following the bombing of Churin. As far as she could tell, the *Dish* only existed where the Autonomy itself benefited from their presence; a corrupt and incompetent organization that sucked the life out of any real resistance.

She touched her temple where there were the traces of another set of stitches. iAm now seemed inevitable. Every citizen would require the *enhancement* within the next two years. The test cycles in Sector 2 and 3 were complete. Next month the implants would be rolled out in a staggered fashion to the general population at a rate of a hundred million a week. LifeScience proudly stated the procedure was now no more invasive than a flu jab, a quick pump through a precision needle and you were done.

iAm was the final step towards mankind's indentured slavery. She was running out of time.

4

SECTOR 1, AVIV

CRUSHING THREE CODEINE into the dregs of last night's coffee, Tristram reflected that a sandman was not supposed to feel fear. It was conditioned out of them; fear, panic, despair, anger, anything that could disturb their judgment or self-control. And yet, despite everything he had seen and done, fear took hold of him now; a deep, paralyzing horror that threatened to twist his soul and unhinge his mind. The emotion took him by surprise. He rarely felt anything these days. He supposed it was one thing to believe something about your existence, quite another to know it.

Reaching for the Luger on the bedside table, he began to strip it down. He must have cleaned it fifty times during the night, sitting in that same hotel chair in the tiny square room. When the sun finally streamed through the windows it caught him by surprise. In the small hours of darkness, it had seemed the waiting would never end.

It was only two days since he landed in Aviv, a Sector 1 mega city of sixty million souls, a sand blasted city with desert and death encroaching on every side. Aviv was within, and yet apart from the Autonomy. Corruption was rife and regulations almost non-existent, a city where in ancient times the world's old religions were born.

His iNet lenses blinked to life. Demel and Cadura, his local contacts, waited for him downstairs. He had met Demel in his first year as a sandman, hunting down rogue traders on the Aviv black market. He was efficient, but limited.

Tristram knew nothing of Cadura and that unsettled him. He didn't like that variable, not for this type of mission. Too much could go wrong. On a mission like this Lara should have assigned the best, not a couple of low pedigree squaddies. It made no sense.

He reassembled his weapon and pocketed it in a heavy leather tool belt. Crossing to the sink, he splashed cold water on his face. The reflection that stared back was alien; the forehead thickened with skin grafts, his eyebrows implanted, black rather than blond, his hair dyed to match them. His nose had been widened at the bottom, his chin broadened, the tattoo removed and his overall complexion altered to a deep brown.

Lara required the alterations so that when his face was broadcast across Media, nobody would recognize him, not even his former colleagues in Securicom.

She sent him to some semi-illegal body shop in Aviv, keeping him off Securicom's books. It was painful, but he was used to pain. Only the retinas were done back in Mansion.

Lara assured him personally that they would put him back *the way he was* right after the mission. However, after what he had discovered there was no going back. They might restore his appearance. They could not wipe the knowledge from his brain.

He tied an embroidered red scarf around his head and put on his hard hat. Show time.

AT THE GATES of Aviv's Academy, Security checked their credentials, exchanged a few words, and then waved the transport through without a second glance.

"That was too easy," Cadura said, too loudly, the windows still wound down. "Who spiked the system?"

"Shut up, and drive," Tristram growled.

The source hacked the system. Anyone who could get deep enough into iNet to rouse *Voice's* attention knew his way around subcode, and cracking into the Academy's records to create a fake HVAC request was child's play. More important than the cover, he also supplied Tristram with a floor plan for the building. Using the source gave Tristram a sense of satisfaction, employing the resources on hand meant less to clean up afterwards.

Cadura swung into the science block, parking about fifty feet from the entrance.

"Not here," Tristram said.

"But we're under the trees," Cadura replied. "It's cover."

"We're too far from the entrance. We may be leaving in a hurry."

Cadura grunted, and pulled the van a few spaces closer.

"Right outside the front door," Tristram said.

"But it says no parking."

"Just do it."

With a sigh, Cadura parked the van and got out, remembering to tie his scarf only once he was outside. Even then he fumbled with it, and it slipped down to his neck. Tristram exchanged a glance with Demel and flicked on the hazards.

Inside, the corridor bustled with students. Nearly all were *i-blind*, letting their lenses guide their steps while simultaneously messaging friends, completing assignments or being otherwise stimulated. Most had their holopads out, fingers floating in the air.

Occasionally two or three would pass by actually talking to each other, their iNet glasses pushed to the top of their heads, but even they seemed to barely register the three figures in white coats.

Later, Tristram supposed, the students would remember them; workmen that didn't quite look like workmen, the red bandana showing under their hard hats.

The building used to be the library and somehow it retained the long ago scent of disinfectant, wooden desks and the paper of books slowly yellowing. There probably hadn't been any physical books here for almost thirty years.

At a sign from Tristram, Demel and Cadura erected four thin cones around a storage closet, all of which emitted a pulse for iNet navigation, and then made a border with hazard tape. Within the perimeter, they placed a step ladder, and pushed a few ceiling tiles away for a touch of authenticity.

Tristram waited for a lull in the foot traffic and then stepped into the storage closet while his men remained stationed outside. It was small but relatively sound proof. Snapping open his pocket scanner he confirmed what the floor plan suggested, no *Earth*.

This was why the floor plan was important. *Earth*'s software was now self-correcting. If the AI identified an open space not covered in a public building it would be logged, and within a week a technician would connect it to the system. However, no AI was perfect and there were glitches if you knew what to look for; such as makeshift closets that served as both a room and storage.

Assuming Lara gave the order, Tristram was about to commit a major crime. Twenty-four hours from now their images would be plastered all over the Media while local squaddies tried to reconstruct their movements and communications in Aviv; from the hotel to the campus and beyond. It was important he laid a false trail, something Securicom could follow, but his interactions with Lara had to remain secret at all costs.

Tristram took a pair of small pliers from his tool belt and pushed them into the back of his mouth. Locating his third molar, he grasped it and gave a sharp tug. A stab of pain passed through his jaw but he ignored it, barely wincing. He needed what the tooth contained; a tiny, point-to-point chip that could bypass iNet's communication infrastructure.

The removal activated the chip with its tiny microphone and speaker, connecting him to an encoded data stream. He paused before he opened the channel, visualizing the protocol. One slip and he would be locked out.

"I need to speak to the operator."

"There is no orchestrator here."

"This is Nostradamus," Tristram said, and repeated a seven digit number.

The line went dead.

This too was part of Lara's protocol. If anything she was even more cautious than Maglan. He waited. Thirty seconds. Sixty. There was a click and the line came alive again.

"Well?"

Tristram had expected Lara, but it was Maglan's voice that crackled from over three thousand miles away.

"The investigation is complete," Tristram said.

"And?"

"The source is telling the truth."

Silence, then, "You saw the evidence?"

"Yes, he had a paper report."

"Who else saw it?"

"Nobody. I burned it."

"What about the other agents?"

"While I interviewed the source, they waited outside."

"But if you spoke about the data, they could have heard you."

"I don't think so."

Another pause.

"Sir?" he said.

"You're a sandman, Tristram, I need you to put them to sleep."

A single fleck of sweat beaded on his brow. "All?"

"There is an old saying, three can keep a secret, if two are dead. We can take no chances. You've seen the data. You understand the implications. We must treat the information as the world's most deadly disease. The only way to contain it, is to eliminate any who might be infected."

There was a click, and Maglan was gone. Tristram stared at the chip. If only one could keep a secret, what would they do with Tristram when he returned to Mansion? He was so far off the grid now, it wouldn't take much for Lara to snuff him out. But would his uncle allow that?

Once again the old suspicion rose in his chest. Gravales' insinuation about Maglan and the night Tristram's father was assassinated. He fought it down.

The dead President was a liar. Hadn't Maglan ensured Tristram received the best medical care after Valencia's last stand, fixing him up as good as new? Hadn't Maglan made Lara bring him in from the cold, the disgraced agent, exiled to Bodia?

On the other hand, Lara needed someone for this mission, and whoever they sent would be 'infected' by the information and a risk to the Autonomy. The assignment of subpar agents now made sense. If a resource was to be sacrificed, better one they could afford to lose. It was a simple question of economics.

Did that include Tristram? Was he expendable?

He shrugged to himself. Too late now. What would be, would be. He dropped the chip and ground it into dust. It was as if the conversation had never been.

Opening the door, he smiled at his men and he smiled for the *Earth* cameras. "Show time," he said.

5

"BUT I DON'T understand," Kolo said. "It is not technology we need, but food, water and access to the Autonomy's vast resources."

Professor Hakim sighed. Not this again. Not today. The subject was too vast and too complicated. Science, not politics, was his area of expertise, and with his lecture just two days away, he didn't have the time for a heated debate.

"Can we possibly just stick to the matter at hand?" he said.

Kolo shrugged. The boy was gifted in so many ways, his intuitive understanding of technology and networks would put most of the other students to shame. But in recent weeks he had become increasingly agitated and quick to anger. Hakim thought he understood why, but that didn't make teaching him any easier. At the end of the course Kolo's visa would expire, and he would have to return home, and home was not a pleasant place.

With a thumb and forefinger Professor Hakim magnified the three dimensional image of the neuron and set it to rotate on the table in front of them.

"To understand the nanotechnology that makes iNet integration into the human mind possible, we must first understand the mechanism of the electrically excitable cell."

"But why do you need it inside your head when you already have it in the iNet glasses you're all chained to?"

And you too, since you've been here, the Professor thought, staying up all night, exploring the other lives, other experiences iNet has to offer. Even visiting the Pleasure Houses, despite your father's strict injunctions. I know Kolo, I know, but I let it pass.

Professor Hakim smiled. "Imagine the entire sum of human knowledge at the flick of a synapse. Communication at the speed of thought. The capacity of the brain increased by a million fold without holographic touchpads, without lenses."

"I understand the science, not the intent."

The Professor sighed. "There is no intent, other than allowing the human mind to benefit from computer intelligence. For example, the almost instant recall of billions of data points, the sharing of knowledge at high speed, instead of using the very slow medium of language. All this functionality is incorporated into iAm."

Kolo stared at the holograph impassively, a bored expression on his face.

The Professor sighed. "Perhaps we should just watch and listen." He touched a command on his air pad and the high definition images came to life.

"In the early 2040s, with the increasing miniaturization of chip technology, the first implants were successfully fused with living brain tissue. In 2048 complete integration of iNet with primate neurons was achieved. A chip less than a millimetre in length . . ."

As the interactive lecture continued, moving through the biological sub structures of the technology, the Professor studied the boy. The other faculty protested when the University accepted him, with a sizable donation of course, from one of the Cut's bloodiest dictators. His father was infamous for his erratic moods, devastating charm, and for murdering an estimated ten million people while coercing a quarter of the continent into a West African bloc.

From Hakim's perspective, he couldn't help being excited by the boy. For a Professor of neuroscience, the opportunity to interact with an adolescent mind from outside the Autonomy, unenhanced by iNet, was fascinating.

The faculty also missed the bigger picture. Top 10 was in negotiations with the Cut to provide its skeletal inhabitants with iAm at no cost. That was the only reason a non-citizen was permitted inside the Autonomy's Sector walls. At the same time Kolo senior was suspicious of their motives, so he sent Kolo to scout out the technology for him.

His train of thought was broken as one of Kolo's bodyguards opened the door, surveyed the Professor's study and closed it again. Every twenty minutes. On the dot. The boy flinched when the bodyguard came in. This jumpiness, like his agitation, was also a recent development.

The Professor couldn't understand it. His father had many enemies, but he was safe from the Cut here.

The brief visi-lecture finished and the image in the centre of the table reverted back to the rotating neuron.

"Well?" the Professor said.

Kolo didn't reply. The boy's expression was blank. Had he even been listening?

"Kolo?" he said, "You have less than two weeks until your exams."

Slowly, the boy turned to him. "You know, when I go home, my father will ask me what I have learned here. He will ask for my advice on this . . . iAm. And I will say it is the control mechanism of their masses, the way guns are for ours."

"There is no control. iAm is simply an expanded memory and communication system. Better data for better decisions."

"But the Autonomy controls the information, controls what people see."

"There is no volition in the information. The user selects what they review, whether academic research, or a game of Steel Ball, or even the Pleasure Houses."

"But nothing can be published outside the system. What if you had something you wanted to say that despite its veracity, despite its importance, was not considered in the interest of the Autonomy?"

Hakim felt a flush of heat. What was the boy getting at? Surely he couldn't know about the lecture. And yet hadn't he returned to his office to discover the paper copy of his data slightly out of place?

Last night, in a fit of paranoia, he made a recording of the lecture, just in case anything went astray. In the cold light of the morning he had felt foolish, and regretted burning his paper copy, but studying Kolo he again felt uneasy.

"We need to get back to your studies," Hakim said, a little unsteadily.

Kolo smiled. "Why? Are you afraid of where this conversation might lead us?"

"No. I'm afraid that you will fail the exams your father paid so much for you to sit."

The boy shrugged. "My father already gave me the best education his wealth can buy, shipping in tutors from the Autonomy, sparing no expense in bribes. He wants me to rise above his achievements and unite the people of the Cut. He doesn't realise the Cut has no future."

The image of the revolving neuron flickered and disappeared. A second later, silence descended as the air conditioning, along with the rest of the building's systems, shut off.

"What's happening?" Kolo said, glancing towards the door.

"I don't know." The Professor pulled up his holopad, "A brown out, I expect. Let me see . . ."

There was a loud crack in the corridor, then another. It was a sound Hakim had not heard for almost forty years, but he had never forgotten it. Gunfire.

"Professor?" the boy said.

They heard one of the guards scream.

"Get down, Kolo."

The boy did as he was told, dropping to all fours and crawling towards the far wall as bullets ripped into the wall outside the office. Hakim wondered at the boy's composure. His guards were under attack. Surely this must have something to do with his father's enemies.

A trickle of dread washed over him. What if this had nothing to do with the boy at all?

Hakim moved behind his desk. His hand shook as he keyed in the combination. Twice he fumbled but on the third attempt it clicked open. He pulled out a box of cigars and ripped it open. Underneath the crenulated paper was a nut-sized rogue. He activated it with a word. Immediately its encrypted data was transmitted to a second, hidden rogue far away. He put the chip in his mouth. If he was wrong, he had just caused himself a lot of inconvenience. If he was right . . . then it was best not to dwell on what came next.

The door crashed open, and a dead bodyguard fell into the room.

The Professor bit down on the chip. To swallow it would not be enough, he needed to break it. The taste of iron filings filled his mouth. He bit it again, and forced the small, metal pieces down his throat.

Three men in overalls charged through the door with raised rifles. Under their helmets were the unmistakable headscarves of the Cut separatist movement, the Lions, the only group not under Kolo's father's draconian control.

Hakim's caution had been for nothing. This was not about him. They were here for the boy. He stepped forward. He wanted to reason with them, but before he could speak, they shot Kolo in the chest.

The boy's eyes widened in shock as he slid down the wall. The man turned the gun on the Professor and squeezed the trigger a second time. A dart hit him in the leg, he tried to pull it out, but didn't make it.

———

THE PROFESSOR AWOKE on the cold, steel floor of a moving van, hands cuffed behind him. The darkness made everything dim, but his eyes quickly adjusted. Kolo blinked beside him, already conscious. The Professor's head swam and he fought to keep himself from vomiting.

"It's all right," he managed. "You're alive. That means ransom, not blood. It will be fine."

"Yes," Kolo replied. "Yes, of course."

"And Securicom will find us. They are good here. The best."

"Yes."

For the second time the Professor wondered at the boy's composure. If these men were his father's enemies, whatever happened next, despite his assurances, would not be pleasant.

The van braked hard and they jerked forward, bouncing off the metal interior. The boy muttered something under his breath. Was it a prayer?

They heard boots crunch on the gravel outside. The Professor didn't know how long they had been unconscious, but one thing was for sure, they were no longer on campus.

The van's side door slid open.

"It will be all right," the Professor said again.

"Yes," replied the boy.

A light shone in, first on his face, then on the boy's. There was a pause, a crack, and Kolo's head exploded.

The Professor screamed. Blood ran from his ears and a high-pitched whine filled his brain. A rifle butt angled towards his head and he lost consciousness for the second time that day.

6

RISTRAM SAT ON the small plastic chair, watching Cadura and Demel take turns prodding the Professor with a shock gun. The Professor made plenty of noise, but not the answers Tristram was looking for.

Ideally this should have been a chemical interrogation, but for that they needed time and a specialist to administer the substances. They had neither. By now the entire university compound would be crawling with local Securicom, and Tristram's fake African image would be all over iNet.

As the Professor screamed again, Tristram's mind wandered back to the boy. Was it just twenty-four hours ago they were in this same house, talking like civilized human beings?

"This information is good, yes?" Kolo had said, pointing to the papers.

Yes, Tristram agreed, very good.

"It will make me safe then, yes?"

Yes.

He did not add that some information was so good, it made you safe in the permanent sense.

The boy's eyes lit up when Tristram promised they would extradite him to Sector 1, away from his father; give him a new identity, a career, a future.

Now his brains were splattered all over the van.

Tristram checked the time. They had been at it six hours. Only two more until the rendezvous and they were no further along.

Studying the scene in front of him, Tristram experienced an overwhelming sense of disassociation. It was as though the figure hanging from the hook was not his brother's old Professor but an actor, pretending to be that man. The makeup was very good, the screams, realistic, and the arm, dangling down like a broken wing, just a clever contortion of the camera.

Cadura shocked the Professor again with a few hundred volts. On cue the actor screamed, before slumping back on the hook, silent again. Cadura turned to Tristram and shrugged. "I can't keep him conscious."

Because you've overdone it.

Demel filled a bucket of water at a large trough and threw it over the dangling figure. It ran off red, into the corner where the drain was already clogged with bits of flesh and gore. Tristram wondered at the poor design. They should have made the spaces in the grate bigger. The Professor remained limp.

Tristram made them wear balaclavas, as though they did not want to be identified by their hostages afterwards, but it didn't fool anyone. Not after Cadura jumped the gun, shooting the boy in plain sight instead of separating them and killing the boy quietly, somewhere in the insulated cellar of this old Mossad safe house.

If the Professor believed the boy was a prisoner, he might have believed cooperation was worthwhile, that at the end of this torture there was the possibility of release. But when the boy's head exploded, the Professor knew it was over, and that set the tone for the interrogation.

"Shall I try burning him again?" Cadura said sullenly. Tristram sucked on his balaclava and nodded.

At first the burning had no effect. Hakim twisted back and forth as though having a nightmare, but he didn't wake. Then suddenly his eyes were open, and he was screaming again, the timbre different this time. It was higher, more like a girl's than an old man's.

Was that a good sign? He wasn't sure. In chemical interrogations, the subjects didn't scream, but a lowering of the voice's tone generally indicated the drugs were working and the subject was lapsing into complicity. A rising pitch, on the other hand, was a sign the lies were still coming, thick and fast.

"Okay, he's awake," Cadura said.

Wearily, Tristram got to his feet and stood next to the hanging man.

"Professor Hakim," he said, his breath wet on the balaclava, "You know the question."

Eyes like egg whites stared back at him.

"Well?"

The man made a noise, very faint.

"What's that? Speak up."

Another noise, more effort this time.

The answer was no. Or nobody to be exact, but the Professor was too weak for the second and third syllable and the consonants were lost through all those missing teeth. It sounded more like "nuhh" followed by a weak susurrus of breath. Still, Tristram understood him.

The first thing the Professor had confessed was that he destroyed a rogue containing the information as they broke into his office. He ground it between his teeth and swallowed. They could check his desk, the box of cigars, the dent the small chip had made. They could check his faeces in a few hours.

Why destroy it? Tristram had asked.

I panicked.

I thought the gunmen were terrorists from the Cut.

I thought they might have found it.

So I destroyed it.

Four lies in one.

"Hardly likely they would find the rogue, given how concealed it was?"

The Professor had no answer.

"And what would they do with the information anyway?"

The Professor had no answer.

"You were planning to make it public in a couple of days, so . . . why destroy it?"

The Professor had no answer.

"Rogues have two purposes: to store information off the grid, and transmit data to other rogues. Where did you send the data? More importantly, who did you send it to? Tell us, and the pain will stop."

I told you I destroyed it. I sent it to nobody.

Which is when the torture began again. The same question had been repeated more than a hundred times, the answer always the same.

Nobody.

About three hours ago Tristram received an encrypted message from Lara. *Voice* had detected an illegal transmission from the building shortly after his own. A message was sent but they could not trace to whom. *Voice* might be able to track it eventually, but it would take weeks, and Maglan needed the answer now.

"Who did you send it to?"

"Nuhh," the Professor grunted.

Cadura put down the butane torch and picked up the shock gun again, his eyes flicking towards Tristram expectantly. Tristram shook his head and leant towards the man on the hook.

"I would like to believe you, but . . . we already know what you sent and who you sent it to. However, for the record I want to hear you say the name. That way, we can patch you up and we can all go home."

Silence.

He leant even closer.

"Difficult as it may be to believe, we do not want to hurt you. But you must understand the world is not ready for your research. Deep down, you already know this, which is why the information was hidden on a rogue, despite the penalties for having such a device. So before you return to your life, to resume your important teaching post, perhaps even pursue certain aspects of your research, I need evidence of your cooperation . . ."

"Nuhh-bah-ee."

Tristram sighed. "I'm afraid that answer is not correct."

He nodded. Cadura stepped forward, shock gun in hand, voltage set to high.

7

HE SCREAM RANG in Professor Hakim's head. His scream. His head. They were burning him again, this time with electricity. He willed himself to pass out, to get back to the comfort of oblivion. He was headed there anyway, his life falling away by inches.

Did he still remember the Shahada from his childhood? No, he had lost his faith long ago.

His mind drifted, and then another shot of white hot pain coursed through him. The man was talking. Asking questions. Always the same question.

"Nobody," he replied.

It was a reflex action.

He even believed it himself now. Good, good.

The man in the balaclava talked about research, and yet he couldn't remember what the research was. That was good too. He didn't know why, but it felt like progress. Like he was slipping away.

When the questions first began he could think and act clearly. That was the dangerous time, when his conscious mind still had a say, when his resolve was assaulted by all manner of pain. But now thoughts only came in intermittent flashes and the end was near. He knew this because for the first time he could not feel it when they burned him, and a coldness had spread across his body. They had over-played their hand.

He should be afraid of death, but curiously he was not. Nor had he ever been. He would join the oblivion that awaited, not kicking and screaming, but with a sigh of relief.

Did he still remember the Shahada?

8

"CUT HIM DOWN," Tristram said.

"There are still other things to try," Cadura replied, picking up a drill. "These old Mossad houses have no end of tricks."

"Cut him down."

Demel began to untie the man's swollen hands, but Cadura slashed a blade across the bindings. The Professor hit the ground with a dull thump, a lump of meat, his fish eyes staring at his own effluvia clogging the drain.

His bowels emptied in an explosive stream of diarrhea and Demel gagged on the stench of human waste and blood, adding chunks of orange and red to the concrete gutter. This kind of work was a sordid business.

"Weak belly!" Cadura laughed.

Tristram knelt down next to Hakim and pulled off his balaclava.

"What are you doing?" Cadura said. "You said to keep them on."

He didn't reply, but pressed his fingers to the Professor's neck. No pulse. Just as he thought.

"Idiot," he muttered and pulled out the Luger. Cadura's eyes widened, and he flung a hand in front of his face, instinctively, as if that would stop the bullet.

Tristram squeezed the trigger and Cadura reeled back against Demel, who wrestled with him like a piece of heavy furniture before letting him slump to the ground.

"What now?" Demel said, coolly pulling off his balaclava.

"Clean up," Tristram said. "Burn the house to the ground, and head out."

"I'll get the gasoline," Demel said. He turned, and walked up the stairs. Tristram read the tension across his shoulders, in his angular, stooping gait.

Even if Demel's mind hadn't worked out what was coming next, his body had no such illusions. Tristram raised the Luger and shot him in the head.

———+———

In a display case, three thousand miles away, an antique Apple iPad 7.4 blinked into life. Solar powered, it had retained a low level of energy for the past thirty-five years. At auction, an antique in this condition might have fetched a few hundred credits until it was examined, and confiscated on the grounds of being a rogue device. In which case it would have been destroyed or sent to the Technology Archive.

The owner had no idea he harboured such contraband. He assumed because the device had never been switched on, that it was not functional, a shell. Professor Hakim, his old friend and mentor, would never have given him something that could end in a treadle mill sentence, or worse. And now it was flashing.

It would take another two weeks before Pasco noticed, and by then it was too late.

9

SIM: CATHEDRAL

L ISTENING TO THE eulogies from those closest to the Professor, Pasco experienced a deep sense of sadness, mainly because it was apparent that closest was a relative term. The Professor was unmarried and had no children or family. He had devoted himself to science at the exclusion of all else, including meaningful relationships.

Three thousand avatars packed into the *Cathedral* sim to pay their last respects. Pasco, having arrived a couple of minutes late, squashed into a bench towards the back. It seemed that most of the avatars were here out of curiosity, rather than any real tie to the great man. Even the overflowing congregation was partly an illusion. Cathedral automatically altered its dimensions to fit the size of the audience so that all services appeared well attended. The breadth of the gothic walls, the depth of the transepts, had been tailored around them for what was, after all, a relatively small affair considering the Professor's standing, and the Media frenzy that followed his death.

The eulogies complete, the *Faith's* in-house AI, a shimmering figure in white robes, made some closing remarks. "Professor Hakim has been taken from the *corporeal* world before his time," the avatar intoned in a sing-song voice. "But let us not forget that he is in a better place now, where the sun shines brightly for all eternity." The digital congregation murmured, *where the sun shines brightly.*

A light ascended from Cathedral's floor, while the three chord anthem, "The Afterlife is My Life" by Dillon Vrain echoed through the vaulted building. Perusing the program notes, Pasco saw that the tune had been chosen by one of the Professor's current students in Aviv. It was an edgy, maverick choice that the undergrad wrote, "would be appreciated by one of the Autonomy's true originals."

All Pasco could think of was how much the Professor hated Dillon Vrain. "You think his songs are anarchistic?" Hakim once said to Pasco's class. "Most of the time he's so jacked up on soma that he's barely coherent. The message gets through clearly enough though; the Autonomy is crap, but protest is a waste of time, so you're better off doing nothing. If that's the extent of rebellion in popular culture then Top 10 is safe. Media couldn't have done a better job if they made him up."

Pasco smiled to himself. As much as the Professor might hate the tune, he would appreciate the irony of Dillon Vrain serenading his final goodbye. As the chords died away, avatars all over the building began to pop and disappear. *Nothing more to see here, folks.*

Pasco remained on his bench at the back, and kneeling – he didn't really know why he kneeled – said a short prayer in memory of his old teacher.

Sitting up a couple of minutes later, he noticed three familiar identikits just to the front of him; old classmates, once friends, now acquaintances.

"Terrible, terrible business," Lisa Elm's avatar said in hushed tones, her hand lightly gripping a champagne glass, pinkie extended.

"Such a shock, such a shock," Sarge DeVries replied in a sort of half-echo.

For some reason, Sarge had chosen a fish to represent himself, a huge grey flounder, incongruous in this room of dark suits and dresses. Avatars were an expression of individuality but at a memorial service, the etiquette was to assume a sober life-like representation. DeVries hovered about three feet off the ground, as if to further accentuate his eccentricity.

"Do you think it's too soon to leave?" Seaton said. His avatar was tall, blonde, and perfectly slim. That was not how Pasco remembered him. Seaton was pudgy and balding, even at seventeen. This athletic figure, as much as the fish, was a fantastic incarnation.

"You've stuck your head in," Elm said, an edge to her voice. "Nobody is making you stay."

"I suppose I'll have one drink," Seaton said and scooped an orange juice from a passing waiter.

The ornate chamber was already less than half full, the avatars returning to their busy schedules, no time for the virtual refreshments laid on by the university. Time spent on death was a poor economic investment.

"I thought there would be more people," DeVries said. His voice even sounded fish-like, all gills, as though he was somehow short of air.

"I don't know," Lisa said, "the sign-in book said almost three thousand."

"Still," the fish replied, "his lectures used to pull in more than a hundred times that figure. He was a great man, a legend."

"*Was,*" Seaton said, fingering his ridiculous blond moustache. "His stock had fallen over the last few years. The term bandied about by some circles in Collegiate was, I believe, *crackpot*."

Lisa's avatar flushed and snapped something at Seaton that the sim beeped out. There was no swearing in Cathedral. Turning away in anger, she stared directly at Pasco, and started in surprise. It was his turn to flush. Half-concealed by a large stone pillar on one side, and a raised porphyry slab on the other, it looked as if he was both eavesdropping, and trying to avoid them.

"Pasco!" Lisa exclaimed. "What are you doing hiding back there?"

How could he explain that he had been too embarrassed to speak to them? That despite the hyper-connectivity of this world, he had lost touch with all of his old friends. Sheepishly he stepped from the shadows.

"Pie-face!" the fish said. "I don't believe it! How long has it been?"

Too long, too long he replied automatically, and realised that he too was doing the funeral double speak, every platitude repeated at least twice.

Terrible business, such a shock, too long.

In another platitude, Pasco heard himself saying how only these terrible events brought old friends together, but Lisa Elm cut him off, hugging him, her long haired, snake hipped avatar beaming. DeVries tried to do the same, but in the absence of arms, just slapped his fishy body against Pasco's skin. Seaton nodded a greeting, looking bored.

"Fish!" Pasco replied, realizing only then the point of the avatar. They had all called DeVries *Fish* at university because he drank like one, despite the fact that, as the Professor once pointed out, fish don't drink. And Pie-face, how long had it been since anyone called him that? His old college nickname, an absurd bastardization of Pasco that the entire class delighted in calling him, just because on his very first morning at Collegiate, he made the mistake of ordering apple pie for breakfast from the vending bot.

A gamine waiter passed by with a tray of champagne and DeVries somehow wrapped a fin around one of the glasses, "Don't mind if I do," he said. Only then did he realise the fin had no way of getting the flute to his mouth, being far too short.

"Seaton, make yourself useful and pour the champagne into my fishy lips, will you?"

Seaton said something, but most of it was bleeped out. The two began bickering, and Lisa, putting her arm through Pasco's, led him away.

"So tell me," she said, surreptitiously wiping her eye with the back of her hand, "what have you been doing for the last few years?"

The familiar lump of lead appeared in his stomach.

Don't think about her.

He made his avatar smile, drawing on an emotional fortitude he couldn't normally muster and the wonders of *soma smile.* Twice during the service he had snuck back to the apartment to push a couple of Mansion's favourite happy pills out of the prescription blister pack.

"This and that," he said. "Some stuff I can't really talk about. I'm sorry . . . I'm sorry I haven't been in touch, with you or Seaton or DeVries. It's just . . ." he trailed off.

She nodded. "I know, I know, job, life, work, it does that. It's my fault too. I only see DeVries because we're both at the Academy in Collegiate. Do you know, Seaton and I have two girls now?"

"Really?" Pasco tried to remember if he ever heard that she and Seaton were married. Were they married? They were an item, back in the day, but he always assumed the relationship wouldn't survive beyond the insular world of Collegiate. But then of course, they had never left.

Lisa Elm sniffed and he noticed then that her avatar was crying, that her questions were just a mask for something beneath the surface, a deep and as yet unfathomed sorrow.

"Sorry, sorry," she said. "It's just the Professor. One minute he was here, the next, this," she gestured around the room.

Perhaps two dozen people remained, lingering in small clumps of twos and threes.

"I had his Collegiate students, you know, while he was on sabbatical in Aviv finishing up that damn research."

She took a large sip of the champagne, and Pasco briefly wondered if she was mirroring; sitting at home with a drink in her hand, her avatar a literal extension of her physical actions. For some people, it was the only authentic way to engage in these real life sims.

"The awful thing is, if the attack had occurred twenty minutes later, the tutorial would have been over, and Kolo – that was the boy's name wasn't it? – Kolo would have been with his bodyguards somewhere else, and the Professor would have been spared." She sniffed again.

"What was he doing in Aviv?" Pasco asked.

"You really have lost touch, haven't you?" She swayed a little. "You know . . . he always spoke highly of you, even after you left. He said our little group was the favourite class he ever taught. I think he was disappointed you didn't stay on along with me and DeVries."

It was the two of you he invited to be his research assistants, not me.

Lisa twirled the empty flute in her fingers. "Aviv," she said. "The Professor said he needed breathing room. There was something about Collegiate that had become too . . . stifling for him. He wanted to complete his research without all the old hacks looking over his shoulder. So he set up a sabbatical with the

Academy at Aviv and he and JP Levy took the next plane out."

"Levy?" Pasco said, "I thought he must have retired by now."

Elm's avatar looked at the ground. "Yes, poor old JP, in his late eighties when he boarded the plane. He actually died a couple of months ago."

"Oh . . . I'm sorry."

"It wasn't a shock. He was terminally ill. His wife had passed away and I think he was looking for something to do. Anyway, the Professor needed his help. The Academy was impatient. If he didn't publish some research soon, he was out."

"Out? The Professor?" said Pasco. "They'd never fire him."

She leant closer. "I wouldn't have believed it either, but Seaton confirmed it. He's on the funding board for Collegiate."

Seaton in the administration and holding the purse strings. It figured. "I guess they don't consider actually *teaching* students a job," Pasco said.

Lisa Elm smiled wryly. "It's a question of productivity. The Academy is more forgiving than the rest of Top 10, but a Professor's primary responsibility is to publish, and Collegiate's finances depend on the economic value of the research."

More avatars popped around the room. The single waiter circulated with tired enthusiasm. Elm took another glass of champagne.

"What was he working on anyway?" Pasco asked.

Elm's avatar hesitated, then pressed her face even closer to Pasco's, as if that actually made a difference to the audio. "Do you remember Lars Pendicott?"

How could he forget him? Pendicott died the night his father was shot. Years later Tristram told him that contrary to the public records, Pendicott hanged himself. Apparently he was one of the *Dish*, or working for them. It was Pasco's father and Maglan who had discredited him.

"It turns out that years ago, one of his charities bankrolled a program to try to resuscitate aborted children," Lisa said. "A very nasty business, but afterwards, the Professor was given access to the data, just in case anything could be commercialized through animal trials."

"You're kidding," Pasco said, whispering himself now.

"He was still working on it when we first came to Collegiate. He and Levy had advanced some of the findings in relation to cell stimulation, but the fundamental issues Pendicott's scientists ran into remained."

"What issues?"

"Although the dead cells could be stimulated back to some level of senescence, the effect was temporary and the mice could only survive a matter of hours without life support."

Pasco whistled. "And we knew nothing about it."

"Nobody did, it was all very hush, hush. The funding was eventually pulled but the Professor wouldn't let it go. He was convinced there was something there. So he kept on in his spare time, shoehorning experiments into mainstream research, but never publishing anything. I helped him on a couple of things, as recently as last year. He was close to a breakthrough."

"Reanimating mice?" Pasco shook his head in disbelief.

Lisa choked on her champagne. "No . . . no nothing like that, a totally different direction, I think."

"What then?"

Seaton appeared at her side. "We need to go. They're shutting the sim down in a minute."

Lisa glanced around her. "Yes. I suppose we better. We don't want to be caught with the lights out, not in this creepy place. Pasco, lovely to see you."

"But what was the breakthrough?" Pasco asked.

"I'll vid you," she said. "You can take me out for a virtual drink one night and we can catch up properly."

Pasco said yes. He would try to keep in touch.

"And me," DeVries said. "I let Lisa hog you today, but we're going to hook up soon, my friend. We'll go on a glorious drunk to astonish the druidy druids."

"I don't even know what that means," Pasco said.

"It means I'm coming to Rhodes in a couple of months and you are going to put me up in Mansion for a debauched weekend."

"Sounds great," Pasco said, wondering how he would fit DeVries into his tiny apartment.

Lisa hugged him, the fish slapped him, and Seaton nodded goodbye, and then they disappeared, back to that tiny strip of an island three thousand miles away, all solemnly promising to meet again.

He wondered if they actually would. As Lisa said, work, family, life, it got in the way of these long distance relationships.

At university Pasco had been good friends with Seaton too, and yet he seemed completely indifferent now. Perhaps he was the only sincere one among them. Still, it filled Pasco with regret. A lapsed friendship was like arthritis, by the time you felt the erosion of the joints, there was no way to make up what had been lost.

10

SECTOR 1, COLLEGIATE

RISTRAM WALKED DOWN the cobbled streets, an early evening fog hugging the ancient buildings. He wore iNet, so as not to appear conspicuous, and brightened the vision setting. Collegiate did not have Atmos and at four o'clock it was already getting dark.

A few years ago, Collegiate, like all Sector 1 cities, began the construction of the vast environmental control system, Atmos. The turbines were washed away in the first bad storm, the sea walls of the small island never quite enough to keep back the rising tides.

The country, formerly known as Britain, was almost fifty thousand square miles at the beginning of the century. It was now about a tenth of that size, with only a few areas free from continuous flooding. Outside of Collegiate, the land was Sector 3, turned over to skaatch production and farmed by nomads who lived their entire life on rafts, cultivating jellyfish for export markets.

The centre of the city was relatively unchanged, a square mile where, despite the intense pressures of population, some of the original buildings had been left intact, the apartment complexes pressing in over their stony cloisters.

The corner of Tristram's iNet scrolled furiously, listing the names of the buildings, the dates constructed, the architects, his high definition lenses like binoculars on a clear, sunny day. He noticed the gargoyles lining the walls, their gurning faces made by pre-digital minds. There was a despairing scholar, head in hands, a laughing fool, a demon, a wizened king. This kind of art no longer existed. If sculpted today they would be less grotesque, less expressive, less individual.

Tristram decided to walk to his rendezvous, partly to get some air into his lungs, and partly because he was curious to see where Pasco had gone to university. It had been five years since they last saw each other. Tristram didn't think about his brother much, but he thought about him today. Pasco knew the Professor. He also knew the target.

Tristram filed along with the professors and students on crowded, raised walkways. Checking iAm, he pinpointed the target's building, a block of towers called the Village.

In the absence of hard information, Lara worked with *Voice* on the likely destination of the Professor's rogue transmission, identifying colleagues who might have touched the research. Although Hakim conducted the final studies in isolation, if someone was considered to have a passing familiarity with the research, it was enough to make them a candidate for sanding.

Just ten days ago, Tristram was exiled in Bodia. Since then he had been to Mansion, Aviv, Rhodes, Dane and now Collegiate, leaving a trail of bodies in his wake.

Someone was bound to link so many deaths, but the President of Securicom disagreed. While having his face put back together in Mansion, Lara convinced him that it was only his perspective that made it obvious.

The world believed the boy's death was the work of terrorists, the Professor, just a case of being in the wrong place at the wrong time. Demel and Cadura would be neither missed nor found; handpicked for their lack of close ties.

Everyone else looked like an accident or natural death. There was the Associate Professor in Rhodes who, prone to depressive episodes, overdosed on soma. There was the old man in Dane who suffered a myocardial infarction. The man almost choked on his cereal when he saw Tristram standing in his narrow apartment holding a syringe. And so it went on.

As he walked, he reached into his pocket and pulled out a couple of tabs of synapse excel. The drug wouldn't do any favours to his liver, but he needed the pick-me-up. It had been a long week.

Immediately he felt the tendrils of energy work through his blood stream and his brain kicked up a couple of notches, overriding his fatigue.

He reviewed the profile. Lisa Elm had worked directly with the Professor and was more likely to have received the data than the others. If the Professor's intention was to protect the research at all costs, to get it out to a critical mass, then what he needed was a radical. She checked that box too. Elm was crunchy to the point of illegality. She wore only recycled fibres, rather than the clothes manufactured in the fluff mills of Sector 2, and according to his brief, her single room apartment was powered by an illicit gas generator so as not to exploit treadle workers.

Elm had a family, which complicated things. Tristram could have worked around them but Lara said no. If Elm had the data then it was possible her family had been exposed. It didn't seem likely that Elm would sit down and go through the research with her seven-year-old child, but Tristram didn't make the rules.

Just as he reached Elm's building, a group of students jostled past him, laughing, exhilarated by their naked eyes and petty law breaking. One of them, an Aspirant, was less sure of himself than the others. He reminded Tristram of Kolo, now no longer a boy but ash, floating around in the dust of Aviv. Tristram took the stairs to Elm's apartment, jumping up them, two at a time.

TRISTRAM WORKED A thin magnetic card between the door and the frame, and pushed back the latch bolt. The Bedouin had been right about one thing, nobody did low tech anymore, they didn't expect it. Half the doors in Sector 1 could be picked with such a card in under ten seconds.

The room had an airless, musty feeling. The windows and door were insulated with plastic to keep in the heat, and limit the use of the small gas furnace in the corner. The furniture consisted of two pre-Autonomy pull out couches, a couple of chairs and a chest of drawers. In these buildings bathrooms and dining areas were communal to limit resource use. The only extravagance was the framed academic posters that adorned the walls. There was a cross section of an atom, portraits of obscure twentieth century scientists and a Vitruvian man. This was what 'Sector Free' living looked like; unhealthy, tawdry, and just a little bit smug.

He knew from *Voice's* records that Elm returned around six after picking up the two children, followed by the father half an hour later. Currently, she was five minutes away.

He checked the single window, which looked out on the wall of the opposite building. There was not much more than two feet between them. Outside was a tiny ledge decorated with a few flower pots. He decided it was wide enough.

He walked over to the couch, inspected the cushions, and briefly sat down and stood up again. He fingered the length of cord in his pocket, which apart from the Luger and a bread knife taken from the communal kitchen, were his only props.

The door clicked. Elm walked in with her two daughters and Tristram kicked into automatic.

"On your knees. Remove the lenses, yours first, then the girls."

Surprise, then anger, then fear as Lisa Elm saw the gun. "W-what is this?"

"I won't say it again."

Elm did as she was told, shepherding the children to do the same. The daughters, white with fear, were too terrified to make a fuss.

Still covering Elm with the Luger, Tristram made a small cut in the back of the couch, pulled out some foam and then tied their hands and feet, using the foam as insulation between skin and cord. He didn't want to leave any marks for the post mortem.

"What is this?" she demanded again, a note of hysteria in her voice.

Tristram put a finger to his lips. *Shh.*

He gagged the children with a swath of cloth cut from his own outer jacket and then pulled up a chair and sat directly opposite Elm.

"Where is it?" he said.

"I d-don't know what you are . . ."

"Professor Hakim sent you something. Where is it?"

Her face didn't flicker and he knew instantly she had no idea what he was talking about. He went through the motions anyway, Lara required it. He pulled the eldest daughter towards him and held the breadknife to her neck.

"Tell me."

"I don't understand what you m-mean."

He nicked the child on the cheek. The girl turned white, her eyes rolled upward and she fainted. Elm choked back a horrified scream.

Tristram smiled and dropped the girl on the ground. The wound wasn't much, could pass as a scratch between siblings. He grabbed the second daughter and put the knife against her throat. "Where is it?"

Elm was on the verge of fainting herself, terrified because there was nothing she could say to satisfy him. She knew nothing.

He put down the knife. "I'm afraid," he said, "that there has been a terrible mistake, for which I apologize. Just let me put this in your mouth" – he pushed a gag into her mouth, tying it behind her head – "thank you, and I will leave you in peace."

Except he didn't leave, but waited three or four more minutes until the door clicked a second time.

Hi honey, I'm home.

The puffy faced man froze as he surveyed his family trussed on the ground. Tristram stepped from behind the door, the Luger pointed at his chest. Tristram told him what he wanted the man to do, and he complied, getting on his knees.

Maybe he believed Tristram when he said there was nothing to be afraid of. Tristram tied him, gagged him and lined him up with the others, four sardines in a can, except there was no can, just Mummy, Daddy, and the two little fishes wriggling on the linoleum.

Intellectuals were not very bright when it came to the practical things in life. His intentions couldn't have been more obvious if he had asked them to dig four graves and stand next to the holes. The father should have rushed him while he had the chance. It wouldn't have made any difference, but that wasn't the point.

He should have tried.

Turning his attention away from the wrigglers, Tristram inspected the tiny gas furnace in the corner of the room. "You realise these things are illegal," he said over his shoulder. "I know, I know, treadle mills are unethical sweat shops, but these old heaters just aren't safe."

Reaching around the back he located the flue that passed out though the hole in the exterior wall. He pulled another chunk of insulation out from the couch and rolled it into a ball. If he had some rodent droppings it would look more convincing, but this would do. He stuffed the insulation into the hole and turned on the gas, waited for the flame to take, and blew it out. An unfortunate accident; the combination of a faulty heater and a mouse nest.

The apartment was about four hundred square feet. iAm estimated thirty minutes before carbon monoxide filled the room. He opened the window, and climbed out, stepping onto the ledge, accidentally sending a couple of the plant pots tumbling to the ground below. He pulled the window down tight.

The sardines twitched back and forth, eyes bulging from their sockets, the parents imploring him with muffled cries. The father wriggled across the carpet and was in danger of banging up against the wall.

Tristram couldn't allow that. He might get a bruise. Tristram held his breath, opened the window and climbed in as quickly as he could. Using his boot to turn him like a sausage on a grill, Tristram pushed him back into the centre of the room. He jammed the family in place, using the couch as a makeshift fence, and loosened the youngest girl's gag so she wouldn't suffocate on her tears and snot. Climbing back out of the window, he inhaled deeply.

He should have blindfolded them before he sabotaged the generator. He could have opened and shut the door, as though he had really left before stepping out onto the ledge. Waiting for help, they would have been relatively calm while they drifted into the abyss without this fear or agitation. Too late now, and the truth was, part of him preferred it this way, preferred to watch the result of his handiwork.

Tristram thought back to the bucktooth girl in Churin, of the mercy he showed her that day. If faced with the same choice again, Tristram would drill her brains against the back of the hotel wall and not think twice. There was nothing inside him now but the killing, and only the killing. He saw man for what he was, just an animal waiting to die.

Lisa Elm and James Seaton began to fade, their faces deathly pale. He thought about how he would arrange them in the room once they were dead. The girls on the couch as though sleeping, the father slumped on the ground, the mother on a chair. Carbon monoxide, the silent killer.

He knew the parents were contemporaries of Pasco, but had stayed on after

Pasco joined LifeScience and then Securicom. Was their acquaintance enough to put his brother on Lara's list? If she gave the order, would he hesitate? Would he feel anything different, or would it be just like those sardines back there, barely sentient objects, culled because that was the way of the world?

A message flashed up on iAm. It was Lara. He needed to finish up. She had another name.

11

SECTOR 1, MANSION

B ALMORAL POPPED A synapse tab, and a rush of energy filled her veins. After subcoding for twelve hours straight she was slowing down, but she couldn't afford to rest, not yet. She was on to something. Something big.

It had begun with a routine hack of Pasco Eborgersen's iNet. She liked to check in on him from time to time, just to take a look around. It wasn't voyeurism exactly, but a precaution, or so she told herself. Pasco was just one of many sources that she tracked to ensure Securicom had found no leads on her. Pasco didn't work for Securicom anymore, but taught children at a local *Faith* school. She sometimes watched his classes. He was a good teacher.

She browsed through his recent history and accessed an archive of Professor Hakim's memorial service from earlier in the week. Intrigued that he had known this murdered academic, she hacked a little deeper, pulling up old correspondence between the two of them. Hakim had once been important to Pasco, both as a mentor and a friend. The communications were full of affection on his side, reserve on the Professor's, as though Hakim never lost sight of whose nephew Pasco was.

From the archive, she flicked over to the Media coverage of Professor Hakim's death. She watched Lion separatists shove two unconscious forms into the back of the van, before accelerating out of the compound, tyres screeching. The kidnapping coincided with a brownout, which meant certain sections of the city lacked *Earth*'s coverage at a crucial moment. Securicom finally discovered it near the site of the bodies, a burned out wreck.

Balmoral checked how often brownouts occurred and was surprised to find that for a Sector 1 region, it was relatively common, especially during periods of high load. Three blackouts and nine brownouts had occurred in the prior year for periods of thirty minutes to seven hours.

Hacking into the grid, she checked the load on the day of the kidnapping. It was relatively flat, certainly not near the level of most of the other system overloads. *Curious*, she thought. The *Dish* were possibly capable of such a stunt, but inhabitants of the Cut?

She watched the footage again and pulled up as much information as she could on the separatist group, probing deep into Securicom's archives on the regional politics of the Cut and the Lions in particular. She returned to the footage, focusing on the third of the separatists. He wore the scarf around his neck, not around his head.

The scarf was inextricably part of the Lions' identity, it covered their head at all times, tied so that the wearer had a red mane down their neck. Even if he had not noticed, the other two would have.

Lions shot members of their own tribe for less. This led to the only possible conclusion, that they weren't separatists at all. And if they weren't Lions, who were they, and what was their purpose? The boy had been killed during the operation, the Professor considered collateral damage, but what if it was the other way around?

She flicked back to the memorial service and listened to Pasco's conversation with Lisa Elm, a current associate of the Professor. She pulled up more information on Elm, and discovered that in the week since the service she too had died, together with her family, in a fatal carbon monoxide leak.

Balmoral researched in earnest then, tracing all of the Professor's acquaintances from the last few years, looking for patterns. Analysing Hakim's social circle it was clear he had few close friends, if any. His contacts were all other scientists. A big name back in the day, he was part of the research team that helped develop the prototype for iAm.

What she discovered shocked her. In the space of two weeks, seven associates from his immediate academic circle had died, the deaths made to look like accidents, but with sandman prints all over them. A bagful of bodies wasn't the Chairman's usual style. The improvised killings smacked of desperation.

Hacking deeper, she saw that after the deaths, Securicom sent in undercover radio teams to sweep the area for rogues. Her first assumption was that they were trying to find something stored on a device. Perhaps details of a new resistance movement originating within the Academy.

Whatever the rogue contained was of critical importance to the Autonomy. It was the only explanation for the frenzied activity. But why eliminate the suspects that were most likely to know the device's location?

If Securicom needed information, they would take time to interrogate the suspects, which meant the searching was about retrieval, not discovery.

Viewed this way the operation was more like a containment exercise, trying to shut down a contagious disease by isolating every possible vector, anyone potentially contaminated by the host. The search afterwards was to find evidence of infection and minimize the chance of another outbreak.

The link to all of them was Hakim. He was the source, patient zero. She guessed that in the two weeks since his death, Securicom, or more likely, one of their unofficial sandmen, had systematically eliminated anyone who might have received an illicit communication from him on a rogue device.

All of the targets had one thing in common; they worked with the Professor, in some capacity, on cell-specific research begun in the 2050s. It was so obvious once she identified the pattern; she wondered why nobody else had made the connection. Maybe they had. Maybe they too had disappeared.

A thrill rushed through her. As far as she could tell, all of the victims were prominent Sector 1 citizens and had no connection to whatever remained of the *Dish*. This was about something else, some intrinsic, possibly fatal threat to the Autonomy. If only she could find out what.

Was it possible that Pasco, of all people, had led her to what she had spent all this time looking for, a way to fulfil her promise to Valencia? Impossible to tell.

Despite the risk, the pattern of deaths led to one inescapable conclusion. She had to make contact with Pasco. It was possible he might have what Securicom was looking for, and if so, he was in grave danger.

Balmoral sent a command to her employer. She would not be coming to work tomorrow, or again. She paused before hitting send. Was that likely? Someone like her, just throwing in the job? What if it raised suspicions?

She embellished. She had been forced out on sick leave by LifeScience. She had cancer, it was terminal. She furnished the update with faked records.

Taking a small pen knife from the inner pocket of her jacket, she reached up to the ceiling and carved a hole in the dry wall. She patted around until her hand alighted on an old cell phone, and next to it, a printed gun. Tucking both into her pocket, she set off for Mansion.

12

SECTOR 1, STERN ROCK

H IS NAME WAS Quincy. He was a Tyro in Securicom and a whiz at retrieving the irretrievable; rogues damaged in fire fights, data packets corrupted beyond recognition and hard drives fried more than three decades before. All of these problem children found their way to him.

This time he had received a rogue removed from someone's small intestine, and sent in a dozen slimy pieces. At first he thought it might be hopeless, even for him. But over the next two weeks he somehow managed to reconstruct it, fragment by fragment. He didn't need the chip fully functional, just operational enough to pull information about the transmission of a specific data packet.

President Lomb herself had briefed him on the project. For ten nights in a row he had been in the office until the early hours of the morning, but he didn't mind. This was the opportunity Quincy had been waiting for. A chance to show off his technical skill to the most senior executive in Securicom.

Tonight he had finally done it, extracted the IP address. He would get a promotion for sure, and he and Jay would finally be able to move out of their sleeping cubes.

Allowing himself a small smile of satisfaction, he snapped off the recovery program and turned to go.

"Oh!" he said startled, "You made me jump. I didn't hear you come in."

A man stood in the doorway. Six three and as hot as you like. The man didn't wear glasses, but gave out a digital signature. *iAm*, Quincy thought, interesting.

"Sorry," the man said, "I didn't mean to startle you."

He had a sexy voice to go with those abs. Shame about the surveillance. At past midnight, and practically alone in this part of the building, this chance meeting had possibilities. Instead, he would have to be boring. "I don't mean to be rude, but this area is très restricted. You shouldn't be here. I shouldn't even be speaking to you."

"I know," the man said, a gleam in his naked eye.

Quincy smiled. Perhaps there were possibilities after all.

13

HE BLOOD POOLED beneath Quincy's head and Tristram unscrewed the silencer. His brief had been to dispose of the body, but fuck that. Lara could find someone else for the mop and bucket. Who did she think he was? A cleaner?

The kid was only twenty-one. Some hotshot tech, recruited into Securicom. His status read he liked to live on the dangerous side.

"Glad to oblige," Tristram muttered, "Nothing so dangerous as plunging into the never-never."

He locked the door and flopped into the kid's vacant chair. He was exhausted, bone tired to the extent that the synapse just made him jittery. He hadn't slept properly for days. That morning he had stepped off the red eye and was on the ground for less than an hour before Lara came up with yet another name for the list.

She considered the tech a risk. As part of the brief, she had instructed Quincy not to review any data from the rogue, and records from *Earth* confirmed the boy had complied. However, Lara wanted to make sure that only she, Tristram and Maglan knew the destination of the Professor's transmission. That meant the kid had to be sanded, but only after successfully isolating the communication. So instead of finally getting some sleep, Tristram had taken a transport to Stern Rock and then waited around until the exact moment Quincy pulled the address.

His iAm flashed to life.

What's the status?

Lara. That bitch never slept either. He sent a visual of Quincy. Sometimes a picture was worth a thousand words.

There was a pause.

Very good. I have the physical address of the Professor's transmission.

"Let me guess," he said. "You want me on the next transport out of here."

Correct.

He sighed. "Go on then."

Another pause.

The location might surprise you.

"So surprise me."

She sent him the address. At first he didn't see the significance, then he realised what she meant and laughed.

Is there a problem?

"No problem. What did Maglan say?"

He has already been informed. It changes nothing.

Of course it didn't. He laughed again. This godless, faithless world had a divine sense of humour after all.

14

SECTOR 1, MANSION

NABLE TO SLEEP, Pasco watched footage from his archives of the four of
them; Lisa, Seaton, Sarge and himself, young research students, yapping
away, high on synapse and each other's company, pulling an all-nighter in
the lab to impress Professor Hakim.

Listening to their voices Pasco experienced a sense of dislocation. He had
to remind himself that despite the tragic death of his two friends those times
couldn't be overwritten, weren't just some sim. After an hour or so, with tears in
his eyes, he closed the archive, dismissing the ghosts back into the past.

It was two am. In the last couple of weeks his insomnia had become even
worse, if that was possible. First the Professor, now Lisa and Seaton. These days
he was on soma all the time, just to get through the day, to put on a brave face
in front of all those impossibly bright, impossibly precocious children.

He reached down beside the bed and pawed around for the case of beer. After
swiping back and forth, his hand alighted on the final bottle. He would have
to make it last until morning, which he supposed was not such a bad thing. He
had drunk three already.

Leaning back on the headboard, he took a swig and pulled the holopad back
out. He wandered aimlessly around the intellisphere, willing himself not to open
any Balmoral archives, willing himself not to obsess, or start searching for anything or anyone linked to her. A year of doing that had driven him half crazy.
He was doing better now; he only ran a cursory search two or three times a day.

To distract himself he reviewed the latest research on iAm. He noted with
some satisfaction that the technology had met all the trial end-points in Bodia,
the test population more productive than their non-enhanced counterparts.

The study also reported on iAm's capacity as a reverse pathway; the creation of a digital profile of an individual's real life actions, thoughts and memories as a side-effect of constant interaction with the chip. It was not clear how this functionality could be used economically, but if the infinite ways of thinking could be hardcoded, wasn't that a form of life beyond death? He wondered what the Professor would have made of it all.

Pasco opened the window to get some air. The noise from the street filtered upwards but it didn't bother him. The window was the best feature of the tiny apartment. These days they were considered undesirable, supplanted by inter-active visi-plates but Pasco liked to look out on the real world, to breathe in un-recycled air. He would have to shut it before he went to bed. The winter week began at midnight and already he could feel the chill as Atmos dropped the temperature to well below freezing.

He finished the beer and dropped it into a recycling tube. As if on cue, his biosquare warned him that he was now over the recommended number of units of alcohol for both the week and the month. At the same time, iNet, responding to a chip in the bottle, asked him if he wanted to order another case for delivery tomorrow.

Yes please.

He removed his lenses and rubbed his eyes. He was tired, but not ready for sleep. He would read a book, but not something reflected on a screen. He opened his battered display cabinet deciding which well-worn novel to pull down.

The Professor's clunky tablet caught his eye. Although solar powered, it had stopped functioning forty years ago, the internal workings fried. He turned it over, thinking of the Professor, and noticed the small green light blinking at its edge.

"Shit!" Pasco almost dropped it in shock. The device was supposed to be a shell, but if it was operational, it was a rogue and contraband. He would have to report it to the Technology Archive in the morning, either that or risk getting picked up in some random aether sweep.

The Professor said the device was dead, so Pasco had never thought to turn it on. Why would he?

Another thought flashed across his mind. The blinking light meant he had been sent a message. There was only one person he knew who had the capacity to do that, and she was the one person in the world he most wanted to hear from.

Suddenly excited, he located the power button and pressed it. Nothing for a moment, then the screen became a flickering white as the device activated. Four boxes appeared. He needed a passcode. He had not expected that. He typed in four numbers, "3333".

Access denied. Please try again.

He tried another. "1234".

Access denied. Please try again.

He tried another combination, then another, and another, until he was locked out and asked to try again in five minutes. He put the tablet down.

What was he thinking? Balmoral couldn't know the . . . what was it? Electronic mail address of the device. The only person who knew that was the Professor. Pasco had got his hopes up for nothing. The light must be a technical glitch. Nobody would try and contact him.

His iNet glasses whined from the bed. He reached across and put them on. There was a message informing him that his pizza had arrived.

Pizza? At two o'clock in the morning?

He opened the audio with the delivery boy. "I didn't order pizza."

"It says here you did," the muffled voice replied.

"I didn't."

A pause. "Did."

Pasco sighed. This could go on all night. What the *Faith,* he thought, easier just to take it. He had the munchies anyway.

With a couple of taps on the keyboard he authorized the building entry and credit transaction.

Waiting for the delivery boy to arrive, a wave of paranoia took hold of him. What if it wasn't pizza at all, but an agent come to arrest him? Surely they couldn't track down a rogue that fast?

Pasco fought down the panic. He was being irrational. If it was an agent, surely he would just announce himself. Unless they thought he would run. Why had he turned on the machine?

The pizza boy knocked on the door and Pasco's heart heaved in his chest. He thrust the tablet under a pillow.

"Coming . . . coming," he said but the door was already opening, the lock overridden from the other side.

The delivery boy walked in, dropped the pizza box, pulling something out of it as he did so. To his horror Pasco found himself face to face with a gun.

"I didn't know . . ." he said, about to proclaim his innocence, but the words died in his throat, and a wholly different emotion took hold of him.

The would-be assassin was not a boy at all, but a petite girl in black leather, a cap obscuring pink hair, mirrored lenses, and a cleavage that popped up and out. Despite the alterations, he was not fooled. His eyes might be deceived, but his heart was not.

"Balmoral," he said, barely able to contain his emotion. "Y-you've changed."

"Move over to the bed," she ordered, her voice cold.

"But . . ."

"Quiet. We haven't much time." She motioned with the gun.

He tried to read her identikit but the name, a transparent ghost, had been hacked and all he saw was a jumble of characters. According to her status she was a shift worker for Subsistence.

The very fact she could access iNet suggested the rumours about retinal implants were true, that the eyes behind her lenses were not, strictly speaking, her own. He wondered what the new eyes looked like.

He was desperate to tell her how good it was to see her again, but the words would not come. She had not even said hello.

She stared around the apartment, her eyes settling on the display cabinet. Would she notice *The Still Point*, stacked neatly with the other books?

"What was there?" She pointed the gun at the space where the tablet used to be.

"A . . . a tablet. What is going on?"

Her mirrored lenses regarded him for a moment. "Before he died, Professor Hakim sent something to somebody, something so important, Securicom have been killing people to find it. I believe he sent it to you."

Pasco's mouth grew dry. She was here because of the Professor?

"Where is it?" She raised the gun.

In a daze, Pasco reached under his pillow and pulled out the tablet. Its green light blinked guiltily.

"I only noticed it because I took it out this evening . . . I thought it might be from you."

Did a ghost of a smile cross her face, or did he imagine it? Either way it was gone in an instant.

"The Professor gave you this device?"

"Yes."

"And you haven't accessed it yet?"

"No. The device is locked, it needs a code."

"Give it to me," she said.

He handed the tablet over. She put down the gun and began tapping on the interface, muttering quietly to herself. "Four digits, almost ten thousand potential combinations. They can be worked through one at a time, but every five entered incorrectly, there is a temporary lock out, and after a hundred incorrect combinations, the lock out is permanent." She looked at the back and muttered, "cellular."

"What does that mean?"

"It means that if I hit emergency call, press the hash key a few times, it tries to dial a number that doesn't exist, on a network that no longer exists, and although the screen is locked . . . yes, here we are, I can access the contacts . . . and there are none except one, and that is your Professor, who contacted this machine through a self-executing rogue file and corresponding temporary network, the day he died."

"What did he say?"

Balmoral shook her head. "To access the message you need the combination for the device."

She no longer pointed the gun. They were having a conversation. It was progress, of sorts.

"What was his date of birth? No hang on, I'll look it up." Her hand whirred across the holopad and then back onto the tablet. She spoke rapidly. "Let's try the year, no it's not that. Day and month. Not that either. Month and last two digits of the year. No. Year backwards, no. Day and year, no, and . . . I'm locked out for another five minutes. There are other codes to try based on his biographical data, but it might be a trigger word, where the numbers 2-9 correspond with up to four letters. What else do you know about him? Did he have any pets?"

"Sorry?"

"Pets and sports teams, used in about fifty percent of passwords from this era. Perhaps he had a pet as a child?"

"I wouldn't know. I don't think so. We weren't that close."

Balmoral stopped tapping and studied him for a moment. "If he sent you the message then you must know how to access the device. Otherwise why send it to you?"

For two years he had prayed for this moment, for the opportunity to see her again. He assumed that if she was alive, she had been prevented from contacting him, or that she was in another sector. Now he wondered if she had been in Mansion all along, but hadn't wanted to see him. Not until she needed something.

Pasco shook his head, "I don't know why he sent it to me."

"Then I'm wasting my time." She picked up the gun and headed for the door.

"So that's it then," he said, his voice shaking. "After two years, you turn up unannounced, rob me, and leave."

She turned and Pasco saw himself reflected back double in the mirrored frames, his face flushed, his lip quivering. In her face he saw nothing, not a trace of emotion.

"Whatever this contains might get you killed. Better not to have it. Better not to know."

"Get me killed?"

"I told you, Securicom are looking for this information."

"There are laws. They can't just kill me. This isn't the Cut."

"No," she said quietly, "it's far more barbaric than that."

She didn't have to add, remember Churin, remember where you took me, what you made me watch.

"And what shall I tell them?" he said bitterly.

"That someone took the device at gunpoint, that you have no idea what it contains, that you have had no contact with the Professor for three years."

"How do you know that? You hacked my vid feeds?"

Balmoral ignored the question. "Your evidence is that they have me coming in on *Earth* with the fake delivery and walking out with the gun in one hand, the tablet in the other, just before I disappear off the grid. It should be enough to save you."

"Save me? I don't believe any of this. You make it sound like the Professor's death was some sort of conspiracy!"

"When a sandman puts a gun to your head and asks who took this device, you can draw your own conclusions."

"And who shall I tell them took it, exactly?"

"You must tell them the only thing that will keep you alive, the truth, and what will remain the truth even under chemical interrogation. Tell them that you thought it was me, but then realised you didn't even know my name." She tapped her mirrored lenses, opened the door and was gone.

Pasco thought yes, he did not know her. All this time, while the past beat inside him like another heart, he had embraced a shadow and loved a dream.

15

WHEN TRISTRAM FINALLY pulled up outside Pasco's building it was still dark. He opened the door of the bubble car and a wall of freezing air hit him. Cursing, he remembered the winter week. The atmospheric change was supposed to be a control mechanism for bugs; a check to those viruses and their hosts that would otherwise thrive in such a highly regulated environment. Tristram didn't see what difference it made. There were always rats and roaches in Mansion, and that wasn't counting the people.

The car's AI pinged his iAm.

Did he want the transport to wait for him?

No.

An idling transport was conspicuous. Passengers trying to get in would remember being told it was reserved, especially on a day like today.

Another part of him thought maybe he should have kept the car. What did he care about operational protocol? There were no rules anymore.

He took a couple of steps to shelter under the building's battered awning, hoodie over his head. The apartment block had seen better days. Scaffolding hugged the wall in some half-hearted attempt at renovation. The entranceway was dingy and exuded failure.

Leaning flat against the wall, he checked the time and decided to give the little bugger a few more minutes beauty sleep. In less than quarter of an hour it would be five am, the doors would automatically unlock, and he could enter without having to vid Pasco first. In the sandman's game, surprise always worked in your favour.

Tristram pulled out a cigarette and lit it, the wisp of smoke almost indistinguishable from his own freezing breath.

He took a drag and a couple of concerned citizens gave him an admonishing look. He stared back with his naked eyes and they shuffled along. Smoking in Sector 1 was illegal outside of designated underground dens, jammed wall-to-wall with Mansion's neurotics. He wouldn't be caught dead in one.

Yes, he thought, when this mission was over he was going to go back to slum-world. He was more at home there. There were none of these rules, none of this crap to deal with.

He stubbed out the cigarette just as a dust bot came down the street. The bot flashed a citation to his iAm stating that he had been booked for smoking together with an automatic fine. It rolled over the stub, hoovering it up.

"Let the robots do the work," he muttered, and in a single swift movement kicked the fucker upside down, so it lay helpless on its back, frozen rat tails sticking out from underneath the industrial brushes.

"Violation! Violation! Violation!" it protested, but before it could shoot off another set of fines, Tristram took out his Luger and unloaded three or four rounds until it finally shut up.

All around him, pedestrians scattered, some whipping out their holopads, others moving as fast as they could in the opposite direction, safe in the knowledge that in another minute the street would be full of squaddies, responding to reports of a man with a gun. Except that today, nobody would arrive on the scene, because Lara would shut down the reports as fast as they came in, and get all pissy about it later.

The building's doors clicked open and he ducked inside, heading for the stairwell. He ran up the ten flights of stairs, not so much to avoid *Earth*, but to get his blood circulating after the freezing weather.

There were a few people in the corridor, going in and out of the communal bathroom. He stood outside his brother's door and listened. Nothing. He wondered what he would find on the other side. If Pasco had seen the information, it would show in every atom of his body.

Tristram knocked. There was no reply. He glanced left and right, then whipped out his magnetic card and shoved it under the jamb, shimmying it up and down until the locked clicked.

A little girl in a nightdress stared at him wide-eyed from across the hall. Fortunately for her, she was not wearing lenses, so Tristram gave her a big smile and whispered, "It's my brother, I haven't seen him in ages and I want to surprise him." That seemed to satisfy her, because she smiled shyly and then skipped away.

He opened the door, banging it against the impractical display case Pasco had taken from their old family apartment. A few feet away was the bed, a pair of thick woolly socks at one end, Pasco's head poking out of the other. He didn't stir.

According to *Voice*, the device must be in here somewhere. Operationally, the simplest thing was to shoot him and then strip the apartment bare. He pulled out the gun and pointed it at the mass of covers. He considered a moment. What if it wasn't here, and he killed the only person who knew where it was?

He pocketed the Luger and kicked the bed. "Rise and shine like a bottle of wine!"

Pasco stirred and suddenly shot up, panicking, before a flicker of recognition. "Tristram!"

"I hope you don't mind me dropping by. I did knock but you were too far gone."

"How did you get in?"

"A door like that? Come on . . ."

Pasco smiled and then stepped forward, awkwardly embracing him. "You've changed, I almost didn't recognize you. How many years has it been?"

"Too long," he replied, and as he spoke Tristram was surprised he almost meant it, that he almost felt something. Almost.

Pasco had changed too, and not for the better. He looked terrible; pale and harassed. Was it possible he had seen Hakim's data? *No*, Tristram thought, something else ate away at him.

The level of alcohol on his brother's breath suggested mild intoxication. Bypassing the privacy firewall he accessed Pasco's biosquare. Scrolling past a bunch of stats on cholesterol, heart rate and blood cell count he focused in on behavioural data and stimulants.

In addition to alcohol, Pasco was on prescription soma smile, and in the last week, he had doubled the already high dosage. Perhaps this was a temporary thing, just grief over the Professor. Maybe he also knew about Elm or some of the others.

"You look like you're doing great," Tristram lied.

Pasco smiled sheepishly. "You look . . . older."

"Life on the open road," he said with a forced laugh.

"I heard you went missing for a while. I was there, you know, when Bruno Mandrax told Maglan you had fallen off the grid."

"Mandrax eh?" Tristram smiled.

Bruno Mandrax, once heir apparent to the Securicom presidency, now worked as an admin dealing with whatever shit Lara felt like feeding him. He probably hadn't seen the light of day in months.

"They said you were badly wounded, I wanted to come and see you, but they wouldn't let me. I left Securicom . . . after Churin."

"Yeah. That was a tough situation." He was bored with the conversation now. He needed to get this over with. He flicked his eyes around the apartment, his gaze fixing on the display cabinet, and a gap where he now remembered a defunct tablet used to be.

PASCO TRIED TO remain calm, but his head reeled. Five years without a word, and yet here Tristram was, the morning after Balmoral turned up, looking around the apartment in exactly the same way she had. He was there for what she had taken, and if they had sent him, a sandman . . . Pasco felt a lump in his throat. "What are you looking for?"

"I'm just checking out your pad," Tristram said casually. "Relax."

But he couldn't relax. He didn't trust that voice, he didn't trust those eyes. As a child they were blue, but it seemed to Pasco that Tristram's irises had become so dark they were almost black, like those of a shark. The sockets had a scored quality around them and the eyes themselves were soulless. Automatically he reached for his lenses. He needed to put a screen between them.

His brother had iAm, of course, which explained his own naked stare. He also toted a blue diamond tattoo on the side of his head, to show the outside world he was already enhanced, an early adopter, and therefore not in breach of any rules concerning the use of iNet, although that too would be apparent to anyone with a connection.

"We were spoilt as kids, weren't we?" Tristram said. "Our bedroom was big enough to play Steel Ball in. You couldn't swing a cat in here, could you?"

Pasco forced a smile. "I suppose it is a little tight."

"Though I have to say," Tristram continued, "it's better than my place in Bodia, about this size but a haven for crawling things and biting things and fighting things." Tristram shook his head. "There is one particular insect we get out there called a gryllacridid. Despite being one thousandth of your size, it lashes out any time you go near it. They can't help it. Cut them in half, and they will suck out their own innards, seeing the other half of their body as viable prey. I keep a few in a cage, just to mess with them once in a while." The soulless pools of black considered him. Pasco felt more afraid than ever.

"Fuck it," Tristram said finally and pulled something out of his pocket. For the second time in less than eight hours Pasco stared into the barrel of a gun. This time, however, he was frightened. For Balmoral the gun had been a defensive mechanism, her way of telling him to respect the boundaries, to let her walk away. For Tristram it was all about attack.

In an instant, Pasco knew Balmoral was right. For some reason Securicom wanted what was in that tablet, and from there, it didn't take too much to deduce that not only did the Professor die on his uncle's orders but that possibly he was next. He didn't doubt Tristram had it in him to shoot, not anymore.

He cocked the gun. "You know why I'm here, don't you?"

"Tristram, please . . ."

"Where is it?"

"Someone took it."

"Someone?"

"Balmoral Murraine, or . . . she used to be Balmoral Murraine. She's changed her identikit somehow."

Tristram paused a beat, as though deciding whether to pull the trigger.

"Do you know what was on the device?"

"I-I didn't even know it was active until last night, when she came looking for it."

Another pause. He was going to do it! He was actually going to kill him!

"Why did Hakim send it to you?"

"I-I don't know, I couldn't even access it. She asked me what the code was. I couldn't tell her."

Tristram studied him intently, keeping the gun trained on Pasco's heart.

———

IAM SAID HIS brother was lying based on Pasco's heightened blood pressure, per-spiration, and rapid breathing, but Tristram knew better. He knew his brother. Pasco didn't have the tablet.

Pasco was shit-scared but he wasn't lying. Neither did he know anything about the research. Even before Tristram pulled out the Luger, he could see something haunted him, but not Hakim's information. Balmoral Murraine perhaps? Come to see him, back from the dead? Maglan said Pasco had developed an infatuation with her. Tristram always wondered whose infatuation it really was.

Maglan thought she could no longer access iNet, but clearly she had found a way. Keeping the gun trained on Pasco, he sent a priority one message to Lara.

Inwardly, he smiled. It was about to get interesting. Maglan would have a fit. Murraine was just about the most dangerous person who could have taken the tablet. Would she be able to flood iNet with the data? Either way, he was done here.

Pasco said something, pleading with him.

"Of course I'm not going to shoot you," Tristram replied smoothly.

One shot to the heart, two to the head. He wouldn't bother with the silencer. He didn't give a fuck anymore. When the noise set off every alarm in the build-ing, Lara could shut it down.

Suddenly, a red haze filled his eyes, as though a screen had just been put in front of them. It was a priority one vid feed. Maglan, incoming. He had to take it now, no choice if he wanted to see properly.

"Stay here. I have to speak with someone," Tristram said, adding with a half-laugh, "If you open the door I *will* have to shoot you."

———+———

Tristram stepped into the corridor, and Pasco thought, *I am going to die.* Those shark eyes knew no mercy. How long did he have? A minute? Five? Oh *Faith*, he was about to die.

Suddenly his iNet screen changed and a single line with a flashing cursor appeared across his lenses.

Do you trust me?

Underneath, the communication was signed, "Still Point." Pasco's breath caught in his throat and a small flare of hope went off in his heart. He pulled up his holopad.

Yes.

Then get dressed. Your warmest clothes. You have less than fifteen seconds.

Pasco pulled on his clothes from the night before, together with an ancient fleece.

Open the window.

What?

If you want to live, open the window.

He did as he was told. For the first time the view made him queasy. A blast of freezing air howled into the room.

Jump.

From ten stories up?

Then he saw it, the scaffold, and a thin, narrow piece of platform three floors beneath him. He didn't know if it could even take his weight. She couldn't be serious.

I can't.

There are only two ways out of this building. One is in a body bag. This is the other. The platform has some give. It will cushion your fall.

He climbed onto the ledge. The platform was so far down, and only a few feet wide. With the wind, he might not even land on it but die in the attempt.

On the platform there is a control box that will lower you to the ground floor.

This was crazy. He would never make it.

When you hit the street, sprint three blocks south as fast as you can. Turn left and I will meet you there.

He looked down again, trying not to focus on the yawning space between him and the six foot platform, and the even bigger space between him and the ground.

If I stay here, I will die. If I miss the platform, I will die.

The door of his apartment opened. Tristram.

He closed his eyes and jumped.

———+———

TRISTRAM REACHED THE window just as Pasco hit the scaffolding and scrambled back to his feet. *Gutsy,* he thought. He watched his brother fumbling with some switches. The platform jolted into action.

Tristram pulled out the Luger. He could still make the shot even with the wind and the difficult angle. Tristram leant all the way out, and let off two quick rounds. The first bullet hit the wall, the second hit the platform, sending splinters flying.

He paused, re-sighted, and shot again. This time he almost took off Pasco's feet, missing him by inches. Better. Those were close enough to convince anyone. Pasco would make it, but it would look like a near thing.

"You need to let him go," Maglan's bulldog face had said to him.

"Why?"

"Because it's our best chance of finding Murraine. Make it look like he slipped through your fingers. Make it convincing."

Tristram had asked, how was he supposed to do that? Pasco was trapped in his apartment, a fish in a barrel.

"Think of something."

He smiled as Pasco made it to the street. Now he didn't have to.

16

F OR THE LAST few hours, Balmoral's old *fisher king* program had attempted to pinpoint any digital signature in the vicinity of the deaths linked to the Professor. She wanted to know who she was up against, and how many.

At first, the program found hundreds of identikits that had been at one of the kill sites. A handful had even been in the vicinity of two of the sites. However, only one identikit was present at all of them.

In the early hours of the morning, the *fisher king* told her not only who that individual was, but that according to the pre-programmed destination of his transport, he was heading straight for Pasco's building. He meant to kill him.

Tristram Eborgersen.

She watched Pasco climb down to street level, and hobble, rather than run, to the edge of the block. She typed out a command on the holopad and the bubble car, which had been idling in and out of slow moving traffic, swung towards the curb.

Three or four pedestrians made a dash for it, desperate for a ride in the freezing air, only to back away puzzled when they saw her inside. Their confusion was understandable, the car appeared vacant on iNet; a neat little hack designed to fool *Earth* when someone came looking for her. During two years as a ToCal flipper, Balmoral had expanded her arsenal of pre-programmed hacks, although few of them were completely reliable these days. *Voice* had become increasingly difficult to fool.

"Get in," she said to Pasco. Dazed, he slumped onto the seat next to her. Reaching over, she slammed the door and the car pulled away.

"He tried to kill me!"

Perhaps, but to her it looked like the shots were wayward. She could tell by the angle he held the gun. The sandman had let Pasco go in an attempt to trace her.

"You saved me," Pasco said, his teeth chattering.

I couldn't just leave you, she thought. "You're my best chance to access the tablet," she said. "I've worked through another fifty combinations, all of which were tied to significant numbers or phrases related to President Hakim. None succeeded. You must know the combination, even though you might not realise it."

"I wish he hadn't sent it to me," he said, rubbing his knee. "I don't know why he did."

"There can only be two reasons," she said. "The first is that he believed you were the one person he could send the data to without putting your life at risk, an assumption that was logical but ultimately incorrect."

"I don't understand what you mean."

"You are the nephew of the most powerful man in the Autonomy. If anyone has immunity from the consequences of sharing whatever it is he sent, it is you. Hakim, born in another century with another value system, made the error of believing that blood counted for something."

"He clearly doesn't know my uncle."

Or your brother.

"And what's the second reason?" Pasco asked.

"That you can be trusted with whatever the device contains. Whatever it is, you will make the right decision about what to do with it."

"But I don't know the code to get in," he said, "I couldn't even begin to guess."

That was a problem. She hoped he might have remembered something, anything, during the night.

"Then we need to move onto plan B," she said.

The car pulled over to the curb. He was too much of a risk while anyone could read his identikit.

"Get out."

"What? But they'll come after me!"

"Don't worry," she said. "It is for your own safety. As you walk away from the car, check your work archive. Look through your most recent applications. You have a new student called Janet Sackville, and buried in her creative essay on advanced sim construction will be your instructions. Follow them exactly and you will be okay. I will see you shortly."

Still in a daze, as though he was sleepwalking, Pasco stepped out and the bubble car sped off.

17

SITTING ON PASCO'S bed, Tristram reviewed his instructions from Lara. She told him to stay in Mansion and remain on alert. It could be five minutes, it could be a day, but *Voice* would locate Balmoral, and as soon as she did, Tristram would bring her in. She was the priority now. There was no margin for error. Fail, and it could mean the end of the Autonomy. They had to retrieve the device before Balmoral released the data and set in motion an irreversible chain reaction.

So what? The truth was, Tristram really didn't give a shit about any of it any more.

Tristram studied the Luger, still warm in his hand. He took the tip of the barrel and placed it against his forehead. The metal felt almost comforting against his skin. He squeezed the trigger slightly, not enough to release another round, but enough to know that he could. He rubbed the tip across his forehead, over his nose, down to his lips and into his mouth.

Would he register anything as the bullet splintered up into his brain? He squeezed a little further, and then slowly pulled it out, experiencing a pang of regret.

He put the gun down and took out a cigarette, lit it, and inhaled deeply, savouring the burn. On a caretaker's lenses, somewhere in the building, a smoking violation would be reported and his brother would receive a citation together with a hefty fine. Pasco might even be kicked out of the building. Tristram smiled to himself and took another drag. It was all so pointless.

18

FOUR HOURS LATER, Balmoral sipped her caf, staying in the shadows of the bar that hugged one of the cross streets in downtown Mansion. She chose this particular venue because of the motley crowd that gathered there. It was somewhere she and Pasco could blend in without too much scrutiny.

From hacking *Earth*, she also knew its internal cameras were offline, not scheduled for replacement until later this week. Even so, if Pasco did not follow her instructions exactly, he would lead the sandman to her.

With some reluctance she had dyed the fringe of her pink hair grey and pushed the rest into a turban, allowing a few wisps to fall across her face. She had also shed the leathers that went so well with Valencia's profile, and instead wore a sombre dark suit, the uniform of lower Mansion.

Acquiring the suit proved trickier than she imagined. Mansion's citizens ordered clothes exclusively through interactive iNet sims; size, shape, colour, all explored in three dimensional high definition, made to order in fluff mills, and shipped to Sector 1.

The only retail outlets in Mansion supplied what amounted to 'wardrobe malfunctions'; a replacement shirt for an accident with a cup of caf, a new pair of shoes for a broken heel. In any given day, in a city thrumming with a hundred million, there were a lot of accidents, but despite this, Balmoral's slight figure was increasingly rare for Sector 1, and after an arduous search in *Wardrobe*, the ubiquitous clothing sim, she was told to wait an hour before picking up the suit so they could retrieve it from an outlying storage facility.

While waiting she did her hair, a quick Vanity Salon job. She also bought a large winter jacket, and made a small slit in the lining at the back into which she slipped the tablet. The gun she discarded. It would never get through security where they were going.

A hunched old man pushed through the door, a band-aid holding together his ancient pair of iNet glasses. He held up two fingers to the bar, and then to the room in general as though confused. His eyes rested on her. For some reason he slapped his forehead, then hobbled over, pulling up a seat at her table.

"What the *Faith* are you doing?" she said.

"You said to dress like this," Pasco whispered back.

"No, that! All those crazy hand movements. Everyone in the bar will think you're demented. Certainly they'll be interested enough to probe your identikit and see you don't have one."

"That's why I have a band-aid!" Pasco rasped. "iNet on the blink."

"Oh yes, of course, genius," Balmoral replied sarcastically and pulling out her holopad, tapped out a couple of commands.

Pasco smiled, his face creasing with old-age lines made from spirit gum. She couldn't help but smile back. His make-up was good. Not too overdone. She had booked him into a Vanity salon where they were used to Mansion's most eccentric customers. They catered to every predilection and didn't ask questions.

"I still don't understand though. Why are we doing all this?"

Balmoral put a finger to her lips as a muscular waiter delivered two cafs and two waters to their table. Only when he left did she begin to speak.

"We have the tablet but no way to access the data. I'm not an expert in ancient hardware, but one way to bypass the code is to hook up the tablet to a compatible computer and upload the contents. However, there is only one place to acquire such a computer on short notice."

"Where?"

"The Technology Archive. Every pre-iNet device capable of creating a network, tracked, labelled and quarantined so it can't be replicated or disseminated as a 3-D blueprint. If you were ever in any doubt that we live in a technological tyranny, suppressing anything that isn't under the Autonomy's control, you need look no further than the archive."

"But that's crazy. You can't undo knowledge."

"Is it? Almost twenty years after alternative networks were made illegal and their associated devices destroyed or archived, there are not more than a few hundred thousand Sector 1 techs who are familiar with how they worked or could construct them from scratch. In another ten years, iAm will be the only communication technology. That is the kind of foresight your uncle has. Every communication will be on the grid, knowledge about what went before severely restricted. The Sector archives are the only physical store, and once they are destroyed, like old works of art, they will be gone forever."

Pasco took a sip of his caf. "But why are we dressed like this?"

"One of the security restrictions is that only citizens over the age of sixty-five are permitted access to the archive. It limits the regular handling of older technologies to those who are already familiar with it."

"No kidding." Pasco pushed his floppy hair back. It would be better if he was bald, his hair was too thick for an older man. Still, at least the hair was white.

"I have hacked into the archive, located the device we need and where it is, but we are going to have to bluff our way in. We'll pretend we are dropping off the tablet for archiving in order to get the computer we need."

She had tried, but although she had accessed an inventory of the archive's contents, she couldn't create the necessary work order to remove a device from the facility. The problem was that the archive's internal communication network was not accessible through the intellisphere. She could have done it with more time, but time was something they didn't have.

"But if they are not expecting us, how are we going to get in?"

"Well first, you need to act the part of the haughty executive from Securicom, not some doddery old man."

Pasco laughed.

"This isn't a joke. One slip, and we are dead."

"I know, I know," Pasco said, still smiling. "It's just so surreal, almost like I'm having a particularly vivid dream, or nightmare. What could possibly be in the tablet worth killing the Professor for?"

"Something that will change the world."

"Do you really think so? I mean isn't it possible that there is another, rational explanation?"

"Something that would explain why a sandman was sent to kill you? Do any of these names mean anything? Henrik Gudjohnson, Delia Sing, Gordon Ukropec, Jin Kwok, Lisa Elm and Sarge DeVries. All research associates of the Professor in some capacity, all dead in the last ten days, with the only agent in the vicinity of each, your *brother*."

The colour drained from Pasco's face. The hand that held the caf trembled. She had been too harsh. He had known some of these people, of course he had. She thought of the correct thing to say. "I'm sorry for any friends you might have lost."

"I knew about Lisa and her family. I thought it was an accident. She had two little girls . . . killed by Tristram? And Sarge?"

"DeVries is not public knowledge yet, but nobody knows where he is and he has not accessed iNet in four days, which coincides with the timing of Lisa Elm's death. I suspect he just hasn't been found yet. He makes sense as a target. He worked on research with Elm."

"I-I couldn't reach him."

She put an arm around his shoulder. She didn't want him to cry. Didn't want his make-up to run. She needed him to be strong. Time was too short.

"You have to understand what we are dealing with. The Chairman is so frightened of what is on Hakim's device, he will stop at nothing to get it back, wipe out anyone who might know anything about it."

Pasco hunched over the table, head bent forward. Beneath the glasses he was crying.

He had to pull it together.

"Their lives need not be in vain," she said hurriedly. "Whatever the Professor sent you is the key to destroying the Autonomy."

As soon as the words were out she wanted to suck them back in.

Pasco glanced up. "Destroy it?" he said through watery eyes. "But surely millions would die if the Autonomy ceased to exist. You can't rip down one infrastructure without another ready to replace it. I've worked in Logistics, I know how brittle the threads are that link together our supply lines. Without food stuffs shipped in from agri-lands, Mansion starves in a week. Without the treadle mills booming in Sector 2, the lights go out for the whole of mankind."

"The alternative is worse," Balmoral said quietly. "In two years, *Voice* will be inside every citizen in the Autonomy's head. In five, inside every person on Earth including the Cut."

"Providing every person in the world a capacity for information, interaction and communication never before dreamt of in the history of mankind! It is our great hope, not the opposite!"

"A world lived through an iAm chip is not life, but slavery, with *Voice* determining what you see, what you know, what you think, and ultimately what you are. When all information is governed by a machine, mankind ceases to exist."

"But why should information be governed? It's not now."

"Tell that to your dead professor."

Pasco reached across the table, picked up his water and drained the glass. His hand shook. "Professor Hakim would do nothing to jeopardize mankind."

Let him think that. It was easier that way. "Perhaps you're right," she said, and put her hand on his. "Now lean in close, I want to tell you our plan."

19

S TEPPING INTO THE Technology Archive was like stepping into another era. The quiet, the high ceilings, the dizzying expanse of space. Inside the doors was a mechanical turnstile and a guard in an elevated booth. He glanced down at them as they approached.

Pasco held out the tablet. The guard squinted at it, then waved them through. Turn, turn, click. Turn, turn, click.

A little further ahead was a front desk where an old curator sat, hugging his shoulders with the cold. As they approached, he held out a tray and motioned for them to remove their lenses, which they did.

"The boiler's broken," he said, stowing the tray. "Today of all days. I ask you. Freeze the knackers off a monkey in here. They should send us home." The curator's nose dripped as he spoke. He didn't bother to wipe it. "Now, what can I do you for?"

Pasco held up the tablet. "We've brought this for the archive. They only just sent over the req. number but it should be in the system: 4462H1."

The curator tapped a couple of commands on his physical keyboard and blinked at the bulky monitor. The computer was hardwired, no iNet devices allowed. Beyond the desk was an elevator and next to it double doors through which a few archivists milled up and down the rows of equipment. Pasco's fingers were numb. It was almost as cold in here as outside.

"I have no record of the consignment."

"My office confirmed the appointment this morning," Pasco replied stiffly. His breath came out in pale wisps of smoke.

The curator blinked at Pasco in the same way he had blinked at the screen and turned back to the monitor with a sigh. He tapped away on the keyboard, hugging his shoulders in between taps, his nose still dripping.

"Nope," he said, "you'll have to ask your office to resend it."

Pasco slapped his hand down on the table, making the curator jump. Some white powder fell from his hair onto the front of his coat. Hopefully it passed as dandruff. The old man looked a bit crusty himself.

"You want us to take it all the way back to the office?" he yelled. "Explain to Madame Devos the desk clerk couldn't find the requisition number for her consignment? Shift the shit back onto her? She wants it done today."

"But there's nothing here." He clicked away again, searching for a non-existent reference, smacking his lips nervously.

Despite the cold, Pasco felt the inside of his palms turn sweaty. This wasn't going to work. The man knew if he let two unauthorized personnel into the archive, it would mean his job, no matter how convincing they appeared.

"You're Graham, aren't you?" Balmoral said.

"What?" he blinked.

"Ogden Graham, mid-level Senator, position up for review in a couple of months?"

"Yes."

She leaned towards him. "I probably shouldn't mention this but right now your file doesn't make the most compelling reading. Your long list of medical issues, your depression, your gambling and your financial worries, they all take a toll on productivity."

He smacked his lips again. "Y-you're on the review committee?"

"I couldn't possibly confirm or deny." Taking the tablet from Pasco she gently laid it on the desk. "This was confiscated last night. Devos wants it archived today. We can't have Wi-Fi enabled contraband like this lying around. You will check bay 49.9 and see that it is empty waiting for the consignment."

He shifted uncomfortably in his seat. "I will have to fetch the engineer. She's working on the boiler right now."

"You better get going then," Balmoral said.

Reluctantly he pulled himself up from the desk and shuffled towards the elevator. As soon as he was out of sight, Balmoral ducked behind the desk.

"What are you doing?"

She tapped a few keys. "It's already locked. I wanted to add a fake requisite that he would stumble upon later. He's bound to keep checking, even when we've gone up."

"Can you hack it?"

"Thirteen digits, a billion combinations? I can't even hack the tablet." She came back around to his side.

"How did you know he would be on duty?"

"I didn't."

"Then how did you pull out all that review board stuff?"

She shrugged. "I made an educated guess."

"I don't believe you," Pasco said.

"His health? Look at him, the constant blinking, smacking of lips. His auto-immune is screwed, synapse abuse for sure. And that ragged piece of paper on his desk, all those scribbles and crossing outs are odds and teams for tonight's Steel Ball game. He's been poring over it for hours, a long-suffering gambler desperate for a win. But over time there's only ever one person who wins, and it's not the person placing the bets."

"So that's how you knew he was depressed?"

"No, the gambling just puts him in financial straits." She gestured to a square picture on the desk. "Look at that antique photo frame."

"The bunch of flowers?"

"The picture came with the frame, back when it was bought. It's the picture you put your photograph over, not the one you keep on display. If there was anyone in his life, their face would be in that frame. He's alone, hence the depression. Being depressed makes him even more worried about his position, because depressives always are."

"That still doesn't explain how you knew his name."

"That one was tricky. It was on his badge."

Pasco laughed, "Name badge? That tab on his shirt? I didn't even notice."

"iNet teaches you not to notice."

The curator appeared in the door, accompanied by a wheezy, barrel-shaped woman with a shaved head. Grease covered her face and hands, tattoos emblazoned her arms. A shock gun hung from her belt. In her hand, she gripped a gas lighter, flicking the flame on and off.

"This better be good . . ." she growled, "I've got an entire building colder than a witch's tits." Her voice was pitched three or four octaves below Pasco's own. "I almost had the old bitch fired back up too."

"I told you," the grey haired curator said, "they need to archive a . . . what is it actually called?"

"An iPad," Pasco said wearily.

"An iPad?" she said, brightening for the first time, "I remember when those first came out I thought it was some sort of electronic sanitary napkin? Eh?"

"Jan, please." The old man flushed. "Bay 49.9."

"Come on then," she growled.

They followed the engineer into the elevator and took it up to the fourth floor.

"Here we are," she said, and wheezed into a corridor with a row of locked rooms on each side. "Oh aye, aye, fucking typical."

"What?" Pasco said.

"They're not here yet, the in-house Securicom farts. They're the only ones who can turn off the alarms so we can install the device." She pressed a button on the wall, holding her stubby finger down. She had a month of dirt beneath the nail. "Paging them," she said by way of explanation. "They'll be in the cafeteria, eating doughnuts, their fat asses up against a space heater."

They stood in the corridor and waited. Balmoral remained impassive, tapping the tablet against her leg. None of them spoke, Jan apparently comfortable in the uncomfortable silence. Pasco probably should have said something obnoxious to reinforce his 'take-no-shit' character, but he had the feeling Jan would see through him. She took much less shit than he did.

What if the desk clerk also saw through him? What if he had decided to check on them and agents were already on their way? He forced himself to calm down.

The elevator door opened and two security men waddled out.

"Finally," Jan said, "the doughnut crew."

Both had shock guns slung low on their waists, and each carried another clunky device in their belt. Pagers, Pasco guessed.

"When are you going to get the boiler fixed, Jan?" one asked, nudging his partner.

"When you get your face fixed." Pulling out a key from a ring at her waist, Jan opened the door into a long thin room filled with a number of glass cabinets, each with a spongy pad on the top surface, and a spike hanging from a frame above it.

"Wait," Jan said, putting an arm on Pasco's shoulder. One of the security guards opened a panel on the wall.

"Floor vibrations won't set off the alarm because nothing is mounted from the ground, but you accidentally knock one of these glass boxes and we're in for a very long night."

The guard fiddled inside and gave a thumbs up. "We're good, Jan, bay alarms off."

"Right you are." Turning to Pasco and Balmoral she said, "Follow me," and set off down the aisle.

There were tablets, laptops, or phones in every single case.

"All portables," Jan said, "with wireless capability, hence the sensors. If any of this inventory got lost, we'd be in big trouble."

"But they are all so big and bulky," Pasco said, studying a black laptop. It was maybe twelve inches by six and looked like it weighed a ton. "How did people carry all that stuff around?"

She stared at him quizzically. "People? You're telling me you didn't use to have something like that?"

Cursing himself for the slip, he remembered he was supposed to be in his late sixties. "Yes," he said, "they just look so much bigger to me now."

"That they do," she said. "How did we ever put up with that garbage, with their load times and keyboards? They didn't even have 4D porn."

Pasco said nothing. He'd never even heard of 4D porn.

"All right, Oggy said bay 49.9." She tapped the side of the empty glass box. "When this thing is wired, even that much vibration will set it off."

"How?" Balmoral said.

"Sensor pads. It's simple tech, but it works. The pad is about three millimetres thick. If it moves at all the vibration registers on the pendulum, the building seals, then it's about . . . how long until the squaddies get here?" She turned to the guard.

"About eight minutes."

"Eight minutes, plus you have to deal with Don in the meantime."

Don growled, and he and Jan laughed.

"You have no idea how serious Securicom takes this shit. To the powers that be, this room is a weapons arsenal." Jan held out her hand to Balmoral. "Give."

Jan stamped the back of the tablet with a device hanging from her belt, then slid the glass top off the small holding unit, placed the tablet inside and replaced the lid, with the sensor pad back in place. The spike hanging from the pendulum came into contact with the waxy substance. Jan nodded to the security guard and he re-activated the box alarms and shut the panel, locking it with a key.

"And we're live," she said.

"See you later, Jan," Don said, "and try to get the boiler up soon, we'd hate to have to sit around in the cafeteria all day." The guards chuckled to themselves.

"Lazy farts," Jan said, and turned to go.

"What's that device?" Balmoral said, pointing to a relatively slim laptop in one of the boxes.

Jan began telling her about the year and make of the device, but Pasco was unable to concentrate on the words. The plan was in tatters. They knew the item would be installed with other devices from the same era, but they had little idea what that meant. Balmoral warned him that once they were inside they would have to improvise but right now, all they had done was give up the very device they needed to break into. Even if they could overpower Jan, they had no way to get it back, let alone locate a computer that might be able to bypass the code.

Jan ushered them back up the aisle and out of the room. She stooped to lock the door. At she did so, Balmoral reached around her side, pulled out the shock gun from Jan's holster and rammed it into her side. Jan gasped, wide-eyed, but did not drop.

"Print activated, bitch," she said, and swung, catching Balmoral full in the mouth. There was a loud crack, and Balmoral crunched to the ground. She stretched her hand out to page Security.

Pasco barged into her, knocking her away from the wall, but not off her feet. She turned to him, pulling out the wrench from her tool belt.

"Jay-sus!" Jan wheezed, "You too?" She swung the wrench at him, aiming for his head. It glanced off his raised forearm and cracked into his ribs. He fell back in agony.

"I haven't had this much excitement in ages!" she cackled, and raised the wrench again.

I'm going to be killed by a wheezy old woman, Pasco thought, but this time, just as the steel bar came down Jan jolted as if stung.

Balmoral had jammed the shock gun into her leg. Jan stared down, disbelieving. "Oh . . ." she said, "oh . . . nice." She crumpled to the floor, twitching.

Balmoral dropped the gun. It was in pieces.

"You accessed iAm!" Pasco panted. Balmoral said nothing, but rubbed her jaw and spat out a globule of blood. "Of course!" Pasco said excitedly, "legal shock guns are connected to iNet, even in this facility. You located the chip and overrode the fingerprint!"

Balmoral stared up at him and he realised the implication of his words. "If you used iAm, then *Voice* will be able to track us down . . ." He put out his arm and pulled her up.

"They will know where we are before that," she said.

"Why?"

She nodded to Jan. "The discharge of a registered weapon pings Securicom. Usually, this triggers a routine report request over iNet, but in this case, an agent will call the front desk to manually document the cause. Graham will page Jan, who will not respond. We'll be flooded with agents."

"How long have we got?"

She shrugged. "It depends what else is going on in Mansion, how many other guns are currently being unleashed on unsuspecting citizens. They may be calling in now, they may take twenty minutes. How's your arm?"

"Fine." His arm ached, but was probably all right. His ribs were another matter, cracked at the very least. They hurt like the *Faith* when he took a breath. "She caught me off guard. She was so strong."

"That's what a lifetime of steroids does for you. She's still packing a huge dose."

"How do you know?"

"She's bald, hairy, talks like a man and is clearly delusional. Couple that with her muscle and it spells steroid abuse, an expensive habit, which is why she is working long days and nights here. The scars on her fist suggest she's been around the block a few times, maybe in some underground fighting circuit. Not exactly the type going into old age quietly." She spat out another gob of blood from her mouth. "I set the stun to max. She should be out for a while."

"Are you okay?"

"I've had worse."

"What do we do now?"

"Follow me," she said.

Balmoral stepped back into the room. "Tread carefully; you heard what they said about the alarm." She tiptoed back to where the tablet was, pointing at the same time to the thin white laptop she had previously asked Jan about.

"That's the one we want. It has a power pack and a cord compatible with our device. We'll have to find an old-fashioned power socket but that's the least of our worries and it's possible the batteries have some life left in them."

She dropped to her haunches, and stared at the pendulum and sensor pad for thirty seconds. "We have to remove the touchpad without triggering the sensor, then slide the box out, taking advantage of the gap between the surface of the box and the pendulum's point. It's the only way."

"That's impossible," Pasco said. "She said the slightest touch would trigger the alarms."

Balmoral ignored him, speaking almost to herself. "The pad is pliable, like wax. It moulds around the point of the pendulum. That's what makes it so sensitive." She walked back over to the door, this time with a pronounced limp.

Pasco thought, *she's getting tired*. The limp was always worse when she was tired. She stepped outside for a moment before returning with Jan's gas lighter.

"What are you going to do?"

Balmoral said nothing but flicked the lighter on, directing the flame at the touchpad.

"You'll set off the alarm!"

Carefully she guided the diamond of blue heat, edging over the pad, staying away from the pendulum itself. Pasco couldn't breathe. There was no way this was going to work. No way.

Slowly the touchpad began to melt, from the corner at first, then down and across. By the time it melted in the middle, the whole pad was liquid and began to run off the top of the glass cube and onto the ground, leaving a tiny space in between the pendulum's spike and the top of the box. She flicked off the gas lighter and gently pushed the box out. If she had set off the alarm, then it was a silent one.

She pulled out the laptop and adapters and told him to shove it under his coat. Then she got to work on reclaiming the tablet.

TWENTY-THREE BLOCKS AWAY from the Technology Archive, Tristram received a priority one communication from Lara. It contained four separate pieces of information. The first was the report of a shock gun release in the Technology Archive. The second, a short vid of two figures entering the building. Neither gave off a retinal signature. He didn't need to be told who they were, despite their disguises. The third was a set of co-ordinates for the building, and the fourth, the authorization code to kill if necessary.

———✦———

BACK ON THE ground floor, the old desk clerk was still hugging his shoulders and complaining about the cold. From somewhere he had pulled out a pair of fingerless gloves.

Pasco approached, trying to conceal the fact that he was fighting for every breath and had a laptop under his jacket. His teeth chattered now, and it wasn't just the cold. The pain in his ribs made him want to vomit.

"Where have you been?" the desk clerk croaked. "The security guys came down almost twenty minutes ago. I was about to send a search party." He stared over Pasco's shoulder. "Where's Jan?"

"She said she was going straight down to the boiler," Balmoral said.

"I didn't see her in the elevator."

"There was a problem with one of the display cabinets. I'm sure she'll be down in a minute."

He blinked. "A problem? Nothing's been reported to me."

"One of the pendulums on an empty box had become . . . tangled. She thought she should fix it while she was up there."

"Any maintenance order needs to go through me," he said, irritated, "and besides her first priority is the boiler. We're going to freeze to death in here."

Did Pasco imagine it or was there a flash of suspicion in the old man's eyes? Balmoral's lip had begun to swell, Pasco was breathing heavily and stood awkwardly with the pain of the bulky device resting against his ribs. They were both more dishevelled than when they went up.

"You know what," the clerk said slowly. "I think I'll just call up security. If it concerns an archive floor, then she should be working under their supervision anyway."

Pasco's sucked in another painful breath. He may not be the brightest, but with a single touch the old curator could lock down the place.

"Not our problem," Pasco said. "Our lenses please."

The curator hesitated, considering them, and then slowly pulled out the tray. "Don't put them on until you're outside." He handed them over.

As they walked away from the desk, Pasco could feel the old man's eyes burning holes in his back. Ahead, the guard at the turnstile glanced down from his booth. Had the curator signalled to him, told him there was something going on here?

Pasco suddenly felt very sick, as if he might faint. The guard was going to ask to search them, he knew it. Concentrating on putting one foot in front of the other, he tried desperately not to labour his steps, tried to look casual. Ahead of him, Balmoral did the same, somehow forcing herself not to limp.

Nothing to hide here.

Balmoral stepped through the turnstile, wincing slightly. Turn, turn, click. He entered behind her; but instead of a click, an ear-splitting whine filled his head.

Instinctively, he put his hands to his ears. The sound immediately cut out, but it was too late. The laptop clattered to the hard, concrete floor and Pasco heard something inside it break apart.

The guard stared at the ground, then at Pasco, and reached for the alarm. Ignoring the searing pain in his side, he bent down to retrieve the laptop, but before he reached it Balmoral yanked him out through the double doors. The security screen crashed down behind them.

"I-I dropped it," he gasped, but Balmoral, lenses on, holopad out, wasn't listening. Her fingers thrummed across the keypad, and a second later a bubble car screeched to the curb.

"But this isn't where I wanted to stop," the man inside said angrily. He was in a severe, dark suit, with two little pins over the top pocket denoting *Elite*.

Balmoral leaned in, "Securicom sir."

"I don't care who you are. This is my car. It's freezing outside and . . ."

She tapped out another command on the keypad, leaned in and whispered something. The man stopped blustering and jumped out. They got in and the car pulled away, just as three guards from the Archive ran into the street after them. Too late.

"What did you say to him?" Pasco asked.

"Belt," she said.

"Belt?"

"Put it on," she said.

Pasco pulled the belt across his chest, letting out a moan as it touched his ribs. Balmoral stared at him through mirrored lenses, and then turned back to the holopad, typing furiously. The car accelerated, cutting a path between lanes, the cars ahead pulling out of the way.

"So what did you say?"

"Nothing," she said, still tapping. "I hacked his iNet memory, pulled a couple of images from his last sim and played them back to him."

"But why would that make him jump out?"

Balmoral shrugged. "Perhaps he wasn't particularly proud of *wheelchair chicks with dicks*."

Pasco felt himself flush. "I don't even know what that means."

"Neither did I, until a moment ago."

The outer shell of the bubble car vibrated in protest. They must have been going double the speed limit. "What do we do now?" Pasco said, watching the buildings blur past.

"First, we get out of the city. They'll be in pursuit, of course. Maybe just the sandman, maybe a whole fleet of Securicom. However, this car is logged as empty, and although *Voice* will be able to hone in on the hack eventually, it might take a while. If we get out of the city, we may be able to elude them, at least for a while."

"But what about iAm? *Voice* will be able to trace you now that it's activated."

"Leave that to me."

Her voice was even flatter than usual, dispirited, as if she didn't really believe escape was possible.

"What was that alarm anyway? Was the device tagged?"

She shook her head. "The guard only reacted after you flinched at the noise. He was watching for it, even before the laptop fell. It wasn't the alarm that alerted the guard, but your response to the sound."

"I don't understand."

"A tiny sonic speaker firing a hundred decibels on the final click of the turnstile, but at a pitch undetectable to those over sixty." She stopped tapping on her holopad. "I underestimated the extent of the Technology Archive's gerontological security protocols. I wanted to warn you after I walked through, but it was too late."

"But you didn't even twitch! I nearly collapsed. I thought my head was about to explode."

"I felt it," she said, adding more quietly, "but I am used to blocking out pain."

"I'm so sorry," he said, "About dropping the laptop . . . I . . . ."

"We'll think of something else," she said, cutting him off.

"You could have taken the computer, left me there."

"The impact probably broke it," she said coldly. "We'll just have to guess the code. There are still a few chances left before the tablet locks us out."

He sighed. Why had the Professor bothered to send him a message, if indeed he had meant to send it to him, without any way to access it?

Balmoral pulled off her turban, the pink hair spilling over her shoulders, casting the few grey wisps at the front into stark relief. She removed her lenses and slowly rubbed her temples.

When she opened her eyes, he was struck by their impossible blue, her pupils like stones in cold, clear water. Suddenly Pasco could no longer hold it in. He needed to say to those eyes what he had been too afraid to say to the emotionless lenses.

"Bal, I need to tell you something. No matter what happens I . . ."

"Don't," she said, cutting him off. "Whatever you are about to say, don't say it."

"Why?"

"Because, I . . ." But she didn't finish the sentence. A transport shot through a sea of bubble cars, and smashed into them. Their car pitched up, rolled, twice and careened into the side of a building, coming to a stop just as Pasco lost consciousness.

20

L ARA BELIEVED THEY would try to escape in a bubble car, try to flee the City, probably using some cloaking program, gambling on the fact that neither *Voice* nor *Earth* would pick up a vehicle that to the outside world had nobody in it. She told *Voice* to get a lock on any empty car travelling over the speed limit, and that would be them.

As a result, Tristram intercepted them exactly where *Voice* said they would be. As much as he hated her, he had to hand it to the President of Securicom, Lara's operational instincts were the best in the business.

He rammed into the bubble car, not really caring who he took out; the targets inside, the pedestrians, even himself. The belts might save Pasco and Balmoral's lives. The three or four pedestrians crushed underneath wouldn't be so lucky. Tristram's military grade transport, with its reinforced shell, was barely scratched.

Tristram pulled away from the wreck, ignoring the screaming pedestrians. His objective was to recover the device, not worry about a few bleating sheep. He stepped out of the transport and flashed a Securicom ID to every iNet in the vicinity, a standardized summary that this was a terrorist operation and that anyone receiving this message should leave the area immediately, or risk being drawn into the crossfire. It didn't stop the screaming, but the rapidly gathering crowd backed off.

He dragged them out of the car. His brother was out cold or worse. With two fingers he checked his pulse. Still beating. He slapped him gently on the cheek. No reaction. Blood seeped out from under the car, and began to freeze on the sidewalk. He didn't think it was theirs.

The girl was also unconscious. She didn't look like much. Typical that his brother had fallen for someone so insubstantial, so petite. The eyes didn't match the face, so Lara was correct about that too, Balmoral had assumed another identity. It took him another moment to realise who that identity belonged to, under all the blood and makeup.

Valencia.

He remembered the room in Styro Town; the bandages, the grenade belted to her head. It all made sense now. Valencia blew apart her skull to cover for her eyeless sockets and give this girl a clean profile.

They never did track down Valencia's iNet identity. There seemed no point after she died. Now, even in death, the leader of the Bedouin mocked him.

In a flash of anger he whipped out the Luger, but then hesitated. Maglan stressed he wanted them alive so he could question them personally, discover what they knew about Hakim's data, what they had done with it.

Interrogation was a waste of time. Tristram could imagine them doing a lot of things if they had seen the data, but breaking into the archive was not one of them.

They knew nothing, had sent nothing, but Maglan wanted to be sure. It pained Tristram, but he could wait. Lara would order him to shoot them both as soon as Maglan was done. He shoved them into the back of the transport, crushing the girl's lenses underfoot.

His iAm flashed to life in his mind's eye. An incoming message from the President of Securicom. Speak of the devil and she will appear.

Status?

He replied with a thought command.

Apprehended.

The device?

Oh yes, that.

He peered inside the upended bubble car. Nothing. He checked through his brother's clothes, but it was not there either. He turned his attention to the girl.

In her jacket pocket was an old cell phone, a model from the early 2000s. It had a thick plastic shell and a bunch of egg-shaped buttons on the front. He pushed a switch on its side and the phone blinked into life. It was a rogue, but not his brother's tablet. He supposed it was meant to be a decoy, a precaution that might have worked if he didn't know exactly what he was looking for. Again he had the urge to put a bullet in her brain.

He patted down her legs and up to her crotch. He flipped her over, working from boots upwards. At the base of her back he found it, hidden in the lining of the jacket.

I have it.

Good. Bring it to the Chairman's office. We'll meet you there. A clean up team is on the way to your site now.

Tell them to bring plenty of equipment.

Do you always have to create so much mess?

He didn't reply. He couldn't tell if she was being facetious. So much mess?

What did Lara expect? He wondered if, when this was finally over, he would be considered just more mess, something to be cleaned away.

He thought of the fatal phrase Maglan had used in Aviv; *three can keep a secret if two are dead*. Would he find a room full of squaddies when he went up to the Chairman's office? Was he taking Pasco and this girl not just to their death, but his own?

Getting into the transport, he pulled out a small backpack and shoved the tablet inside. The car was still on manual control. For a moment he wondered about heading out of Mansion and bolting for the hills. He could use his knowledge as a hostage, what he had done, and what they had asked him to do. He dismissed the thought. iAm made flight impossible. Once activated, *Voice* knew where he was until the day he died. He should never have let them put the bastard in.

But would he run if he could? Before his time in the tunnels, before he found his father's killers, he would have fought all comers, and believed that somehow he was still on the side of right. But something in those dark passages changed him, even before his exposure to Hakim's data.

The transport flipped to automatic, pulled away from the curb and set a course for Securicom.

Peering into the rear-view, he noticed the girl was conscious now, blood dripping from her nose. She knocked on the plexiglass panel that separated them. He touched a button next to the steering wheel rendering the panel opaque. Whatever she wanted, he didn't want to know.

21

ER JAW WAS broken, a small fracture that made it painful to move or speak. Her nose was broken, smashed by Pasco's elbow as the transport hit their vehicle. Her neck was whiplashed, and pain shot through her body just trying to keep her head up. From a more positive perspective, she was still functional, and beginning to think clearly again. And if she could think, there was a chance.

Balmoral rapped on the window, trying to get the sandman's attention. He stared at her, and she thought, no they are not alike, these twins. Pasco's eyes with their hidden depths, his brother's with their hidden shallows. He darkened the screen, blocking her out, and that was precisely what she wanted.

She felt around on the floor and her hand alighted on the cell phone. The sandman had turned it on. She pushed it back into her coat. It might come in handy later.

Beside her Pasco moaned, his words unintelligible, something about the Professor, but words nevertheless. She squeezed his hand. He would be all right.

She thought again of the sandman, and his features, a twisted shadow of the face she had grown to know so well. For all his physical presence, there was a weakness there too, a weakness which Pasco did not possess. She would have to use that flaw, devise a plan and find some way to get the tablet back. The problem was she felt so sick, and as another wave of nausea washed over her, she thought her head might split.

22

HE TRANSPORT PULLED into the underground garage and parked in the bay next to Maglan's private elevator. Pasco lay propped against the back seat, still unconscious. The girl must have pulled him up from the floor. Cute. The girl herself was in worse shape than before, lapsing back into semi-consciousness. Blood trickled from her ear. She had vomited in the corner of the car and passed out.

Perhaps the belts had not helped them. Perhaps inside those heads they were haemorrhaging, and neither he nor Maglan would have anything else to do. It made sense now, the girl knocking on the glass. She wanted him to open the door so she could be sick. Too bad. He pulled her out by her collar and half-dragged, half-carried her towards the elevator. It took a full three minutes to reach the heady peak of Securicom's tower, the doors opening directly into Maglan's office.

"Tristram," Maglan said. He sat behind his huge mahogany desk, fingers steepled.

Strange, he thought, no Lara. She should be there. This was the culmination of the mission after all. Perhaps she was about to step through the door, gun in hand.

Three can keep a secret if two are dead.

He noticed Maglan had removed his iNet glasses as soon as Tristram entered the room. No record.

"Put her here," Maglan said, gesturing to the chair in front of him.

"Do you want me to bind her hands?"

Maglan raised an eyebrow. "I think I can handle her."

Tristram dropped the knapsack in the centre of the table. "Hakim's rogue," he said.

Maglan reached inside and pulled out the tablet, weighing it in his hand. "Solar powered, latter teens of this century by the looks of it, and ah . . . yes password protected. So Lara's theory was correct, they broke into the archive because they needed to find a way into the device."

"I told you Pasco had not seen the information. I could see it in his eyes. Hakim's data, it changes you somehow . . ." Tristram caught himself too late. He had been too expansive.

Maglan's eyelid twitched. "Really? Lara's reasoning was a little less . . . emotional. She thought if Pasco had accessed the data, then so would the girl and it would be too late, the impact apparent all around us." Maglan paused. "Pasco is still unconscious?"

Tristram nodded.

"Do you have stimulants?"

"A couple of shots of *half-life*, in the transport's medkit."

"Administer one and bring him up. Keep to the elevator, and the bay. I don't want any record of you entering the building. We end this tonight."

"What about her?" He indicated to the slumped form on Maglan's desk.

"She looks just fine to me." The Chairman put out his hand and picked up a few strands of the pink hair. "Officially, Balmoral Murraine no longer exists. This is . . . what was her name? Valencia. Only you, me and Lara know different."

Like Hakim's data, Tristram thought. He turned to go.

"Tristram, leave your . . . firearm here. You know how I feel about guns in my office."

He pulled out Gravales' gun, and placed it on the table next to the knapsack. This time, as he turned away, he wondered if he was about to feel a bullet rip between his shoulder blades.

23

A s THE ELEVATOR doors swished closed, Balmoral lunged for the gun, pointing it directly at the Chairman's heart.

He blinked. "You don't ah . . . appear to be as injured as you seemed a moment ago. Let me guess. A bleeding nose dabbed into the ear hole, then fingers down the throat. Enough to dupe that boy, although believe me, he's no slouch. Recently though, he has become a little . . . sloppy."

He smiled. "Do you know there is a snake that shits, vomits and bleeds from the eyes to convince would be predators that it is dying, only to whip around and deliver a fatal bite?"

"Don't speak," Balmoral said.

"Or what? You'll kill me? I don't think so. I know how your mind works. If there was no reason for me to live, you would have already pulled the trigger. But we're still sitting here, which means you want something. Whatever you think you've got planned, I assure you, it's over."

"I'm the one holding the gun. Not one of your Autonomy weapons with an eye control chip, but something that will rip off your head no matter how many times you blink at it."

He smiled placidly, one eye on her, one eye searching for her. She tried to hold the gun steady, but it was unnerving, how much he hated her, how much he wanted to destroy her. He could barely stop himself from reaching across the table and throttling her, despite the gun. Instead he stood up, hands raised slightly, so she could see them.

"You will excuse me if I fix myself a drink? It's been a long day."

He opened the crystal decanter and poured. At the same time he picked up a couple of olives from one of the silver trays and popped them into his mouth. He replaced the stopper in the decanter, then paused. "How rude of me," he said. "Would you like anything? Olives, salami, walnuts? A whisky perhaps?"

"No," she replied, disconcerted. She held the gun, but somehow he held the initiative.

The Chairman smiled again, tipped his glass to her, took a sip and resumed his seat.

She had to gain control of the situation. "I am going to tell you what I want," she said, hearing her voice falter. "I want the sandman . . ."

"Pasco's brother," Maglan interrupted.

". . . to take Pasco to the roof and place him inside the copter that's sitting there."

"Copter? My s-class, long range VTOL, you mean. Hardly a *copter*."

"And I want five thousand clicks of fuel in the tank."

"It's always fuelled. I never know when I might need it."

"And you and I will follow them up there, with you in my sight all the way, until I'm in the air."

"I see . . . and for all of this, I get what exactly?"

"Another few years of life, and" – she nodded to the tablet – "that."

He took a sip of the whisky, smacked his lips and replaced the tumbler on the table. "I already have *that*." He sighed. "Tempting as it is, I don't think I will accept your deal. I am an old man, you are a young woman, and you have far more years to lose than me if you pull that trigger. Besides . . . how do I know you won't just shoot me and take back the tablet when we reach the roof?"

"I will give you one chance to reconsider." She cocked the gun. "Agree or I will shoot you, then I will shoot the sandman, then I will take the tablet and find a way to extract whatever it is you don't want the Autonomy to know."

"Do it then," Maglan said, "but understand this, you will be dead before the bullet works its way into my skull. You have a gun trained on me; what you might not realise is that I have a gun trained on you. I will die but so will you and your precious Pasco."

"You're bluffing."

"Really?" He turned, and stared out of the window. "Lara?"

"Yes, Sir." The President of Securicom's voice filled the room.

"Can you explain to this lady what a synaptic haemorrhage is?"

"A fuse in iAm's primary circuit board, a diodic implosion, causing instantaneous aneurism."

"And do you have a lock on Murraine's digital signature?"

"Yes, sir."

Maglan turned back to her. "You see, our President of Securicom had you covered the moment you activated your iAm chip and got that biochemical charge flowing. It's just one small pop apparently. We've taken the digital death to the next level with iAm. Instead of erasing one's digital persona for crimes against the state, we can now erase them in the physical sense."

He leaned forward, drink in hand.

"I know, it is genius. It was an innovation of Lara's, the kind of lateral thinking that made her head of Securicom. Though it pains me to admit it, she has achieved more in the last two years than I achieved in ten. No more *Dish*, no more real resistance of any kind, all the Sectors habituated to their various functions, record productivity figures, economy booming, population growing again, and that's even before the Autonomy-wide installation of iAm. A Chairman couldn't ask for more."

He smiled again. For the first time, it reached his eyes.

"If you want to interact with the world, you need iAm. But if you have iAm, we have you. The ability to identify an enemy is the *only* tactical piece of information we need. Think of it! Disharmony and conflict will be a thing of the past. You look at me, and you see a monster. You cannot possibly grasp that with this technology I have ensured the future of mankind. I look at you and see a monster, and cannot possibly grasp how someone with your intellect could ever imagine that there is another way. Fortunately, Lara does not think as you do."

Her hand trembled as her finger tightened on the trigger.

"Look on the bright side," Maglan said. "Even if you didn't have the chip, it would still be no good."

She said nothing. Had lost the ability to speak.

"Lara, how many fingers am I holding up?" Maglan gave the V-sign, V for victory.

"Two, sir," the voice echoed back.

He leaned towards her, oblivious to the gun barrel a few inches from his skull. "Two, sir. Try to do anything without my authorization and a hundred agents will be on you before you know it. Oh, you need me, and you need me breathing."

Balmoral was hardly listening. She was focused on Lara. The voice seemed to come from the room itself. She had an uncanny sensation of the ground yawning beneath her feet, about to swallow her up.

"W-who is Lara?" she said.

"I think you know."

And in that instant she did, and all the fight fell away. The gun clattered to the table.

24

U NCONSCIOUSNESS, BY DEFINITION, was a trick of the mind. Time became meaningless, concepts bent. Pasco's first thought was that he should be in pain but his body felt light, so insubstantial he almost floated. He realised then he had been administered *half-life*; an emergency drug that blocked off pain pathways, accelerated blood pressure and flooded the muscles with adrenalin and the brain with endorphins.

His second thought was that while he was out cold, his subconscious had stumbled on an answer his waking self had strained for but been unable to grasp. But what was it? He could not remember.

The room swam into focus. Slowly he became aware of the distinctive aroma of Maplewood, leather and the vague tang of whisky. His reaction to these familiar stimulants was Pavlovian, except that instead of hunger, he felt stone cold dread.

He couldn't immediately make sense of the scene. Tristram stood by the door, arms folded. Behind the desk, Maglan, his massive bulldog face impassive. Opposite him, Balmoral, her naked eyes staring straight forward, her shoulders slumped. In between them lay a gun, the tablet computer, and an empty glass of whisky.

Incongruously, Pasco thought; *it was Professor Plum, in the library, with the tablet computer.*

The tablet!

In the dark recesses of the unconscious he had deciphered the access code! He knew it now as surely as he knew his name. He also knew that whatever happened next wasn't going to be good. Pasco was thankful for the *half-life*. The chemical's contortions overrode his panic and he remained focused.

Why didn't Balmoral pick up the gun on the table? She could reach it. Had Maglan drugged her? Some sort of tranquilizer perhaps. If this was the end, they could at least go out fighting. His uncle had damaged her, sucked the fight right out of her body, but how?

"Pasco," his uncle said. "How good of you to join us."

Pasco felt a rush of anger overtake him. "What have you done to her? Y-you killed the Professor, you killed my friends; you have done such terrible things . . . such terrible wrong."

"Don't tell me about right or wrong," Maglan said. "I have spent my whole life measuring such questions in factors of millions. My generation has not had the luxury to think in any other way, so that your generation could survive and thrive. If a million people had to die so two million could live, that was the decision that had to be made. In the case of your precious *Professor*, I didn't think twice. The death of a few researchers does not compare to the destruction he wanted to unleash on the world."

The Chairman rose. His bulky form towered over the room. "I have never taken a life that was not ultimately for the good of mankind. A life taken for no reason, that is the true . . . inhumanity."

With a single, vicious swing Maglan slapped Balmoral's face, and held his hand out as if to do it again, but controlling himself, cupped it behind his back. His scar, usually inconspicuous, was thrown into pallid relief, a livid blotch on his forehead.

Balmoral's head jerked to the side when Maglan hit her, but then slowly returned forward, hardly blinking. Pasco tried to stand up, to help her, despite his wobbling knees, but with a firm hand Tristram pushed him back into the chair.

"I am afraid I have to leave you and your, ah . . . girlfriend soon. Tomorrow, the slumbering billions will welcome in a new Chairman and this," he gestured to the panoramic view of Mansion, "will no longer be my concern."

Leaving them. He was retiring?

"President Lomb will assume the Chairmanship, as well as retain her position as President of Securicom. If there is one thing I know for a fact, the Autonomy is secure in her hands."

Still Balmoral did not move, but just stared down at the gun. What was wrong with her? Why didn't she fight?

Maglan walked over to the Maplewood side table and filled his whisky tumbler.

"Do you want to know why no AI, not even *Voice*, has ever managed to pass themselves off as human? I don't mean answer a few Turing Test questions, but integrate as a fully functioning member of human society, undetected."

Pasco said nothing.

"No?" Maglan suddenly threw his glass against the wall. Pasco jumped as it smashed into pieces, the whisky streaking down the damask paper.

"The problem with an AI is that they lack the peculiarly human trait of unpredictability. Over time, it betrays them for what they are. For seventy years an AI has known the answer to the riddle about combining a politician's rant and a frothy dessert – the answer, by the way, is a meringue harangue – and yet integration into human society has ultimately proved elusive."

His uncle stared at Pasco as he would an insect. "One of your many treasons was that you took classified information and shared it with the terrorist under your charge. What was it you told her that *Voice* concluded after analysing her brain? I think it was, 'Balmoral without her iNet is nothing'."

Balmoral slumped further into her chair.

"You know, Pasco," Maglan said, staring at Balmoral with satisfaction, "*Voice* doesn't use punctuation, not when, to the AI at least, the statement is self-evident. The conclusion was not: Balmoral without her iNet is nothing, but: Balmoral, without her, *iNet is nothing*."

"I don't understand," Pasco said.

"During her coma *you* helped *Voice* create a digital imprint of her mind. The result, Lara Lomb, an AI with the capacity to manage the security of thirteen billion people through iNet; flawlessly, effortlessly, without guilt, or passion, or vanity."

Pasco felt nauseous. Balmoral, the digital imprint for the President of Securicom. Balmoral, who hated the Autonomy with every inch of her being. In a sick twist, his uncle had even used her name, rearranging the letters into Lara Lomb.

"She passed the test, Pasco. There is not a single person in the Autonomy who suspects President Lomb is an AI. She is a dictator, but what a dictator."

Maglan picked the gun off the table and threw it to Tristram. "We leave Mansion in fifteen minutes," he said, "You know what to do." His uncle glanced at Pasco one last time, and was gone.

25

T RISTRAM KNEW EXACTLY what to do, his orders were explicit. He pointed the Luger at Balmoral, "On your feet." Without a murmur she obeyed, resigned to whatever came next.

How changed she was, how little like her Bedouin namesake. The face, at once so angular and defiant, had sunken in on itself, become closed and dull. Maglan had finally achieved his end. He had broken her.

"You too," he said to Pasco, "over to the elevator."

In a daze, his brother stood and took a couple of woozy steps before collapsing. He grabbed the table in an attempt to break his fall, but succeeded only in knocking everything onto the floor; Maglan's precious decanter of whisky and his trays of midnight treats. At least the new Chairman wouldn't miss them.

"Get up!" Tristram said.

"Y-you don't have to do this," Pasco pleaded from the carpet, tears welling in his eyes. He was on the verge of going into shock, despite the *half-life*.

"Get up," he repeated, cocking the gun.

Gingerly, Pasco obeyed. "W-where are you taking us?"

Tristram put the gun to his lips. The time for words had passed. Maglan wanted to see the bodies before they left Mansion.

Lara had relayed the plan to him. The Hakim operation over, she said accompanying his uncle into retirement, after all Tristram had been through, was the best solution for both of them. On a remote island in Sector 1, his uncle would have his whisky and books and Tristram would have his memories.

Tristram wondered if his uncle really meant to take him, or whether his body was also destined for a cleaner, to be picked up with the others, driven to the sea wall and cast into the ocean.

With Pasco unsteady on his feet, Balmoral reached out to take his hand, but he shook her off with a shudder. Not so lovey-dovey now. Perhaps Pasco blamed her for this, or perhaps, now death was near, his brother could only think about himself.

The elevator opened onto the roof. Tristram poked them out, gun in hand. It was freezing cold, despite the late afternoon sun silhouetting the Chairman's VTOL plane.

"Over to the helipad," Tristram ordered, slipping the silencer out of his pocket and affixing it to the barrel of the Luger.

"That's far enough," Tristram said and they both turned around.

"You really mean to do it then," Pasco said weakly.

Tristram raised the gun.

26

A S PASCO STARED into death, it seemed that time slowed, every micro moment elongating before him. He looked across at Balmoral. She was completely still, her eyes half-closed. She had withdrawn so deeply into herself it was as though she was dead already. What had she thought when he pulled away from her, when she reached out to him for comfort? If they died now, that rejection would be her final memory.

He turned to Tristram. "You know what our father would say if he could see us now?" He forced tears to well again. "Our father would say that if this is the end of the game, we must part as gentlemen."

"Gentlemen?"

"Despite everything, our father would have expected that." Pasco put out his hand.

Tristram registered no emotion, but continued to stare at him with the dark, dead-eyed stare of the sandman. Surely, deep inside, his brother felt something. Or if he didn't, he knew that he should. Tristram hesitated, then flipped the gun to his left hand, and extended the right.

Pasco grasped it. "Good game, my brother, good game."

Automatically, Tristram echoed, "Good g-" but as he did so, Pasco pulled him forward with every ounce of energy he could summon and rammed his free hand into his brother's mouth.

Tristram's eyes widened. Recovering quickly, he swung the gun at Pasco's head, using it like a club. It caught him on the temple and stars blazed in front of his eyes. The blow would have knocked Pasco unconscious but for the *half-life* still coursing through his veins.

Tristram took a step backwards and squeezed the trigger, but the bullet sliced into the tarmac. Mouth foaming, neck constricting, his attention turned from Pasco to the adrenalin shot he kept secreted in his boot, but he was already too out of control to reach it.

As a child, the only physical advantage Pasco possessed over his brother was that he didn't go into life-threatening shock whenever he came into contact with nuts.

When Pasco pretended to faint in the office, he scooped a handful of walnuts from the silver salver before knocking the tray and everything else onto the ground.

Those nuts were now in Tristram's mouth. He writhed back and forth, gasping for air.

"Get in the copter," Balmoral shouted, "Quickly!"

Wiping away the blood that dripped into his eyes, and shivering uncontrollably, Pasco followed her into the copter. Balmoral pulled the iNet glasses from the cockpit, and furiously typed out commands on her holopad. The rotary blades began to turn.

Fifty feet away, the elevator doors opened. Pasco watched in horror as his uncle appeared on the roof, still carrying the knapsack. His eyes darted to Tristram, clawing spasmodically at his boot, then to the copter, its blades picking up speed, and finally to Balmoral in the pilot seat, lenses in place.

Maglan roared something, repeating it again, and again. Pasco didn't need to be a lip reader to understand what he said.

Kill Murraine!

Who was he talking to?

Maglan cursed, pulled out a revolver and shot at the cockpit. The bullet missed, ripping into the undercarriage. A couple of inches lower and he would have taken out a fuel tank. He shot again. A side window shattered. Glass sprayed across them.

"How long until we can take off?" Pasco yelled.

"Two minutes."

Too long. If Maglan hit the tank, it would all be over. Pasco climbed out and ran towards his uncle, arms outstretched, obscuring the shot. Balmoral would get away, even if he did not. Another bullet ripped over his shoulder, missing him and the copter. Maglan's eye twitched. He aimed at Pasco's head and squeezed the trigger.

Nothing happened.

Maglan looked at the weapon in surprise, then at Balmoral, and threw it down. He lunged towards the copter, his eyes fixed on Balmoral. In his hand flashed a stiletto blade.

Desperately, Pasco grabbed Tristram's gun from the ground. Maglan climbed the steps, his huge figure framing the doorway. Another moment and he would have her.

Pasco had one chance. Wiping the blood from his eyes, he pulled the trigger.

The Chairman flinched as though stung by a hornet, his hand reaching around his back before he toppled backwards.

To Pasco's left, Tristram gasped. He kicked out at Pasco's shins, not purposefully, but in the final spasms of asphyxiation. His lips were blue, the last of his life choking away. Pasco hesitated, then reached down and pulled the pen from Tristram's boot, jamming it into his leg.

"Not for you," he said quietly, "but for our father."

From the cockpit, Balmoral yelled. He couldn't hear her. He couldn't hear anything now except the roar of the rotary blades. She pointed to the knapsack. His uncle had dropped it as he fell. It lay half covered by his prostrate form and as Pasco pulled it free, he almost slipped on the pool of blood that welled around him.

He climbed into the copter. Balmoral threw him a pair of iNet lenses. He put them on and immediately heard her voice through the implant telling him to buckle up. It was going to be a bumpy ride.

Pasco fumbled for his belt as they rose into the air. Below he saw Tristram climb woozily to his feet, while at least a dozen agents flooded onto the roof from the Presidential elevator. Tristram said something and they pulled out their weapons and began to shoot, but it was too late. They were away.

27

OR THE NEXT ten minutes, neither of them spoke, Balmoral manoeuvring the craft in and out of Mansion's crowded skyline and over the sea wall, Pasco attaching a makeshift brace to the broken window panel.

"Where did the agents come from?" he shouted. iNet fed his words directly into Balmoral's implant, but even so he struggled to hear himself over the noise of the rotaries.

"When your bullet ripped through the Chairman's spine, his biosquare automatically requested back up."

"Will he live?" he said, feeling his throat constrict, not knowing what he wanted to hear.

"If he does, you just saved his life."

"What do you mean?"

"This aircraft was going nowhere but the bottom of the ocean. I am trying to hack the flight plan now, forcing a reroute. Until then, I'm navigating on manual."

"The bottom of the ocean?"

"Apparently *Lara* believes that whatever is on the laptop is so deadly nobody can know of its existence, so she made the logical decision. Eliminate your uncle and brother."

"But he is the Chairman of the Autonomy!"

"*Was.* Even so, I have sent him the flight plan, so that if and when he regains consciousness, he can peruse what Lara's retirement plans looked like. It might make him think twice about his protégé. It is not too late for him to shut her down, but it soon will be." Balmoral hesitated, "She is . . . is too dangerous for this world."

Pasco looked away, hearing the pain in her voice, not wanting to catch her eye.

"You should remove your iNet now. I don't want *Voice* to track us through your identikit. It's the only reason why you're not digitally dead. She's hoping to pick up your signature."

"But I won't be able to hear you."

"When we hit the right altitude, the rotaries will turn off and the jets will fire up. It will be quieter then and we can talk."

"But surely Lara can track you through iAm?"

The copter veered to the right and downwards. Pasco's stomach lurched into his chest. Balmoral tapped out a flurry of commands on the holopad until the aircraft levelled off again.

"Unless you want to get very wet," she said, "I need to concentrate."

Pasco removed his lenses and stared out of the window. Slowly the lights of Mansion faded into the background until all he could see was the blue black water of the Atlan Sea. They continued to ascend, shaking with turbulence.

Were they shaking too much? Were they were going to plunge into the ocean? He panicked as the rotaries cut out completely, until he realised they were now cruising, the jets engaged. Almost unconsciously he said a quiet word of thanks to the *Faith*.

Balmoral stopped typing. "I managed to overwrite the flight plan." She nodded to his hands. "You can relax now."

He stared down at the white knuckles and released his grip on the chair. He noticed for the first time that Balmoral's hands were covered in blood, injuries sustained from the window, glass lodged deep into the skin. Her face didn't look too hot either; her jaw was swollen and purple with contusions, her nose too had blood caked underneath it and was bent at an angle.

"What a mess," he said under his breath.

She smiled. "You should take a look at yourself." She mirrored her lenses so he could see his reflection; the gash on his head, the red crusted eyebrows, the peeling makeup. He looked half zombie, or like someone who had played a game of Steel Ball without a helmet, if such a sport actually existed.

"You need to shower so we can attend to your wounds, and then you can attend to mine," she said. "I've taken a look at the copter's inventory and there are substantial medical supplies in the back. I'll tap into your biosquare, and get an avatar to walk us through the appropriate protocol based on your injuries."

"And if it demands I stay in bed for at least two weeks?"

"Then you are, as they say, shit out of luck, because once we land we're going to have to keep going, at least for a day or two, if we're to have any chance of evading Lara."

"But how do we run? She can track you through iAm."

"Worse than that. *Voice* can reverse the biochemical current in any activated chip and cause it to implode."

Pasco stared at her in disbelief. "Aneurysm?"

"Lara's invention," she said quietly.

He remembered now, his Uncle's erratic shouting. *Kill Murraine.* It wasn't invective, but a command.

"But she didn't do it . . ."

"Only because the chip is not in my brain."

"What? I don't understand."

"A surgeon called Mr. Glass removed the chip and left it taped to the underside of my wrist, before putting me in a body bag and kicking me down the side of an embankment."

Pasco's head reeled with the risks associated with such a procedure. iAm had been designed for easy implant, not easy removal. "But in the Archive with the shock gun? You overrode the thumbprint recognition."

"By prizing off the sensor, that's all. Without the sensor pad, the shock gun functioned normally."

"And you said you were no good at hardware."

"I said I was no good at ancient hardware. Remember, I worked the technology lines of Churin for years before becoming the Autonomy's most wanted."

"But surely Lara knew you hadn't accessed it? Why did my uncle think you had?"

Balmoral reached inside her coat pocket, wincing as she did so, and pulled out an old cell phone. "Because I kept the chip and embedded it in here. Run a small electronic current through it, and it gives off a pulse. I had this in case we needed a decoy. I was planning to activate the device and tape it to a transport heading out of Mansion, something to buy us some time. It seems your brother turned it on when he was looking for the tablet. In the end, he did us a favour. Maglan thought he had me, but the pulse from iAm emanated not from my head, but from my pocket."

She turned over the phone, inspecting it.

"The chip is dead, imploded within its case, as it was supposed to implode inside my brain." A grey shadow passed over her face, and he was afraid she was going to withdraw into herself again, like she had in Maglan's office.

He put an arm on her. She gave him a small smile.

"Attend to your wounds," she said. "You need stitches in your temple. The needles are tipped with morphine so they don't hurt. But no other painkillers or stimulants, you can't take anything within twenty-four hours of *half-life*."

"I know that. I *am* a trained medic."

"Pre-doc," she muttered.

"While you were in a coma I did most of your routine procedures."

"You shouldn't have a problem patching yourself up then," she said, but this time with a ghost of a smile.

"You're back," he said quietly. "In the Chairman's office, I thought for a moment . . ."

"He had broken me?" She looked away. "In a way, he did."

"Lara is not you."

"The AI is a digital imprint of my mind. The difference is that she is governed by economic laws. When I was in that room, when your uncle told me who Lara was, I guess I kind of lost it, phased out, shut down. I had failed, but in a way I could not possibly have imagined."

"And now?" he said.

"I will never lose hope with you at my side again."

He grinned. "You mean because I took out a sandman with a fistful of nuts?"

Balmoral blushed. "No . . . because now I know why you didn't take my hand when I needed you."

———— ✦ ————

SHE FINISHED TWEAKING the flight route, calculating exactly how far they could go before the plane ran out of fuel. She then put the controls on full auto, and left the cockpit.

At the back of the plane was the Presidential suite, complete with office, bedroom and bathroom. Pasco had showered and now sat on the bed, inspecting the medkit. He was stripped to the waist, but he had found clean clothes to change into.

She patched into his biosquare. She sucked in her breath as she cast an eye over his readings; the elevated blood pressure, the liver toxicity, the trauma. The *half-life* had wreaked havoc on an already compromised system.

She deployed the program and then relayed instructions to Pasco, thankful for the avatar. It meant she didn't have to think, just read off whatever was on her screen as the avatar interacted with his biosquare.

She watched as Pasco cleaned the wound on his forehead, bandaged his midriff, taped a cut here, sewed a gash there, before getting to work on her. He removed the shards of glass from her arm with tweezers, and stitched up the holes.

They were silent, concentrating on the work in hand, Pasco focused on thread and skin, Balmoral on sucking in the pain, despite the morphine tipped needles. Apart from her cuts, her jaw ached, her nose ached, and a dull thud at the back of her brain made it difficult to concentrate.

Pasco tried to be so careful, so tender, finally wrapping her arm and hand in a neat bandage. He was like a mother, fussing over a child. Not her mother, but what a mother was supposed to be. He cared for her more than anyone ever had.

"Everything okay?" he said.

"Fine." She hesitated. "In the car, before we crashed, I know what you were going to say, but I couldn't hear it, not then. I-I think *Voice* is right, my reasoning is tied to an emotional, rather than physical equilibrium, and I . . . I can't afford to feel, any more than I already do. Not until this is over."

Pasco didn't reply, but leant over and very gently kissed her on the lips, and she realised as he did so that she enjoyed the sensation.

She couldn't remember being kissed before, properly kissed, the warmness of it, the softness of it. She wanted to kiss him back but an overwhelming tiredness pressed down on her.

Pasco smiled. He too looked exhausted, the *half-life* having stripped every ounce of energy from his system. He helped her onto the small bed and lay down beside her.

Her last thought was that it was possible they would not wake from this slumber. Perhaps her concussion had ruptured a vessel in her skull and she didn't know it, perhaps the *half-life* would induce a stroke in Pasco, perhaps Lara had traced them, and would send a faster aircraft to shoot them out of the sky. So many potential ways to die, but she was happy. Pasco held her hand.

28

WHEN PASCO AWOKE, Balmoral sat cross-legged on the floor, typing on her holopad, her face a mask of concentration. His skull pounded, and as he sat up, black dots filled his eyes.

"How long was I out?"

"Almost six hours."

He rubbed his neck. "I didn't know a copter could fly for that long."

"This is a VTOL x-type, the twin rotaries are just for vertical take-off and landing. At altitude, its cruising distance is equivalent to a plane. We still have about two hours of flight."

Cold, factual, removed. When Balmoral fell asleep, he had watched her, savouring the proximity, the tenderness in her smile when they kissed. He must have lain there half an hour before a wave of nausea overcame him, his heart racing like it was about to explode. He had taken a couple of soma, just to come down from the speeding side-effects of the *half-life*, before finally passing out.

The empty blister pack was still on the floor. He should have thought to throw it out. Was that why she was suddenly so short? She was concerned about him? Inwardly he smiled. It was the first time he had known her to have a *mood*.

"Where are we going?" he said.

"Milton, in Sector 3. A remote desert outpost of the Autonomy, five hundred square miles of skaatch territory just west of the Cut."

"Why there?"

"Because it's the furthest we can travel before we run out of fuel."

"And then?"

"We walk over the Sector crossing and into the Cut."

"The Cut!" Pasco said, alarmed.

"The West African bloc, to be precise."

"Why?"

"Because that part of the world is loyal to a man who hates the Autonomy even more than we do. The father of Kolo, the boy who was murdered with the Professor. When we explain what we know, he will help us."

"Or we might be picked up by hungry savages and thrown into a pot and roasted."

"Only if we don't make it clear we have something to trade."

"You mean they might?" Pasco said. "I was . . . joking."

"Don't worry, you're statistically far more likely to die from the volume of chemicals you have recently ingested."

Pasco said nothing.

"The Cut is the only place free from *Earth*," she continued. "Which means it is the only place we will be able to stay hidden for any length of time. We will find Kolo's father. We will show him the tablet. Perhaps we can even locate the materials to access the machine."

The professor. The tablet. The code!

How had it slipped his mind?

"Where's the tablet?" he said urgently. "Still in the cockpit. Why?"

"I know what the code is."

"What are talking about?"

Pasco was already on his feet, heading to the front of the plane. The knapsack was on the passenger seat. He pulled out the tablet, tapped the screen. Nothing. A pang of disappointment shot through him.

"It's solar powered," Balmoral shouted up to him, "and it's been in a black bag. It will need a minute."

He walked back to the passenger quarters. "Professor Hakim was an avid etymologist," he said. "The first day I met him, he told me he didn't like my name. I thought he was making a reference to me being an Eborgersen but he actually meant my first name. He told me, 'Pasco means to *pass over*, a walking gentleman, an actor without a part to play. Not at all fitting for one of my students.' And the strange thing was by the end of that week, *nobody* called me Pasco, the Professor included, thanks to Sarge DeVries making up a stupid nickname because I had apple pie for breakfast."

Balmoral looked at him, her expression confused. Does not compute.

"They all called me Pie-face. It's obvious."

She shook her head.

"Don't you see? It must be 3.142. That is the combination."

"Pi?" Balmoral said. "It can't be. There is no decimal option in the tablet's combination."

"Just because Sherlock didn't suggest it," he mocked.

"Sherlock?" she said, puzzled.

"Right," he laughed, "that reference she doesn't get."

The screen sprang to life and Pasco held his breath as he typed in the numbers.
3142

There was a click and the interface opened. "At your service," he said, handing her the tablet. She cradled the device, her eyes wide with surprise.

There were a bunch of square icons that were meaningless to him; a compass, a jagged line, musical notes, a cloud and a sun. Balmoral tapped the one that was an envelope. Inside was a single message entitled, 'End Game'. It contained documents and a media file. She tapped the file, and it began to play.

29

T HE PROFESSOR STARED out at the camera. He was in a small, dark room. Was
it a store cupboard? The date stamp showed it was the night before the kidnapping, at two am. His face was thin, his eyes sunken and his complexion
sallow. Whatever he was doing in Aviv had taken its toll. For the first time, he
looked more than his seventy years.

"It is a few days before the lecture," he said quietly. "I believe my data has
been compromised, and I am in danger. Perhaps it is an old man's paranoia,
someone trying to scare me or throw me off my stride. Academic jealousy is
legendary, after all." He gave a small chuckle. "Someone trying to scare me," he
repeated. "The question is, has it worked?"

He pulled out a cigarette and fumbled with a match. He inhaled deeply,
arranged his face, and began again.

"These past few days I have wrestled with the research and its implications.
I am afraid that if my findings were leaked before the public lectures, Top 10
would do everything in its power to suppress the information, ignoring a basic
law of physics in the process. Once a phenomena has been observed, there is no
going back, the universe has already changed. Like a dead cat in a box, while
unobserved, it could be alive or dead, but once observed dead, it can only be
dead."

He took another drag.

"These are my findings, substantiated by the documents included with this
transmission, in case . . . something happens. Perhaps my future self will one
day pull up this recording and laugh at my caution, or perhaps my future self
does not exist."

"What is this?" Balmoral sounded disappointed.

"Shh," said Pasco. He had never seen the Professor like this before, his usually
calm eyes frantic, his tone guarded. Even without an audience, the Professor was
reluctant to begin, reluctant to convey his message.

"Take one." The Professor cleared his throat in that affected way he had. Behind him the wall lit up with a two dimensional projection of the title of the lecture series, "End Game".

"Today I am going to ask you to open your mind to the implications of three scientific principles that together, change everything we think we know about the world, and man's purpose in it. The first is already accepted as fact by the scientific community, and that concerns the origin of the universe. Simply put, that given infinite time and space, the universe can be created from negative gravity. There is no requirement of pre-existing elements for creation, or even some sort of mythological prime mover, *nothing* can indeed be a catalyst for everything."

Hakim stepped out of the line of sight of the camera as the references for this well-established theorem scrolled across the screen. Hawkins seminal 2011 work, Stadler's 2022 experiments using negative gravity, and Hodder's equations of 2024 that proved a vacuum with minor negative energy, if left for an infinite amount of time, in an infinite amount of nothingness, would eventually create the big bang. The probability was mind boggling; something like a trillion, to the power of a trillion to one, but in infinite time, any probability, no matter how small, eventually occurs.

It was hardly controversial. The only point of contention was over where negative gravity came from. Advocates of the *Faith* thought they knew, whereas a dwindling number of diehard atheists countered there was no way of knowing. Dwindling because in the Autonomy, it had become very important to believe, to have A-points, to aspire beyond the corporeal world.

Even Pasco did daily devotions. His job at the school would be impossible without them, and personally he agreed with the *Faith* on the origins question. The simplicity and beauty of the equations explaining the big bang was all the evidence one needed for a power beyond man's understanding.

"Before I discuss the second scientific principle," Professor Hakim said, re-entering the line of sight, "I would ask that you indulge a brief transgression, a historical allusion if you will."

The screen behind him darkened. Everything became brown and smoky, mud covered the ground and guns boomed.

"The Academy doesn't go in for history these days," the Professor said, "believing that it has little economic merit or purpose. However, in *my* youth we learned about the events that shaped the world. What you see before you is a recreation of the Somme battlefield from the First World War of 1914-18, also known as the Great War. An apt title, as I will go on to show."

He dropped his cigarette, stepping on the stub. "Over four months, over a million and a half soldiers lost their lives for less than seven miles of territory."

The screen filled with graphic images of soldiers peppered with machine gun fire and young men draped across barbed wire.

Professor Hakim recited, "*What passing bells for these who die as cattle? Only the monstrous anger of the guns. Only the stuttering rifles rapid rattle, can patter out their hasty orisons.*" He paused. "The use of orison by the poet, Wilfred Owen, means prayer. Essentially, the soldiers prayed for comfort before being cut down by machine gun fire."

Balmoral shook her head and Pasco experienced a sinking feeling. People had died for these rambling pontifications. He could not see what possible importance this presentation had.

The sound of the guns, screams, and groans rolled into an almighty crescendo, and the screen panned over body after body, some badly mutilated. The camera pulled back to a bird's eye view, showing the tiny strip of territory over which so many lives were lost, a whole world on either side. The screen became blank, and for a couple of seconds there was nothing but silence.

"Now picture the human race. We estimate that more than a hundred and thirty billion people have been born on this planet, thirteen billion of whom are alive now. Ten percent of those who have ever lived, all created from nothing, from that improbability of negative gravity, all living their lives, whether for a few seconds, or a hundred years. A woman born in Sector 1 today, who governs her health through biosquare technology, and completes three cycles of cell replacement therapy in her post-menopausal years can expect to live to a hundred and ten; thirty-seven percent longer than at the beginning of this century. Men are close behind."

"That brings me to the second principle." Several complex equations appeared behind him, each solving themselves with a precise answer. This wasn't Pasco's area but he recognized the calculations showing the rate of decay in the human metabolism.

"Robust Human Rejuvenation," Hakim said, "a term first coined by Aubrey de Grey in 2005, proposed the theory that if scientists could find a way to prevent or offset the systemic damage that metabolism wreaked on the human body, we could slow and even stop the aging process. At its most basic, our biological structure is a brain on a stalk, maintained by cells and organs that eventually break down due to wear and tear. Stop the wear and tear, and maintenance can be extended indefinitely."

"The Vanity Salons have already proved that certain cells can be replaced with younger, healthier clones, or in the case of larger, more complex structures, from genetically compatible human subjects. However, to date, expanding the science to encompass man's entire genetic structure has proved both elusive and incredibly expensive."

Hakim stared out of the screen as if studying his audience. Again, the visual behind him shifted, and showed a new set of data, some parts of which had been blacked out.

"In the early 2040s, unofficial experiments, excluded from the Academy's official canon of data on rejuvenation, proved that intensive cell replacement could revive a pre-term foetus, although the results were short term and very painful for the subject."

"Pendicott's data," murmured Pasco. Surely that wasn't the reason for all the caution?

"With adults, and our pesky, ever-shortening telomeres, the process is far more complex. However my own studies over the last ten years show that it is theoretically possible to restore cells in all major organs, reversing the effects of metabolic breakdown, effectively creating an environment for the brain in perpetuity."

Empirical data scrolled across the screen.

"The evidence to support this claim is on the screen behind you, but no need to rush for the notebook just yet . . . I will review all of the experiments and their corresponding data in the subsequent two lectures of this series. For now, let me finish this elucidation of the second principle with a tangible example."

He held up a small cage to the camera. It contained a white mouse, excited and running around.

"This is Mini," Hakim said. "Mini celebrated her twelfth birthday two weeks ago. What is remarkable is not so much that this is six times longer than the average mouse life span, but that she shows all the characteristics of a young adult."

The screen filled with Hakim's face.

"With appropriate funding, we can replicate animal studies in humans and double life expectancy within the next twenty years. In other words, if you are lucky enough to be alive for the next three decades, most of us can expect, no matter what our age now, to have another lifetime ahead of us. I estimate that once we have achieved double life span, we can achieve triple in about half the time, quadruple in half again, until we eradicate metabolic damage altogether. Put another way, if you are under the age of fifty, it is possible that you may never have to die."

Hakim stared hard into the screen.

"All it takes is investment. For many of you, and perhaps even for me, death can become a concept of the past, a choice, not a necessity. The aging process can be not only slowed, but indefinitely reversed through ongoing treatment."

"That's not possible . . ." Pasco muttered. He looked over to Balmoral. She stared at something behind her lenses and he knew she had frozen the experimental data and was reviewing it line by line. She said nothing.

An image of the Somme filled the screen again.

"I believe the hitherto history of mankind can be equated to the Somme offensive. Man, throwing himself against annihilation, when all the time, all our effort, resources, will, should have been mobilized against avoiding death, rather than charging headlong into the line of fire."

The screen blanked for a second time and Balmoral and Pasco stared into the darkness.

"Was this what they were trying to squash?" Pasco rasped.

"I don't know," Balmoral muttered. "I suppose it could destabilize the Autonomy, to dedicate all funding towards what his data proves is possible. Think of it, Sector 1 citizens stockpiling credits for treatment, lower Sectors rioting at the inevitable squeeze on resources, potentially even at the fact that, at least initially, they cannot hope to benefit from the research. Then again, such disparities already exist. The life expectancy for a woman in Sector 3 is less than half of that in Sector 1, the mass of the population are more interested in *where the sun shines brightly* than their hardship on earth."

Pasco wondered again why so many people had died for this. Trying to stop progress in an area in which LifeScience stood to make trillions made no sense. There might be issues of overpopulation, but they had twenty years or more to figure that out. With synthetics and innovations in skaatch farming, the Autonomy had the capacity to feed an even larger population, and in terms of habitat, man could find a way to repopulate the Cut, or the seas, or underground, or even, in time, outer space. So what was the big fear?

Hakim's face appeared again and Pasco realised the lecture was not over. Another cigarette burned between his fingers. He was still in the store cupboard, although the time stamp showed it was almost four-thirty in the morning.

"The third principle," he said. "In 2025, a scientist called JP Levy submitted a doctoral thesis that probed the very nature of death. Little is known of this thesis because it was rejected by the Academy, and in his fifties, when he should have been at the height of his career, Levy found himself marginalized and relegated to the lower echelons of academia, developing modules for Sector 2's Prep. This thesis had been his life's work."

Professor Hakim sucked on the cigarette.

"In defence of the Academy, the data was highly speculative and based on theory rather than empirical evidence. However, by observing how particles behave in the universe and performing numerous tests on his hypothesis, Levy posited that an after-life could not exist. He argued that what exists beyond the veil is exactly the same as the state prior to the big bang, which, if you will recall requires an almost infinite amount of time to pass before anything happens. Not exactly what the *Faith* promises to those with the requisite number of A-points."

Hakim smiled thinly, but he looked exhausted.

"Levy further argued that if ever science advanced to the state that a recently deceased cadaver could be rejuvenated, then the hypothesis could be proved. Though far-fetched in 2025, the possibility of stimulating the brain back to a brief functionality after a period of death, death here defined as all vital signs gone, for a period of at least one hour, is . . . now possible. I draw your attention back to the suppressed data on what had already been achieved with a recently aborted foetus."

He took another drag on his cigarette.

"To be clear, I am not talking about the Lazarus syndrome; the supposed miracle where a subject's heart stops beating and then resuscitates. Most of these cases can be explained by a fault in tracking the vital signs in the first place. No, I am talking about clinical and absolute death."

The back-screen lit up again, this time with a hospital ward.

"Fifty years ago, this was a functioning emergency room, designed to administer critical care on campus. A product of a different time, it was located underground, safe from long forgotten wars." He leaned in confidentially. "Forgotten, and with nothing above ground level, it has no *Earth*. This is where I have been working with Doctor Levy. Over the last year, we found five subjects, including Levy himself, willing to be euthanized for the sake of scientific enquiry. None of the subjects except Levy, who was ill, were under ninety or believed they had their best years ahead of them. Their profiles, statistics, background and recorded assent statements are all available in the lecture notes."

Images of various procedures filled the screen.

"We euthanized the subject, and each was confirmed clinically dead for a period of three to five hours. With a pixel analysis of this footage, a third party can confirm that the readings and process are valid. After death was confirmed we initiated the complex process of rejuvenation. In each case the subject became conscious for a period of up to three minutes."

One after another, the subjects appeared in front of the camera. They spoke with significant difficulty, the faces of two of them, the longest dead had the signs of rigor mortis, and the muscles of their faces were stiff.

Each confirmed, in almost identical words, what they had experienced, and that was a dark, silent expanse of nothing. Except that they were not in an abyss, but *were* the abyss, or at least part of it.

Another noticeable feature was that each of the subjects, including Doctor Levy, who was the final candidate and for whom this had been the great question of his life, wanted to be left alone. They did not want to speak but were irritable and short, as though already beyond worldly cares; the questions, an irrelevant concern of the living.

Hakim dropped the stub of his cigarette and stepped on it. "There is a single, inescapable conclusion. The eternal bliss promised by the *Faith,* which so many of our citizens crave is in actuality an eternal blank. Perhaps the two concepts are not mutually exclusive. However, that is my third scientific truth."

He took a long sip of his water.

"Over the course of the lectures I will go through the data step by step, and prove that humanity has the capacity to control the duration of existence in this world, in the full knowledge that what follows is an eternal sleep. Perhaps a fifth of the current population of the Autonomy will be in a position to extend their life indefinitely, the others will join their fallen comrades in eternity. Thank you."

Again, the screen went blank, and this time, the presentation was over. For a moment neither of them spoke. Pasco became conscious of the aircraft again, of the low hum in the background. "Is it credible?" he said.

"Credible? Do you think they would have killed so many people if it wasn't?" Balmoral scrolled around the attachments. "All the backup data is here. If this information could be discredited on a scientific basis, then the whole weight of Media could be trusted to do exactly that. The research would have died as another crackpot theory. No, truth has a way of sticking, and this was a truth Lara could not afford the world to know."

"It changes everything of course, but is it really a threat to the Autonomy?"

"You have never been outside Sector 1. Not really. In Sector 1, the *Faith* is important, of course it is. It has become a way of life, but in general, people cling on to their lives as something worth living in themselves, something precious. In Sector 2 and 3, people don't live but exist. They accept this because the hardships of the corporeal world only augment what is due to them in the next. Remove that dream, and their slave-like existence no longer has any meaning. Do you think the eleven billion people of slumworld are going to put up with that? It doesn't take a genius to figure out that this idea would effectively end the bargain that makes the Autonomy possible."

He visualized it then, Sector walls broken down, the possibility for an uprising on a scale never seen before or since. This information was like a new class of weapon, an i-bomb; a single idea as powerful and devastating as a nuclear warhead. It would unhinge civilization and potentially leave a barren wasteland in its wake. Even though he did not agree with Maglan, for the first time, Pasco understood the hard logic that drove his uncle's actions.

"What should we do?" he asked.

"Flood every Media channel with the data. No matter how much propaganda they throw at it, the message will get through. Top 10 will be overthrown, and mankind can start again."

"But so many will die . . ."

Balmoral cut him off. "We do not know that. Any outcome is possible. Besides, your Professor was right. By observing something, you change it. Like shining a light on a particle, it changes the substance of what you observe. Don't you see? This isn't a question of morals or ethics or even trade-offs. The fact is a fact and whether propagated or not, it has already changed the world. Once the first person realises the world is round, it is round and nobody will ever fall off its edge. The next phase in man's existence began the moment Hakim observed these results."

"Won't they shut down whatever you release?"

"Lara will try. Right now we have two things in our favour. She still has no way to pair me and my clean persona of Sophie Valencia, so I am free to subcode without fear of digital death, at least until I upload the data. Secondly, she has no idea we managed to unlock the device, so she won't rush in as soon as she finds us, but will take us out with a sandman. Involve others and you widen the circle, with more to clean up afterwards. She will avoid that if she can."

"So what now?"

"We head straight for the Cut. Outside of the *Earth's* glare, I will begin on the subcode that will unlock every single Media channel on iNet, directly routing the information from this rogue. It will take time. At least seven hours. Hopefully we will get that long."

"What do you mean?"

"Lara will be right behind us."

He felt a jolt and gripped the arms of his chair as the aircraft began its descent towards the dusty wasteland of Milton.

30

SECTOR 3, MILTON

HEY LANDED ON a small patch of dirt that bordered one of the gigantic skaatch farms. The plane aroused curiosity, but not as much as might be expected. The population was too exhausted for curiosity. There were shifts to complete, joules to burn. Supervisors patrolled the fields, driving the productivity of the workers as they tended to the swarms, but nobody stopped them as they began to make their way east along the perimeter.

"Why are the Supervisors ignoring us?" Pasco wondered aloud.

"My identikit reads we are on official Securicom business. Not to be impeded."

"How far is it until the Sector crossing?"

"Five miles. I took us in as close as I could," Balmoral replied.

Five blistering miles.

"Can we take a transport?" Pasco said, having to shout. The sound of wings and whatever else insects click and rub was deafening. "A bubble car maybe?"

"There are none out here."

So they trudged through the dry, baking air. In every direction were huge black nets, under which skeletal figures farmed billions of insects. Some of the nets billowed almost half a mile in the air. The workers were bent double with the backbreaking work. Welts and scars decorated their skin from repeated collisions, bites, and stings.

They were probably on a gram of cut synapse just to get through the day. The rumour was that skaatch workers hardly ate, couldn't bear the sight of the stuff, so they lived on opiates until their bodies expired sometime in their early thirties.

Outside of the nets, ramshackle slums sprawled in every direction, with tradesman selling tepid water, slices of skaatch, or a sack to sleep in. Mothers ferried children back and forth to Mamfac, or if they were older, to a lodge where they could shell insects and prepare maggot cultures.

Many of the faces had grotesque skin cancers caused by the relentless sun that burned the ground around them. Whole families camped in the dirt next to communal outhouses. In the heat, the stench was overwhelming, and as they walked an unhealthy miasma coated Pasco's tongue, eyes and lungs.

Despite the deprivation, every single person wore iNet, their glasses not only shading out the sun, but providing a twenty-four hour world of alternate reality. In Logistics it was estimated that the level of physical conversation in Sector 3 was down to less than a couple of sentences a day. Life was conducted in a realm of fantasy, through sims that took the individual anywhere but this barren skaatchland.

Pasco struggled for breath. The pain in his ribs returned with a vengeance. He fantasized about lying down in the middle of the dirt, just to sleep for a while. Twice they stopped for water at one of the ramshackle stations that bordered the fields, but it was brown, warm as soup and hardly refreshed them.

Finally, they saw it in the distance. The border crossing; a patchwork of rusted fences separating one wasteland from the next. The fence was largely symbolic. The real deterrent lay elsewhere, turrets every few hundred meters, manned twenty-four hours a day with machine guns pointing towards the Cut.

In the first years of the Autonomy, starving masses would rush the fences, suffering huge fatalities in the process, but eventually breaking through. What they discovered on the other side were endless miles of insect farms and no way to process the potential joules. Exhausted, most died before Securicom reached them.

He followed Balmoral, heading for a part of the fence where the mesh had fallen away.

"You don't think they'll try to stop us?" Pasco said as they approached.

"There is no law about breaking into the Cut. The problem is coming back the other way."

He stepped through with a sense of trepidation, staring into the desert. It was the first time he had looked out at an expanse of land and not seen any people. They would be there of course, tribes of them, seeking safety in numbers, staying as sheltered as possible during the day, coming out at night to hunt each other or to trade.

Balmoral and Pasco had no water, no food, nothing to sell. Even if their story was believed, would the starving natives take them to Kolo's father? According to Balmoral his settlement was more than two hundred miles away.

With a shudder he thought of the more likely outcome for joule rich outsiders. As he watched Balmoral limp ahead he wondered if she really had a plan beyond releasing the data. Perhaps they didn't need one. The data was their end.

"We can shelter up there," she said, pointing to an outcrop of jagged rocks at the top of a small ravine. Although not more than a few hundred meters from the fence, it provided cover, somewhere they could hunker down. Neither spoke as they ascended, too exhausted now for words, and when they finally reached the summit, both collapsed under the overhanging rocks, desperate for shade.

Balmoral pulled out her holopad and set to work, her hands trembling with fatigue. Pasco knew that she, like him, would be in terrible discomfort now, the dulling effect of the heavy grade analgesics beginning to recede, leaving only the raw pain of their injuries. He watched her assume that rigid mask of concentration, a focus that took her above and beyond the physical world, and her fingers blurred across the keys.

Pasco sat beside her, his back to the rock. He nodded once, then twice and he was out.

HE AWOKE TO the *whump, whump, whump* of a copter. It was close and getting closer. The shadows around him had changed, a late morning sun turning to late afternoon. He felt as though a thousand muggers had stomped on his head, while a thousand more worked away at his ribs. "A copter," he wheezed, mouth dry as dust.

Balmoral didn't reply, but continued to code. Her fingers like small, nimble animals, her face drained of all expression except the slight frown of concentration.

"Balmoral," he rasped. "Someone's coming."

"I know," she said. "It's a sandman. I have been following his movements since he left Milton's export hub. Lara managed to track us once we landed. He came in on a chartered flight then commandeered a copter."

"Is it . . . is it him?" he asked, despite himself.

"Yes."

It figured. Somehow Tristram had always been there, always right behind him. Was this their destiny? Set from the moment they were born, predetermined by some universal world order that was not God?

"We need to run," he said, realising the futility of his remark before the words were out of his mouth. Run? Could either of them even walk? They were only hours away from fatal dehydration.

"I am almost done," she said. "I just need a few minutes more."

"You said you needed at least seven hours!"

"You've been passed out for over six. At one point you stopped breathing."

"What?"

"I cut a few corners with the code," Balmoral said, ignoring him. "Lara will be able to shut me down as soon as I dump the data, but by then it will be too late."

The copter landed at the foot of the ravine, throwing up dust.

Oblivious, Balmoral continued to type, her legs crossed, her face devoid of all expression.

Pasco peered down over a rock and watched Tristram jump out, low to the ground, his jacket billowing as the rotaries came to rest. His brother knew they were up there, informed by the eyes in the turrets. He climbed cautiously. Perhaps he thought they had a weapon. Either way, in another minute he would be on them.

"I'm ready," Balmoral said, looking up and in that instant, Pasco wondered if they would be remembered as the greatest terrorists of all time, or if there would be anyone left to remember at all.

Her hand hovered over the holopad. "Hold me," she said. He crawled over, and put his arms around her, hugging her tight. She smiled at him, and pressed the key.

"Is it done?" he said.

"Yes."

"How long?"

"The chain reaction has already begun. *Voice* has a contingency, a program to bring down the whole of iNet, but it was hacked. Lara will not be able to get it online before a critical mass of communications has been sent and by then, it will be too late."

"Hacked? By who?"

She raised an eyebrow. They both laughed, but he was conscious of how thin their voices sounded. Yes, even if there was no sandman, they would surely die out here.

She gazed up at him, the fading sun streaking across her deathly pale face. The words from *The Still Point* came back to him. "It is possible," he said quietly, "that here, now in the garden, in the green, she is as lovely as she will ever be."

Balmoral suddenly tensed. Pasco didn't need to turn around. He sensed the gun on his back.

"Do it," he heard himself say, still holding Balmoral. "Gladly, little brother," Tristram rasped.

31

AS HE AIMED the gun at Pasco's head, Balmoral saw Tristram for what he was, a lost creature from whom all emotion had drained long ago; a husk without a soul. After Rhodes, she had sworn never to kill again, and yet she didn't hesitate. He needed to die. She executed the piece of subcode, and prayed she hadn't already been locked out by *Voice*.

It was the ugliest hack she had ever done, but the program served its purpose. Instead of firing, Tristram's knees buckled and he collapsed. It was her last action. Her interface froze and died in digital death.

Pasco turned around and stared in shock at his brother's lifeless form. "What happened?"

"Synaptic implosion," she said.

"You?"

She nodded. Pasco scrambled over to his brother and picked up his limp hand. Tears shone in his eyes. "He could have been so much more," he cried. "It was our father. He never got over his death."

She didn't argue, but she knew that if Tristram had been brought up in the most functional family in the world, he would still be capable of pulling the trigger on another human being without feeling the slightest pang of remorse.

Psychopaths were born, not made. Who knew that better than her? She, who fought to unmake herself every day, to feel something more than the cold logic that filled her brain. And perhaps she had finally succeeded, because didn't she love this person in front of her? Not a theoretical love but a deep, all-encompassing need to be with him and part of him.

Pasco stood up, glanced at her, and then without a word he walked away. She didn't call him back. She didn't have the strength. Her exhaustion had reached a critical level.

Balmoral removed her useless glasses and lay down on the dirt. She must have passed out because a moment later he was back, gently holding up her head as he poured ice-cold water into her mouth. She had never felt so thirsty.

"There were three flasks in the copter," he said. "I checked the gas too, and there is enough to get us a couple of hundred miles into the Cut. Put some distance between us and whomever might come after us next."

"Pasco, I can't fly a copter, not without iNet. Not with a . . . stick and everything."

He laughed. "Of course. I . . . I didn't think."

The flasks would last them a day, less if they actually tried to move.

"I also found this," he said and held up a large backpack. "I guess Tristram thought he might have to track us. There is a shelter, medical supplies, a condensation unit for water and rations for two weeks."

A dim hope kindled inside her. "He was going to do a runner," she said, "after he killed us."

"But he had iAm."

"Maybe he thought Lara would let him go. Maybe he didn't care anymore."

"There's um . . . even a rolled up sleeping bag. Only one, I'm afraid." He gave her a sheepish, crooked grin.

She realised then that she wanted to kiss him, so she did. It was long and soft and salty and a flush of warmth passed through her. "I think we'll manage," she said, smiling.

He smiled back and together they watched the sun set before slowly making their way east.

The world, it was all before them, where to choose

Their place of rest, and providence their guide:

They hand in hand with wandering steps and slow

Through Eden took their solitary way.

Paradise Lost

ACKNOWLEDGEMENTS

Thank you, Christine, for your unerring faith and patience. Thank you to my children for being so understanding during the times I had to write, rather than play with you. Thank you to my father for proofreading and your helpful suggestions, and to my mother for your support and encouragement. Thank you to the team at Kristell Ink, especially Sammy Smith, without whom this novel would not be possible.

A SELECTION OF OTHER TITLES
FROM KRISTELL INK

SPARK AND CAROUSEL BY JOANNE HALL

Spark is a wanted man. On the run after causing the death of his mentor and wild with untamed magic, he arrives in Cape Carey where his latent talents make him the target of rival gangs. It is there that Carousel, a wire-walker and thief, takes him under her wing to guide him through the intrigues of the criminal underworld.

But when Spark's magic cracks the world and releases demons from the hells beneath, two mages of his former order make it their mission to prevent his magic from spiralling out of control. They must find him before he falls into the clutches of those who would exploit his raw talent for their own gain, forcing Spark to confront a power he is not ready to handle.

Meanwhile, a wealthy debutante learning magic in secret has her own plans for Spark and Carousel. But the sudden arrival of the mages throws her carefully laid plans into disarray and she unleashes a terrible evil onto the streets of the unsuspecting city – an evil only Spark's magic can control.

Everyone wants a piece of Spark, but all Spark wants is to rid himself of his talents forever.

NON-COMPLIANCE: THE SECTOR BY PAIGE DANIELS

I used to matter . . . but now I'm just a girl in a ghetto, a statistic of the Non-Compliance Sector.

Shea Kelly had a brilliant career in technology, but after refusing to implant an invasive government device in her body she was sent to a modern day reservation: a Non-Compliance Sector, a lawless community run by thugs and organized crime. She's made a life for herself as a resourceful barkeep, and hacks for goods on the black market with her best friend Wynne, a computer genius and part-time stripper. Life is pretty quiet under the reigning Boss, apart from run-ins with his right hand man, the mighty Quinn: until Danny Rose threatens to take over the sector. Pushed to the edge, Shea decides to fight back . . .

IN SEARCH OF GODS AND HEROES BY SAMMY H.K SMITH

Buried in the scriptures of Ibea lies a story of rivalry, betrayal, stolen love, and the bitter division of the gods into two factions. This rift forced the lesser deities to pledge their divine loyalty either to the shining Eternal Kingdom or the darkness of the Underworld.

When a demon sneaks into the mortal world and murders an innocent girl to get to her sister Chaeli, all pretence of peace between the gods is shattered. For Chaeli is no ordinary mortal, she is a demi-goddess, in hiding for centuries, even from herself. But there are two divine brothers who may have fathered her, and the fate of Ibea rests on the source of her blood.

Chaeli embarks on a journey that tests her heart, her courage, and her humanity. Her only guides are a man who died a thousand years ago in the Dragon Wars, a former assassin for the Underworld, and a changeling who prefers the form of a cat.

The lives of many others – the hideously scarred Anya and her gaoler; the enigmatic and cruel Captain Kerne; the dissolute Prince Dal; and gentle seer Hana – all become entwined. The gods will once more walk the mortal plane spreading love, luck, disease, and despair as they prepare for the final, inevitable battle.

In Search of Gods and Heroes, Book One of Children of Nalowyn, is a true epic of sweeping proportions which becomes progressively darker as the baser side of human nature is explored, the failings and ambitions of the gods is revealed, and lines between sensuality and sadism, love and lust are blurred.

www.kristell-ink.com

CPSIA information can be obtained
at www.ICGtesting.com
Printed in the USA
LVOW04*0123161216

517421LV00011BA/189/P